RYMELLAN 3

SARAH ETTRITCH

THE TRIAD

NORN PUBLISHING
TORONTO, CANADA

Library and Archives Canada Cataloguing in Publication

Ettritch, Sarah, 1963–
Rymellan 3 : the triad / Sarah Ettritch.

Short stories.

ISBN 978-1-927369-03-6

I. Title.

PS8609.T87R97 2012   C813'.6   C2012-901796-5

Editing by Marg Gilks
Internal design by Fiona Raven
Cover design by Boulevard Photografica/Patty G. Henderson

First Printing April 2012
v1

Published by Norn Publishing
www.NornPublishing.com

For Monica and Alison

ACKNOWLEDGEMENTS

.....

The usual suspects: Jennifer Brinkman, my partner and beta reader; Marg Gilks, my editor; and Patty Henderson, my cover designer. Thank you.

CONTENTS

.....

NO GOING BACK

.....

LESLEY SANK INTO HER CHAIR AND flicked on her comm station, relieved that she was finally behind a closed office door. While striding through the lobby and corridors, she'd felt as if she were an impostor. How could she have denied her Chosen? What would her peers think, if they knew? She'd initially looked forward to her day off after the awards ceremony, but had spent it cringing as others admired the Medal of the Protector. Even Jason had dropped by to see it, after he'd beeped Mama to make sure Jayne wasn't around. Lesley had desperately wanted the day to end, but had also dreaded returning to duty.

With a sigh, she viewed her schedule for the day. Two reminders deepened her shame: the orientation for the commander training program would start in three days, and she and Jayne were due for another forced outing to satisfy Berry—and annoy Mo. Merely seeing Jayne's name made Lesley feel like a failure; spending time with her would be excruciating. Last time they'd met alone, Jayne had confided that she didn't believe they were Chosens. Could Lesley blame her? Everyone seemed to forget about the Way when dealing with Jayne, so she could be excused for suspecting that the Chosen Council had deliberately thrown her into a triad. The logic behind her conclusion couldn't be denied. Lesley, on the other hand, had no excuse. None whatsoever.

Someone rapped sharply on the door, then swung it open. Lesley's heart sank when Laura stepped into the office. She wished she could talk to her, unload the shame and confusion that had distracted her since the awards ceremony. But although Lesley hadn't committed a violation, Laura would be terribly disappointed, perhaps angry, if she found out how easily Lesley had dismissed Jayne. Lesley didn't want to lose the respect of someone she considered a role model. The shame was already difficult enough to bear without others knowing about her weakness.

"Good morning," Laura said cheerfully. "I know you're trying to wrap up two opinions for Blair before the training program, but do you have time to investigate a situation in B3? I doubt it's anything, but we need to check it out and everyone else is busy."

"Sure," Lesley replied, hoping she'd be able to concentrate on Blair's cases when she returned.

"Great, I'll dispatch the details," Laura said as Lesley rolled back her chair. "I've set up a meeting with Blair tomorrow, to discuss how we'll work things while you're doing your training. I have the impression she wants to cling to as much of your time as she can."

Lesley could hear the amusement in Laura's voice as she turned and reached for her cloak, and felt relieved that, with her back to Laura, she didn't need to force a smile.

"She's insisting that we meet over lunch. She wants to take us to that new eatery everyone's raving about, to congratulate us on our medals."

"That's nice of her," Lesley said, managing to sound enthusiastic.

"I'll put it on your calendar. And I'll let you get going. I know you have lots of work waiting for you." With a nod, Laura left.

Lesley braced herself before leaving her office to walk the corridors again. Not in the mood to talk to anyone, she groaned when her comm unit beeped. She glanced at it, prepared to let the beeper leave a message—she was in the middle of rushing to investigate a tip, after all—but then changed her mind when she read the name.

"I beeped Ross to let her know I'll do the Basic Maneuvers 1-B practicum," Mo said after they'd exchanged greetings. "She wants me to be more involved this time. Apparently they want to make a few changes to the requirements and she wants my input, so she suggested I attend a couple of meetings. I said I would. They're hands-on meetings, otherwise I would have tried to get out of it."

Lesley chuckled.

"The thing is, she's on 72 for the next couple of weeks, so that's where they're meeting. I said I'd go up on Friday and stay until Monday."

An idea formed as Lesley pushed open one of the double doors and stepped into the morning sunshine. "Why don't you take Jayne with you?" If Mo agreed, Lesley could delay her forced outing with Jayne until next week.

Mo hesitated. "I don't know, she went up with me not that long ago. And this time I won't be around as much. The meetings sound like all day affairs."

"Oh." Lesley wasn't proud of what she was about to do, but she did it anyway. "Then perhaps it is better that Jayne stay down here. She might not want to be on 72 for three nights, and we're due for another lunch for Berry. I'll suggest that we meet while you're away. There, I'm telling you in advance." She held her breath.

Silence, then, "You know, you're right, it wouldn't be a bad idea to take Jayne with me. I was only going on Friday because we're meeting at 10:00 on Saturday. But I can pick Jayne up early Saturday morning, so it'll only be a two-night stay. I'll be around in the evenings, so she won't be alone all the time. And she has to get comfortable being by herself on the station."

"If you're sure. But now I'm thinking that I really should see her for lunch, before Berry gets upset."

"No, no, that can wait," Mo said quickly. "I doubt Berry will care if you wait a week. I'll beep Jayne as soon as we disconnect and arrange for her to go with me."

"All right," Lesley said evenly. "I'll let you do that, then. I'm almost at my aviacraft."

"Your aviacraft?"

"I'm on my way to check something out for Laura."

"I won't ask what. I'll see you later."

They disconnected. Lesley shook her head and slid the comm unit back into its holder. Manipulating Mo. Yet another reason to be disgusted with herself.

JAYNE PRESSED THE comm station's disconnect button and dropped onto her sofa with a thump. If only she could have come up with a good excuse to not go with Mo to 72. Another trip to 72 didn't intimidate her, but being with Mo for two days did. It was so unfair! She cherished her growing friendship with Mo and was starting to believe that Mo valued it too. The Chosen Council had forced them together, but Mo had put aside her preconceived notions; her open-mindedness had allowed a genuine bond to form. Jayne no longer felt as if Mo spent time with her solely for duty's sake. For the first time in her adult life, she had a friend, and she'd meant it when she'd said that friendship would be more than enough. She didn't want those other feelings!

Breathe! Nobody had to know, most of all Mo and Lesley. The danger wasn't that she'd become involved with one or both of them—neither would ever be interested in her in that way. No, the danger was more insidious than that. If they were to suspect how she felt, it could affect their relationship, the foundation of the triad. Protecting their relationship had to be her priority—nothing else mattered. If she was careful not to let her feelings show, everything would be all right. Lesley and Mo would be none the wiser, they'd all be friends, and the triad would succeed. This Adams would *not* be involved in a failed Joining.

Fortunately Mo would be in meetings for most of their time on 72. Jayne wanted to spend time with her, but hours on end might be a strain. Oh, if only these feelings would pass! She had to believe they eventually would. Surely they wouldn't hang around for years when—

The comm station beeped. She tensed, hoping it wasn't Mo again, or Lesley. Her muscles tightened further when she read the name: *Cdre. L. Finney.* With trepidation, she pressed the connect button. "Yes, hello."

"Good morning, Jayne," Laura said. "I'm going to ask you a question, and you can say no. You're under no obligation to agree, all right?"

"All right," she said, her curiosity piqued.

"I've spoken to Kevin Stewart's counsellor, and he wants to arrange a session with you and Stewart. He believes it will help Stewart."

Help him to do what? Vent his hatred of Papa on her? He couldn't berate him, so instead he'd berate her?

"As I said, you're under no obligation to agree," Laura said into the silence. "I'll understand if you'd rather not."

Jayne understood what she symbolized for Stewart. Given Papa's behaviour, she sympathized with him to a degree. But hadn't she already endured enough because of the Incident? What did he want from her? He was an overseer. He'd lost his sister, but he still had a life. She'd lost her parents and most of the rest of her family, endured jeers and insults for thirteen years—two men had tried to kill her! He'd said his piece at the awards ceremony. What more did he want?

She couldn't make it right for him. How could she do for him what she couldn't do for herself? "I don't think I can do it. I understand why he's—it's hard to accept that someone you love . . ." Her eyes welled up. Argamon! She took a deep breath and slowly exhaled. "Tell the counsellor no."

"I will." Laura didn't sound upset or surprised.

They said good-bye and disconnected. Deflated, Jayne stared into space. Despite making what she believed to be the right decision, she felt guilty. What if he fell from the Way because she didn't meet with him? No! She had to stop blaming herself for everything. He'd had thirteen years to deal with the Incident. It wasn't her fault the triad had put her name on the tip of everyone's tongue, opening old wounds for some. She had enough problems of her own without trying to solve everyone else's. Stewart had his family and counsellor to help him.

But that afternoon, as she was about to set off for the Trading Centre to obtain painting supplies, her resolve to not get involved wavered when her comm unit beeped. *G. Stewart.* No, she wouldn't answer. She couldn't. Why wouldn't they leave her alone?

She groaned when the message indicator appeared on the comm unit's display. Too conscientious to delete the message without listening to it, she steeled herself and played it:

Yes, um, I probably shouldn't be doing this, but I don't know what else to do. I'm Kevin's—Kevin Stewart's—Chosen. I know his counsellor asked if you'd meet with him and you refused. Would you reconsider? Please? I don't know what else to do. He just can't seem to move past it. I shouldn't ask, but I'm afraid of losing him. If you won't do it for him, do it for me and the children. Her voice choked off. *Please,* she whispered. *I'm sorry.* The message ended.

Jayne's hands shook. The woman sounded so despondent. But what could Jayne do? Would meeting with him really help, if all he did was rant at her? What difference would it make? Stewart's sister would still be dead, Papa would still be a monster, and she'd still be his daughter.

Stewart wouldn't be satisfied until she was executed, and Robert too, for good measure. The man had actively called for her death, not once, but twice!

But it wasn't his Chosen's fault. If there was even the slimmest chance that meeting with him would prevent the Incident from taking another papa away from his children . . .

She felt torn. Deciding she needed time to think it over, Jayne buttoned her cloak and left for the Trading Centre. Applying for art college still didn't sit well, but neither would linking accounts with Lesley and Mo when she wasn't doing anything with her life. These days, it felt as if everything she did was to help satisfy other people. It had been easier when she hadn't had to worry about anyone else. But also lonelier.

JAYNE YAWNED INTO her hand and fought the urge to stretch out on the sofa and nap. They'd only just returned from supper in the canteen, but Mo had picked her up at 6:45 that morning.

Mo gave her a sympathetic look. "I guess hearing about the launch area isn't all that exciting."

"No, it's not that," Jayne said, mortified. She relaxed when Mo grinned. "I'm just tired." Waking at 6:00 wasn't the only reason behind her fatigue. After spending the day working on the painting for her college application, she was mentally exhausted. The act of painting would have exhilarated her if she hadn't had to fight against the part of herself that thought applying for college was a bad idea.

"Are you sure you're just tired?" Mo leaned forward in her chair. "You were very quiet over supper."

Painting had also kept her mind off the message from Stewart's Chosen. She still didn't know what to do. He wasn't her responsibility, but could she ignore his Chosen's plea and then live with herself if he fell from the Way?

"Did something happen today? You said you stayed in our quarters, but . . ."

"I did stay here."

"What's wrong, then?"

Mo looked genuinely concerned, but could Jayne talk to her about Stewart? Did Mo want to hear about yet another problem related to the

Incident? Jayne was sick of it herself, but she needed advice and Carol wasn't here. "Laura Finney beeped me a few days ago."

"What did *she* want?" Mo asked, surprise raising her voice.

"I guess she talked to Kevin Stewart's counsellor about what happened at the awards ceremony, and the counsellor said it might help Stewart if I met with him."

Mo's mouth dropped open. "Why? So he can get everything off his chest? And you're supposed to just sit there and take it?"

"That's what I thought too," Jayne said. "Laura said I wasn't under any obligation to do it, so I said no."

Mo thumped the arm of her chair. "Well, good for you!" She frowned. "You're not regretting saying no, are you?"

"I wasn't." Jayne sighed. "Until his Chosen beeped me."

"She beeped you! She had no business beeping you! You said no."

"She's worried, Mo. You didn't see him at the ceremony. If he hadn't come to his senses . . . I didn't talk to her. She left a message." Jayne reached for her comm unit. "Here, I'll play it for you."

"Wait." Mo rose from the chair to come sit next to Jayne, who didn't mind. To her surprise, she still felt comfortable with Mo. She didn't understand why, but Mo didn't rattle her like Lesley did. When she was with Mo, she didn't feel as if her brain had stopped working, wasn't worried that something horribly embarrassing would come out of her mouth every time she opened it. But there was no denying that she cared very much for Mo and about what Mo thought of her, so—

"I'm ready." Mo stared at her.

Jayne quickly pressed the play button. What had she just been thinking about her brain not working?

Mo's expression grew sombre as she listened to Stewart's Chosen. "She sounds desperate," she murmured when the message ended.

"Yes, she does."

They sat lost in their own thoughts. Mo broke the silence. "Meeting with him might not help him, though. It could make things worse. You can't stop him from falling from the Way."

"But if he does fall from the Way, I'll always wonder if meeting with him would have helped. You didn't see him. You weren't there when he confronted me. I saw—" Jayne stopped. Normally she'd only open up to that extent with Carol.

"What did you see?" Mo prompted.

She either trusted Mo, or she didn't. "I saw myself. We're both victims of the Incident."

Mo snorted. "Come on! He lost a sister. You lost both your parents. It affected you a lot more than it did him."

Jayne wasn't sure they could assign value to lives like that. "But it did affect him. He can't understand why it happened." Just as she couldn't. "We both belong to a club nobody wants to belong to."

"But he hates you. If you meet with him, he'll just pile on the abuse to make himself feel better."

"But I'll know I did what I could," Jayne said quietly.

Mo's forehead creased. "You can't stop him from falling."

"Perhaps not. But if I meet with him, maybe I won't feel guilty about it if he does fall." She looked down at her lap. Tears sprang to her eyes when she felt Mo's hand on her shoulder.

"It sounds like you need to meet with him," Mo said. "I'm not sure it's a good idea, but it sounds like that's what you need to do."

Jayne silently cursed when a tear rolled down her cheek. She brushed it away, then leaned forward and dislodged Mo's hand when more tears threatened. Just as Jayne thought she'd mastered her composure, Mo's arm slipped around her shoulders. The tender gesture disarmed rather than bolstered. "I just wish it would all go away, so I could be like everyone else," she said, sniffling. "It never ends. It never—" She sobbed, and almost dissolved into a flood of tears when Mo's arm tightened around her. Then she shook herself and furiously wiped at her cheeks. She'd always fought against wallowing in it. If she allowed herself that luxury, she'd spend all her days crying. "I might regret it, but I have to meet with him," she said, steering the conversation back to the less upsetting topic.

"Tell them you'll do it, but only if you can bring your Chosen," Mo said.

Jayne turned to her. "What? You don't have to."

"I want to," Mo said firmly. "You don't have to face him alone. You're not alone anymore."

Jayne's vision blurred. She wanted to close her eyes and draw strength from Mo's compassion and support; wanted to reach for her, hold her, bathe in the comfort of Mo's arms. But that would be wrong. She tore her gaze away and stood. "I need a handkerchief." Jayne could feel Mo's eyes on her as she retreated into the bedroom, hoping a handkerchief was in her knapsack. Relief flooded through her when she found one shoved inside a side pocket. On the way to the bathroom to splash water on her face, she stole a glance at Mo, who was sitting exactly where Jayne had left her, staring pensively at nothing.

After making herself somewhat presentable again, Jayne hesitated in the bathroom doorway. What would Mo think if she were to sit in the chair, rather than next to her?

Mo's comm unit beeped. Jayne seized the opportunity to move closer to her and hover, still not sure where to sit.

"So are we going to show Jayne how pilots play cards tonight?" a woman's voice said as soon as Mo hit the connect button.

"Les and I have already played cards with her," Mo said, then mouthed "Ann" at Jayne.

Jayne nodded and sat next to her. Ann's interruption had broken the mood.

"I meant pilots who don't play like wimps," Ann said, making Mo roll her eyes. "Come on, when I ran into you earlier, you said you'd be up for it."

"I said we *might* be up for it. But I'm tired. Maybe another time."

"You sure? How about just the three of us? We can play in your quarters, if you want."

"Not tonight." Mo paused. "But thanks for asking."

"If you wanted to play, we could have gone," Jayne said when Mo disconnected, though the thought of playing cards with Mo's fellow pilots—or even just Ann—intimidated her.

Mo shook her head. "I feel like a quiet night in."

That suited Jayne fine, but . . . "I won't be good company." And she no longer wanted to talk about Stewart. "I'll meet with Stewart," she said, hoping that would put an end to the subject for now. "And I can meet with him alone. You don't have to come."

"I'm going with you." Mo's tone made it clear that she wouldn't be swayed. "Make sure you tell Laura that."

"Actually, I was thinking of telling Lesley and asking her to tell Laura, so Lesley knows what's going on." Was that true, or did she want an excuse to write to Lesley?

"Good idea." Mo slid forward to perch on the edge of the sofa and stretch. "And don't worry about entertaining me. I brought my violin for a reason. My audition is only a few weeks away, so I need to practice." She turned to Jayne. "I can go to a music room, if you think I'll get on your nerves."

"No, don't do that. I'm all painted out for the day, and even if I wasn't, your violin wouldn't bother me. Once I've finished the dispatch to Lesley, I'll just lie here and close my eyes and listen."

Mo's face lit up. "Really?"

"Yes, really." She wouldn't mind being serenaded by Mo and her violin every night.

MO GLANCED AROUND her empty quarters in alarm, then turned to Ann. "She said she might go for a walk, but I didn't think she would."

Ann snorted. "Why not? Because you wouldn't be there to hold her hand?"

Something like that. "She's still getting used to the station." And might be lost. Panic gripped Mo. "We have to find her!" She hurried into the corridor.

Ann grabbed Mo's arm. "Calm down! Beep her."

Of course. Feeling stupid, she pulled out her comm unit. When Jayne answered, Mo felt like scolding her and collapsing to the floor in relief. "Where are you?"

"I found that observation deck you told me about, the one you said is never busy," Jayne replied.

"Observation Deck 5?" Ann murmured.

Mo nodded. "Stay there. We'll come and get you." She disconnected and blew out a sigh. Ann grinned at her. "What?" Mo snapped.

"Nothing," Ann said, still grinning. "Are we going to get her, or not?"

By the time they reached the observation deck, Mo's heart had slowed to its normal pace. Jayne was sitting calmly, her sketchbook open on her lap. But no coloured pencils. Stubborn woman.

Jayne flipped her sketchbook closed. "Sorry, I didn't realize I was supposed to meet you in your quarters."

"You weren't. I guess I just expected you to be there."

"And she was in quite the panic when you weren't," Ann added.

Mo glared at her. "I thought you might be lost," she said to Jayne. When Ann grinned at her again, she almost wished they hadn't agreed to have supper with her. But she'd turned down Ann's invitation to play cards the previous evening, and not many on the station had reached out to her and Jayne. Mo couldn't deny that she appreciated Ann's support. "Anyway, let's go eat. My stomach was grumbling during the last half-hour of the meeting."

When they entered the canteen, Ann suddenly pivoted and walked back toward the entrance, motioning for Mo and Jayne to follow her. "Leeds," Ann hissed before Mo could ask. "I spotted her at a table."

"Oh. Let's go to the eatery on Deck 8, then. It'll take forever to get our food, but we're not in a hurry."

Ann nodded. "I didn't think you'd want to eat in the same room with Leeds."

Jayne's brow furrowed. "Why not? Who is he?"

"She was kicked out of the Military Academy because of Lesley!" Ann said, her eyes bright with excitement.

"She wasn't kicked out *because* of Les." Mo fell into step with her. "She wasn't kicked out at all. She was sent to the Indoctrination Academy for a refresher because she couldn't control herself."

Ann's attention remained on Jayne. "She couldn't keep her hands off Lesley. Interior had to step in. I had to meet with them, because I caught Lesley and Leeds together in Lesley's room."

Mo's temples pulsed. "You didn't catch them together. You merely confirmed that Leeds was in Les's room and that Les didn't want her there, as you flaming-well know!" Though when Ann had first told Mo about what she'd seen, she'd made it sound as if Les was all over Leeds. "We'll tell you over supper," she mumbled to Jayne, who was probably filled with questions. "Speaking of Les, have you heard from her today?"

"She replied to my dispatch about—" Jayne glanced at Ann "—the counsellor, but she didn't say much. Just thanks for telling her and she'll see us tomorrow."

So Jayne had also received a terse dispatch. Les had been acting weird since the awards ceremony, but every time Mo asked, she insisted nothing was wrong.

"That reminds me, I'm going off rotation tomorrow. Do you think I can fly with you to, uh, your house?" Ann asked.

Mo's jaw tightened. "We've arranged to meet Les for supper, but I suppose we can drop you there first. But you're not having supper with us!"

Ann gasped. "What a disappointment! I guess I'll have to settle for spending time with my boyfriend, you know, the one I haven't seen for a week."

Fortunately Mo wouldn't have to witness the happy reunion. As she followed Ann and Jayne onto the elevator, her thoughts returned to Les. At least Les had agreed to Mo's suggestion that they all meet for supper. Since Jayne would be with them, Mo wouldn't pry over the meal, and hopefully Les wouldn't drop a nasty surprise on her, as she had the last time they'd met for supper upon Mo's return from 72.

Her comm unit beeped twice. Les! She opened the dispatch. *Mama wants to talk about the Joining Ceremony. She suggested we all meet with her after supper tomorrow. What do you think?* Mo looked up at Jayne. "Adelaide wants to meet with us about the Joining Ceremony tomorrow after supper. Is that okay with you?"

Jayne hesitated. "That's fine."

"We'll have to do it sometime, so it might as well be tomorrow." Mo ignored Ann's smirk and quickly typed a reply. *Tell her okay. I'm looking forward to seeing you.* Before sending it, she deleted the last line. What would she have hoped for in response? Reassurance that everything was okay? Considering Les's insistence that nothing was wrong, maybe it was best to leave it. Les would eventually deal with or talk about whatever was bothering her. No matter what it was, Mo would support her, as always.

LESLEY HUNG HER cloak and led the way to the Thompsons' informal dining room. Mama looked up from her chair at the head of the table. "I expected you about half an hour ago."

"It was busy," Lesley answered as she sank into the chair next to Mo, who had pulled out one of the chairs next to Mama. Jayne hesitated.

"Sit here!" Mama slapped the table with her right hand. Jayne slinked behind her and sat in the chair to Mama's right. Lesley silently apologized for neglecting to guide her to a seat. Jayne was a guest—and her Chosen. She reached for Mo's hand.

Mama tapped the pad in front of her. "I think I've worked out most of the guest list. About five hundred so far."

Mo's jaw dropped. "Five hundred!"

"Your papa suggested about two hundred names," Mama said, shrugging. "Now, I have the lists you two gave me." She picked up her pencil and turned to Jayne. "How many guests will you want to invite?"

Jayne swallowed and tucked her hands under her legs. "Two."

Mama stared at her. "Two." She held up a couple of fingers. "Two guests?"

Jayne nodded.

"Two." Mama frowned. "You won't invite your cousin and her Chosen?"

"Those are the two I want to invite."

"Don't you have a brother?" Mama pressed. "I assumed you meant him and a guest. And you must have other family—aunts, uncles, other cousins? Are your grandparents alive?"

"No, I—I'm not close to them. I just want Carol and Ronald there."

Mama gave her a long look. "Your brother has to be there," she said in the deceptively quiet voice Lesley knew meant trouble. "What do you think it will look like if your brother isn't there? You'll be on the steps by yourself."

"Nobody will know he's not there," Mo said.

Mama twisted to look at her. "We'll know! The Chosen Council will know! Anyone who knows she has a brother will know!" She turned and pointed at Jayne. "If your brother isn't on the steps, there will be whispers."

Jayne shrugged. "I'm used to whispers."

"I don't care if you're used to whispers!" Mama threw down her pencil. "This isn't just about you. This is Lesley and Mo's Joining Ceremony too, not just your Joining Ceremony."

"I know. But I'm not close to my brother. We don't get along. I don't want him there."

Mama's face tightened. "Sometimes you have to do things you don't want to do. It's a Joining Ceremony. Everyone invites people they can't stand!" She jabbed her finger against the table. "And this family has stood behind you. In return, I expect you to support this family by following tradition."

Mo straightened. "Oh, come on, Adelaide, you make it sound like you're doing her a favour by accepting her into the family!"

"No, I am merely pointing out that we have supported her 100 percent. Now it's her turn."

"Who cares if her brother isn't there?" Mo countered. "You won't care if her brother isn't there."

"Yes, I will!" Mama glared at Mo. "Have you ever been to a Joining Ceremony where the siblings weren't present?" When Mo remained silent, Mama said, "I didn't think so." She turned to Jayne. "Perhaps your parents didn't properly instruct you in the etiquette regarding Joining Ceremonies."

Mo shot up from her chair. "Jayne should be able to invite whoever she wants to invite! It's her Joining Ceremony, too!"

Mama's face reddened. "Yes, and that's why I expect her brother to be there!"

Lesley looked on in shock as Mama rose and leaned across the table. Mo rarely stood up to Mama like this. She put her hand on Mo's trembling arm and hoped Mo would sit back down, but she didn't.

"Jayne, in particular, can't afford to deviate from what's expected," Mama said quietly.

Mo snorted. "Oh, so you're forcing her to do something she doesn't want to do because you're worried that Rymellans will look down on her. That makes sense!"

"I am trying to help her!" Mama screeched.

"What's all the shouting?" Papa asked from the doorway. "I can't hear myself think."

Mama sniffed. "It seems the younger generation doesn't understand tradition. Jayne doesn't want to invite her brother to the Joining Ceremony, and Mo doesn't seem to care."

Papa frowned and looked at Jayne. "Why don't you want to invite your brother?"

"She doesn't get along with him," Mama said. "As if you're supposed to get along with everyone you invite. What do you think, Lesley?"

She'd hoped Mama would settle it without involving her. "I have to agree with Mama. It's tradition to stand on the steps with the immediate family." She met Jayne's eyes. "And she's right, you really shouldn't deviate from tradition. It will be odd if the only living member of your immediate family isn't there. Those who know will wonder."

"I wish Carol and Ronald could stand with me," Jayne mumbled.

"Well, they can't!" Mama sat back down. "So invite your brother. What's his name again?"

"Robert."

"Invite him. You'll stand on the steps with him for five minutes and then you don't have to bother with him again. All right?"

After a moment, Jayne nodded.

"And invite more relatives. You won't have to talk to them. There will be hundreds of people there." She twisted toward Mo as Papa, apparently satisfied the storm had passed, left the room. "Are you going to sit down?"

Mo blew out some air and plunked back into her chair.

"Good. Let's move on. We have so many details to discuss!"

Lesley glanced at Mo, and relaxed when Mo caught her eye and shrugged. Mo usually respected tradition, so it must have been Mama's attitude that had angered her, not Mama's insistence that Jayne invite her brother. An hour later, Lesley's suspicion was confirmed as they put on their cloaks.

"I'm sorry about the fuss I caused," Jayne said. "I was being stubborn. You shouldn't have stood up for me, Mo. I know I should invite him."

"I couldn't just sit there while she talked to you like that. Yeah, you probably should invite him, but she could have been less rude about it. That crack about etiquette—" Mo shook her head. "Totally uncalled for."

"I don't want to cause problems between you and Adelaide."

Mo waved her hand dismissively. "Ah, she's already over it. She got what she wanted."

Jayne sighed. "Yeah." She bit her lip; her eyes looked moist.

"Hey." Mo touched Jayne's arm and gazed up at her. "Adelaide was right. You'll only have to stand with him for five minutes. And I told you, you're not alone anymore," she said tenderly. "You have us. Right, Les?"

Lesley couldn't breathe. She felt as if a tidal wave had uprooted her anchor and swept her out to sea. Why hadn't she seen it before? How could she have missed something so obvious? It was in Mo's voice, in her concern, on her face—in her touch! No wonder Mo had stood up for Jayne. She had feelings for her. Mo had feelings for Jayne!

"Les?"

Lesley swallowed. "Right." Then she somehow managed to put one foot in front of the other and follow them out the door, even though her heart had been ripped from her chest.

LESLEY WANDERED AIMLESSLY on the patio behind the Thompson house, her hands shoved into her pockets. The orientation for the commander training had ended; tomorrow she'd begin the actual training. Somehow she'd have to focus, force herself to ignore the dull ache in her chest that wouldn't go away.

The back door swung open. Papa emerged with a mug in his hand. "Oh!" he exclaimed when he spotted her. "I didn't know you were home. I figured you were over at Mo's."

Usually she'd jump at the chance to spend a day off with Mo, but it was painful to look at her right now. "Mo's at the Military Academy flying sims with a friend." She and Ann had invited Lesley along but, not in the mood, Lesley had declined and encouraged Mo to go without her.

Papa lowered himself onto the wooden bench swing on the patio and blew on his tziva. "If I'd known you were here, I would have made you a mug."

She shrugged. "That's okay, I don't feel like tziva."

He studied her. "Worried about the training tomorrow?"

Only that she wouldn't be able to concentrate. "No."

"Then what is it?"

Pretending that something in her peripheral vision had caught her eye, she pivoted away from him and forced another shrug. "Nothing." She felt his eyes on her back.

"You've been moping around for a couple of days now. Talking about it might help."

Could she reveal something so awful to Papa, tell him that she wasn't special to Mo, that their years together hadn't mattered? Lesley had thought they had a bond that nobody else could touch, that their love was unique, that Mo couldn't love anyone but her. A few days ago, she'd been one of a kind. Now she was one of a pair. Not so special, after all. And there was no going back to believing that she owned Mo's heart. No more drawing on the strength of Mo's love when she was feeling down, or someone was disappointed with her, or her day just wasn't going well.

During their separation Lesley had always hoped that, no matter what happened, she'd always hold a special place in Mo's heart. They'd turned out to be Chosens, but she'd lost Mo anyway. She'd lost her.

"Here," Papa murmured, nudging her leg.

When Lesley looked down at the handkerchief he offered, she realized she was weeping. Embarrassed, she mumbled a thank you and wiped her eyes.

"Come sit down," he urged. "Tell me what's wrong."

Still dabbing at her eyes, she sat next to him and wondered how to start. There was no point dancing around it. "Mo has feelings for Jayne," she said flatly, then stared at her lap and played with the handkerchief. She felt sorry for him. What was he supposed to say? He couldn't make it go away or make her feel better.

He set his tziva on the bench's wide arm. "When did she tell you?"

"She didn't. I figured it out when they were over to discuss the Joining Ceremony." Her voice sounded nasal, but if she blew her nose, she'd have to give up the handkerchief. "I know this sounds bizarre, but I don't think she's figured it out yet."

As she'd lain awake at night, Lesley had gone over her last few conversations with Mo. If Mo was aware of her feelings, wouldn't they be ripping her apart inside? Wouldn't she be torn between her growing feelings for Jayne and her love for Lesley? Or had Mo already stopped caring about her? No! Mo wasn't a deceitful person. She couldn't carry around a secret so huge without it affecting her demeanour. As far as Lesley could tell, nothing had changed between them. Mo was acting as she usually did and hadn't come across differently in the conversation they'd had two hours ago, or any other conversations, for that matter.

But it was easy to torment oneself in the dark, and Lesley had, relentlessly. One path she'd started down and quickly abandoned was to blame Jayne. It had crossed her mind that perhaps Jayne *was* like her parents: manipulative, secretive, able to smile while stabbing someone in the back; someone who could ensnare Mo without Mo recognizing the threat. Then Lesley had berated herself for almost falling into a trap that could doom the triad. She didn't know Jayne well, but based on what she did know—and her gut—Jayne wasn't deceptive and manipulative. And with CT134 technically still on the table—no.

Then Lesley had moved on to berating herself for stupidly encouraging Mo to take Jayne to 72—twice! After imagining what could have taken place there and vacillating between wanting to cry into her pillow and pound it into a pulp, she'd calmed down. Neither of her Chosens could lie through her teeth while carrying on behind Lesley's back. To pull that off, they'd have to be master manipulators who had absolutely no regard for her. She couldn't see it. Definitely not in Mo, and Jayne? Where would it lead? What did they think would happen when Lesley found out? Love sometimes made people stupid, but both were smarter than that. They'd know that hiding it would be riskier in the long run than telling her. They were in this triad together, and they had to work together to hold it together. As absurd as it was, any betrayals had to be out in the open.

"Maybe you're seeing something that's not there," Papa said gently.

No. She'd just torn down one whopping lie by accepting that the triad was real. She wasn't about to tell herself another one. "I wish that were true, but it's not. I'm not imagining things." She sighed. "So what do I do now? How do I deal with this? I thought I meant something to Mo."

"You do! She loves you."

"She doesn't love me as much as I thought she did. How could she? She's interested in someone else!" Her anguish forced her to her feet. Papa tugged at her arm. "No, I can't sit. I can't sit." She shoved her hands into her pockets again, one hand still clutching the handkerchief.

"Just because Mo . . . may have feelings for Jayne doesn't mean her feelings for you have changed."

Lesley wanted to believe that, but if Mo was still satisfied with their relationship, with their love, why would she develop feelings for someone else?

Papa shifted on the bench. "This was bound to happen eventually."

"I didn't expect it to happen." Lesley hesitated. "I only really just accepted the triad. I know that sounds weak in the Way, but—"

"Lesley, being strong in the Way doesn't mean you'll accept a triad, just like that." He snapped his fingers. "Of course it would take time. Everyone would have been numb for a while, needed time to wrap their heads around it."

But she'd actively denied it. She'd even told Jayne that she didn't believe they were Chosens.

"It can be tough when you have only one Chosen," Papa added.

She didn't dare ask if he spoke from experience. "I've just told you that my Chosen has feelings for someone else. I could say that on the monitors, and nothing would happen." She sank onto the bench next to him and slumped her shoulders. "Nothing prepared me for this."

"It would have been easier if you'd started out as three strangers."

She turned to him. "You think so?"

He grimaced. "Well, I'm speculating, trying to imagine what it would be like. You probably wouldn't take it so personally."

"Of course I wouldn't!" she snapped. "It wouldn't be the woman I've loved for the past thirteen years." She pulled the handkerchief from her pocket and played with it again. "This is probably going to sound stupid, but I thought we were different. We've been together for so long, and been through so much, that I thought . . . I thought we were untouchable." She pressed her lips together and shook her head. "I really thought we were different, that we had something special."

"You do."

"Not anymore." She brushed away new tears.

Papa's arm slipped around her shoulders. "I know you can't see a bright side right now, but you'll get through this. And when you do, you'll have something that only two other Rymellans have. Two Chosens. Two women who'll love you and cherish you above everyone else."

Right now, she felt as if she didn't have anybody. When Papa pulled her close, she didn't resist, but even as she wept into his shoulder, she felt numb. She felt as she had during her separation from Mo, when the world had become two-dimensional, grey, devoid of laughter and joy. Even then, there had been hope—deeply buried, but there. Hope that their separation would end, that their love couldn't be denied, that the Chosen Council would choose them for each other, as they'd chosen each other for themselves.

But now there was no hope, no chance for a reprieve. They couldn't go back. Their relationship wasn't special. She wasn't special. This grey world would be her home for the rest of her life.

HEAVING A SIGH, Lesley rose from the pilot's seat and slid open her aviacraft door. Meeting Jayne for lunch was the last thing she wanted to do, but the timing couldn't be helped. If they didn't get together on their own initiative, Berry would force the issue, and avoiding Jayne wasn't an option anyway.

Jayne was waiting for her, her sketchbook tucked under her arm. Lesley forced a smile and made herself meet Jayne's eyes. On the way, she'd wondered if seeing Jayne would anger or hurt her, but she felt . . . nothing, except that ever-present dull ache. "Shall we?" She motioned for Jayne to start walking. They'd agreed to go to the same eatery as the last time. "I really do only have an hour this time," Lesley said, meaning it. "I have a class at two."

"How is the commander training going?" Jayne fell into step with her.

"So far, so good. It's a lot of work. Every day starts off with a test, so I have to study every night." Her schedule gave her the perfect excuse to not see Mo. They talked to each other daily, but hadn't spent any time together for five days now. Lesley missed Mo, but dreaded seeing her. Would Mo's touch feel the same? Would Lesley blurt out what she suspected? Would looking at Mo make her weep? She glanced at Jayne, and resisted her stirring resentment. It wasn't Jayne's fault. It wasn't Mo's fault. Even if Lesley could assign blame, it wouldn't matter. It wouldn't make everything go back to how it was before.

She forced herself back to the conversation. "It'll be even busier when we start the practical training exercises. I'll be back at the Military Academy for those."

"Will that seem weird?" Jayne asked.

Her throat tightened. "It will bring back a lot of memories." She recalled their excitement when they were accepted into the Military Academy and then into the pilot training program. And living together for the first time—late nights playing cards; the parties Mo had dragged her to; their duets in the music rooms; quiet nights in. But it hadn't all been good; Mo's trouble with Ann and Lesley's run-ins with Leeds and Morton also came rushing back, along with how she and Mo had supported each other through the rough times. "I met Laura there," she said as she recalled her reluctance to go to Mo's first concert. "Well, not there exactly, but that's where she became my mentor."

Jayne's brows shot up. "I didn't know she taught at the Military Academy."

"She didn't." Normally Lesley wouldn't talk about her failures, but she didn't want to silently wallow and long for times gone by. "She offered to mentor me when I got into trouble for going to a concert." She recounted what had happened, glossing over the problems she and Mo had experienced because of her confusion around how Mo had fit into her life. "I'm glad I went to the concert," she said as she pulled the eatery door open.

Jayne responded after the server had seated them. "If I'd heard that story before I met you, I might have been surprised that you chose the concert over the study group. Now I'd be surprised if you hadn't."

"Why?" Lesley asked as she picked up the menu.

"You never would have missed Mo's first concert."

For a moment, she wanted to reach across the table, grab Jayne's shirt, and . . . She tightened her grip on the menu. It wasn't Jayne's fault. Lesley couldn't resent her Chosen, someone she had to spend the rest of her life with—and someone Mo cared for. The woman across the table was important to Mo.

Jayne was also important to Lesley, but not in the same way. Still, she reminded herself that Jayne *was* her Chosen. Up to this point, Lesley had treated their time together as an obligation to fulfill, not as an opportunity to grow closer to her Chosen. If Jayne had been her only Chosen, wouldn't she try to get to know her on a more personal level? Perhaps if she focused on Jayne and learned more about her, she wouldn't see Mo every time she looked at her.

"What do you like to do?" Lesley asked after the server had taken their orders. "I know you like to draw, but what else do you like to do?"

"Paint." Jayne grabbed her napkin and unfolded it. "Read. Uh . . ."

"What do you like to read? Aside from art books." When Jayne hesitated, Lesley cursed herself for relating. She hated personal questions, too.

"The usual dramatizations. The odd space adventure." Jayne smiled at the surprise Lesley couldn't quite mask. "The ones about solving a mystery, when they come across an abandoned ship or colony or something like that. I've tried the space battle ones, but I can never follow what's happening. There's no point when you skim all the action scenes." She placed the napkin on her lap. "I bet Mo likes to read those."

"No, she doesn't." Lesley couldn't help feeling smug. "Mo's not much of a reader."

"Do you read them?"

"No." And she wasn't about to admit that she liked the mystery ones too.

After a moment, Jayne said, "Carol occasionally passes me a notification story she enjoyed, but they don't appeal to me."

"Me, either," Lesley admitted. It would help if the mere action of Jayne opening her mouth didn't irritate her. She took a deep breath. "Do you like music?"

Jayne nodded. "Very much." She gazed at Lesley. "Mo plays the violin beautifully. I really enjoyed listening to her practice when we were on 72."

Blood pounded in Lesley's ears. Was Jayne deliberately tweaking her nose at her? "Mo and I enjoy playing together," she blurted. *Top that!* Though her sense of victory quickly died. Now she'd have to reveal something she'd rather have kept private. "I play the flute."

And she was acting like a five-year-old! Resenting Jayne, competing with her—what would it accomplish? But meekly accepting that Mo had eyes for someone else was asking too much. Lesley couldn't . . . she just couldn't—and she didn't want to talk about her flute, either. "Did you enjoy your last stay on 72?" Despite her inner turmoil, she kept her voice even.

Jayne nodded again. "Though I upset Mo at one point."

"Oh?"

"I went to one of the observation decks while she was on a shift. When she returned to her quarters, she thought I was lost. I think she was a bit worried."

Was she, now? Lesley's jaw clenched. It shouldn't grate that Mo was looking out for Jayne on 72, but it did.

"It's nice of Mo to invite me to go with her. Do you think you'll ever come? It would be nice if you . . . I'd—Mo would love it." Jayne picked up her water glass and took a gulp from it.

Lesley wasn't so sure that Mo would want her along. "It will be difficult while I'm doing the training. I don't have many days off." Which meant Mo and Jayne would enjoy many cozy trips to 72. Lesley reached for her water glass. This wasn't working, and she couldn't see how it ever would. Every time Jayne mentioned Mo, Lesley felt as if she were being pummelled, and there was no escape. They were all stuck together.

Somehow she had to accept Mo's feelings for Jayne, but how? And what would she do if Mo wanted to act on those feelings? Would Mo care about how it would affect Lesley and their relationship? Perhaps she wouldn't. What had been unthinkable at their notification meetings was now a possibility for Mo. Her feelings for Lesley had obviously changed, diminished in some way. The dull ache in Lesley's chest flared. She couldn't believe it! They were Chosens, but she'd lost Mo anyway.

The server arrived with their lunches. Lesley wasn't hungry, but she picked up her fork and jabbed at a lettuce leaf. "What did you think about those CT134 cases I sent you?" she asked, falling back to a familiar and comfortable topic. She'd had enough of getting personal. Papa believed that having two Chosens meant that her life would be filled with love, but all she saw ahead of her was pain.

LESLEY FINISHED STUDYING the final page of her notes and closed the file, confident that she'd pass the next morning's test. Since it was only 20:30, she checked the course syllabus, and was searching for articles related to the next day's topics when the front door thudded shut and familiar footsteps pounded up the stairs. She tensed and stared at the monitor.

Mo burst into the bedroom. "Oh, you *are* studying. I was starting to wonder if you're avoiding me."

Apprehensive, Lesley twisted in her chair and met Mo's eyes. Argamon, she'd missed her, and could have cried with relief that nothing had changed—for her. Her life would never make sense without her love for Mo. Loving Mo came as naturally as breathing; stopping either would drain Lesley's life away. "We have a test every morning."

"Yeah, I know. But you're in this training for a while." Mo peered at the monitor, then quickly averted her eyes. "I'm not looking at anything I'm not supposed to see, am I?"

Lesley couldn't help but chuckle. "No, I was just searching for something to read, to prepare for tomorrow's class."

Mo rolled her eyes. "No, no, see? This is where you stop for the night and beep me, otherwise we'll never see each other. Preparing for the next class is optional, right?" Apparently meaning it as a rhetorical question, Mo slipped her arms around Lesley and hugged her from behind the chair. "How did your lunch with Jayne go?"

Lesley recognized the underlying tension in Mo's voice. But was it for the usual reason—Mo's jealousy—or because Mo was interested in Jayne?

"I know, I know, I shouldn't ask, but I can't help it!" Mo let her go and flopped onto the bed. Lesley swivelled in the chair to face her, and Mo sighed. "I trust you, okay? But—I don't know, it's hard not to think of them as dates."

"They're not dates." Lesley narrowed her eyes. "Is that why you're here? Because you want to hear about the lunch?"

"No, I'm here because I haven't seen you for almost a week. I figured I'd given you enough time to calm down about your course and I better come over and make sure you don't neglect me." She gave Lesley a wry smile. "But since you had lunch with Jayne today and she didn't say anything about it when I beeped her—"

"You beeped her?"

"Just to arrange to pick her up tomorrow." Mo swung her legs off the bed and sat up. "It's too bad you can't come with us, but on the other hand, having an Interior officer there would probably put a damper on the whole thing."

Or maybe Mo didn't want her along.

"I don't even think she should do it. Stewart sends letters wanting us to execute her and then insults her at the awards ceremony, and now she's supposed to help him?" Mo shook her head. "She thinks she's responsible for everything." Her brow puckered. "I'm glad I'm going with her, to make sure she doesn't let him walk all over her."

Only slightly irked, Lesley studied Mo's concerned face. She agreed with Mo. She wasn't entirely comfortable with Jayne going either and was glad that Jayne wouldn't face Stewart alone. But she didn't have feelings for Jayne. She liked her, and because Jayne was her Chosen, she cared about what happened to her. That was as far as it went.

Mo wagged her finger. "But you're sidetracking me. Tell me about your lunch."

"Why, because you're worried I might run off with Jayne?" Lesley asked, hoping Mo would clarify why their lunch bothered her. She regretted her question when Mo slapped the bed.

"Don't joke about it, Les! I know you don't understand it, but I can't help worrying that Jayne will take you away from me. I know, I know . . ." She frowned down at her lap.

Lesley wanted to leap from the chair and punch her fist into the air. Mo still loved her, or at least cared enough that she didn't want to share her. Could Lesley have been mistaken, seen something between Mo and Jayne that wasn't there? Perhaps her epiphany at the awards ceremony was colouring her perception. She'd thought she'd seen something in Jayne's eyes outside Government Hall, too. They were all Chosens, but that didn't mean they were falling for each other.

Mo had seemed awfully tender and concerned, though. Lesley didn't want to lull herself into another comfortable lie. "Why don't you and Jayne come over here after the counselling appointment tomorrow? You can tell me how it went." Not only that, she needed to see Mo and Jayne together again, and would prefer to do it here, on her territory. If her initial impression was confirmed, she might feel like a third wheel over at the Middletons'. "I won't be here until around 18:00, but you can stay for supper."

"Enough!" Mo's eyes blazed. "Stop trying to dodge the lunch thing. Yeah, I'll suggest to Jayne that we come over, but I want to hear about the lunch. Now!" She patted the bed next to her.

Lesley abandoned her chair for the bed and slipped her hand into Mo's when Mo reached for it. Mo's touch always bolstered her, and tonight was no exception. How would Lesley concentrate tomorrow? Supper with her Chosens couldn't come fast enough! But even if her suspicion turned out to be true, at least she'd learned one thing about herself that partly made up for her stumble regarding the triad: no matter how deeply Mo's feelings for Jayne would hurt her, no matter how betrayed and lonely and inadequate she'd feel, she'd never stop loving Mo. No matter what happened, she'd always love the Chosen next to her.

STIFF WITH TREPIDATION, Jayne followed Counsellor Nolan into his office and dropped into the chair the farthest from the Stewarts. Mo took the remaining empty chair and crossed her legs. Fortunately the chairs were arranged so that everyone faced the counsellor, rather than each other. Relieved that Mo would act as a buffer between her and the Stewarts, Jayne glanced her way for reassurance. Mo met her eyes and smiled, but it didn't help. The tension in the room was already palpable.

Nolan settled into his chair and surveyed them. "Before we begin, let me introduce everyone. This is Kevin and Gwen Stewart." He gestured in their direction. Jayne nodded, but kept her eyes on Nolan. "This is Lieutenant Commander Middleton."

Mo shifted in her seat. "Just Mo. I'm not here as a member of the military."

Nolan nodded. "Mo. And this is Jayne Adams."

As if they didn't know who she was. Jayne tucked her hands under her legs. This was a mistake! She never should have agreed to come.

Kevin Stewart sniffed. "Only one Chosen with you?"

"Lieutenant Commander Thompson is on duty," Mo said. "Otherwise she'd be here."

Would she? Lesley had seemed bored over their lunch. Their dispassionate conversation about the CT134 cases had contrasted sharply with their animated discussion during their first lunch together. Lesley's commander training was probably draining her energy, making it difficult for her to act interested during social obligations she could do without.

"Let's focus on who is here," Nolan said. "I thought it might be beneficial if we were to have a conversation, get to know each other a little."

Someone snorted. Jayne suspected the only person who believed—hoped—the conversation would do any good was Gwen Stewart.

"I don't want to get to know her," Kevin Stewart declared.

Nolan turned to him. "Then why did you talk to her at the awards ceremony?"

"Not to make friends, that's for sure! She needed to know her place!"

When Mo straightened, Jayne shook her head and rested her hand on Mo's arm. On the way, she'd told Mo not to be offended on her behalf, that Stewart wouldn't say anything she hadn't heard many times before. But Mo was used to polite exchanges; even the mildest insults would shock her.

"What *is* her place?" Nolan asked.

"The Wall of Offenders."

Gwen Stewart gasped. "Kevin!"

Jayne gripped Mo's arm. "It's all right," she murmured.

"No, it's not!" Mo hissed back, but she didn't round on Stewart.

Nolan shifted his attention to Jayne. "Would you like to respond to that?"

Anything she said would be a waste of time. When Kevin Stewart looked at her, he saw Papa. He couldn't berate Papa, couldn't get his revenge on him, so she was supposed to serve as Papa's substitute. Well, she wouldn't. As much as she understood Stewart's pain, she wasn't Papa. She couldn't fix what had happened, couldn't absolve Brenda Stewart of responsibility, and wouldn't apologize for something she didn't do. Gwen Stewart's plea had persuaded her to come, but now that Jayne was here, she could see there wasn't any point.

She couldn't help him, but perhaps he could help her. "What do you know about the Incident?" The moment she spoke, she felt as if she were under a bright light, her inner self bared for all to see.

"What?" Kevin Stewart said.

"What do you know about the Incident?" Hot tears of shame and humiliation welled, humiliation because she had to ask for details—especially from Stewart. Without thinking, she moved her hand down to Mo's, needing to hang on to something—someone. The moment her fingers touched Mo's, she realized what she was doing and snatched her hand away. "Sorry," she said, probably too low for Mo to hear.

"You don't know what happened?" Nolan asked softly.

"No, I don't." It was easier to speak to him than to Stewart. "I didn't even know about his sister until . . . Lieutenant Commander Thompson told me about the letters and who'd sent them."

The room fell silent. Nolan turned away. "What *do* you know about the Incident?" he asked Stewart.

"I know her papa killed my sister!"

Mo tutted and glared at Nolan.

"What *else* do you know about the Incident?" Nolan asked, his expression pained.

"Why's she asking me? I don't believe for a second that she doesn't know what happened."

"Contrary to what you might believe, they didn't discuss their violations around the supper table," Jayne said through clenched teeth. "Did you know what your sister was up to?" When he didn't reply, she glanced at him and cringed at his anguished face. His Chosen rubbed his back and murmured to him. Jayne regretted her harsh question.

Why were they at each other's throats? People they'd loved had betrayed them; both their worlds had changed in an instant. Though Rymellans hadn't painted him with the same brush as her. Oh, no! He still had a reputation, had still managed to become an overseer. Yet here he was, eager to vent his spleen and blame her for his sister's behaviour, to make himself feel better. Despite understanding the reasons behind his venomous attitude toward her, she'd had enough. "I think we should go," she said to Mo. "I don't see any point in staying."

Mo instantly rose. "I agree."

"I'm sorry," Jayne said to Nolan.

He didn't try to persuade her to stay. "Thank you for—"

"I didn't know what she was doing," Kevin Stewart said quietly. "All I knew was that she was taking art lessons from . . ." His nostrils flared; he trailed off. "I found out when military showed up at the house, to search it."

Halfway out of her chair, Jayne lowered herself back down. Mo silently followed her lead. "Military came to our house, too," Jayne said, wanting to keep the conversation going. "I didn't understand what was happening. I was only twelve." She paused, to emphasize that last point. "They ushered me out of the house and took me to relatives, but they didn't tell me anything. My uncle explained it later. Well, he told me they'd fallen from the Way, committed Chosen Violations. He didn't give me any details."

"It's *never* appropriate to discuss the details of a Chosen Violation, especially with a child," Nolan said. "Your uncle was doing what he thought best for you."

She'd figured that out years ago. And no, she wouldn't want to hear the sordid details of exactly what took place. But . . ."I understand that, but it's been difficult not knowing anything, even the basic facts. If you look up the Incident," as she'd done many times when younger, futilely hoping that more information would suddenly appear in the public record, "you'll read that four people were executed for committing Chosen Violations, and that it's called the Adams Incident because the Adamses, Joined Chosens, were two of the four."

It had always seemed so unfair that the entry didn't name the other two offenders. Yes, it was shocking and almost unthinkable that both Chosens in a Joining had fallen at the same time, but that shouldn't minimize the involvement of the other two. They'd also committed Chosen Violations. They were just as guilty, regardless of what Kevin Stewart thought. The announcements on the monitors would have named them and their names would be on the Wall of Offenders, but she didn't have access to either. Archived announcements weren't available on the public network, and historical records usually didn't dwell on those who'd fallen. Her parents were an exception.

"Knowing names won't help you." Stewart shook his head. "It doesn't help. The Incident would still be incomprehensible. You'd just have more information to torture yourself with, still ask yourself why."

He was right. On one level, understanding would frighten her—wouldn't that mean she'd fallen from the Way? But that didn't stop her from asking why, though perhaps what she really wanted to know was: why her? Why her parents, her family? Why hadn't they been stronger? Hadn't they loved each other? Hadn't they loved their children? *Why didn't you love me? Why wasn't I enough to stop you?*

She shook herself. "I'd still like to know what happened." It irked her that other Rymellans knew more about events that had radically changed her life than she did.

"If you know something, you should tell her," Mo said.

His Chosen nodded. "Tell her, Kevin. What will it hurt?"

He released a heavy sigh. "I don't know much. I asked, but nobody would tell me anything. I was only her brother," he said bitterly. "My sister took art lessons from . . . your papa. I don't know how they met.

I don't know when they," he grimaced, "crossed the line. I don't know how their violations were discovered."

"But you do know something else," Jayne pressed, wanting to shake it out of him.

"Only because I overheard military talk about it, and more than once, so I'm certain it's reliable."

What? What did you overhear?

"The fourth offender . . . his name was Joseph Hill. That was on the monitors, but most Rymellans probably don't remember. I do, though. I'll never forget." He pulled a handkerchief from his pocket and patted his brow.

Every muscle in Jayne's body tightened. She finally had a name, but what had Kevin Stewart overheard?

"I heard the military say . . ." He glanced at Nolan. "I heard them say he was your mama's counsellor."

Her counsellor? At least he hadn't been fourteen, but—her counsellor? Was there a connection between the counsellor and Brenda Stewart? How could Mama and Papa have fallen from the Way at the same time? Her counsellor? She looked at Nolan, who had a fixed smile on his face. Jayne wanted to roll her eyes. If that revelation made him feel awkward, could he imagine how she'd felt for the past thirteen years? "Did you know him?" Jayne asked Stewart.

"Of course I didn't know him!" Stewart blustered. "Why would you ask such a thing?"

"I was wondering if he was connected to your sister."

"Oh, so you'd like to blame Brenda for the Incident!"

"No, I . . ." Why bother? He'd twist anything she said. "No connection, then." Maybe her parents *had* been monsters who'd enticed two naive Rymellans to their deaths.

Nolan cleared his throat. "Thank you for the information, Kevin. It was kind of you to offer it."

Jayne silently fumed. She was entitled to know!

"Kind?" Mo said indignantly. "I'm sorry, but he's caused her nothing but grief, or have you forgotten that he's asked for her execution—twice—and was rude to her at the awards ceremony? And now he gets a pat on the head for telling her something she has the right to know? He owes her a big flaming apology!"

"I'm not apologizing to her!"

Mo leaned over the arm of her chair and jabbed a finger toward Stewart. "Then look her in the eye and tell her you think she should be executed—a Rymellan who hasn't committed a capital violation or done anything to you. Tell her!"

Admiration and gratitude surged through Jayne. Mo wouldn't feel a restraining hand on her arm this time!

Nolan motioned for Mo to sit back. He turned to Stewart. "Do you still think she should be executed, Kevin?"

"I—I—I need time to think." Stewart lowered his head.

"Perhaps we should break for today," Nolan suggested.

Mo's jaw dropped. "You mean, you want us to come back? Why should we?"

Gwen Stewart met Jayne's eyes. "Now that you have the information you want, you'll wash your hands of this? Is that the only reason you came?"

"No. I'm not like that." Jayne wanted to touch Mo, take her hand and squeeze it. She gripped the arm of her chair instead. "My Chosen is only trying to protect me." Her throat tightened; she blinked back tears. In her heart, she believed what she'd said. Mo honestly cared. *You're not alone anymore.* "We'll be back."

"Good," Nolan said with a satisfied nod. Through him, they arranged their next appointment. Jayne and Mo quickly left the office and the Stewarts.

"Jayne!" Nolan called as they walked up the corridor. She turned. "Did you receive counselling after the Incident?" he asked when he caught up to them.

"No." Well, she had, but it had been obvious from the first appointment that the counsellor was forced to take her on and wasn't comfortable with her. Jayne hadn't helped. Still numb, she hadn't wanted to talk about feelings she didn't have, especially with a stranger. After the fourth session, she'd begged her aunt and uncle not to take her back. Nobody, including the counsellor, had tried to change her mind.

"You might want to consider it. It's never too late."

"I'll think about it," she mumbled, knowing she wouldn't. The Incident was personal; she wouldn't discuss it with just anyone. She'd only agreed to the appointment with Nolan because of Kevin Stewart's personal connection to the Incident—and his Chosen's plea. If Jayne wanted to talk about her feelings, she'd talk to someone she trusted, someone she felt safe with and who wouldn't judge or hurt her. Someone like Carol. Someone like Mo.

HOPING SHE WASN'T agreeing with something she shouldn't, Lesley nodded when Laura paused to sip her juice. What had they been talking about before Lesley tuned out? The sight of Lieutenant Pierce at the cafeteria's hot meal counter reminded her. He coached Laura's son's swimming team. "When is Ben's next competition?" She knew she'd erred when Laura frowned and stared at her.

Laura drained her glass, then dabbed at her mouth with a napkin. "I could use a walk after that lunch. Come with me."

It almost sounded like an order. When Laura rose and picked up her tray, Lesley followed suit. Five minutes later they strolled along a path behind headquarters that was accessible only to military. Laura clasped her hands behind her back. "All right, we're not in my office. We're outside, and we're alone. What's wrong? I'm asking as a friend, not as your commanding officer."

"Nothing." Everything. Supper with Mo and Jayne the previous evening had confirmed her suspicions. The subtle clues were obvious, at least to Lesley. Mo hadn't touched Jayne much—if they'd dined at an eatery rather than at the Thompsons', other diners would have assumed they were a couple and a friend, with Jayne being the friend. Lesley would have been tempted to write off her earlier impression as a mistake, if not for the strain in Mo's voice when they'd discussed the appointment with Nolan. It went beyond the usual concern shown for a friend. Mo cared deeply and felt personally involved, even slighted, on Jayne's behalf.

Thanks for not insisting that we leave when Stewart started talking, Jayne had said to Mo.

Of course we weren't going to leave! I know how important it is for you to find out more about the Incident. Are you sure it's a good idea to go again, though?

Jayne had hesitated.

Are you sure you're not doing it just to prove you're not a bad person?

I know how much he's hurting, Jayne had said, shaking her head. *But that doesn't mean the next appointment will help him. If you're uncomfortable with what I'm doing, you don't have to go with me.*

No way are you going alone! We're in this together, Mo had declared, her voice infused with sympathy, conviction . . . passion.

At that point, Lesley had excused herself to go to the bathroom so she could clench her hands and calm herself in private. But before pushing back her chair, she'd had to move Mo's hand back to her own lap. It didn't make sense!

"See, this is what you were doing all through lunch," Laura said, startling Lesley. "Zoning out. You asked me about Ben's next competition three times. The second time, I thought maybe you hadn't heard me the first time, but three times?" Her smile didn't mask her concern.

Lesley's stomach churned. Perhaps she should have eaten a lighter lunch. "Nothing is wrong."

Cool eyes studied her. "It's eating away at you. Talk to me."

Since Laura wouldn't accept another denial, Lesley considered making something up to appease her. But that would only add guilt to the burden Lesley already carried. She forced out the words. "Mo has feelings for Jayne." She stared miserably at her feet as she walked. Humiliation hadn't coursed through her when she'd told Papa, but she was his daughter. He wouldn't think less of her because she hadn't turned out to be special to Mo. She fought tears. Argamon! She felt as she had when she'd first flown maneuvers on automatic pilot in the simulators—helpless, out of control, flung without warning in every direction—except she'd had a seatbelt back then. "I don't think she realizes it," Lesley said, to forestall the more obvious questions. "But she definitely does."

"She hasn't said anything to you?"

Lesley shook her head. "As I said, I don't think she realizes it."

Laura was silent for a moment. "She probably doesn't recognize her feelings because she loves you, so she's—"

"Her feelings for me have obviously changed," Lesley snapped. "She hasn't figured that out yet, either." She didn't know what tore her up more inside: that Mo didn't love her as much—or at all—or that Mo had feelings for Jayne.

Laura stopped walking. "Why do you think her feelings for you have changed?"

Lesley jerked her head up and whirled to face Laura. "She has feelings for someone else! What else am I supposed to think?"

"That she loves one Chosen as much as she always has and is developing feelings for her other Chosen?"

"If she still loves me as she always has, why would she develop feelings for someone else? I know Jayne's her Chosen, but we've been together for thirteen years and shared so much." She shook her head. "No, her feelings must have changed." Though Mo was still jealous when Lesley saw Jayne. Habit?

"Love isn't finite," Laura said gently. "If it was, I wouldn't love all my children. I'd only love Ben."

Lesley wanted to scream. "It's not the same thing."

"Why is one type of love limited and the other isn't?"

"Laura, we're taught to love our Chosen and nobody else."

"You have two Chosens. So does Mo. So does Jayne. The Chosen Council obviously believes you can love two."

Lesley believed that loving more than one person was possible—just not at the same time.

"Do you remember your lessons about the Danlion colonies? Because of fertility problems, the women had to bond with more than one mate."

"Yes, I do remember. I also remember how they slaughtered each other." If not for a handful of Danlions who'd managed to escape on a cargo ship before the rest turned deadly biological weapons on each other, none would have survived. Hundreds of years later, Danlion still wasn't safe for humans.

"That had nothing to do with their mating customs."

Lesley had never been convinced of that. And who cared about the Danlions? They were human, but not Rymellan.

"We had our own problems before the Way," Laura pointed out.

"And the Way solved them." Rymel was stable. Rymellans were one. War wasn't the norm here anymore, which had allowed Rymellans to flourish and become the most technologically advanced human world in the known universe. If the Danlions hadn't spent so much time fighting each other, perhaps they would have found a solution to their fertility problems. "Our ancestors were right."

"Yes, they were. The Way saved us. And the Way has given you two Chosens."

"The history of triads isn't exactly stellar."

"It's improving." Laura smiled ruefully. "Yes, I'm biased. I know triads can work."

"Your triad met as strangers." Lesley was starting to agree with Papa on that; it would have been easier. "I don't know, Laura. I've always seen myself as strong in the Way, but . . ." Accepting a relationship with Mo and Jayne felt beyond her. She couldn't even imagine it. How could she and Mo continue to have a relationship? "Right now, it seems like an impossible situation."

"You're expecting too much of yourself. You *are* strong in the Way, but that doesn't mean you'll never struggle. It means you'll follow the Way no matter what, and I know you'll do that. You do, too."

Of course she would, but what about happiness and love? Lesley had always believed they'd flow naturally from following the Way. They had, until she'd stopped deluding herself about the triad.

"Have you talked to Mo?" Laura asked. "It sounds like you're talking to everyone but her."

What would she say: "I've noticed you're falling for Jayne"? And then what—Go ahead and have a relationship with her? "I'm not ready. I can't face them having a relationship. I know that's disappointing."

Laura's forehead creased. "Stop it! I'd probably feel the same way. I'm only suggesting you talk to her because it needs to be out in the open, not because I expect Mo and Jayne to jump into a relationship tomorrow. Mo might not want that. And what about Jayne?"

Lesley shrugged. "I have no idea how Jayne feels." Jayne's behaviour toward Mo hadn't changed. Then again, she didn't seem to mind Mo's sympathy. But what was she supposed to say—"Stop worrying about me, stop touching me"? Mo wasn't pawing at her or anything like that.

"You know, Mo might not be recognizing her feelings for what they are because she's not ready, either," Laura said.

"Then my pointing them out to her could do more harm than good."

"Perhaps you should have a more hypothetical discussion about how you'd both feel if one of you were to develop feelings. Right now, you're making all sorts of assumptions because you're not talking to her about it." Laura folded her arms. "Frankly, it's a discussion you probably should have already had."

Lesley's denial of the triad, and their arrangement, had made such a discussion unnecessary. But now . . . despite how Mo's feelings for Lesley must have changed, Mo was still jealous when Lesley saw Jayne. How would she react if Lesley were to raise the possibility that one of them might fall for her? Would a piece click into place, or would she fly into a rage? There was only one way to find out, but Lesley would rather return to being in denial—about the triad, and Mo's feelings for Jayne.

JAYNE CARRIED HER mug over to the counter and, while her back was turned, asked the question she'd been dying to ask since Carol arrived. "Did you know it was her counsellor?"

"No. I would have told you." Carol paused. "I haven't kept anything from you, honest. Remember all those times we tried to eavesdrop when we thought they were talking about it?"

"We weren't very good at it." Jayne smiled at the memory. She turned around and leaned against the counter. "They always heard us."

"Stupid creaky hallway," Carol muttered. "They never discussed it with me. I tried, but they wouldn't." She lifted her mug and drank, took a moment to swallow. "I've always wondered why you've never asked Robert what he knows."

Jayne rolled her eyes at Carol's feigned ignorance. "You know why I haven't." She sighed. "They want me to invite him to the Joining Ceremony. The Thompsons," she clarified when Carol drew breath. "They think it'll set tongues wagging if he's not there."

"They're probably right."

"I don't want him there. I don't want him anywhere near Lesley and Mo." She didn't want him on the steps or in her life. His presence would spoil the day. Just the thought of inviting him sickened her.

"Don't you think it's time to put it behind you? He's your brother."

"He didn't want to be my brother, remember?"

"He was seventeen. He panicked."

"He abandoned me when I needed him the most."

"And he realizes that. He—"

Jayne pushed herself away from the counter and leaned over the table. "No, he doesn't!" She jabbed a finger at Carol. "*You* want him to realize it, you and Kelly. If he has any regrets about it, where is he? Why doesn't he beep? Why hasn't he shown up on my doorstep? The few times I've seen him, you and Kelly have forced us together. Did he beep when the triad was announced? No. Did he visit me in the infirmary? No. Did he even ask if I was all right when you told him I was in the infirmary?" Carol's silence was ample answer. "*He* decided he didn't want to be my brother. If he's changed his mind, he'll have to come to me." She hoped he would, so she could slam the door in his face.

"And you've explained all this to the Thompsons? If you don't invite him to the Joining Ceremony, they'll want to know why."

Her anger left her. Drained and dejected, she sank into a chair. How would she explain her family to a family that always stuck together? Lesley's brother had moved out over the triad, but misguided or not, he believed his refusal to accept the triad—or, more specifically, Jayne—was a refusal to stand by and watch while his sister ruined her life.

Robert's reasons for running away had been all about him. Jayne had never doubted that if he could have changed his name and removed all traces of their relationship from the records, he would have. She was surprised he hadn't blamed her for the Incident. He'd certainly told anyone who'd listen that he'd finished all his levels at the Indoctrination Academy, while she was still at an impressionable age. He'd never explicitly said that if either of them was a threat to the Way and should be executed, it was her, but he'd meant it. She may have been only twelve, but she hadn't been stupid. At first she hadn't understood why he'd insisted on staying with their other uncle, but it hadn't taken her long to figure it out.

While the petitions for their executions were on the table, everyone talked about nothing else, except when she was around. Robert only visited when he knew she'd be in bed, not out of consideration for her, but so he could spew his poison behind her back. At night, everyone would gather in the living room, instead of huddling in the kitchen or outside in the garden. While they did lower their voices, she could hear them from the shadows at the top of the stairs. The more guests present to listen to his nonsense, the more vigorously Robert argued his position: he was strong in the Way, while she was still learning the Way and vulnerable to "alternative viewpoints." Not once had he asked about her. Not once had he come upstairs to peer into the bedroom, probably afraid of being painted with the same tainted brush he enthusiastically brandished.

Once the overseers had denied the petitions, the frequency of Robert's visits had dropped dramatically. She'd asked for him, but he never came. He'd turned against her when she'd most needed her brother, and now he had to live with that . . . But Carol was right. If Jayne stubbornly refused to invite him to the Joining Ceremony, the Thompsons would expect—demand—an explanation. Did she want to tell them that her own brother had hoped to offer her as a sacrifice to appease those who wanted retribution against their family?

"I'll have to invite him," she said to Carol, feeling as if she was betraying herself.

"It could be the beginning of a reconciliation," Carol said.

No. It would mar her Joining Day. On the other hand, if it marked the last time she ever saw him, she'd have two reasons to celebrate the date every year.

After Carol left, Jayne reluctantly looked up Robert's code and punched it into the comm station. He worked nights, so he should be home.

Robert didn't bother to say hello. "I did a double-take when I saw your name."

"I'm beeping to invite you to my Joining Ceremony," she said flatly. "The Thompson family would like you to be there."

He chuckled. "It'll be a bit of a farce, won't it? You and me, on the steps together."

"If you don't want to come, then don't. I'll tell them I invited you, and you declined." She regretted the words the moment they left her mouth. Robert would never allow her to paint him in a bad light.

"I didn't say I wouldn't go, just that it will be a farce. When is it?"

"I don't know yet. We've submitted a few dates to the Chosen Council. I should know in a few weeks."

"I assume I can bring Kelly."

"Yes."

"Well, when you know the date, let me know. Or have Carol pass it along. Doesn't matter to me." He sounded bored.

"I'll tell Carol—"

"Anyway, I have to go. Bye." The connection went dead.

Jayne blinked back tears as she sank onto the sofa. She hated talking to Robert. Whenever Carol badgered her about him—*Why won't you see him? Rejecting him isn't the answer. The two of you need to talk*—Jayne always said she no longer cared. But despite what she told herself and Carol, that wasn't why she avoided him. The hope that he'd regret how he'd treated her and understand how he'd failed her, that he'd reach out and try to make amends, had always existed deep within her. But every time she spoke to him, that ball of hope shrivelled. He wasn't remorseful. When he'd moved on with his life thirteen years ago, he'd truly left her behind. There would never be a tearful apology, an acknowledgment of her isolation and pain, a vow to do better. He didn't care. He never would. Speaking to him only drove home the reality that she wasn't rejecting him, and he wasn't rejecting her. To him, she was nobody. Nobody at all.

KEVIN SCOWLED WHEN Gwen pushed open his study door. He'd heard her greet Cynthia, and had hoped Gwen would come up with an excuse to put her off seeing him. She knew he wasn't in the mood to socialize. "I'm working on a case," he growled.

Gwen frowned at him. "It's only Cynthia, and she's concerned about you." She lowered her voice. "I told her about the appointment."

"You *what?*"

"She's your sister."

"I suppose you told her about what happened at the awards ceremony, too." His jaw clenched when she nodded. "You had no right to tell her anything!"

"She's your sister, Kevin. You need your family, all of us. Shutting yourself away and brooding won't help. Now, come on." She beckoned to him. "You can't avoid her forever."

Startled, he pushed back his chair. Gwen was more perceptive than he'd thought. Did she know that he'd discouraged Cynthia from visiting because seeing her reminded him of his meeting with Finney? He'd been so sure that he was acting in the best interest of the Way, yet everyone was disappointed with him, including his Chosen. His behaviour at the awards ceremony had mortified and frightened Gwen, who'd wept the entire way home. If not for her, he never would have agreed to meet with Adams.

Cynthia smiled up at him from the sofa, compounding his guilt for neglecting her. "Glad to see you," he mumbled.

She met his eyes. "How are you?"

"Fine," he said, knowing she wouldn't believe him.

"Tziva?" Gwen asked.

Cynthia shook her head. "Not just yet." Her eyes grew bright with curiosity. "Gwen told me about your appointment. What's she like, Kevin?"

He sat in one of the chairs across from her and shrugged. "I don't—"

"Not quite what you were expecting, was she, Kevin?" Gwen plunked herself next to Cynthia and pointed at him. "He knew more about the Incident than she did."

Cynthia's brows rose. "Really?"

"Apparently she didn't know about Brenda until Lieutenant Commander Thompson told her. Kevin had to tell her about Hill. Apparently nobody told her anything. She was only twelve. The counsellor said they were protecting her, but it must have been hard on her, not knowing."

His hands didn't clench when they both grimaced and nodded. Before the appointment, seeing them sympathize with an Adams would have shot his blood pressure through the roof. But now he didn't know what to think. Gwen was partly right—Adams hadn't been anything like he'd imagined. He'd expected her to swagger into the counsellor's office, arrogant and hostile.

"She almost left when it looked like Kevin wasn't going to tell her anything," Gwen said.

Cynthia turned to him. "Why wouldn't you tell her?"

"I thought she was playing games."

"Why?"

"It sounded fishy to me, her not knowing anything."

"Why would she lie about something like that?"

To irritate him.

Cynthia's mouth pressed into a disapproving line. "It must have been difficult for her, having to ask *you* for the information."

At first he'd wanted to stretch out Adams' agony, make her beg him to divulge what he knew. Then he'd looked at her, seen the longing and the hurt in her eyes . . . Peter Adams' eyes. No! Her eyes. *I didn't understand what was happening. I was only twelve.* Her quavering voice had barely masked her pain. For the first time, he'd seen *her*, not her papa. A Rymellan deeply hurt by the Incident, like him. Remembering the moment he'd empathized with her made him squirm; he folded his arms and leaned forward.

"Don't get angry," Cynthia said, misinterpreting his discomfort. "To her, *we're* the bad family."

Kevin glared at her. If she'd said that to him before the appointment . . . He took a deep breath. "I don't think Adams sees us that way."

Gwen gave him a pointed look. "Her name's Jayne. And I don't think she sees us that way, either."

"What else did you talk about?" Cynthia asked.

"Nothing," Gwen said, before he could reply. "Mo—Lieutenant Commander Middleton—got upset because Counsellor Nolan thanked Kevin for telling Jayne about Hill. She wanted Kevin to look Jayne in the eye and tell her she should be executed."

Cynthia gasped. "Did you, Kevin?"

He swallowed. "No."

She nodded. "Looking someone in the eye isn't the same as sending letters."

Her voice was reproachful, but he read the sympathy in her eyes. When Nolan had proposed the appointment with Adams, Kevin had quickly rejected the idea. That would have been the end of it, if not for Gwen's distress over his behaviour at the awards ceremony and the effect Adams—and everything else dredged up by the triad announcement—was having on their relationship.

He'd arrived at Nolan's office skeptical that any good would come of the meeting with Adams. The appointment had initially gone exactly as he'd expected. The sight of Adams had enraged him; his hands had balled into fists and he'd wanted to lash out, pound into her, make her acknowledge that her family had devastated his—until he saw the hurt and bewildered twelve-year-old girl who hunched her shoulders, spoke in a trembling voice, and cried out for answers.

When Middleton had demanded that he look Adams in the eye and tell her she should be executed, all he could think about was the girl who'd had her parents ripped away from her, through no fault of her own. But could he let it go, read announcements about the Thompson triad without seething over how Peter Adams had taken advantage of Brenda? What if Adams had children? What if she moved past the Incident and found happiness?

He was torn between his desire to eradicate every trace of Peter Adams, and his growing understanding of how the Incident had affected Adams' daughter. All he knew for sure was that he wanted to talk to Adams—Jayne—again.

AS LESLEY WALKED from her aviacraft to the house, she listened to the message Mo had left earlier that afternoon: *Les, it's me. Do you want to come over tonight? We'll have the house to ourselves. I know you have a test tomorrow*—Lesley could hear the sigh in Mo's voice—*but it feels like we haven't seen each other for ages. You don't have to study for hours on end. Study for an hour and then come over, okay?* She winced at Mo's pleading tone. *Oh, and we should see Jayne on your day off. We haven't seen her together since we had supper after the counselling appointment. Beep me later!* Mo *would* bring up Jayne.

She blew out some air and pondered what to do. That was the third time she'd listened to the message, hoping a clear winner would emerge from the war between the part of her that wanted to follow Laura's advice about talking to Mo, and the part that wanted to go on as if Mo's feelings for Jayne didn't exist. While the battle raged, she'd avoided Mo, feeling paralyzed. Something had to give.

Logic dictated that she talk to Mo. Deep down, she knew she didn't have a choice, that Mo's feelings for Jayne would eventually come between them no matter what she did—it was already happening. But raising the subject with Mo could be disastrous. Would their relationship survive the conversation and remain strong, or would it be irreversibly weakened? Did Lesley want it to survive? Mo had feelings for someone else!

And Lesley still loved her. All these years, Mo had never fully trusted her, but every time Lesley had insisted that she'd never leave, that she'd love Mo no matter what, she'd meant it. Only the Chosen Council could ever have torn them apart. But Lesley had never imagined the situation she was in now—Mo potentially having a relationship with someone else. She'd just known that her love for Mo would never die. So here she was, looking at being a third wheel as Mo's feelings for Jayne deepened. What did that say about her? Did it make her pathetic? Should she go over to Mo's tonight, lay down the rules, tell her to stick to their arrangement? Or else . . . what?

Jayne wasn't a passing fancy, some woman up on 72 who'd caught Mo's eye and was only a crush that would eventually burn itself out. She was Mo's Chosen—their Chosen. They would be together for the rest of their lives. Demanding that Mo resist her feelings for Jayne would only hurt her relationship with Lesley. Not only would Mo resent her, but Lesley would feel like a tyrant. But what was the alternative—telling Mo to go ahead and have a relationship with Jayne? Could Lesley honestly read a book downstairs while they were carrying on upstairs? Would she feel the same when Mo touched her? Would she believe it when—if—Mo said she loved her? If Lesley did what the Way expected and told Mo that it was all right to honour her other Chosen in *every* sense of the word, how could their relationship survive? Would *she* survive? Lesley would never violate the Way, but she didn't feel alive in this grey world in which she was no longer special to Mo. She felt like a walking shell, as she had during their separation, but with no hope for a reprieve.

Knowing she had to reach a decision, Lesley paced outside the house. She appeared to have two choices: talk to Mo, or avoid her. Seeing her without bringing up her feelings for Jayne couldn't go on for long. Laura was right; it would eat away at Lesley until it came out in a horribly emotional way that would do more harm than good. If she went over tonight and didn't talk to Mo, it would only hang over them, with Mo unwittingly hurting Lesley every time she showed concern for Jayne. Lesley had to believe that they stood a better chance of weathering the coming storm if they were open and honest with each other.

She beeped Mo.

"Hey, I hope you're beeping to tell me you're coming over," Mo said.

"I am."

"Good! Bring your flute. My audition's next week. I've already practised today, but I wouldn't mind playing with you for good measure."

"Uh, not tonight. I thought it would be nice to spend a quiet night together, and maybe talk. We haven't talked—really talked—in a while. You said everyone else will be out, right?"

"Yep." Mo paused. "I hope you'll stay over."

"I don't know. I'll see how I feel." It would depend on how their conversation went. "I have to be up for my course."

Mo groaned. "I hope you're busier with this course than you will be when you're a commander."

"I don't know, the commanders I know are pretty busy."

"I guess it's a good thing I have another Chosen, then."

Mo's tone was light. She'd clearly meant her words as a joke, but Lesley felt as if she'd just been knifed in the gut. "I'll be over around 20:00. I'll see you later."

"I'm looking forward to it."

Lesley closed her eyes. "Me too."

They disconnected. Lesley slid her comm unit back into its holder, but didn't go inside. She walked around the house, into the back garden, and onto one of the paths. There, hidden by the trees, she dabbed at her eyes when tears blurred the path. Talking to Mo was the right thing to do, but it felt like the beginning of the end of everything she held dear.

LESLEY ALMOST HIT Michael when she swung open the Middletons' front door. "Sorry, I didn't know you were there."

"I'm just on my way out." He turned to Mo, who was standing behind him. "Don't forget to tell her about the supper next week."

"I will," Mo said, rolling her eyes. "Why's it so important that we all be there?"

"Because we haven't eaten together as a family since . . ." Michael screwed up his face, then brightened. "Since your notification lunch!"

Mo snorted. "And what a great meal that was." She frowned. "Is Andrew inviting his girlfriend?"

"He asked if he could, but I told him no. I only want family there. Anyway, I have to go." He nodded to Lesley and slipped out the still-open door. She closed it.

Mo stared after him. "He wants us all here for supper next Thursday—even Jayne! He's catering it! It'll be served around 19:00, so even if you have to study, you should—" Her comm unit beeped. "Who's that?" she mumbled as she pulled the unit from its holder.

"Archer here. Mo, I hate to ask you this, but is there any chance that you can do five morning shifts, starting tomorrow at 10:00?"

"Five?" She glanced at Lesley. "I don't think so. It's too short notice, and I don't want to be away for four nights right now."

Archer sighed. "That's what everyone's saying."

"You could order someone to do them," Mo pointed out. "Including me."

"I want to avoid that, if I can. I still have more supply pilots I can try. Thanks anyway."

They disconnected. "Too short notice," Mo repeated. "And I'd have to be up too early to get there in time, or go tonight, and I don't want to do that." She reached for Lesley.

Lesley quickly hugged her, so she wouldn't have to force a smile. "What were you saying about supper next week?"

"Just that you should have time to study afterward," Mo said into Lesley's shoulder. "You can even do it here. Jayne can keep me company."

It was now or never. Lesley drew back. "Actually, I want to talk to you about Jayne."

Mo looked up. "What about her?"

"Let's sit down." She followed Mo into the living room, sat next to her on the sofa and, after hesitating a beat, took her hand. How to open *this* conversation? Not wanting to give herself an excuse to put it off, she'd deliberately not rehearsed what she'd say. "Do you remember what I said after our notifications, that Jayne probably wasn't our Chosen? That the triad could be a sham?"

"You're not going to bring up CT134 again, are you?" Mo's voice was hushed.

"No. But I was wrong. She is our Chosen. I guess it was my way of coping with it, until I could face it."

"I was never comfortable with that. If our Joining won't be real, what would that imply about the rest?"

"I know. And I know how weak in the Way it was to—"

Mo shook her head. "No! You said it yourself, it was your way of coping. Come on, Les. We were both in shock after our notifications. We weren't thinking straight. We told ourselves whatever we needed to believe to understand it."

Lesley swallowed. "Does that include our arrangement with Jayne?"

"What do you mean?"

"She's our Chosen."

Mo remained silent. Her tight face and intent stare told Lesley to tread carefully. How could she get Mo to open up about her feelings toward Jayne without bluntly asking about them? She squeezed Mo's fingers. "Since the three of us are Chosens to each other, I thought we should talk about whether our arrangement is realistic, just to see how we're both feeling about it, now that we know Jayne a little better. Perhaps we'll decide that our arrangement still makes sense." Lesley would love that to be true, but it would be weak in the Way for them to refuse to even consider the possibility that Jayne might become more than a friend—especially since, for Mo, she already was.

But Lesley needed time to come to grips with Mo's feelings for Jayne. She needed reassurance. Had Mo's feelings for her changed? Could Lesley hold it together and at least tolerate a relationship between Mo and Jayne, or would she be utterly despondent and die inside every time she was in a room with them? The stability of the triad had to be their primary concern, and agreeing to take things slowly and not act on any feelings until they—Lesley—had time to adjust might be the best way to ensure it. But they couldn't talk about that, or anything related to it, until Mo acknowledged her feelings for Jayne. "But we should talk about how—and I'm not saying this will happen—but how we'll deal with it if one of us starts to—"

Mo yanked her hand from Lesley's and leaped to her feet. "I knew it!" she screamed. "I knew you'd do this! From the moment we found out we're in a triad, I knew this would happen!"

"Nothing's happening." Lesley slowly rose and motioned for Mo to calm down. "I just thought—"

"You just thought you'd have a relationship with Jayne!" Mo burst into tears. "I knew this would happen," she wailed. "I knew it . . ." She doubled over.

Horrified, Lesley put her arm around Mo and drew her close. "I don't want a relationship with Jayne. I just want to talk—"

Mo pushed her away and backpedalled. "You didn't think Jayne was our Chosen. Now you do, and you want to talk about our arrangement. What do you think I am, stupid? Don't treat me like a flaming idiot!"

Lesley heaved a sigh. "I don't want to have a relationship with Jayne! But . . . since she is our Chosen, it's possible that one of us might develop feelings for her. It doesn't have to be me." She hesitated. "It could be you." Cringing, Lesley stared at Mo. No matter how much she suspected Mo had feelings for Jayne, it would devastate her to hear Mo confirm those feelings.

Mo pointed a trembling finger at her. "Don't you dare put this on me," she said firmly and quietly. Then she shouted so loudly, Lesley's ears rang. "Don't you dare!"

The anger—hate?—in Mo's eyes brought tears to Lesley's. She stepped toward her. "Mo—"

Mo curtly shook her head and reached for her comm unit. Lesley opened her mouth to ask what she was doing, but Mo motioned for silence by slicing her hand across her neck. She punched in a code. "It's Mo. Do you still need someone to do those shifts?"

"I haven't found anyone yet," Archer said, sounding hopeful.

Lesley vigorously shook her head, but Mo ignored her. "I've changed my mind. Arrange quarters for me. I'll be arriving tonight."

"Great! Thanks, Mo!"

"What are you doing?" Lesley cried when Mo disconnected. "We need to talk!"

Mo whirled and marched into the hallway.

"We need to talk!" Lesley repeated, chasing after her. She watched in disbelief as Mo grabbed her cloak from its hook and flung it over her arm. "Mo! Don't do this."

Mo opened the front door, then turned to Lesley. "Have fun with Jayne."

"You've got it all wrong!"

"I am sick of your lies! I'll tell you what I had wrong. You! Wanting you as my Chosen." Mo lowered her head and muttered under her breath, then looked up. "During our separation, I couldn't imagine my life without you. I pined after you. I felt . . ." Her lips trembled. She clenched her free hand and held it against her heart. "I felt as if I couldn't survive without you, that I'd never be happy. Then it turned out we were Chosens, and even with the triad, I couldn't have been happier." She dropped her hand to her side and yelled, making Lesley jump. "Especially since you seemed as eager to shut Jayne out as I was! But that's all changed now, hasn't it, Les?" She sneered. "You don't care about *me*. All you'll do is hurt me. You'll hurt, hurt, hurt me! I was hoping for the wrong thing. I should have hoped I'd never see you again."

"You don't mean that," Lesley whispered, barely able to see Mo through her tears. "I love you. I've *always* loved you. We belong together. Don't we?"

Mo stared at her for a moment, then turned away and stepped through the doorway. The door slammed behind her.

Intending to go after her, Lesley reached for the door's handle, but her knees buckled the moment her fingers touched it. Mo's feelings for Jayne, Mo's spiteful words, the seemingly impossible task of honouring the Way without losing her sanity and Mo's love—it finally proved too much for her. She slid to the floor and wept, her sobs echoing around the empty hall.

CROSSROADS

.....

M O KEPT HER HEAD DOWN AS she strode through 72's waiting area and into the elevator. Nobody had sat next to her on the shuttle, but she wasn't sure if her demeanour or the abundance of empty seats had ensured her solitude. She felt sick, mortified, and frightened. Les's shocked face taunted her again; Mo cringed over how much the harsh words she'd uttered at their parting must have hurt her. She hadn't meant them, and it hadn't taken her long to regret them, or her decision to run away to 72 at the worst possible moment. What a mess!

She groaned aloud when the elevator doors opened on Deck 6 to reveal Ann loitering in the corridor. "Archer told me you're filling in for Ian," Ann said. "D6-242, if you're wondering. I was just about to head up to the waiting area. Want to play some cards?"

Having checked Archer's dispatch on the shuttle, Mo already knew the location of her quarters. She hoped she looked all right. She hadn't cried on the way to 72, but her head throbbed. "I'm tired. I'm going to bed," she mumbled, hoping to dissuade Ann from following her.

But Ann tailed her. "It's only 21:45. You're usually good until about 23:30." Her voice sounded shrill. "Why are you walking so fast? Are you okay? You're not in uniform! Where's your bag?"

Mo winced and grabbed the side of her head with her left hand. "Will you please be quiet?" When they reached quarters D6-242, she shifted her cloak to her left arm and punched the *Open* button. "Look, I'm tired, okay? I'll see you tomorrow."

"You sure you're okay?" Ann stepped over the threshold after her.

Mo couldn't take it anymore. She flung her cloak across the room. "I'm fine!" she yelled. "I'm flaming fine! Now will you please leave me alone! Just leave me . . ." Tears welled in her eyes. "Leave me alone," she managed to whisper, then sank onto the sofa and buried her head in her hands.

Her relief at hearing the door swoosh shut was short-lived. Footsteps approached her. "What's going on?" Ann asked.

Mo raised her head. Ann stood in front of her, her hands on her hips. "If I say 'nothing,' will you leave?" Mo asked. *Oh, what's the point?* "Les and I had a fight. I won't be surprised if she never wants to see me again." Not that Les had the choice.

"Is that why you changed your mind about doing the shifts? Archer said you originally told him no."

Mo nodded.

"So you and Lesley had a falling out, and you decided to handle it by running away to 72, leaving her down on the planet with Jayne when she's mad at you." Ann snorted. "I wouldn't hold your breath for the Genius of the Year award."

Mo shot to her feet. "Can you be supportive, for once in your life? Can you? Do you know how to do that?" She glared at Ann, then thunked back down on the sofa and buried her head in her hands.

Ann didn't move. "Is it about Jayne?"

Now who wouldn't be getting the Genius of the Year award? "Yeah. And I was so angry at Les, I said some horrible things." Things she wished she could take back. "I wasn't thinking straight, okay? If I was, I'd still be down on the planet."

"Wait! You were angry with *her*?"

The surprise in Ann's voice made Mo look up. "Yeah. Is that so hard to believe, that I can get angry with her?"

"No. But . . ." Ann hesitated. "Well, I thought if the two of you were going to fall out over Jayne, it would be because she was upset with you, not the other way around."

"Why?"

"What do you mean, why?"

Mo threw up her hands. "Exactly what I said! Why would she be upset with me?"

Ann gaped. "You don't know?"

Mo wanted to throttle her. "Stop playing flaming games! I'm not in the mood."

"I'm not playing games! What's the matter with you? If Lesley and Jayne got together, you'd lose it. So don't pretend you don't know why she's upset."

She had no idea what Ann was talking about. "What does that have to do with anything?"

"You and Jayne." Ann let out an exasperated sigh when Mo shrugged, still drawing a blank. "Your relationship!"

"What relationship?"

"Come on, Mo. The two of you are close." Ann drew her hands together. "I assumed you were . . . involved."

Mo couldn't believe her ears. "We're not! Whatever gave you that idea?"

"Hanging out with the two of you when you're both up here. The way you talk about her. It's obvious you care about her."

"Of course I care about her. She's my Chosen. She's my responsibility."

Ann shook her head. "No. I mean *care*."

No. No way. "You're seeing something that's not there."

Ann barked a laugh. "You really are clueless. You should see yourself with her. You don't hang off each other, exactly, but she's usually on your arm. You worry about her, you're protective of her, you're happy when you're with her. I've certainly noticed it, and I'm not the only one. Some of the other pilots—"

"What?" Mo blurted. "What are they saying?"

"Nothing bad. Just that the two of you seem to be getting along well. Really, really well."

No. No, no, no. "I'm just being supportive. She's not familiar with 72. She's shy, she doesn't feel comfortable with people she doesn't know. And she's dealing with that idiot Stewart right now."

Ann rolled her eyes. "Okay, why don't you go out there right now and be supportive to someone else's Chosen in the same way you are to Jayne, and see how that works out for you."

Mo clenched her hands and stood, but then sank back down. She *was* just supporting Jayne . . . wasn't she? She enjoyed Jayne's company, and yeah, she did worry about her. So many people had let Jayne down. Mo wanted to reassure her that she was no longer alone, that Mo would be there for her . . . that she wanted to be there for her. But that didn't mean . . . No, she was just being a good friend. They *were* friends, right? And since they would—did—share each other's lives, of course they'd grow close and develop a certain . . . intimacy with each other, but . . . no.

Ann shifted her weight. "Okay, let's say I got it wrong. If I did, so could Lesley. *Something* is making me and everyone else think you and Jayne are closer than friends. Whatever we're seeing, she's probably seeing."

Fear snaked through Mo. "You think she thinks Jayne and I are together?"

"Mo, the cook in the canteen probably thinks you're together," Ann said, jerking her thumb over her shoulder. "Of course she's noticed there's something between you."

"There's nothing to notice!" But what if Ann was right, and Les had put two and two together and got five? "Argamon!" She covered her face with her hands and flopped against the back of the sofa.

"What did Lesley say? What happened?"

Mo parted her hands enough to peer at Ann. "She said she wanted to talk about Jayne."

"And?"

And she didn't know—she'd assumed Les wanted a relationship with Jayne and so hadn't given her a chance to say much of anything. *But . . . since she is our Chosen, it's possible that one of us might develop feelings for her. It doesn't have to be me. It could be you.* Had Les been trying to find out if she had feelings for Jayne? If Les believed that she did . . . "I've screwed up, Ann. I've screwed up real badly." So badly that she wouldn't blame Les for hating her. She desperately wanted to see Les, throw herself at her feet and beg for forgiveness, but she was stuck up here for five days. She was a complete *idiot*. "I might have totally misinterpreted everything." Les was doing the same, except she hadn't told Mo that she wished they weren't Chosens. *Idiot!* "I didn't give her a chance to tell me what she was concerned about. I thought she wanted permission to have a relationship with Jayne, but that's not what she wanted. Yeah, I know, I'm stupid."

"You know, I've never understood your attitude toward Lesley." Ann folded her arms. "She's never so much as looked at anyone else, as far as I can tell. There would have been no shortage of eager takers if she had, but for some strange reason, she's only ever wanted you."

Mo opened her mouth to tell Ann that she already felt guilty enough, thank you very much, but changed her mind. She deserved whatever Ann flung at her.

"Did she beep you on the shuttle, try to reach you?" Ann asked.

"No. I've really blown it this time." She fought another round of tears.

Ann cleared her throat and turned toward the small kitchen. "Do you want tziva?"

Not really, but her blubbering was making Ann uncomfortable. "Sure."

While Ann busied herself with the tziva, Mo sat slumped on the sofa, worrying about Les. How was she? What was she thinking? Would she forgive Mo's horrible parting words? Did she think her two Chosens were carrying on behind her back? Why did they have to end up in this stupid triad, anyway?

"Here." Ann handed her a mug.

"Thank you," Mo murmured. "Would you mind checking to see if there are any painkillers in the bathroom? I need something for my head."

"Why don't you go to the infirmary? They'll take care of it a lot quicker than painkillers will."

But that would mean venturing into the corridors, looking like a wreck. By not cracking jokes about Mo's appearance, Ann was proving she could be diplomatic. "I don't want to leave my quarters," Mo mumbled. Plus, her throbbing head served her right. *Idiot!*

Ann shrugged and disappeared into the bathroom. "Good news," she said, returning with a bottle. After handing it to Mo, she picked up Mo's crumpled cloak and threw it over the sofa's arm. Mo tipped a couple of pills into her hand and washed them down with tziva. She leaned back and closed her eyes.

"You're Chosens, so you'll have to work this out," Ann said.

That was probably the only reason Les would talk to her. If Les hadn't wished they weren't Chosens before, she probably did now.

"I don't think I'm wrong about you and Jayne."

Mo opened her eyes a crack. Ann sat in the chair across from her, a mug of tziva in her hand.

"Maybe you don't see it, but—"

"Right now, I'm worried about me and Les." She'd worry about Jayne later . . . her feelings for Jayne . . . *whether* she had feelings for Jayne.

They sipped their tziva in silence. Mo had to admit she was grateful for Ann's presence. If she was alone, she'd probably be prostrate on the bed and sobbing into the pillow, believing Les wanted a relationship with Jayne. Maybe Les did. Maybe Ann was wrong and Mo hadn't misinterpreted. But at least now, she wouldn't rage at Les about Jayne when she next spoke to her. She'd listen, as she should have done in the first place. A glance at her comm unit told her it was almost 22:30. As soon as Ann left, she'd beep Les. She wouldn't sleep until they'd talked. "Thanks for following me in here."

"Well, you are Andrew's sister." Ann lifted an eyebrow. "And maybe this would be a good time to mention that you'll fly three of your five shifts with me, including the one tomorrow morning. I figured I'd better make sure you're all right, so I don't have to play counsellor when I'm in the cockpit. And I don't want to have to crank up the music to drown out your crying."

Mo almost chuckled. "Good. I'm glad it'll be you," she said, temporarily abandoning their game of pretending they weren't really friends and didn't care about each other. Maybe someday they'd both abandon it permanently.

The door chimed. Mo groaned. "Can you get that?" She set her tziva down and lay on the sofa so she couldn't be seen from the door. "Tell whoever it is to get lost—nicely. Tell them I'm tired and I'll see them tomorrow." Then she realized how bad it would look if Ann remained in her quarters. "And I'll see you tomorrow, okay? Thanks for staying with me."

The door swooshed open. "Come on in," Ann said.

What? Mo wanted to kill her. She struggled to a sitting position, furiously rubbed at her eyes, and ran her hands through her hair in a futile attempt to make herself look presentable. "I'm really tired," she began, gearing up to quickly shoo the visitor out of her quarters. Her

     RYMELLAN 3

breath caught in her throat when the newcomer rounded the sofa and looked down at her. "Les!"

"See you at 10:00," Ann said. The door swooshed shut behind her.

Still in her cloak, Les set Mo's violin and the knapsack she shrugged off her back onto the floor. She dropped into the chair Ann had vacated. "Your violin." Her voice lacked its usual vigour. "You'll need to practice. I brought you some clothes, too. I figured you have a uniform in your locker. If not, you'll have to get one from supply."

She couldn't have made Mo feel worse if she'd tried. "Thanks," Mo murmured, shocked by how tired and defeated Les looked. Her eyes were puffy, her skin mottled, and she remained slumped forward, as if buckling under an unbearable weight. Mo slid to the edge of the sofa, then stood, waited for her head to stop pounding, and went to her. She crouched, placed a tentative hand on Les's leg. "I said some terrible things to you."

Les continued to stare at the floor.

"I wish I could take them back. I wish we could start the conversation over again. I shouldn't have run out like that."

Still no response.

"I should have listened." She hesitated, then said what had to be said. If Les laughed and called it absurd, Mo would laugh along with her and blame Ann. "Ann thinks you were going to ask me about Jayne . . . how I feel about her."

When Les jerked her head up and met Mo's eyes, Mo expected to be blasted for discussing what had happened with Ann. She resisted the urge to shrink back, gripping Les's leg instead.

"How do you feel about her?" Les asked.

So Ann was right. But anger wasn't fuelling Les's intense stare. It was pain; a pain so raw that it ripped through Mo too, exacerbated by the knowledge that she'd deeply wounded the woman who mattered to her more than anyone else ever could—including Jayne.

Les was waiting for an answer, her eyes shining with tears. "I said I'd love you no matter what, and I will. But I need you to be honest. Don't . . . don't make this worse by not respecting me." When she blinked and returned her gaze to the floor, Mo grabbed her hand and squeezed it. Les's fingers felt lifeless; they didn't curl around Mo's.

"Les—" She had to stop; Les wasn't the only one struggling with her composure. Mo pressed her lips together and closed her eyes until she was sure she could speak without breaking down. She'd never imagined that she could hurt Les like this. "Les . . . I do respect you." So she'd be as honest as she could be, and not give the answer she'd want to hear in Les's boots. "I don't know how I feel about Jayne, and I'm not saying that because I'm trying to dodge the question. I don't know! I—when Ann said—I don't know. I'm confused, okay?"

"So you might have feelings for her." Les's voice was flat.

"Yeah." The word hung between them. "Why don't you take off your cloak and we'll talk. I'll make you tziva." What she wanted to do was wrap her arms around Les and hold her, but . . . Oh, who cared how Les might react? Mo squeezed Les's hand, then let go of it and used Les's leg for support as she pushed herself up. She reached for Les, then sucked in her breath when Les grabbed her wrists.

"You don't have to do that," Les said. Mo's confusion turned to horror when Les clarified what she meant. "I said I wanted honesty. I don't want you acting out of habit. I know . . ." Les's shoulders heaved; she let go of Mo's wrists and dropped her hands to her lap. "I know your feelings for me have probably changed."

What? "Les, my feelings for you haven't changed! I love you! You mean everything to me."

Les shook her head. "That can't be true. You care about someone else, Mo."

No, no, no! This was worse than any nightmare she'd ever had. "No! I mean, I might, but that doesn't mean I don't care about you. Any feelings I might have for Jayne have nothing to do with you. It has nothing to do with us."

Les's skepticism was written all over her face. "How can it not have anything to do with us? If you were happy with us, you wouldn't want someone else."

Fear gripped Mo. If the tables were turned, she would have thought the same; she would have interpreted Les's feelings for Jayne as a rejection of her. But it wasn't like that! She loved Les, still wanted Les, would die for her without a second's hesitation. She wasn't sure what she felt for Jayne, but she flaming-well knew how she felt about Les! But would

Les believe her? "Les." She crouched again, gazed up at her. "I love you. My feelings for you haven't changed." Her fear that Les would never believe her deepened at Les's dubious expression. How could she get through to her? Saying the same words over and over again wouldn't do it.

Les glanced at her comm unit. "I have to go."

When she pushed herself up from the chair, Mo straightened. "Stay."

"I can't. I have my course tomorrow."

"So take an early shuttle." Mo knew she was being selfish, especially since they would have had hours to talk if she hadn't run out on Les like an idiot. "As it is, you'll get home really late. You'll get around the same amount of sleep whether you're here or at home."

"I can't risk it. If I oversleep here, I'll have to wait for another shuttle. At home, I can be in my aviacraft within twenty minutes."

Was that why, or did Les no longer want to share a bed? "Les, I am so sorry I ran out. We *do* have to talk. I hate to see you leave like this. I'm worried about you." Her hopes rose when Les appeared to think it over.

"I'd like to stay, but I can't."

At least that was something. "I'm coming with you to the waiting area."

"You don't have to. You look . . . tired."

She wanted to cry. That was her Les, ever polite and thoughtful. "I don't care how I look. I'm coming." Les didn't protest.

As they walked down the corridor and then stood silently in the elevator, Mo felt as if she were with a stranger. Normally she'd think nothing of taking Les's hand, but Les would think she was acting out of habit or obligation, that she didn't really care. What could Mo do to make it right?

When they reached the waiting area, the shuttle was already boarding. Mo grabbed Les's sleeve, afraid that Les would proceed right through into the boarding tunnel without breaking pace. They faced each other. "Thank you for bringing my violin, and the clothes," Mo said. "I'm glad you came. Will you beep me when you get home?"

"No. You're flying a shift in the morning. You need to sleep."

"I won't sleep, Les."

Les sighed. "I'll beep you tomorrow, after my training."

Mo couldn't resist the urge to touch her any longer. She reached for her, and blinked back tears when Les's arms wrapped around her. "I'm sorry." She pressed her cheek against Les's, held her tightly. "I do love you. You have to believe that."

"I want to," Les murmured.

Mo's heart sank at Les's unspoken *But I can't.*

Les stepped back. "I have to go. I will beep you tomorrow."

Mo stood in the waiting area and stared down the boarding tunnel long after Les had disappeared. On some level, she felt worse than when they'd parted outside her aviacraft at the beginning of their separation. Back then, they'd been right with each other; an external force had ripped them apart. But now . . .

All those temper tantrums Mo had thrown at Les's perceived disloyalty to her—how stupid and childish! Had she ever truly doubted Les's fidelity and love? No. But Les was honestly struggling and questioning Mo's love for her, and Mo didn't know how to make her see that she loved her as deeply as she always had.

Back in her quarters, Mo sat at the comm station and typed a dispatch: *I'm not worried and concerned about you out of habit. I love you. I'll show you how much I love you for the rest of our lives. I thought maybe I'd come down tomorrow, be there when you get home. We'll only have a few hours, but I can't bear not being with you when I know things aren't right between us. If I have to, I'll come down every night. Coming up here is one of the dumbest things I've ever done. I won't blame you if you think I'm stupid, but I won't let you get away with thinking I don't care about you. I do.*

Love, Mo.

With a sigh, she pressed the send button, then forced herself to get ready for bed. She lay awake, watching the time change on her comm unit and desperately hoping for a reply from Les.

None came.

MO OPENED HER locker after her shift and eagerly grabbed her comm unit. She checked her dispatches, hoping to see one from Les. *Yes!* But she wouldn't read it here, with others milling around. Guilt stabbed through her when another one caught her eye, from *J. Adams.* She wanted to read that one, too. Argamon!

Ann eyed her from a nearby bench. "You want to grab lunch?"

She wasn't hungry, but not eating wouldn't help. "I'll go with you to the canteen, but I'll eat in my quarters. I need a nap." After she'd read the dispatches. "I might go down to the planet, nap on the way."

"I thought you might." Ann hadn't said anything about the previous evening; she made small talk on the way to the canteen. Mo almost wished Ann would be her usual annoying self. Her restraint showed that she knew how serious the situation was with Les—not that Mo needed anyone to confirm that for her.

Back in her quarters, she set her sandwich on the sofa and anxiously pulled up Les's dispatch: *Please don't come down. I have to study for my test, and having you here will make that difficult. I need some time alone right now, and I don't want you running yourself ragged. How about I come up when I'm off?* Les wouldn't be off until Friday! But it was better than nothing. *I do appreciate your concern.* Ugh. That sounded so stiff and formal, as if she were writing a flaming "thank you" dispatch. *I said I'd beep today, but I need some time. I'll beep you Friday morning, to let you know what shuttle I'll be on. Mo, somehow we'll get through this. I don't know how, but we will. Love, Les.*

Mo's vision blurred. She brushed away tears and read Les's dispatch again. Les's closing words offered the first glimmer of hope that Mo hadn't destroyed the precious bond between them. No mention of the Way, no trotting out their obligations to one another as Chosens. Les had spoken from the heart; her statement that their love would endure was more powerful than any articles she could have quoted. Unfortunately, it was also an indication of how much she was hurting, and Mo had been the one who'd stripped her defences and struck a critical blow. Without realizing it!

She unwrapped her sandwich and took a bite, then typed a reply: *Les, I'd love it if you'd come up on Friday. I shouldn't ask this, but would you consider coming up Thursday night? Don't feel you have to, but it would give us more time. And yes, we'll get through this, because I will never give up on us. You want honesty, so here it is: I am a little confused about how I feel about Jayne, but not about us and how I feel about you. I love you. You mean everything to me, and I can't wait to see you.* Words wouldn't be enough this time, but Mo wrote them anyway. *I'll be thinking about you. Love, Mo.*

Not wanting to over-tinker with it, she pressed the send button. Now Jayne's dispatch beckoned to her; Mo hated how much she wanted to read it. To prove to herself that she could wait, she ate half of her sandwich before opening the message: *How are you today, Mo? How is your violin practice going? I was thinking that, since you're going with me to the Stewart appointments—Argamon, they were supposed to see Nolan tomorrow!—maybe I should go with you to your audition, if you want me to. I don't know if having me waiting will make it easier or harder for you, so don't feel you have to take me along. I'll be cheering you on, no matter where I am.*

Aw, how sweet. Mo wouldn't mind taking Jayne with her at all, but how would Les feel about it? How could the three of them even be in the same room now? Mo would feel she had to watch everything she said and did, aware that Les might interpret innocent words and gestures as something deeper. Could Mo only be herself with Jayne when Les wasn't with them? But wouldn't that be a different type of betrayal? Les had made it clear that she'd rather be hurt than protected.

And what about Jayne? She could inadvertently upset Les or embarrass Mo by being friendly and supportive—like offering to go to Mo's audition with her. But the only way to prevent that would be to tell Jayne about Les's suspicions—no, about Mo's feelings for her, and that Les knew. Enough with the denial. She *did* care about Jayne. Her interest went beyond friendship. But how far? Was she in love with her? Maybe Jayne's history and vulnerability brought out her maternal instincts. Maybe the fact that Jayne was her Chosen naturally heightened her concern for her. Or maybe she was falling in love. Mo wasn't sure. But to deny that *something* was there, to herself and to Les, would only make things worse. Les wanted to face it head-on, so Mo would too.

She wasn't sure she wanted to tell Jayne about her feelings, and wouldn't without Les's permission, anyway. In a moment of clarity, she realized that Les would have to be involved in every step she might take concerning Jayne. Les would have to know about it, be ready for it, and agree to it. Not that Mo wanted to take any steps. Right now, her priority was Les.

She refocused on Jayne's message: *I'll almost be finished my painting around the time of your audition. I'd like to show it to you and Lesley. I know you're not art critics, but I guess I just want some reassurance that the applications committee won't laugh. I was thinking maybe I could make supper for the two of you. Don't expect much; it won't be a grand meal. But I'd like to do it. Would you come for supper? If I send a dispatch to Lesley asking her, do you think she'll mind?*

"No, no, don't send her a dispatch!" Mo said aloud. While Les wouldn't lash out at Jayne, she wouldn't appreciate a chirpy dispatch from her, either. Mo read the last two lines of Jayne's message, then quickly typed a reply, worried that Jayne might write to Les before she could stop her: *Jayne, I'm on 72. I was ordered up here last night—a little fib wouldn't hurt—and I'll still be up here for a few days, so you'll have to reschedule the appointment with Nolan. I'm sorry I didn't tell you sooner. I'll let you know how I feel about my audition when it's closer.* Mo wanted to take Jayne with her, but it would be up to Les. *As far as supper and your painting go, yes! I'd love to see your painting and to come for supper.*

She was touched that Jayne wanted to share her painting and cook for them, and knew that Les wouldn't refuse Jayne on either count. Les might hate the idea of seeing Jayne right now—Mo didn't know—but Les wouldn't let that get in the way of honouring her Chosen. Just as she hadn't let her anguish get in the way of reaching out to Mo last night, of agreeing to come up on her day off, and of promising they'd get through it. Mo wanted to hug her. Argamon, she loved her *so* much. How could she make Les believe her? Les deserved to believe her.

Mo heaved a sigh. *I'd hold off on asking Les, though. She's really distracted with her course work right now. Why don't we talk about it next time we're all together?* Mo cringed at the prospect. And . . . *Oh, we're having a family supper next week, on Thursday. Papa's upset because we haven't eaten together for so long. If you can't make it, let me know.* Though she'd be surprised if Jayne was busy. *I'll talk to you soon. Mo.*

At the same time she pressed the send button, her comm unit beeped twice. She read Les's reply—*I'll come up on Thursday night*—and tried not to feel deflated by its terseness. Les had agreed to come up earlier, and they often sent each other one-liners. Plus, if anyone needed reassurance right now, it was Les, not her. She sent a single line back: *I can't wait.*

Then she finished her sandwich, crawled into bed, and stared at the ceiling for the rest of the afternoon.

MO BUZZED AROUND Les, taking her cloak and knapsack and asking if she wanted tziva. She felt as if she were entertaining a guest she desperately wanted to impress. At least Les hadn't shrunk away when Mo had reached for her in the waiting area; Les's hug had even felt warm. But she hadn't said much beyond *How are you?* and *Have you been practising for your audition?*

She hung Les's cloak and optimistically took her knapsack into the bedroom. The sofa would be a little cramped for someone of Les's height. "I'll just get the tziva started."

"No, let's talk first. I don't want to sit around and sip tziva as if I'm visiting an acquaintance."

So Les had felt it too.

Les lifted an eyebrow. "Any doubts I might have had about whether you love me disappeared when you took my cloak and knapsack. I think I can count on one hand the number of times you've done that."

Mo's eyes welled up. "Of course I love you." She bit her lip, then fought the tide when Les's arm slipped around her. She had no right to cry.

"Come on, let's sit down." Les steered Mo to the sofa.

Mo expected Les to sit in the chair. When Les sat next to her, Mo searched her face. Les looked tired, but otherwise okay, though she was practiced at masking her feelings. Her lack of concern about her appearance last time she was here had indicated how devastated Les had been—and probably still was.

"Les . . ." Mo tentatively took her hand, then tightened her fingers when Les didn't pull away. "What we have . . . I could never have with Jayne what I have with you. We have so much history. We've been through so much together. Our lives are entrenched on a level I don't think can happen with Jayne. And I don't mean you're a habit. I mean that . . ." She struggled to find the right words. "I mean that my love for you runs deeper than it could for anyone else. Nothing else can touch it, including . . . including anything I might feel for Jayne."

"If the situation was reversed and I said that to you, you wouldn't believe it."

No, she wouldn't. She would have completely lost control of her senses, berated Les, lashed out at Jayne, made everyone around her miserable. Yet Les, on the surface, appeared calm. Sure, she was the more rational one, but that didn't mean she never hurt. "How are you feeling, Les? Talk to me. What scares me the most right now is how this is affecting you and how you feel about us. Yeah, maybe I'd deserve it if you couldn't stand to look at me, but—"

Les vigorously shook her head. "I told you the other night, I'll always love you, no matter what." She looked down at her lap. "I don't have a choice. About that, or about how to deal with you and Jayne."

"There is no me and Jayne!"

"Not yet, but there will be," Les stated.

"I'm not so sure. I don't think there can ever be anything between me and Jayne, not without me feeling as if I'm betraying you." Les's awareness of Mo's feelings for Jayne already made Mo feel as if she'd let Les down, that she was doing something wrong. "It doesn't matter that we're all Chosens. I can't behave as if our relationship, our love for each other, doesn't exist."

"And I hope you won't, or this triad will be in serious trouble." Les's grip on Mo's hand tightened. "Realistically, you won't be able to see Jayne and pretend you don't like her in that way, not for long. And I can't be resentful. I can't be angry with either of you. That's not to say I won't be, but I'll have to learn to live with it."

"Les—"

"There's no other way, Mo. If I can't accept it, we'll be at each other's throats for the rest of our lives. We'll be like those triads I read about in the CT134 cases. For us to have a chance at a decent life, I *have* to accept it. Ironically, the only way I can see us getting through this without hating each other is for me to accept your feelings for her."

Knowing Les, she'd put on a brave face while internalizing her pain. "If accepting it means bottling it all up, I don't think that'll work."

"I didn't say I'll never get upset about it." Les snorted softly. "I already am. But I know what I have to do." She met Mo's eyes. "It'll be hard. I can't guarantee I won't take it out on you sometimes."

"Les . . . I know this is a double standard, but when it happens for you, I don't think I'll be able to handle it at all." If Les had developed feelings for Jayne first, it would have taken them a lot longer to sit down and have a civil conversation about it. Mo would have been too absorbed in her pain to rationally discuss it.

"It's not happening for me, Mo. I'm not sure it'll ever happen."

"I thought the same thing. I honestly believed our arrangement would work because I never expected this to happen. Maybe that's why I didn't realize I was developing feelings for her. I wasn't—I mean, I didn't—ugh." *But this Adams woman, she's not just anybody. She's Lesley's Chosen. The Chosen Council says they're meant for each other.* What had Mo said in response? Something like, *she's my Chosen too and I'll never be interested.* But she was! Mary had been right. The Chosen Council didn't make mistakes. Since Jayne was Les's Chosen, it was only a matter of time. Mo's jaw clenched. She had no right, but she couldn't help it. Was it happening for Jayne yet? Had she developed feelings for either of them?

"Are you going to tell her?" Les asked.

"No. Right now, things feel too fragile between us. I meant what I said. I won't risk our relationship." And maybe she was afraid of what Jayne would say . . . Mo had never been in this position. She and Les had fallen into their relationship; she'd never had to tell someone how she felt and asked if they felt the same. She hoped Jayne reciprocated her feelings, but it would be easier if Jayne didn't. "And Les, even if I was to tell Jayne and she felt the same way, I don't think I'll ever be able to . . . act on my feelings when you're not there. I can't see it! I'll feel like I'm doing things I shouldn't be doing behind your back, even when you know about it." She would always think of Les. How could she not?

"That might change over time."

Mo doubted it, but said, "Maybe. But you know what? Right now, I'm concerned about us, and about how we'll ever be able to sit in the same room with Jayne together. For me, the priority is us. I'm not saying I don't care about her. I do. But even she said that *our* relationship is the foundation, and she's right. So right now, I want to feel like we're okay again. I don't know how, because I feel like I've hurt you in a way that can't be healed." She blinked back tears. She'd hurt Les so severely that Les doubted her love. "I love you, Les. I really do. That will never change. You said you'll love me no matter what, and I'm saying the same thing to you. Maybe you're finding that hard to believe right now, but I mean it."

"I admit, one of the reasons this is so difficult for me is that it's made me feel less special to you." Les's lips trembled. She cleared her throat and quickly rubbed at one eye.

Mo wanted to cry out in frustration. If only she could reach into Les's heart and make her see! Words were so flaming useless at times like this,

 RYMELLAN 3

but they were all Mo had. "You are *not* less special. You're everything to me. Maybe that sounds impossible—it would have sounded impossible to me—but it's true. It's true, Les." She pulled Les into a hug, buried her face in Les's shoulder, and closed her eyes when Les held her close. At least Les hadn't said *I want to believe you* as she had the other night. But her silence worried Mo.

When they finally drew back, they wiped away tears, but the tension between them had lessened. "We should see Jayne soon," Les said.

"I know, but it's going to be awkward."

Les nodded. "But we need to do it. *I* need to do it. We should see her before your papa's family supper."

"Yeah, we should." A family supper wasn't the place to find out how they'd react when they next saw Jayne together.

"I was thinking we should meet her for a late supper the day you're back."

"Okay." Mo wasn't surprised that Les had already given the matter some thought, and was willing to go along with whatever she wanted—not that Les was the only one who wanted to see Jayne. Mo did too, though unlike Les, she'd be pleased to see her—and feel guilty about it.

"Why don't you ask her? I'm not trying to avoid her," Les quickly added. "You always arrange things with Jayne."

"I'll send her a dispatch." And she'd hold off on asking Les about taking Jayne with her to the audition.

Les slapped her knees. "Enough about this for now. Do you want to play together, take our minds off it for a while?"

Les's abrupt desire to end the conversation didn't alarm Mo. Nothing they'd say would make it better; they'd go around in circles and wallow in it. "Did you bring your flute? I didn't see it."

"No, I didn't. Why don't you make the tziva while I go and borrow one from supply?" Les stood and stretched.

So Les already wanted some time on her own. Whatever she wanted right now, she could have. "That sounds good." There would be more heart-wrenching discussion, maybe as soon as tomorrow. But now it was time for action, and Les's suggestion that they play together was a positive sign. Mo wasn't fooling herself—playing with Les would feel a bit like going through the motions—but if they were to heal the bond between them, they had to start somewhere.

LESLEY LEANED OVER the railing on the raised platform that ringed the arboretum and watched the Rymellans below her. They relaxed on the benches, examined the various shrubs, or strode through the area without so much as a glance at the greenery. When Mo's shift finished in a couple of hours, they'd have a late lunch. Lesley had quietly planned to leave for Rymel in the late afternoon, but now she intended to stay and have a late supper with Mo. She wanted to stretch out their time together, for Mo's sake, more than hers. Mo had practically burst into tears when Lesley had climbed into bed with her last night, and was treading around her so carefully that Lesley wouldn't have been surprised to catch her actually tiptoeing. She couldn't bear Mo's acquiescence, or the reasons behind it. She wanted the feisty old Mo back, the one who wasn't so afraid of disagreeing with or irritating her. She wanted the Mo who loved only her, too, but that wasn't going to happen.

Their talk last night had helped, but only a little. Lesley couldn't deny that Mo still cared about her—Mo's love was evident in her words and actions—but she still felt empty. Would this feeling that nothing mattered eventually lift? She was asking herself the same questions she'd asked during their separation, except this time, she had Mo. Perhaps she should focus on that—what she had, rather than what she'd lost.

In addition to Mo, Lesley had something else she hadn't had when they were separated: control. Last time, their fate was in the hands of the Chosen Council; all she and Mo could do was hope. This time, their fate was in their own hands. They were at a critical crossroads; the path they would take was up to them, but every direction could lead to disaster. The best they could do was choose what they believed was the least hazardous route, then work together to overcome the obstacles they met along the way.

Lesley had meant it when she'd said that she'd love Mo no matter what, and that the only way she could see the triad working was to accept Mo's feelings for Jayne. That was the path she had to take, but could she do it without resenting Mo and Jayne, without wanting to make them hurt as much as she hurt?

At the moment, she wasn't sure she could, but she'd have to try, starting with their upcoming supper with Jayne. Lesley remembered the palpable awkwardness at their last lunch, when she'd only suspected that Mo had feelings for Jayne. Now that she knew for sure . . . The supper would be the first test of many, one she hoped she wouldn't fail.

JAYNE LIFTED HER mug and tried not to stare when Mo grabbed Lesley's arm and laughed. Mo's mirth sounded forced; Jayne didn't see it in her eyes. The entire supper had felt weird. Usually Lesley and Mo were relaxed with each other; they bickered and teased and sometimes completed each other's sentences. Tonight, despite their frequent outward displays of affection, they were choosing their words carefully, and one often looked at the other after speaking, as if seeking reassurance. They might be fooling everyone else in the eatery, but not Jayne. She'd spent enough time with them to know that something was wrong

The way they were interacting with her was also different. They were distant, polite, wary—how she'd expected them to behave when they'd first found out about the triad. The three of them had grown more comfortable with each other—especially her and Mo—but tonight it felt as if they'd gone back to when they first met. Though, back then, Lesley and Mo hadn't worked so hard to put on a show. There was no need; they'd felt secure and confident about their relationship.

Jayne almost dropped her mug when it suddenly hit her. They no longer were.

Her mind raced. What had happened? The last time she'd seen them together, after the appointment with Nolan, they hadn't behaved like this. Lesley had been quieter than usual, and Jayne's lunch with her had been more strained than the first one, but Mo had been her usual self.

Mo had just come back from 72. Had they argued before they'd picked Jayne up, and were still angry with each other? No, a simple argument wouldn't have them pretending to be a lovesick couple because they were worried about their relationship.

Worried about their relationship . . . Fear tightened her throat just as she swallowed some tziva. She grabbed her napkin, pressed it against her mouth, and coughed into it. "Sorry," she said hoarsely. "Wrong way."

She didn't mind that her face was probably red and her eyes watery. Now they wouldn't see her panic.

Mo and Lesley's relationship was the triad's foundation. *What happened?* She had to somehow find out, see if there was anything she could do to support them. She couldn't stand by and watch them fall apart. She would *not* be involved in a failed Joining! And she cared about them; they cared about each other. They were good together! What had come between them, to the point that they couldn't act naturally with each other?

Jayne tried to calm herself. Before she blundered in like an elephant, she should give them time, see if they resolved whatever it was on their own. But she wasn't going to sit in her apartment and wonder how they were doing. She'd last seen them over a week ago, and had been content to let them decide when they'd get together. Now she needed to see them more often, so she'd know whether things between them were improving or, if they weren't, know when to help them.

The supper at Mo's was coming up, but everybody would be formal and polite then. Jayne needed to see them alone. Mo had advised her to hold off on asking Lesley about coming over to her apartment for supper, that they'd talk about it next time they were together—and here they were. Usually she'd wait for Mo to bring it up, but . . . Jayne cleared her throat. "I mentioned to Mo that I'm almost finished my painting for my application. I'd like to show it to you and . . . well, you've had me over for supper, and taken me out several times. I'd like to invite you and Mo for supper at my apartment. Maybe next Sunday?"

Their faces froze; they looked at each other. Jayne had the feeling she'd said something terribly wrong. "You don't have to. I just thought—"

"I was going to mention it to you." Mo lifted her hand to touch Lesley's cheek, then hesitated.

Mo's fear, her uncertainty about how Lesley would react if she touched her, spoke volumes to Jayne. She didn't understand what was causing the tension between them, but her gut told her that her supper invitation should wait. "I'm sorry. Mo told me to wait until you weren't as busy. We can talk about it another time. It's not urgent."

Lesley grasped Mo's fingers and lowered Mo's hand to her lap. "Let me check my course schedule."

"We'll let you know." Mo's smile didn't mask her strained tone.

Jayne wanted to reach out to them, but how? They were both trying so hard to hide their uneasiness with each other—or maybe with her. Was that it? *This is how I expected them to behave when they first found out about the triad.* Oh, Argamon! Had they changed their minds about her, decided that maybe they didn't want to be in a triad after all, or couldn't overlook her family history? What had changed? Had someone said something or threatened them?

No, that wouldn't make sense. They'd invited *her* out to supper tonight, not the other way around. Why would they do that if they were having a change of heart? She'd grown to trust them, to believe that they'd never violate the spirit of the Way. She still believed that, and even if she were wrong, it wouldn't explain why they were so uncomfortable with each other. Wouldn't they just be uncomfortable with her? Her first instinct must be right. Something was wrong between them, and being with her was probably the last thing they wanted to be doing right now. They should be talking, sorting out whatever was bothering them.

Jayne feigned a yawn. They didn't disappoint her. "I guess we should get going," Mo said. Lesley was already rising. Jayne nodded and silently followed them to the cloakroom.

She didn't try to engage them in conversation in Lesley's aviacraft; she'd passed the point of worrying that they'd think less of her if she sat quietly. "Thank you for supper," she said when Lesley landed the craft. She slid the door open.

Mo glanced over her shoulder, then at Lesley. "Uh . . ."

"We'll walk you to your apartment." Lesley reached to unfasten her seatbelt.

"No, I'll be fine. You have your course tomorrow," Jayne shifted her attention to Mo, "and I know it's been a long day for you. Good night." She hopped off the craft and slid the door shut before they had a chance to protest.

At the Middleton supper, she'd look for signs that they'd resolved whatever difficulty they were experiencing, but she wouldn't be surprised if there weren't any. They weren't angry with each other, they were floundering. Jayne had to do something, but what? Intervening might make things worse, but she couldn't stand by and watch them drown.

JAYNE KNOCKED ON the White home's front door. The moment it swung open, she said, "I'm sorry. I know it's short notice."

"No." Carol beckoned her inside. "You saved me from a dull afternoon. Ronald's over at a friend's, helping him put down new flooring." She took Jayne's cloak and sketchbook. "I'd agreed to go with him, even though Martin's Chosen bores me to tears. So I didn't mind bowing out at all. Told her I have to deal with a cousin crisis."

"You didn't say that, did you?"

Carol chuckled. "Of course I didn't. Come through to the kitchen. The tziva's ready."

Jayne sat at the kitchen table and murmured a thank you when Carol set a mug in front of her.

"So, what's so important that it couldn't wait *and* you wanted to talk about it in person?" Carol asked as she pulled out a chair.

"It's Lesley and Mo. Something's wrong with them." She curled her hand around her mug for something to hang onto.

Carol's brows drew together. "Can you be a little more specific?"

"They're having problems. Relationship problems."

"So they've had an argument. It happens. No relationship is perfect."

"It's more serious than that! They're acting weird with each other. They're uncomfortable—they aren't—they—" Her fear and frustration strangled her.

Carol lifted her hands. "Slow down, okay? Start from the beginning. When did you notice it?"

Jayne took a deep breath. "Last night. I had supper with them. Mo had just come back from 72 and I guess they figured we hadn't seen each other for a while. I knew something was off right away. They were too affectionate, too . . . happy. Every action came across exaggerated, as if they were putting on a show. They seemed uncomfortable with each other." Actually, Mo had been the more ill at ease of the two. Her behaviour had been too exuberant when responding to Lesley, and less spontaneous than usual with Jayne. "Lesley was quiet, withdrawn, almost," as she'd been at their lunch together, "and Mo almost seemed afraid to say anything. I've got to do something, Carol. Their relationship can't fail!"

Carol pensively sipped her tziva. "And you have no idea what the problem might be?"

"No. It crossed my mind that maybe *I'm* the problem, that they've had a change of heart and now we're back to how it was right after we met. But if that were the case, I could see them being uncomfortable with me, but not with each other. They've never acted this way before."

"Maybe they're uncomfortable with you for another reason. Maybe—" Carol's eyes widened.

"What?"

"Nothing," she said quickly, then gulped down some tziva.

"What?" Jayne repeated.

"Nothing. I suddenly had a catch in my throat I needed to moisten."

"Carol."

"Jayne, whatever it is, it's up to them to sort it out. It's their relationship."

"Their relationship is the foundation of the triad! I can't just sit by and do nothing!"

"You're overreacting. So they had an off night. That doesn't mean—"

An off night? It was more than that! "Carol—"

"Or maybe they're going through a rough patch. It doesn't mean their relationship is falling apart. They're Chosens. They'll work it out."

"Like Mama and Papa did?" Jayne's heart pounded.

"Is that why you're in such a panic? Because you think the triad will fall apart?" Carol's forehead creased. "Jayne, your parents were an exception."

She picked up her mug with a shaking hand, then quickly put it down when the tziva almost slopped over the mug's edge. "I know Joinings can fail."

"They were an exception," Carol repeated. "You can't think that way. You can't take everything on yourself, including all the responsibility for the triad, because of what your parents did."

Jayne groaned and buried her head in her hands, then forced herself to look up. Hiding wouldn't help.

"Is that the only reason you're so upset about this?"

"Why else would I be upset?" Jayne asked dully.

Carol eyed her over the rim of her mug. "Because you care about Lesley and Mo?"

Heat travelled up Jayne's neck to her face.

Carol's eyes brightened. "Which one? Or is it both?"

"Of course I care about them. I'm in a triad with them. I have to care about what happens to them."

"I meant—"

"No. Not at all." She hated lying to Carol, but it was the only way to ensure that Lesley and Mo would never find out about her feelings.

"Are you sure?"

"Yes! Even if I did care—in that way—nothing could ever happen."

Carol drew back in surprise. "Why not?"

Why did she have to explain the obvious? "Because they're a couple, and have been a couple for thirteen years. It doesn't take a genius to figure out that they'll never be interested in me. Not only that, I'd never do anything to threaten their relationship. We have an arrangement, one that makes sense."

"Jayne, you're all Chosens. Your arrangement won't last."

"We're not Chosens."

"Yes, you are," Carol said firmly. "The Chosen Council says you are. Why aren't you accepting that?"

Her head felt as if it would explode. "I'm not weak in the Way," she said through clenched teeth.

"I know," Carol said evenly. "So why? Is it because you feel you don't deserve anyone?"

"No!"

"Isn't it? You've convinced yourself that nobody could possibly be a match because you're not good enough for any of them."

"No." But her voice lacked conviction. She sighed.

Carol patted her hand. "You're all Chosens. That's something to celebrate and be happy about."

It terrified her. "If I ever develop feelings for them, I'll never act on them."

"Why not?"

"Because I wouldn't want to be responsible for destroying the triad." And if she were to give herself permission to act on her feelings, she wouldn't know how. Why bother, when Lesley and Mo would be horrified? Perhaps she'd convinced herself the triad was a sham so she'd never have to seriously consider a relationship with them. She could dismiss her feelings, push them down, pretend they weren't there. Did it matter? If she admitted they were Chosens, she'd handle her feelings in the same way. Lesley and Mo's relationship was the foundation. She would do everything she had to, including locking away her feelings for them, to support their relationship. "I won't do anything that could hurt their relationship. I won't allow this Joining to fail."

Carol's voice grew gentle. "Jayne, don't deprive yourself because of what your parents did. If you do care for your Chosens . . . deeply care for them . . . you're not doing anything wrong. And if you were to want a relationship with them, that wouldn't be wrong, either. Don't twist what you think the Tradition expects of you because of your parents. It'll only lead to grief."

Jayne would prefer the grief of unrequited love to that of losing her Chosens at an execution site.

"If they'd been in a triad with anyone else, that other Chosen would have expected relationships with them. And you can't control what Lesley and Mo do. They're your Chosens." Carol paused. "You're not the only one who can develop feelings."

Now Carol was being silly. "Forget about what could happen. I care about what is happening. They're having a problem, and I need to know how to help them."

Carol leaned back in her chair and folded her arms. "I already told you what to do. Nothing."

"But—"

"You asked for my advice, so listen to it! Don't do a thing. You have no idea what's going on. Depending on what the problem is, you might be the last person they'd want interfering."

Something in Carol's voice piqued Jayne's curiosity. "Why?"

"Trust me on this, Jayne. You're panicking. If you only just noticed, it's too early to get involved. So let them deal with it, all right?"

"But what if it keeps up? What if they're not dealing with it?"

Carol's brows shot up. "I thought you wanted to talk about what *is* happening."

"You're right," Jayne admitted. She'd follow Carol's advice—for now. But she suspected that Carol had a theory about what might be wrong between Lesley and Mo. She wished she had practical experience with relationships! Since Carol could be stubborn, Jayne would let her keep her secret for today. But if the situation between her Chosens didn't improve, she'd badger Carol, beep her relentlessly, until Carol voiced her suspicion.

MO UNBUCKLED HER seatbelt when the aviacraft touched down in the Middleton estate's holding area. Les had seemed okay with her picking Jayne up, and should be at the house by now. Mo looked forward to seeing Les; if it was up to her, she'd beep ten times a day and be over at the Thompsons' every night. But since their supper with Jayne, which had been difficult for both of them, Mo hadn't wanted to push Les.

When she followed Jayne off the aviacraft, she was surprised to see Les waiting for them, shielding her eyes against the glare. "I thought since it's a big family supper, we should make our entrance together."

Or was Les keeping an eye on them? Mo felt as if Les was scrutinizing her every word and action—not that she blamed her. If she were Les, she'd do the same, and she wouldn't be so rational about it.

"No sketchbook?" Les said to Jayne.

Jayne pointed over her shoulder. "It's in the craft."

Les grunted and slipped her hand into Mo's. "Mo says you'll be going with her to the audition."

Mo tensed. Less than a minute together and she was already worried that Jayne would say something to inadvertently upset Les. At least Mo *knew* she was being scrutinized. Poor Jayne didn't. "I told Les you'd offered to come with me," she supplied quickly, then squeezed Les's hand and said to her, "It's too bad you can't come too."

"Having both of us there might make you nervous," Les said.

Mo gave her a sidelong glance, but Les's expression offered no clue about what she'd meant.

"Did Mo tell you we'll come to your apartment for supper on Sunday?" Les asked as they walked to the house.

Jayne nodded. "Don't expect something on the scale of this supper, though. Do you have these family suppers often?"

"No. I can't remember Papa ever catering a meal." Mo swallowed. Mama had always taken care of those details. What Mo wouldn't give to talk to Mama about Les and Jayne! She was being as honest as she could with Les, her usual confidante, but obviously she had to tread carefully. She couldn't talk to Jayne. Papa? No, not about this. Ann? She already knew more than enough. Maybe she should visit Mama's crypt, pour her heart out, and hope the silence would answer her.

"So it's nobody's birthday or anything like that?" Jayne asked, dragging Mo back to the conversation.

"Nope, I would have told you. I think Papa just wants to see us all around the table for once."

"And the whole family will be there?"

Mo could hear the anxiety in Jayne's voice and resisted the urge to touch her arm. "Don't worry about Mary and Matthew. They were fine when we went to the Dance Hall, and they haven't caused any trouble since." Mo kept her eyes forward, despite wanting to look at Jayne.

"We should go to the Dance Hall again," Les said.

"Yeah, we should," Mo said slowly. Why did Les have to be so flaming dutiful, even when it hurt her? Les didn't have anything to prove. She didn't have to show that she could go to the Dance Hall and watch them dance. Mo wanted to scream at her, and hug her. But for now, she'd hang onto her hand and hope tonight's supper would be more bearable than the supper with Jayne.

When they reached the house, Mo glimpsed a few faces through the living room window. As soon as she'd hung her cloak, a caterer ushered her into the living room and offered her a drink. "I feel like I'm at someone else's house, not mine," she murmured to Les as she surveyed the room. Everyone was here except Matthew . . . and Papa! *Figures.* "Where's Papa?" she asked Nathan.

"He's here. He said he had to go to the study and not to disturb him."

"He's probably asleep." Mo glanced to her left, to make sure Jayne had followed them into the living room and received a drink. Would the caterers seat Les between them? That seemed to be the seating arrangement everyone had adopted for the triad, though it wasn't the one they observed when they were alone. She and Les tended to sit across from Jayne, and when they walked together, Mo usually ended up in the middle. She hadn't thought anything of it before, but now . . .

The front door thumped shut. "You just made it," Andrew shouted when Matthew entered the room.

"I missed the train by a minute," a harried-looking Matthew replied. He glanced around. "Where's Papa?"

"Supper is ready," a caterer announced from the hallway. "If you would follow me to the dining room, please."

"Does she think we can't find it?" Nathan murmured, making Mo smile. As she walked to the dining room with everyone else, Mo wondered why Papa was making such a fuss. This was the sort of meal she expected at the Thompsons', with caterers bustling around and everyone acting as if they hobnobbed and ate gazillion-course meals all the time. Mama had only ever arranged catered meals to mark significant social events, such as Neil's notification lunch. True, they hadn't eaten together for a while, but that had never bothered Papa before.

The pretentious table settings reinforced her impression that the supper was way over the top. There were place cards! And, as expected, hers was to Les's right and Jayne's to Les's left. After everyone had taken their seats, Mo noticed that the caterers had made a mistake. There was a table setting at Mama's place, which wouldn't be a great start to the supper for Papa. Mo glanced around for a caterer, hoping to rectify the error before Papa arrived.

But she was too late. Papa strode into the room, stood behind his chair, and gripped its back. "I'm glad to see everyone." He cleared his throat. "I wanted us to gather here, as a family, because I want to introduce you to someone. Someone special to me." His cheeks flushed a deep red.

Mo stared at him. He couldn't mean . . .

"I met Peggy on one of my government committees. We have a lot in common and enjoy each other's company. I'd like you to get to know her." Despite his obvious nervousness, he managed to smile. "I know she'd like to get to know you. So I'll just go fetch her from the study." He wheeled and left the room.

Everyone started to whisper, but Mo wasn't listening. Her fingernails dug into her palms. If not for Les's firm hand on her leg, she'd push back her chair, march from the room, and not look back. *Am I the only one who didn't know?* No, everyone looked as shocked as she felt. Except Nathan. She narrowed her eyes. He didn't look surprised. When she got him alone . . .

She wanted to close her eyes when footsteps approached, but forced herself to watch as Papa escorted his new "friend" into the dining room, his hand lightly touching her waist. "This is Peggy," he announced.

Peggy nodded. "Hello." Murmured greetings answered her.

"I'll start here and go around the table. This is Neil, and his Chosen, Barbara."

Peggy smiled. "Pleased to meet you."

Mo couldn't deny her smug satisfaction when Peggy's smile remained fixed. Nervous, was she? Finding it nerve-wracking to force her way into someone else's family? Mo tried not to frown when Papa gestured in her direction.

"And this is Mo, my youngest daughter."

Peggy nodded. "Pleased to meet you, Mo."

Mo hung onto Les's hand and returned the nod.

"And Mo's Chosens," Papa said with a chuckle, "Lesley and Jayne."

"Oh, yes, the triad. I'll look forward to chatting with you later."

Well, that made one of them. When Papa finished his introductions, he motioned for Peggy to sit. She did—in Mama's place. Mo whipped her napkin off the table and angrily unfolded it. Fortunately she was seated several chairs away from Peggy, because the urge to spill something on her might have been irresistible.

The caterers rolled in the first course. Mo half-heartedly stabbed at the salad with her fork and didn't bother participating in any of the small talk. Papa was lucky she was still here. Every time she heard Peggy's voice or glimpsed her, she thought of Mama . . . and how she'd died.

Les's attentive behaviour throughout supper only made Mo feel guiltier. Les didn't need this, either. Papa's timing couldn't have been worse—not that there ever would have been a good time. Why hadn't he warned her? Did he honestly expect her to welcome this woman into the family? Peggy would be a constant reminder of one of the worst periods in Mo's life. Mo couldn't deal with that, not when her life was already going through another rough patch. She didn't have the energy or the inclination to cozy up to Papa's flaming girlfriend when her own relationship was struggling.

FROM ONE END of the sofa, Jayne watched everyone else in the room socializing, noting who made the effort to speak to Peggy and who skirted around her. Mary's nose was definitely out of joint, Neil and Barbara weren't sure, and Andrew kept his eye on her from a distance. Only Matthew and Nathan seemed comfortable around her, making sure her drink was topped up and quickly engaging her in conversation whenever Michael was distracted with someone else.

As for Mo . . . upset was an understatement. She hadn't spoken to Peggy once, and if looks could kill, Peggy's family would be planning her farewell ceremony and Mo would be at an execution site. Mo's uncharacteristic reticence as they'd flown to the Middleton estate had already deepened Jayne's concern about whatever was going on between her two Chosens. Now this.

Jayne felt shut out. Mo had never talked about her mama, and Jayne hadn't wanted to ask. It would be an awkward conversation, when your own mama was an embarrassment. Had Mo and her mama been close? Had she died when Mo was young? How had she died? As far as Jayne could recall, Mo's mama had come up in conversation only once, when Mo was talking to Ann about Andrew. Why did Mo never speak of her? Jayne realized with a start that Mo knew more about her mama than she did about Mo's.

Maybe Peggy's sudden appearance would force Lesley and Mo to deal with whatever was troubling them—or make it worse. Mo wasn't the only one acting strange. Jayne had grown used to Lesley's restrained manner and was learning how to deduce her mood and opinions based on her subtle body language. When Jayne had first met her Chosens, Mo's ability to read Lesley had seemed uncanny; Jayne could almost have believed that Mo knew how to read Lesley's mind. Now it wasn't so mysterious, though were she and Mo to have a *guess what Lesley is thinking* contest, Jayne would still lose.

But as in the restaurant, Lesley's manner may have fooled those at the supper table tonight, but not Jayne. Lesley was distant, indifferent, concerned about Mo but emotionally flat about everything else.

She seemed . . . sad all the time. What was wrong? Carol said to stay out of it, but how long could Jayne watch them struggle? It wasn't only a matter of ensuring the triad survived—she cared about them! But they didn't care about her, not to the same extent, and so she was in the dark, and wasn't surprised to still be sitting by herself twenty minutes after they'd mumbled that they'd be back in five. Were they talking about Peggy, about their problem—whatever it was—or had they just wanted some time to themselves? All Jayne could do was sit and sip her drink, and hope they'd soon return, to her and to their normal selves. She missed them.

MO LIFTED THE pile of socks in her top dresser drawer and pulled out the small case hidden beneath them. "Mama's commendation," she said with a sigh. "I haven't looked at it in months. I haven't visited the crypt lately, either." She lifted the lid and stared at the silver badge, then held out the case.

Lesley took it and gazed down at the commendation she'd only seen once. Apprehension filled her as she remembered when Michael had presented it to Mo. Mo's depression, her struggle to move beyond the accident and her mama's death, the emotional visit to the crypt with the Middletons—why did Michael have to choose now to introduce Peggy to the family?

"If it wasn't for me, Mama would have been at the supper table, not what's-her-face." Mo folded her arms and shook her head.

Not again. "If it wasn't for you, hundreds of children would have died." In an instant, the same overwhelming futility she'd felt on the *Falcon* when she'd said those words for the hundredth time returned. Lesley quickly moved on. "It's been almost five years, Mo. He's not an old man."

"Why didn't he tell us before—" she lifted her hands and flexed them, as though she were strangling someone "—forcing her on us like that. Nathan said the only reason he wasn't completely surprised was because he'd run into them at the Trading Centre a few months back, and then here, in the study. He fell for their 'we're working' line. Come on!"

Lesley chuckled to herself and handed the commendation back to Mo. "Maybe your papa wanted to wait until he was sure about her. Introducing her to the family . . . that's a big step."

"He should have warned us." Mo placed the case back in its hiding place and slid the drawer shut.

"Perhaps, but what would you have said if he'd told you in advance? You probably would have told him you didn't want to meet her."

"Maybe," Mo mumbled. "I mean, every time I look at her, I'll think of Mama."

If Lesley was forced to choose between Mo sinking into a depression and Mo acting on her feelings for Jayne, she'd choose the latter. She couldn't bear to see Mo go through that again. "I don't want you shutting yourself away."

"I won't, unless *she's* around." Mo met Lesley's eyes. "So you'd care if I shut myself away?"

"Of course I'd care." She instinctively stepped toward Mo, reached for her—and closed her eyes when Mo fell into her arms. She could almost believe that everything was right between them.

"Do you think she's noticed that I'm not happy about her?" Mo said into Lesley's shoulder.

Lesley wondered if Mo could feel her smile. "Yes, I do." She hesitated. "You have to give her some credit for not forcing you into conversation with her. She's had plenty of opportunity, but she's given you a wide berth."

"Maybe Papa told her about the accident, which he had no right to do."

"Mo, he had every right to tell her how his Chosen died. You know that."

After a moment, Mo grunted. "I guess Jayne's noticed too."

So much for their brief respite from the storm. Lesley drew back. "I'm sure she has."

"I have to tell her about the accident. Tonight."

"Tonight? Are you sure?"

Mo nodded. "We're already keeping Jayne in the dark about everything else. It won't be fair if she's the only one who doesn't know why Peggy makes me want to throw up."

If not for the memory of Mo's drawn face, the body swallowed by clothes that no longer fit, and the hours, days, and weeks Mo had spent staring vacantly at her comm display while she neglected her quarters, career, friends, and lover, Lesley would have resisted, advised Mo that telling Jayne could wait. But she wouldn't dare risk aggravating Mo's depressive tendency. "It's your decision."

Would Jayne understand how severely the accident had affected Mo? She wasn't there; she didn't live through it. She didn't see Mo shrunken and defeated; didn't sit through countless conversations listening to Mo torment herself with "what if" and "if only." Hadn't hated her helplessness and been overwhelmed with guilt because she wished the old Mo would resurface. Hadn't cheered Mo on as she clawed her way out of darkness.

"Will you come with us when I take Jayne home?" Mo looked up at her. "I don't want to tell her here, not with Nathan and Andrew and maybe—uh, can I stay with you tonight?"

Lesley's throat tightened when she realized that Mo assumed they'd tell Jayne together. "Sure." She not only wanted to be there for the conversation with Jayne, but afterward too, so Mo wouldn't be alone to brood. Mo still needed her, still wanted her support. Perhaps all wasn't lost.

JAYNE UNBUCKLED HER seatbelt, picked up her sketchbook, and rose. "Thank you. I'll see you on Sunday." Though if the flight home was any indication, it would be a quiet supper table.

Mo twisted around. "Can we talk for a minute?"

"Sure." She sat back down, hopeful that she was about to find out what the problem was between them. Maybe they'd resolved it? Or were they upset with her and the disagreement was over how to handle it? Was that why they couldn't seem to relax and be themselves around her? "What is it?" she blurted.

Mo glanced at Lesley. "Do you mind if we talk in your apartment?"

Her heart pounded. "No, not at all." It must be serious. It wasn't as if they'd never held an uncomfortable and difficult discussion inside one of their aviacrafts; Jayne had found out about Brenda Stewart while in Lesley's.

By the time she swung open her apartment door, all sorts of scenarios had run through her mind, including CT134. If not for their recent behaviour, she wouldn't entertain that possibility, but now . . ."Would you like tziva?" she asked evenly.

They shook their heads, and also turned down her offer to take their cloaks. She led them into the living room, invited them to sit, and perched on the chair across from them.

"You probably noticed I'm not that thrilled about Peggy." Mo's grin was too wide.

Jayne nodded. "It must be strange to see your papa with someone else." *Especially out of the blue.*

Mo sighed. "Yeah, that's part of it. But . . ." She swallowed. Lesley took Mo's hand and gave her a reassuring smile. "I haven't told you how my mama died." Mo looked down at her lap. "She—she died in an accident. An aviacraft accident. I crashed it. The craft."

Now Jayne understood why Mo hadn't wanted to talk in the aviacraft. How horrible! What could she say that wouldn't sound flaming inadequate?

"On purpose," Mo clarified. "I crashed the craft on purpose."

What? Jayne blinked at her.

"I had to." Mo's shoulders heaved. "I . . ." Her lips formed a thin line and she shook her head.

"The aviacraft's navigation system failed," Lesley said, rubbing Mo's back. "It was headed right for a learning academy. The only way to avoid hitting it was to ditch—bring the craft down before it reached the building. Unfortunately a gentle landing wasn't an option." She paused, perhaps to allow Mo to pick up the story, then continued. "Mo and her mama had been to the Trading Centre and were on their way home. They were both brave, both willing to give up their lives to save the academy. Unfortunately Susan didn't make it. Mo almost died too. She was awarded a medal for saving so many lives."

The horror of it left Jayne speechless. Not only would Mo have felt responsible for her mama's death, but guilty for surviving. Perhaps she still did.

"I didn't handle it well." Mo's eyes were moist, but her voice was steady. "I blamed myself, and almost threw everything away." She turned to Lesley. "Including Les. It got so bad, my commanding officer invoked Article 844."

It must have been serious. Jayne finally found her voice. "I'm sorry."

"Without Les's support, I wouldn't have made it. Seriously, Jayne, I wouldn't have made it. And she didn't have to stand by me. We weren't Chosens then."

Yes, they were, and right now, with Lesley comforting Mo, they were behaving naturally with each other. Jayne suspected it wouldn't last; this conversation wasn't about whatever was upsetting their relationship. But they'd managed to put their relationship problems aside—an encouraging sign that they might eventually overcome whatever the other issues were. They clearly still loved each other; that wasn't the problem. But Jayne would think about that later. She wanted to focus on Mo and this conversation.

"Having my papa drop Peggy on us like that . . . I couldn't help but think of my mama and how she died. I don't know if I'll ever be able to stop."

Jayne understood; she'd had the same problem after the Incident. Every time someone referred to the Chosen Tradition or Joinings or anything along those lines, thoughts of her parents intruded, along with feelings of humiliation and shame. Over time her mind had stopped automatically dredging them up whenever someone mentioned an article number with "CT" in front of it. She wouldn't have been able to function, otherwise. But would drawing on that experience upset Mo? "Your experience is very different from mine," she said, wanting to make it clear that she wasn't comparing Mo's mama's death to her parents', "but after the Incident, I was plagued with reminders. If I could have shut them all out, I would have. It was tough in the beginning, but it eventually passed. If Peggy becomes a frequent visitor, you'll stop thinking about your mama at some point. When you see Peggy, I mean." When Mo stared at her, Jayne wanted to take the words back. "Will you show me your medal?"

Mo's answering smile was self-mocking. "If you remind me next time we're at my house."

"No need." Lesley stood up and pulled a box from her cloak pocket.

Mo's face slackened. "You brought it?"

"I thought Jayne might ask."

"Thank you," Mo breathed, her voice a curious mix of surprise, gratitude, and . . . admiration?

Sensing an undercurrent between Lesley and Mo, Jayne tried to decipher what wasn't being said, but remained puzzled. She accepted the box from Lesley with a murmured thank you, opened it, and gazed at Mo's award.

"My mama got a commendation," Mo said. "The Commendation of the Way, for bravery and selflessness."

The highest possible civilian commendation. "You must be very proud. I wish I could have met her." The feeling wouldn't have been mutual.

"We may visit the Middleton crypt soon. Perhaps you'd like to come with us," Lesley said.

Mo rose from the sofa and grabbed Lesley's hand. "That's a great idea, Les. Thank you."

Again, that undercurrent. Jayne didn't understand why Mo was so grateful to Lesley. Would she have found it difficult to invite Jayne to visit the crypt or show her the medal herself? "If you won't mind, then yes, I'd like to go with you." She left the chair to move closer to them. "Do you mind if I take the medal out so I can have a closer look?"

Mo shook her head.

"I'm sorry about your mama, Mo," Jayne said as she turned the medal over and read the inscription on its back. "It must have been a terrible time for you."

"It's not really good for me to dwell on it, but I thought you should know in case we see more of Peggy." Mo rolled her eyes. "It's not Peggy, per se. I don't even know her."

Jayne placed the medal back in the box, closed it, and handed it back to Lesley. "Thank you for telling me." She suspected they'd only scratched the surface when recounting the crash and its aftermath, especially since Article 844 had been invoked. But she wouldn't torture Mo by prying; she was grateful that Mo—and Lesley—trusted her enough to share the little they had. Jayne could wait for the rest. "Are you sure you don't want tziva?"

She wasn't surprised when they both shook their heads. "I have a class tomorrow," Lesley said. "We should go."

They said good night. Jayne shut her apartment door behind them and thought once again about what a terrible time Mo must have had. Tonight had reminded her that she wasn't the only one whose parents had died under horrible circumstances. Poor Mo. And Lesley had supported her through it all.

Jayne saw her two Chosens as an inseparable unit. She'd met them at the same time, was coming to know them at the same time, and was developing feelings for them at the same time. Having two Chosens no longer seemed strange at all. She couldn't imagine one without the other and would always see herself as an appendage to their relationship. Fortunately they didn't seem angry with her and still trusted her, so maybe the problems they were experiencing had nothing to do with her. So what was going on, then? She wanted to be there for them, just as Lesley had been there for Mo.

MO HUNG HER cloak in the Middleton hallway and listened for voices. Silence. She breathed easier. Les had left for her course a couple of hours ago, but Mo had hung around the Thompsons', hoping to give Peggy plenty of time to leave—if she'd stayed overnight. At some point, Mo would have to make an effort to talk to her, but not today.

She went into the kitchen to pour herself a glass of juice, and was mid-sip when she suddenly tensed and quickly set the glass on the counter. The approaching footsteps grew louder. Papa appeared in the doorway. "So. You're home."

"Yeah, I'm home." Mo folded her arms. "And I know what you're going to say, but you should have warned us first. Okay, we still would have been shocked, but at least we would have been shocked without her staring at us. You probably figured we'd tell you we didn't want to meet her, but you still should have told us first. And I know it was difficult for you to bring your . . . her home to meet us, but just springing her on us like that let you off the hook and put it on us."

He sniffed. "Well, I guess I'll just go back to the study."

"What? That's it?"

"You don't seem to need me. You're doing just fine carrying on a conversation between us without me opening my mouth!" He turned to leave.

"Okay, okay!" The amusement in his eyes irritated her. "Why didn't you tell us, especially me? How do you think I felt? Every time I looked at her . . ." She blew out a sigh.

Papa's brow puckered. "I didn't tell you because I wasn't sure you'd agree to meet her. I'll admit to that. And I didn't want you to worry. If I'd told you about her, you might have . . . I don't know . . ."

"Needed a counsellor again? I won't." Ironic, how her problems with Les would prevent her from brooding over this latest twist in her life. "But that doesn't mean I won't find it difficult to warm up to her. Though it's not her, per se."

"I know." He stepped into the kitchen. "I delayed bringing her home as long as I could," he said quietly. "And when I couldn't wait any longer, I thought it might be easier for you—for everyone—if you all met her together, so you'd all find out at the same time and none of you would be trapped in conversation with her."

"Why couldn't you wait any longer?" Mo asked, desperately hoping he wasn't about to move Peggy in.

"I'd like her to spend the Festival of the Way with us."

Was it that time already? "Doesn't she have family?"

"She's a Solitary. While she does have family, we'd like to spend it together."

The Middletons and Thompsons had continued the tradition of spending the festival together while she and Les were separated. This would be Mo's first festival at home since her time on the *Falcon*. "Have Adelaide and Alan met her? Do they even know about her? I assume we'll be eating with them again."

Papa nodded. "I'll drop in on them later. I wanted you to know about Peggy first."

Mo would love to be there, especially to see Adelaide's face. The Festival of the Way supper could turn out to be livelier than usual this year, with Papa's girlfriend and Jayne reading from the Chosen Tradition. Oh, yeah. This would be one supper to remember. Poor Jayne. No more Festival of the Ways with Carol and Ronald—or had she passed festival days alone? Wait. The mandatory morning program included the skits about the Adamses. Argamon! Mo didn't care what Les said, they were definitely sitting in the back this year.

"So can I assume you'll be pleasant at the festival? I don't expect you to spend copious amounts of time with her, but it would be nice if you'd at least say hello and exchange a couple of words."

"I'm not rude, Papa. If you're serious about her . . ." he nodded ". . . then

I'll try. I don't know when—" or if "—I'll be able to sit down with her and have a serious conversation, but I won't ignore her. She's important to you." He'd moved on. She tried not to feel betrayed on Mama's behalf, but she couldn't help it. Yes, it was unreasonable and unfair; she couldn't expect Papa to pine after Mama for the rest of his life. But a girlfriend would take some getting used to. "Give me some time. I'd like to hear about . . ." How their relationship had developed? Ugh. "About when you met and when you . . . I don't know, realized you liked her. Just not yet."

He gave her a small smile. "That's fair. She knows that it may take time."

"Did you tell her how Mama died?"

"I had to! I—"

She held up her hand. "I figured you had. I don't even know why I asked." They stared at each other.

Papa cleared his throat. "I should go to the workshop. I told Andrew I'd be in." He hesitated. "I hoped to catch you, to make sure you weren't too angry with me."

"I'm not angry." Not really. "Go make some pants or something."

She twisted to pick up her glass and didn't straighten until she'd heard him leave the kitchen. Why were her eyes tearing up? Was she grieving for Mama, for Papa, for herself? Or was she trying not to weep over her relationship with Les? The only positive thing about Peggy's abrupt entry into her life was that she and Les had something new to talk about. Last night—telling Jayne about the accident and then staying with Les—it had almost felt as if things were back to normal between them. But they weren't. Les had only temporarily put aside the mess around Jayne to support Mo. If only Mo could put aside her feelings for Jayne. If only they weren't in a triad. If only Mama weren't dead.

MO OPENED THE audition room door and stepped into the waiting room. Normally she'd feel relieved, but the audition had been so far down on her worry list that it had felt like an afterthought. Hopefully she'd managed to infuse her performance with emotion and energy, regardless. She scanned the waiting room, her eyes briefly resting on Jayne before moving to a young ensign sitting across from her. "Patrick Davis?"

He gulped and nodded.

"They said you can go in."

Davis picked up his violin and gave Mo a sickly smile as he walked past her, his face white and his chest heaving. It was a good thing he didn't play a wind instrument.

Her gaze settled on Jayne again. Jayne's pencil was poised over her sketchbook, but still; she stared expectantly at Mo. Mo quietly sighed and walked over to her.

"So?"

Mo shrugged. "I think I did all right. Nobody covered their ears."

Jayne chuckled. "Did they say when you'll find out?"

"In a couple of weeks." Not that she cared one way or the other. Her life was a flaming mess! She'd deeply hurt one Chosen and didn't know what to do with the other. Every minute she spent with Jayne felt like a betrayal. Was Les thinking about them? If their positions were reversed, Mo wouldn't be able to concentrate when Les was out with Jayne. She'd sit in class wondering what they were talking about—and doing. On the other hand, Mo wanted to be with Jayne. Sort of. She could do without the unfamiliar awkwardness and the sinking feeling that she was hurting her relationship with Les every time she said something complimentary to Jayne or cared about what she thought. Would she ever relax when she was alone with Jayne? It would be impractical for her and Les to only see Jayne together, and Counsellor Berry wouldn't approve.

Mo realized with a start that Jayne had closed her sketchbook and was now standing. On the way to the aviacraft, she struggled for something to say to fill the silence. Jayne must already have noticed that she wasn't in a talkative mood, but with luck she'd put it down to pre-audition nerves. Now that the audition was over . . . "I talked to my papa about Peggy." And had already told Les about it, so the flaming scorecard she now kept in her head was even. "She'll spend the Festival of the Way with us, that's why he wanted us to meet her." She turned to Jayne. "I guess you'll be spending the Festival of the Way with us, too."

"I hadn't really thought about it," Jayne said, not looking thrilled with the idea.

"We always have our festival supper with the Thompsons. We usually attend the morning program with them, too." Except when Mama had been on duty at the Indoctrination Academy, but that hadn't been an issue for several years now. No, this year, they'd all get to spend it with Peggy. Okay, talking about her family was a bad idea. "What do you usually do?" she asked Jayne.

Jayne shrugged. "Go to the morning program and then go home."

"By yourself?"

"Carol has her family, and now Ronald's family."

"Carol's family is your family too."

When Jayne sighed, Mo wanted to touch her arm. Her grip tightened around her violin case. "Okay, I guess I'm not surprised they don't invite you along." Fortunately they'd reached the craft. Mo stored her violin in a cargo holder and slid into the pilot's seat. Jayne sat in the passenger seat, where she usually sat when Les wasn't with them, but again, Mo felt as if she were doing something wrong. She kept her eyes on the nav panel as she powered up the craft.

"Do you want to hang out at my apartment for a bit? Have a tziva?" Jayne asked.

Oh yeah, Mo could imagine recounting their afternoon to Les. *I had my audition. I think it went okay, but I won't hear for two weeks. Oh, and then we went back to Jayne's apartment and were alone there for a while. Nothing happened. We talked. Just talked. Yep, talked.* And Les would see guilt written all over her face, even though nothing *had* happened. "Um, why don't we go to an eatery? I'm a little peckish." She'd force down a dessert, or two.

"I think I have chocolate cookies at home."

"No, no, don't worry about it. Come on, let's go out. Change of scenery. We'll go to a nice little eatery in C5." To forestall further protest, she made a great show of punching in the coordinates. The craft lifted off. "It has delicious cupcakes," Mo said, for something to say. What would they talk about while eating? Maybe she'd just keep shoving cupcakes into her mouth.

Jayne leaned toward her. "How do you feel about Peggy, now that you've talked to your papa? Any better, or still the same?"

Mo swallowed and forced herself to turn and meet Jayne's eyes. Argamon, she wanted to tell her how she felt! Not just about Peggy. Everything! For honesty's sake, not because she wanted to act on her feelings—not now; not yet; perhaps not ever. Certainly not while her relationship with Les was tenuous. But at least Jayne would understand why Mo no longer felt at ease around her. Then again, telling her would probably increase the awkwardness between them. Best to keep quiet about it, so only one of them was acting like a moron.

What was Jayne's question again? Oh, yeah. "The same. But I won't be rude to her or anything like that. I'm glad Papa and I had a talk, because I won't feel like I have to force myself to flutter around her during the festival."

"I'm sure he wouldn't have expected that, even if you hadn't talked. He understands how difficult it is for you. It must have been difficult for him to take the step of . . . dating someone."

Mo hadn't thought about that. When Peggy had caught his eye, had he felt as if he was betraying Mama? Had he agonized, gone to the crypt, wondered what Mama would want for him? Would she want him to remain alone for the rest of his life? Probably not. But that didn't mean Mo could easily accept Peggy, not with Mama's death still preying on her conscience during weak moments.

She slowly exhaled, then tensed and used every bit of willpower she had to not flinch away when she felt the warmth of Jayne's hand on her arm. But it was too late. Jayne quickly lifted her hand and straightened in her seat.

Argamon! She'd noticed. Mo wanted to bash the nav panel in frustration. It wasn't fair that Jayne didn't know what was going on! Now she'd think Mo hated her, which couldn't be further from the truth. Could Mo make things any worse? She was a complete idiot at relationships. Fortunately she was a Chosen. Without the Chosen Council, she'd have spent her life alone because she would have botched every attempt to date anyone. As it was, she was making life a misery for her two Chosens.

This couldn't go on. Something had to give. But what?

JAYNE DRAPED A sheet over the canvas and led Lesley and Mo into the living room. Her two Chosens had praised her work, pointed out little details, and asked questions, but all in the name of politeness. They were distracted, indifferent, going through the motions. If she didn't suspect that their behaviour had nothing to do with her painting, she'd be crushed. They'd made polite noises about her cooking, too; in fact, her guests had been the epitome of graciousness all evening. She felt like a distant relative they visited on occasion out of obligation, where they sipped tziva, made small talk, and surreptitiously checked the time every chance they had. How long had they agreed to stay to be polite? Two hours? If so, they'd soon make their move.

"Would you like another tziva?" She could see the hesitation in their eyes. As usual lately, Mo looked to Lesley. Why? She'd never had a problem making decisions on her own, or speaking her mind. Why was she suddenly worried that she'd say the wrong thing?

"Sure," Lesley said, surprising Jayne. Maybe they'd decided on three hours.

"Why don't you sit in here and I'll bring it through when it's ready." Jayne escaped to the kitchen, relieved to have a few minutes on her own and sure they felt the same. Nothing made sense. Every time she saw them, her confusion deepened. Jayne desperately wanted to know if they were too wrapped up with themselves to worry about her right now, or if she was somehow part of their problem.

And what about Mo? They'd had a comfortable friendship, but now Mo was stiff and quiet around her, and she'd almost recoiled when Jayne had touched her in the aviacraft. Jayne leaned against the counter and threw her hands in the air. What had she done? For a panicked moment, she'd wondered if Mo couldn't relax around her anymore because she'd let her feelings for Mo show, and if that also accounted for Lesley's indifference toward her. But Jayne had been careful, and it wouldn't explain why their behaviour toward each other had changed.

Plus, they didn't seem upset with her, and Jayne was certain they'd be angry if they found out how she felt about them. It was as if they just didn't care. She had the feeling that, if they could, they'd never see her again. Suddenly she'd become an inconvenience, someone they'd rather avoid. Had they found out something else about the Incident? Had she said something really stupid or offensive and they'd decided they could do without her friendship, after all? They wouldn't execute her, but they'd tolerate her presence, occasionally pat her on the head, and hope she'd amuse herself most of the time? What was going on?

How long was she supposed to stand on the sidelines and hope they sorted it out? What if they weren't even trying?

The water boiled. She prepared the tziva and carried it into the living room on a tray. Lesley and Mo accepted their mugs ever so politely. Jayne stared at them from her chair, her two courteous Chosens sipping their tziva while probably hoping they could make her disappear, and who knew what they were thinking about each other?

Enough! Forget Carol's advice. Jayne didn't know what she was going to do, just that she had to do something. She might annoy them, but outright animosity would be better than polite indifference; at least she'd know where she stood.

MO LEANED BACK in the passenger seat and groaned. "That was probably one of the most painful evenings I've ever spent in my life." Poor Jayne had worked up the nerve to host them for supper, only to be faced with two uncomfortable guests.

Focused on the nav panel as the craft ascended, Les nodded. "It was awkward."

"Awkward? You call that awkward?" Mo sighed. "We can't go on like this."

"What do you suggest we do, then?" Les snapped.

Mo could hear the unspoken *This is all your fault*. "Maybe we should tell her what's going on."

"You *would* say that." Les's mouth pressed into a thin line.

"Just so she's not in the dark, Les." And so Jayne would understand why Mo was treating her like a biohazard. She still felt awful about tensing up when Jayne had touched her. "It's not fair right now. We're so uncomfortable around her that she must have noticed. She probably thinks it's her."

"It *is* her!"

"No, it isn't."

"You honestly think that telling her will make us more comfortable around her?"

Probably not. "At least she won't be in the dark."

Les folded her arms. "I don't know. I don't see what it will accomplish."

"Okay, things would probably still be awkward." Especially with

Jayne knowing how she felt. "But, I don't know, they couldn't be any worse than they are now."

Les remained silent.

"Aren't we supposed to be honest with each other? Communicate? Work together?" Mo frowned when Les smiled and shook her head. "What?"

"Have you thought about how I'll feel when you tell her you care about her in that way? What happens afterward? How will I feel when we're all together? How will I feel when it's just you and her?"

"I'm not suggesting I get involved with her, just that I tell her what's causing the tension. I'd suggest the same thing if the issue was something else."

Les turned to her. "Would you?"

"If it was making us so uncomfortable to be together, yeah, I would." She could see the skepticism in Les's eyes. "Be with me when I talk to her."

"No! I can't be there for that conversation. It's between you and her. It's not something you have an audience for." Les's shoulders hunched. Her arms were folded so tightly that Mo wondered how she could breathe. "You say you don't want to get involved, but telling her about your feelings is crossing over into relationship territory. Once you tell her, you can't go back. What if she says she feels the same way? What then? Am I supposed to say, 'Oh, that's wonderful, I'm delighted for the two of you'? 'I hope you have many happy years together'?" Before Mo had a chance to respond, Les continued. "That's what I'm supposed to say, right? That's what I have to say. I just have to take it. It doesn't matter how I feel, I just have to take it."

"Les—"

"I'm not ready for that. I don't know when I'll be ready. How would you feel?"

A lump formed in her throat at the sight of Les's distressed face. She'd handle it badly, so badly that conversations like this wouldn't be possible. The second Les mentioned feeling anything for Jayne, Mo's world would collapse and any hope of a mature conversation about the issue would evaporate. She'd demonstrated that by running away to 72 when she'd merely thought that Les wanted a relationship with Jayne. So yeah, maybe she was asking for too much, too soon. Maybe she was too worried about Jayne and not worried enough about Les. Les masked her feelings so well that it was easy—maybe convenient—to assume that she had everything under control. But she obviously didn't, and Mo should know better.

She hesitated, then placed her hand on Les's leg, which felt hard as rock. "Okay, I won't say anything. I guess we have enough problems as it is." If she'd hoped for reassurance that the situation wasn't that bad, she wouldn't have received it. Les stared stonily ahead. "We need things to be right between us, first," Mo said.

"If you mean 'how they were before,' I don't think that's possible."

Mo's heart sank. "You can't mean that."

"I do mean it." Les finally unfolded her arms. "I'm not saying things can never be good between us again, just that they'll be different. But who knows? Maybe time will prove me wrong. I wouldn't mind being wrong about this." Her mouth turned up at the corners, but her eyes remained dull. "I understand what you're saying about Jayne. It isn't fair, but I need more time before you take that step."

"You have it. I told you, our relationship is the most important thing to me. We have something special."

Les nodded. "Yes, we do."

The lack of enthusiasm in Les's voice was a knife through Mo's heart. But what else could she expect? She should have stayed away from Jayne, should have been polite, but distant. Les had managed it, but then, Les hadn't been so insecure that she'd crowded Jayne to keep Mo away from her. Maybe Les should have been more diligent; she would have been right! And now she believed that Mo's love for her had grown shallower or even died.

Mo wanted to lower her head and have a good cry. Would things ever be right again, between any of them? Giving Les the time she needed meant shafting Jayne. Being honest with Jayne would mean hurting Les. Even the staunchest of optimists would have a problem finding a glimmer of hope, and Mo tended toward doomsday scenarios in the best of times. She had no problem coming up with one now: two Chosens, two permanently broken relationships.

JAYNE LIFTED THE knocker on the Middletons' front door, then quietly lowered it. This was her last chance to give up on a course of action she'd waffled over for days. Maybe she should turn around, slink back to the train station, and stay out of it. But then what? Endure more awkward, painfully uncomfortable times with Lesley and Mo? For how long? She'd considered talking to Carol again, but Carol could only hypothesize about what was wrong. Jayne needed to know for sure. With a groan, she lifted the knocker and rapped at the door. Enough of going around in circles.

The door swung open. Nathan's brows rose. "Jayne! Hi. Mo didn't mention you were coming over."

Mo couldn't mention what she didn't know. "Is Mo here?"

"Yeah." He stepped aside and motioned for her to enter. "Mo!" he yelled.

Jayne's stomach fluttered as she waited in the hallway.

"Mo!" Nathan shouted again.

Mo came bounding down the stairs. "What do you—Jayne! What are you doing here? I mean, if you wanted to come over, I would have picked you up."

"I felt like taking the train."

Mo's eyes widened. "Nothing's wrong, is there?"

"No. I wanted to talk to you." She caught Nathan hovering in her peripheral vision. "Privately."

"Oh. Okay. We can go to my bed—the study. Papa's not here, right?" Mo asked Nathan. Nathan shook his head, and she turned back to Jayne. "Let's go into the study. Hang your cloak."

Jayne did so, wondering how long her cloak would remain on the peg. Depending on how Mo reacted, she could be leaving within five minutes. She followed Mo to the study, her apprehension rising.

Mo shut the door and leaned against one of the desks. "What's wrong?"

Jayne took a deep breath. "That's what I was going to ask you."

"What do you mean?" Mo's shrill tone and her refusal to meet Jayne's eyes belied her feigned ignorance.

Jayne had decided to ask first about Mo's behaviour toward her, rather than about problems between Mo and Lesley. Hopefully the answer to the first question would illuminate the latter situation. "I've noticed that you don't seem comfortable around me lately. Have I done something? Offended you in some way?"

Mo's shrug was exaggerated. "No."

"Then what is it?"

"Nothing. I don't know what you're talking about."

"Maybe it's just me, then," Jayne said, managing to keep her voice even despite her stirring frustration. She hadn't expected Mo to lie outright. "I thought—well, we seemed to be getting along all right. We were at least comfortable with each other. But lately . . . it's pretty obvious to me that you can't relax around me. You can't tell me you didn't feel the tension at my apartment on Sunday."

Mo stared at her. The silence stretched.

"Mo—"

"Leave it alone, Jayne," Mo said quietly. "Just leave it alone, okay?"

"I can't leave it alone."

"Why not? I'm asking you to drop it."

And then what? She was supposed to go home and wonder why Mo didn't feel comfortable around her? Because Mo had as good as admitted that, yes, there was a problem! So why wouldn't Mo tell her what it was? Every fear she'd had upon receiving her Chosen Papers came rushing back. At the time, she'd never dreamed that her Chosen—of course she'd expected only one—would become her friend, her ideal scenario. The best she'd expected was to be tolerated. Then Lesley and Mo had come along, and to her surprise and delight, they'd more than tolerated her, especially Mo. Were her initial fears now being realized? As they'd come to know her, had their early impressions of her soured? It did feel as if the triad had moved backward to a polite acceptance of her existence in their lives, rather than any genuine desire to include her. It must be her—what else could it be? Then, yes, she could see why Mo would be hesitant to say, "Sorry, Jayne, but we just don't like you." It wouldn't be polite!

"I can't drop it." Her voice quavered a little, but she didn't care. "I need to know what's going on. I enjoyed spending time with you, and Lesley. If I could just understand . . . at least know if there's anything I can do . . ."

"There's nothing you can do."

Her frustration boiled over. "What is it? Tell me! I thought we were friends."

"We are."

"If you don't like me anymore, just tell me. At least I'll know—"

Mo shook her head. "No, that's not—"

"I know I'm not very exciting, especially compared to pilots and—"

"It's not—"

"—everyone else in the military." Tears stung her eyes. "Yeah, I'll be disappointed, but I can't stand this awkwardness."

"Jayne—"

"If you're honest and it's out in the open, maybe we'll at least be able to spend time together without feeling uncomfortable." She brushed away a tear.

"Jayne, it's—"

"I'm used to it. I can handle it. I know you tried. I—"

"Jayne, it's not that I don't like you, it's that I like you too much!" Mo shouted.

What?

Mo groaned and clenched her hands. "Argamon!"

Shocked, Jayne turned away and brought trembling hands to her face. She must have misheard. "What are you saying?" She forced herself to face Mo.

Mo gulped. "Well, you know, we're Chosens, and things develop between Chosens, and they have developed. For me." Mo swung her arms toward Jayne. "Toward you."

Jayne gaped like an idiot.

"And if your face is any indication of how you feel about that, I think I'll crawl into a hole and die now," Mo said, her face suddenly beet red.

"No! I—I'm surprised. I—that is—" Her mouth gave up. How many possibilities for their change in behaviour toward her had she come up with? And not once had she considered this. Not once had this possibility occurred to her. Wait. Change in *their* behaviour, not only toward her, but toward each other. Her blood ran cold. "Lesley knows, doesn't she?"

Mo hesitated, then nodded.

Jayne grabbed her head. Flaming Argamon, this was bad. No wonder! It all made horrible sense now. "How long has she known?"

"Uh, she's known for sure since around the time I was—" Jayne silently completed Mo's sentence at the same time she said it "—last on 72. But I think she guessed a couple of weeks before then."

Lesley had known all this time? It must be killing her. Jayne had known Lesley was strong in the Way, but how strong could someone be? The lunch, the supper at her apartment—what had Lesley thought when Jayne had gone with Mo to her audition? What would she think if she knew they were together now?

"I'm not supposed to be talking about this," Mo said. "I told Les I wouldn't. She's . . . not happy about it."

That was probably the understatement of the century. Now she understood why Mo had wanted her to back off, but Jayne didn't regret pressing her. It would have come out eventually . . . if Mo was telling the truth. Jayne had never imagined that this scenario would arise. Mo liked her in *that* way? Really? "I know I forced the issue, but I needed to know what was going on. I've noticed that you and Lesley seem to be having problems, and around the same time, you were suddenly both acting differently toward me, so I figured I must have done something, or that maybe you didn't want to be around me anymore."

"You didn't do anything. It's me." Mo examined her fingernails. "How do you feel? About me?"

Argamon's flaming valleys, no! Don't do this to me! What had she told herself? As long as they never found out about her feelings, the triad would survive, tick along nicely with Lesley and Mo in love and she the doting friend. Their relationship was the foundation of the triad! It couldn't falter—but it was already in trouble. Would telling the truth help, or put them all into a more precarious position? Mo and Lesley's relationship was paramount and must remain strong! Jayne would *not* belong to a failed Joining. *Say, "I don't feel the same way." Say, "It's too early." Say, "I don't believe we're Chosens. Your feelings will pass." Say, "I don't feel that way yet, but maybe in time. Say, "Please, please, don't do this to me! Don't make everything I've always feared come true."* She wanted to drop to her knees and beg Mo to take it back, to tell her that she wasn't like her parents and hadn't doomed the triad to failure. *Please!*

Mo lifted her head. The hurt in her eyes took Jayne's breath away. "It's okay. I figured . . ." Mo's voice choked off, then she squared her shoulders. "Anyway, now you know and, uh—"

"I feel the same way, Mo. I feel the same way." Jayne couldn't allow Mo to believe that she didn't care. If that doomed the triad, then maybe it deserved to die. Not wanting to hurt your Chosen, wanting to be honest . . . that must count for something.

"You do?" Mo squeaked.

Jayne nodded, not entirely surprised by how dejected she felt. If she'd ever allowed herself to imagine someone confessing their feelings for her and confessing hers in turn, she would have seen herself bursting with happiness and sealing the moment with a passionate kiss. But that wasn't possible, not when so much was at stake, and when someone else she dearly cared about must be hurting badly and going through one of the most difficult periods of her life.

"Okay," Mo breathed. "Okay. But—"

"I know. Lesley."

"She didn't want me to say anything. She said she needed more time."

"How bad are things between you?"

Mo's eyes welled with tears. She gulped, struggled with her composure. "Not good," she managed to whisper, confirming Jayne's worst fear.

Jayne ached to hug her. She shoved her hands into her pockets.

"She doesn't believe I love her anymore." Mo's voice conveyed her bewilderment. "She doesn't think she's special to me, when nothing could be further from the truth."

With things as they were, Jayne could see only one course of action that would work best for both herself and Lesley. "Will it help if you tell her you've told me and we're both committed to sticking to our arrangement?"

Mo shook her head. "No! I can't tell her you know. She'll be horrified."

"Mo, we can't keep this from her. She needs to know."

"It'll just upset her. I told her I wouldn't tell you."

"And you didn't intend to." Jayne slipped her hands from her pockets and pressed one against her chest. "I forced the issue, not you."

"She won't believe me."

"Then let me tell her."

Mo thrust out her hands. "No! Not a good idea."

"I need to talk to her about it."

"Why?" Mo asked, eyes wide, clearly thinking Jayne insane.

"To reassure her that my priority is her relationship with you."

"You think that will help?"

"I don't know, but I do know that I can't see you, or her, or both of you, without having a conversation with her about all this. I just can't." It would be impossible to sit through another polite lunch with Lesley, to see Mo without feeling guilty, and to carry on stilted conversation with them while an elephant lumbered about the room. Jayne checked the time on her comm unit. "What time does she usually get home?"

"You're going to talk to her *today*?"

"Why not? I'm here." And she'd probably chicken out if she allowed herself time to think about it.

"I'll go with you," Mo declared.

"No, let me talk to her alone." Maybe she *was* insane. "I don't want her to feel as if we're ganging up on her." And she wanted Lesley to be honest, to call her every name under the sun, if that would help. Mo's presence would only deter Lesley from speaking her mind.

"Jayne, Les doesn't like to get personal with people she doesn't know well. And she likes to work things out on her own."

"I'm her Chosen, and yours. As much as we all hate it, I'm involved in this. I wish I wasn't. I wish the two of you had been Chosens to each other and had never met me, but that didn't happen. I can't stay silent this time. This is too important."

Mo slowly exhaled. She opened her mouth, then threw up her hands in resignation. "Do what you have to do."

Jayne had almost hoped Mo would talk her out of it.

Mo gazed at her. "So you think the best thing to do is to stick to our arrangement?"

"Yes. Don't you?"

Mo hesitated. "For Les, yes."

But not for *us*? Argamon, there was an *us*. Jayne couldn't believe it, but she'd worry about that aspect of this mess later. "It's best for the triad." But now, when she spent time alone with Mo . . . Her hands went back into her pockets. She should have brought her sketchbook, but she'd wanted to think on the train, not draw. From now on, she'd be sure to have it. "So what time does she get home?"

"By six, usually." Mo's brow furrowed. "Are you sure about this?"

"Yes. Don't warn her."

"I won't. But you better beep me afterward and tell me what happened."

"I'll see how she feels about that. Anyway, it's already 5:20. I should head over there."

"At least eat supper here," Mo said.

"No, that's all right." She'd probably throw it up; her stomach was already churning. "I want to go speak to her." Before she lost her nerve. "If I'm there when she comes home, I can talk to her and then leave her to eat her supper in peace."

"At least let me fly you home afterward," Mo said as they walked to the foyer.

"Let me see how it goes, okay?" She stopped herself from patting Mo's arm. "Thanks for the offer."

Jayne slipped into her cloak, aware of Mo's eyes on her and grateful that her hands weren't shaking half as much as her insides were. "All right. I'll beep you later, no matter what." *Just to let you know I'm still alive.* She wanted to groan. "Bye." She opened the front door and stepped outside.

"Jayne."

Jayne turned.

Mo leaned through the open doorway. "I'm glad—I mean—"

"Me too." But they both also cared about someone else, though Jayne wasn't about to admit to that. "I'm glad we're still friends."

They held each other's gaze. So many unsaid words hung in the air. A new kind of awkwardness might now exist between them, but at least Jayne would understand the reason for it. She winced at the concern and apprehension in Mo's eyes and clasped her hands behind her back. "Don't worry. Things can only get better."

The mocking smile Mo gave her in return said it all. "If you need me, if talking to Les doesn't go well, you know where I am."

Running to Mo because Lesley was upset would be the worst thing Jayne could do. "Worry about Lesley, not me. She needs you right now." She tore her gaze away and steeled herself. *Wish me luck* died on her tongue. Too trite.

As Jayne walked away from the Middletons', she resisted the urge to look over her shoulder to see if Mo was still there. The moment she was confident that nobody could see her from the house, she sat on the path, not caring if her cloak got dirty. She needed to slow down her racing mind, or her conversation with Lesley was guaranteed to go badly.

Mo liked her in *that* way? She never would have suspected in a million years! Under any other circumstances, her elation would have had her believing that she could leap into the air and land on 72. But Lesley and Mo's relationship was in trouble, both of them were hurting—the triad could fail! All leaping into the air would gain her was a sprained ankle. The triad had to come before any foolish romantic notions. Bolstering it would require hard work, commitment, and honesty. And she was sitting here wasting time.

Jayne pushed herself to her feet, brushed off her cloak, and quickly overruled the cowardly part of her that wanted to forget the whole idea and go home. She'd promised herself that she would do everything in her power to prevent the triad from failing, so retreating to her apartment and hoping it would all go away wasn't an option. It was put up or shut up time, and she, for one, was not going down without a fight.

CONVERGENCE

.....

JAYNE WAITED NEAR THE THOMPSON ESTATE'S empty holding area, trying not to pace. Maybe she shouldn't ambush Lesley the moment she stepped off her craft, but the alternatives—hanging around outside an empty house, or sitting in the living room with Adelaide and Alan staring at her—weren't any better. Mo had said that Lesley was usually home by six; according to Jayne's comm unit, it was almost that now. She shielded her eyes and scoured the sky. Was that dot growing larger? Yes! Assuming it was Lesley, this was Jayne's last chance to make a run for it, but she resisted the urge and made sure to stand far away from where the craft would touch down. Despite the apprehension that now gripped her, she didn't want to be squashed.

A minute later she watched the aviacraft descend and land. The door slid open. Lesley hopped from the craft, swung a knapsack over her shoulder, and slid the door shut. She walked a few steps, then stopped short. "Jayne! What are you doing here?" Her face tightened. "Is Mo all right?"

"She's fine." Jayne gulped. She was about to find out if talking to Lesley was the smartest or dumbest idea she'd ever had. "I just came from Mo's, actually."

If Lesley was surprised or upset, she didn't show it. "Why isn't she with you?"

"I wanted to talk to you alone." She could barely hear herself over the pounding in her ears.

"What do you want to talk about?"

Jayne wished they were walking, rather than facing each other. "I went to see Mo because I'd noticed that she seemed uncomfortable with me, and that you two seemed uncomfortable with each other," she said, struggling to keep her voice even. "She told me . . . what's behind it all."

Lesley's eyes bored into Jayne. "What did she tell you?"

Argamon! She'd expected Lesley to react at this point, not force her to say it. No matter how gently she spoke, Jayne would feel as if she was gloating. She considered hedging, but instinct told her to be honest. "She said she has feelings for me. And . . . I told her I feel the same way about her."

Lesley's expression didn't change. When she didn't say anything, Jayne continued. "I pushed her into telling me. She didn't want to. She told me to leave it alone, but I was worried. About both of you." Still no reaction. Would Lesley just stand and stare? "I thought I'd better come and talk to you about it."

"Why? Are you here to ask my permission to have a relationship with her?"

"No! I—"

Lesley suddenly marched off toward the house. After a moment's hesitation, Jayne hurried after her. "I thought it would help if we talked," she said breathlessly.

"There's nothing to talk about," Lesley said without looking at her. "You and Mo are Chosens and you want to be together. There's nothing I can do."

Finally, a chink in her armour. "We're going to stick to our arrangement," Jayne said.

"What arrangement would that be? You and Mo together and me the friend?"

"No!"

Lesley stopped and whirled toward Jayne. "Why not? We both know that's where it will end up."

"No, it won't!" Jayne cried, shocked by Lesley's anguished eyes. "Mo's feelings for you haven't changed."

"How would you know?"

"Because I see the two of you together." She wouldn't dare mention that she'd discussed the subject with Mo.

Lesley's eyes narrowed. "You said you spoke to Mo because the two of us seemed uncomfortable with each other."

"I could see there was something wrong, but I never doubted that you still love each other."

Lesley's chin came up. "I didn't realize you were keeping track."

"I'm not!" They glared at each other. "Lesley, we're all Chosens. I do have more than a passing interest in the two of you."

"You obviously do in Mo."

Jayne scrambled for a response that wouldn't give away her feelings for Lesley, but couldn't come up with one.

"If you're planning to stick to our arrangement, why are you talking to me?" Lesley asked. "Why are you here?"

"Because I wanted to make sure you knew I'd pressed Mo into telling me about what's going on. I don't want more trouble between the two of you, and I don't want you to think we're talking about you behind your back."

"Mo could have told me," Lesley retorted. "Did she tell you to talk to me?"

"No. She tried to talk me out of it, but . . . Maybe you hate me right now, but I couldn't see myself having lunch with you, and seeing you and Mo, without talking to you about this."

Lesley sighed. "Maybe it will be easier with you knowing. I don't know."

"I want this triad to work."

"So do I. But nothing prepared me for this, Jayne. I know you can say the same, but not quite. You don't have to figure out how to accept that the woman you've always loved now cares for someone else." She raised a finger. "Not only that, walking away isn't an option. No, you have to honour both of them, respect them, live with them, see them together. Would you know how to do that?"

Jayne swallowed. "I don't know."

"Neither do I. I was hoping to have time to figure it out."

"Maybe we have to figure it out together, the three of us."

Lesley shook her head. "It's not your and Mo's problem."

"Of course it's our problem! If one of us isn't happy, how can the other two be? Mo clearly isn't."

"I'm sure she was happy when you told her how you feel about her."

"No, she wasn't. How can she be, when she's worried about you and your relationship? We're all—"

Lesley frowned and looked past Jayne. "Do you want to stay for supper?"

"What?" A stone crunched behind her. Jayne looked over her shoulder, expecting to see Mo.

Adelaide strolled up to them, carrying a satchel. "I didn't know you'd be visiting today," she said to Jayne.

Jayne waited for Lesley to step in, but apparently Lesley wasn't going to help her. "It wasn't planned. I was on my way to the train station from Mo's when I thought I'd drop in and say hello. Lesley landed just as I was passing by."

"Are you staying for supper?" Lesley asked.

"No, I just wanted to say hello. I'll be heading home now."

"Don't be silly!" Adelaide snapped. "How long does it take you to get home? Three hours? You'll be starving by then. I'm surprised Mo didn't invite you to stay for supper."

"She did. But—I mean—" Argamon, she was a lousy liar!

"Stay for supper. I'll beep Mo, tell her to join us too," Lesley said.

What? Jayne wanted to gape at her.

"Well, I'm hungry, so let's get a move on." Turning, Adelaide strode down the path.

"Why?" Jayne murmured to Lesley as she fell into step with her.

"Mama wouldn't have accepted no for an answer, so it was supper with me, or supper with me and Mo."

"You don't have to do what you think I want."

Lesley lifted a brow. "I'm not. I'm doing what *I* want."

MO CHEWED HER thumbnail and wondered for the hundredth time if she should hop on her bike and hightail it over to the Thompsons'. She should have tried harder to talk Jayne out of it, or at least gone with her.

Jayne feels the same way about me.

Not now! She should be worried about Les and Jayne, not feeling all sentimental because Jayne cared about her. Would she ever think of Jayne without feeling guilty? Mo sighed. Seeing her would be worse.

Her comm unit beeped. Finally! She frowned when she saw the name, and wondered if she should hold the comm unit at arm's length. "Les?"

"Do you want to come over for supper?" Les said calmly.

"What?"

"Supper. Jayne is staying, too."

"Uh, sure. I'll head over now." They said good-bye. Bewildered, Mo didn't waste any time in throwing on her cloak and hopping on her bike.

Jayne must have chickened out at the last minute. Mo agreed that they had to tell Les about their conversation; what she'd objected to was the timing. She would have preferred to tell Les herself before the three of them got together again. Now she and Jayne would have to sit through supper together without Les knowing.

At the Thompsons', she found Jayne sitting in the living room by herself. "I don't blame you for not telling her," Mo whispered.

Jayne looked up at her. "I did tell her. Then Adelaide showed up and roped me into supper."

Great. "Where is she?"

"Changing." Jayne pointed at the ceiling. "Though she's been changing for fifteen minutes now."

"I better go talk to her."

Mo climbed the stairs but hesitated outside Les's bedroom. Normally she'd knock and walk in, but this time she rapped on the door and waited. "It's Mo." Silence. Mo opened the door a crack and peeked into the room, then stepped inside and closed the door behind her.

Les sat at her desk, still in uniform. She swung the chair around to face Mo. "I said I needed time."

"I know. She came to me, not the other way around."

"You didn't have to tell her."

"What did you expect me to do? She asked me point blank what was going on." Mo could feel a headache coming on. She hated being caught in the middle, but she couldn't see any escape. "I tried to put her off, but she's not stupid. You know how uncomfortable we were at her apartment. She thought I—probably both of us—had soured on her. I couldn't let her go on thinking that."

Les folded her arms. "So you care more about what *she* needs."

Mo slapped her thighs. "No! Argamon, Les, if I defend her or say anything that suggests that I care about her, you take it as a slight against you. It's not you against her. If that's the way you're going to think about it, we won't be able to talk about her."

"How would you think about it?"

Her irritation fizzled. "I wouldn't be thinking. I'd probably break everything I own and refuse to speak to either of you." Was it her imagination, or did Les's face soften? "Look, I know this is difficult—okay, understatement of the year. It's flaming impossible! But we're Chosens. Somehow we'll find a way to live with all this. I just don't know how."

"That's why I wanted time. To figure it out."

"I don't think this is something you'll figure out by thinking about it. We'll have to muddle through." And hope they somehow made it to the other side in one piece? But what else could they do? There *was* no escape, for any of them.

Les stood and rolled the chair under her desk. "I'd better get changed before Mama comes looking for me."

"Les—"

"You should go and keep Jayne company." She met Mo's eyes. "We don't have time to talk about it now."

Mo wanted to apologize, but for what? She hadn't forced the issue. She'd tried to dissuade Jayne from talking to Les, and she hadn't intentionally developed feelings for Jayne. But she couldn't help feeling guilty because she was the one who'd fallen for Jayne first. She'd blinked; she'd betrayed their relationship. She was the weak one, but she wasn't bearing the brunt of this mess. Les would have to go downstairs and sit through a civil meal with her Chosens and her parents. How would she feel, with Mo on her right and Jayne on her left? How could she bear it?

"Lesley!" Adelaide yelled up the stairs.

"I'll tell her you'll be down in a few minutes." Mo reluctantly turned to leave. She wanted to stay here for Les; she wanted to go downstairs for Jayne. Would it always be this way? Would she ever think of one Chosen without thinking of the other? In a way, she hoped not.

LESLEY SANK INTO one of Counsellor Berry's comfortable chairs and crossed her legs. "Thank you for agreeing to see me at such short notice."

Berry smiled. "No problem."

Mo and Jayne were disrupting Lesley's concentration during class and keeping her awake at night. The need to talk—to have someone tell her she wasn't weak in the Way and provide her with a nav map to follow—had driven Lesley here, but it was difficult to admit that she was struggling. She was an Interior officer on her way to becoming a commander. "I hope it didn't inconvenience anyone else."

"Don't worry about that." When Lesley remained silent, Berry leaned forward in her chair. "What's bothering you?"

"It's Mo and Jayne."

"What about them?" Berry prompted.

Now to say the words that would make her feel inadequate. She wasn't special enough. She wasn't attractive enough. She wasn't satisfying enough. Mo wanted someone else. "They've developed feelings for each other."

Berry's expression remained neutral. "Did they tell you this?"

"Yes." If Berry asked how she felt about it, Lesley would throttle her. "When?"

"Mo told me a few weeks ago." Well, Mo had acknowledged her feelings after Lesley had pointed them out to her, but Berry didn't need to know the details. "I asked her for time. We agreed that she wouldn't say anything to Jayne, but it was difficult to see her—Jayne—and she noticed we were uncomfortable. She went to see Mo to find out what was wrong, and that's when it all came out. Mo told Jayne about her feelings, and Jayne said she feels the same way."

"And then they talked to you about it?"

"Jayne talked to me about it."

Berry's eyes widened slightly, but she nodded.

"She said she couldn't see me, alone or with Mo, without having a conversation about it."

"When did that happen?"

"A couple of days ago, right after she talked to Mo."

"Have all three of you had a conversation about it?"

Lesley shook her head. "Jayne said they'll stick to our arrangement."

"Do you think they will?"

"No." Her eyes welled with tears. Not wanting to cry in front of Berry, she fought them and lowered her head. "I don't mean they'll go behind my back," she said, keeping her voice even with some effort. "I expect them to eventually come to me and say they want to throw our arrangement out the window." She inwardly cursed when a tear ran down her cheek, then took the handkerchief Berry held under her nose, where she could see it. "I'm sorry," she said as she dabbed at her eyes. "I should be handling it better."

Berry's brow furrowed. "How do you think you should be reacting?"

She drew a shaky breath. "We're Chosens. We're in a triad. This was bound to happen. I should have prepared myself." But she'd avoided the issue by telling herself the triad was a sham.

"You can't prepare yourself for something like this, Lesley. You can think about how you'll feel and react, but until it happens, it's not real."

"Still, I shouldn't be struggling so much. I'm—I thought I was strong in the Way."

"Are you worried that you'll violate the Way?" Berry asked evenly.

Horrified, Lesley shrank back against her chair. "No!"

"Of course you're not. I wouldn't worry about your strength in the Way. It's unreasonable to expect yourself to automatically accept the developing relationship between Mo and Jayne, just like that. Of course you'll struggle, and hurt. It's only natural. I'd be worried if you were taking it in stride." Berry's mouth turned up at the corners. "You took the step of making this appointment, and I know that probably wasn't easy."

No, baring her pain to a counsellor wasn't something she'd normally do; it made her feel weak. But she had to talk to someone. "How do I accept their . . . developing relationship?" She winced at the term. "I thought Mo loved me."

"She does."

"Not enough, apparently."

"Lesley—"

"She says her feelings for Jayne have nothing to do with me, that she doesn't feel any less for me, but it's hard to believe that."

Berry nodded. "It's one of those things you'll accept over time, when you see that nothing's changed between you."

But something had. Mo deeply cared for—perhaps loved—Jayne. Then again, if Lesley could forget about that when she was with Mo, would things feel as they always had between them? Right now, Mo's feelings for Jayne hung over them and invaded every conversation. If Lesley could somehow block the knowledge of them from her mind, would she still believe that Mo's love for her had diminished, or was her awareness of Mo's feelings for Jayne colouring her perception? Was it making her see, or expect, changes that weren't there, in terms of Mo's love for her and Mo's commitment to their relationship? She couldn't forget about Mo's feelings for Jayne, but the possibility of perception versus reality was food for thought.

"How do you feel about Jayne?" Berry asked.

"I like her. We do seem to have a few things in common. But I don't like her in that way." And now she wondered if she ever could, or if she'd resent Jayne—unfairly. She was here partly because she didn't want to blame Jayne for something that wasn't her fault. "Mo's seeing Jayne in a couple of days. She offered to cancel, but it's the appointment with Nolan. I know Jayne needs the support, and I know I can't keep them apart. I have to get used to them seeing each other." She squeezed the handkerchief in her right hand. Was she supposed to give it back? Crying in a counsellor's office was a new experience. "I'm not worried that they'll act on their feelings . . ."

"Earlier, you said you expected them to come to you to break your arrangement."

Lesley nodded.

"I agree that they won't act behind your back. From the way they're handling it so far, it's obvious that they want what's best for the triad, and for you."

If they'd wanted what was best for her, they would have kept their feelings in check! Yes, unreasonable. But Lesley couldn't help feeling that way.

"You want what's best for the triad, too."

"Of course I do. And I want us to be happy, not just follow the Way in misery. But I don't know if that's possible."

Berry's eyes grew distant for a moment, then they met Lesley's. "You know the arrangement won't last."

"I know." A certainty that cut to her core.

"And you want to do what's best for the triad, long term."

"Yes." Suspecting what would come next, she braced herself.

"Holding them back, trying to control their relationship, will hurt all of you. They'll grow resentful. You won't feel right about denying them. It'll eat away at all of you. They need control of their own relationship."

Their own relationship. Lesley wanted to stand and pace.

"You don't want to make them come to you. I think you know that."

To her horror, her eyes welled again. Argamon! She bit her lip.

"I don't expect you to go to them today and tell them the arrangement is off. You need to get yourself there mentally, first."

"I don't want to be the tyrant that holds them back. But I can't . . ."

"I know." Berry's forehead creased. "Easier said than done. But that's what we have to work toward. I know you're busy, but I'd like to see you alone at least once a week for a bit—twice, if you can manage it."

"Will you see them alone?"

"Not unless they want me to. And you don't have to tell them you're seeing me. You can if you like, but you don't have to."

Lesley had never expected to need a counsellor twice a week, but she'd never expected to be in a triad, or to be Mo's Chosen and find out that Mo had fallen for someone else. "Around this time is usually best for me," she said, pulling out her comm unit.

They arranged appointments for the next three weeks and then said good-bye. When Lesley reached the door, she realized she still clutched the handkerchief.

"Keep it," Berry said. "I have a whole cabinet full of them. Tools of the trade."

Lesley knew her smile didn't reach her eyes, even though she felt more hopeful than she had when she'd entered Berry's office. She'd known what she had to do, and hearing someone else say it had offered reassurance. There wasn't an easy way out. She hadn't missed the obvious. It would be cruel and uncaring to insist that Mo and Jayne stick to their arrangement, but tell that to her survival instinct. Nobody wanted to die a slow, painful death.

ANNOYED, JAYNE CLENCHED her hands as Kevin recounted his bewilderment, anger, and sense of betrayal after the Incident. She tried not to trivialize his experience; after all, his sister had been executed, and her Chosen Violation had shocked and devastated his family. But he'd been an adult and had understood what had happened. He hadn't been taken from his home by military, lost both his parents, been dumped on relatives who wanted to be supportive but were afraid of guilt by association, left to fend for himself at seventeen, bullied at the Indoctrination and Learning Academies, and held up as an example of being weak in the Way. Oh, and his sibling hadn't turned her back on him. It hadn't been about him.

She'd fought bitterness and resentment, determined not to let the Incident dictate how she behaved for the rest of her life. Otherwise she could have turned out like Kevin. He was glossing over what he had—a Chosen who loved him, children, and a prestigious position—to focus on what he'd lost. He was carrying around a burden largely of his own making. Though here she was, getting angry with him.

At least he wasn't venting at her anymore; he was talking to Nolan. If Nolan expected Jayne to pour her heart out next, he'd be disappointed. She'd tell him the truth. She didn't feel the need, not here, and it would only take one word to sum up what she'd lost: everything. That wouldn't be terribly interesting.

Focus on the positive! She gave Mo a sidelong glance. Jayne's life had recently taken a turn for the better, the opposite of what she'd expected at her notification meeting. Rather than having two Chosens who resented her, she had one who cared about her, and maybe one who resented her for reasons Jayne hadn't anticipated. How *was* Lesley? Jayne hadn't spoken to her since that night at the Thompsons'. Lesley hadn't appeared upset during supper and had flown Jayne home. If she'd wanted to talk to Jayne and Mo about their feelings for each other, that would have been the perfect opportunity, but the three of them had sat in a silence fraught with unsaid words.

Jayne had also submitted her application to art school. The news had delighted Carol, but Jayne's heart sank every time she thought of it. It wasn't that she was afraid of being rejected—though she'd prefer to be accepted, of course—but that she'd handed Rymellans an opportunity to put her in her place yet again. If the rejection letter was cruel, she'd feel as if she were back at the Learning Academy, wondering if the criticism was genuine, or a reflexive reaction to her last name. After all, nothing good could come from an Adams.

Nolan's voice snapped Jayne back to her surroundings. "... difficult to reconcile the sister you loved with the woman who committed the Chosen Violation," he was saying. "It's natural to ask why she didn't think of you, of her family. A Chosen Violation is such a selfish act."

Why hadn't she thought of Papa's family? Had Brenda Stewart known that he had two children? *Don't blame her.* He hadn't given his children a second thought, so why would she?

Nolan turned to Jayne. "Can you relate to what he's saying?"

Jayne stifled a snort. Again, she had to fight her rising irritation. She could understand how shocking it would be to find out that one's sister was committing Chosen Violations right under one's nose, but that paled in comparison to being rejected by one's parents. Of course she'd struggled to reconcile the two people she believed had loved her with the two who'd violated the Way with no thought to how it would affect her. She still did. Hadn't they wanted to see her grow up? Hadn't they realized what life would be like for the children of two executed criminals, especially two executed for Chosen Violations?

She dug her fingernails into her palms. This session might be helping Kevin, but it wasn't doing anything for her. She'd learned to live with the questions that would never have answers, and for the first time in a long time, she had a chance at happiness. The sun might finally chase away the oppressive gloom that had surrounded her since the Incident—but she'd never forget what she'd lost.

She jumped when Mo squeezed her arm, then drew courage from Mo's reassuring presence. "I'd rather look forward, not back. And I'm not needed here anymore."

"Why not?" Nolan asked.

"I was under the impression that I'm here because hearing about the triad, about me, brought back bad memories for Kevin Stewart." She glanced at Kevin, not wanting to talk about him as if he wasn't there. "We've moved on from that. You can counsel him privately now."

"Talking about it *is* helping," Kevin said.

"You don't need me here for that."

Gwen leaned forward to peer past Kevin at Jayne. "It might be good to have a joint session every once in a while."

Not good for her. "I don't need to talk about the Incident. I wondered who the fourth criminal was, and I'm grateful to you for telling me," she said, nodding at Kevin. "But now it's time for me to leave." She rose and turned to face the Stewarts. "I expect you'll see news of our Joining Ceremony on the monitors."

Mo stood at Jayne's side. "Yeah, you will." She told the Stewarts the date they'd Join.

"That's only a couple of months away!" Gwen said.

The Chosen Council had agreed to the earliest date Lesley had submitted, probably eager to Join the triad. Jayne hadn't been looking forward to living under the elder Thompsons' roof, but now . . . Given recent developments, it would be better to avoid long periods of time at home alone with Mo. Adelaide and Alan would make that easier, and Lesley would probably appreciate their presence, too. "Yes, it's soon," Jayne said to Gwen, forcing a smile. If not for her worry about Lesley, it would have been genuine. "After that, you're more likely to hear about my Chosens' accomplishments than you are about me. I have every intention of staying *off* the monitors." Her name would *not* be added to the Wall of Offenders.

"So that's it, then?" Kevin stood and cleared his throat. "I never thought I'd say this, but thank you." He inclined his head.

Gwen pushed herself up from her chair. "Yes, thank you. I know you weren't sure about meeting with us. I'm glad you did."

Jayne nodded at them, then curtly at Nolan. "Good-bye." She strode from the stuffy office, knowing Mo would follow, and didn't slow her pace until they'd almost reached Mo's aviacraft. "I suddenly needed to get out of there," she said when Mo caught up with her. Maybe Kevin wasn't the only one who'd benefitted from the two sessions. She *was* ready to look forward.

"So do you feel you've done what you needed to do?" Mo asked.

"He seems to be dealing with it now."

"I don't care about him. As far as I'm concerned, you did more for him than he deserved. I want to make sure you won't blame yourself if he does anything stupid."

"I won't." They boarded the craft and belted themselves into their seats.

"So what now?" Mo asked.

Good question. This time last week, she wouldn't have thought anything of suggesting that they go to her apartment or spend the rest of the afternoon together.

"It's only 14:30. Do you want to get a tziva somewhere? Maybe the eatery in c5 that we went to last time?" Mo suggested.

"Sure. The desserts were scrumptious."

Mo punched in the coordinates; the craft lifted off. "I have a feeling the servers are going to see us there quite often," Mo said, making Jayne chuckle. They'd have to find other public places to hang out. "I'm doing a few shifts on 72 next week, so I'll be staying over a couple of nights. I know you sometimes come with me, but . . . with the way things are . . ."

"I know. It wouldn't be a good idea." It would be unfair and self-ish to ask Lesley's permission, and there wasn't much point. If Lesley said to go ahead, that she didn't mind, Jayne wouldn't believe her. Not only that, Jayne couldn't forget how close she'd come to cross-ing the line when she and Mo had discussed Gwen Stewart's message on 72. The overpowering desire to touch Mo, to lose herself in Mo's arms . . . The conviction that Mo would be horrified had been a powerful deterrent—one that no longer existed. That didn't mean Jayne would give in next time; she believed that sticking to their arrangement was the best course of action for the triad, and she wouldn't hurt Lesley and sabotage their tenuous friendship. But the tension would grow unbearable. Why put themselves into a pressure cooker? "Has Lesley said anything about . . ." *Us?* ". . . the other day?"

Mo shook her head. "But that's not unusual. When she's wrestling with something, she stays silent for a while, then talks."

There wasn't a tidy solution to the situation, though. Lesley wouldn't suddenly know what to do to make everything okay again. Jayne felt for her. She wanted to grow closer to Lesley, but would that be possible now? How could Lesley not resent her? Jayne turned to Mo. "We're due for another lunch for Berry." She was probably the last person Lesley wanted to see, but they couldn't let a permanent rift develop.

"I know." Mo shrugged, but her face tightened. "You'll have to get together again at some point." She clearly didn't like the idea, perhaps worried that the lunch would upset Lesley and create more problems between them.

"When she beeps me about it—" Jayne wouldn't dare take the

initiative and ask Lesley to lunch "—do you want me to suggest that we wait?"

"No."

"But you'd rather we didn't meet for lunch."

"A little." Mo raised her hand. "And I know I have no right." She sighed. "I also know that Les has never deserved my jealousy. I don't want to start making the same mistake with you."

Jayne fought the sudden urge to grab Mo and kiss her. Yes, 72 was definitely off-limits; Mo's aviacraft would be too, if she couldn't trust herself.

AFTER LESLEY FINISHED reading her dispatches, she leaned back in her office chair and laced her fingers behind her head. Class wouldn't begin for another twenty minutes. Normally she'd review her morning notes, but her thoughts turned to Mo on 72. Jayne hadn't gone with her, a fact that upset, rather than appeased, Lesley. She couldn't stand that Mo and Jayne were obviously discussing her—how she felt, and how much they thought she could bear. It didn't matter that she would have been distracted, and perhaps angry, if Jayne *had* gone with Mo. They shouldn't have to worry about her.

Someone tapped at the door and swung it open. Laura peered into the office, then stepped inside when Lesley beckoned for her to enter. She sank into one of the guest chairs. "I thought I'd let you know that I'll spend the Festival of the Way in C3. I doubt there will be trouble, but since it's the first one with Jayne in attendance, having a commodore there won't hurt."

"You can sit with us, though we'll be in the back," Lesley said, wondering why Laura was really here. She wouldn't have batted an eye at seeing Laura at the festival; she would have been surprised if Laura hadn't decided to keep an eye on C3ers as they celebrated the Chosen Tradition with an Adams in attendance. "The Adams skit. If people want to gawk, they'll have to make the effort to turn around."

Laura chuckled. "Maybe I should sit next to Jayne."

Lesley smiled in turn. "You could. I'm always in the middle, so . . ." She trailed off. Would she be in the middle, or would Mo? "The chair next to her should be free. I'm sure she'd appreciate the support."

"Ben and Megan always beg me to sit in the back. I'll surprise them."

"Daniel will be out of the Indoctrination Academy next year, right?"

Laura nodded. "And Megan will be in." She paused. "With your course, we haven't had a chance to speak much lately. How are things going?"

Finally, the reason for Laura's visit. Lesley leaned forward and rested her elbows on her desk. "I was right about Mo."

"She has feelings for Jayne?"

Lesley nodded, then forced out her next words, knowing Laura would find out at some point. "Jayne feels the same way about Mo." She controlled her breathing with difficulty.

"I see."

"I'm having extra sessions with Berry," something Laura could discover at the press of a comm station button, if she didn't already know, "but they don't know that."

"It must be difficult," Laura said gently. "Don't push yourself. You have time. I know you're Joining in a couple of months, but I also know that you want to put an end to CT134 once and for all." Her mouth turned up at the corners. "Nobody will be checking the sleeping arrangements."

Lesley lifted a pencil from her desk and rolled it between her fingers. "I don't know where everything will stand in two months, but I've made it clear to them that I won't be upset if they . . . enter into a relationship."

Laura's brows drew together. "Really?"

"Yes." Or at least she'd make it clear next time she saw them. She wanted them to stop avoiding each other because they thought her too fragile, too weak, to cope.

Perhaps if she told them about her appointments with Berry, they'd know she was dealing with it and worry less about how their relationship would affect her. Berry had said that Lesley had to reach the point where she could handle discarding their arrangement, but Lesley was starting to believe that talking about it wouldn't get her there. Nothing would. It was time to move the triad in the direction it had to go. When she was backed against a wall, she'd have no choice but to accept whatever happened. Delaying the inevitable was wallowing in it. She was stronger than that.

As Jayne followed Mo and Lesley from Berry's office, she wondered why Lesley hadn't asked her to lunch yet. They were overdue, but Berry hadn't called her on it. The entire session had been boring, mainly a recounting of their activities since they'd last seen Berry two weeks ago. Not wanting to upset Lesley, Jayne hadn't brought up her feelings for Mo, and was sure that Mo hadn't said anything for the same reason. Jayne would have been flabbergasted if Lesley had raised the subject.

"So where are we meeting William?" Mo asked, breaking into Jayne's thoughts.

"On our land." Lesley smiled when Mo did, but was she genuinely looking forward to it?

Half an hour later, Jayne dutifully listened to William as he tapped the blueprints Lesley and Mo held open against the side of Lesley's avia-craft. It was hard to believe that a house would eventually sit in this empty field, the house in which she'd live with her Chosens and their children, grow old, and die. "Whatever you think is best," she murmured, when Mo asked if she agreed with a suggestion Lesley made to William. They'd tell her it would be as much her house as theirs, but she didn't feel that way and would agree to whatever they wanted. Anything would be better than her small apartment, and the estate was lovely—and private. Another reason she shouldn't have applied to art school: if she got in, she'd have to leave the estate three or four times a week. But she wouldn't be accepted, so it was a moot point.

"When will construction start?" Lesley asked.

"Next week." William rolled up the blueprints and slid them into a cylindrical case. "But I wouldn't bother coming to look. There won't be much to see for a while. Oh, Karen wants you all for supper again. I'm supposed to tie you down to a date."

"You said Carol wants us over, too," Mo said to Jayne.

She nodded. "But if you want to go to Karen's first—"

"Tell Karen I'll beep her later," Lesley said to William. "We have to put our three schedules together to figure out a date. And we haven't been to supper at Carol's yet."

"All right." William slung the blueprints over his shoulder and picked up his bike.

"Just a sec," Lesley said as he mounted it. "We haven't talked about the interior design."

William shielded his eyes from the sun and gazed at her. "It's a little soon for that."

"I know. But . . . Jayne."

Jayne turned to Lesley.

"Will you work with William's team when they're ready to think about the interior design—choose the colours and the furniture? Run whatever you want by Mo and me, but we're hoping you'll take the lead on it."

Jayne gaped. "But—I don't know anything about interior design."

Lesley shrugged. "You'll have a better eye for it than we will."

But what if they hated a colour she chose, or loathed a piece of furniture? Then again, Lesley had said that Jayne could run whatever she wanted by them—which Jayne would take to mean everything. Despite her fear that she'd make a mistake, she couldn't throw their trust back in their faces, or their generosity, especially Lesley's. Any attempt to include her must be difficult for Lesley, and this gesture was huge. "Okay. I'll, um, take the lead."

William looked at Jayne. "Catherine Moss oversees the interior design. I'll let her know. When it's time, she'll contact you." With a wave, he rode off. "Don't forget to beep Karen," he shouted over his shoulder. Lesley nodded, even though he could no longer see them.

"So what now?" Mo said. "It's only 15:30."

"I have that meeting with Commander Blair in an hour," Lesley said.

"Right. That was pretty inconsiderate of her, scheduling it on your day off from your course."

"Don't blame her. This was the only day I could fit her in."

"How long do you think you'll be? We can meet you afterward, have supper somewhere."

Lesley pursed her lips. "I shouldn't be longer than an hour. But let's talk first. Why don't we sit in my aviacraft?"

Jayne tensed. Last time Lesley had suggested they talk in her aviacraft, she'd dropped the Brenda Stewart bombshell. Apprehensive, she followed her Chosens onto Lesley's craft and sat in her habitual seat. Mo twisted the passenger seat toward Lesley. "What is it?"

Lesley sighed. "I've been seeing Berry a couple of times a week, to talk about how I feel about everything. Obviously I had to tell her about . . . you two."

No wonder Berry wasn't prodding Lesley to invite Jayne for lunch and hadn't pried as much as usual during their session. She knew everything! Jayne noticed Mo's eyes widening and saw her jaw tightening. Was it because Lesley hadn't told her first, or was she just surprised?

"So it's okay to talk about it during our sessions. You don't have to hide it because of me." Lesley lifted her hands, then dropped them to her lap. "I should have asked you whether it was okay to tell her, but I needed to talk about it, and I didn't want you to know I was seeing her, not at first. I hope you're not upset."

"I'm not," Mo said. "That's what counsellors are for. She can't tell anyone."

Jayne felt relieved that Lesley had told Berry for her. "I agree."

"But as far as *our* sessions go, I don't think we should bring something up unless we've agreed to it," Mo said.

Lesley grimaced. "She's supposed to help us. She can't do that if we keep problems from her."

"I'm not saying we hide stuff, just that we don't surprise each other by bringing something up out of the blue. I'd like to think we'll have discussed it amongst ourselves first." Mo leaned forward and put her hand on Lesley's knee. "Les . . . I'm glad you're going. And that you told us."

Lesley's face flushed. She twisted toward Jayne. "I did tell her we'd go to lunch soon."

"Sure. Just let me know when you have time."

"I'm on 72 in a couple of days. Go then," Mo suggested.

"You won't be taking Jayne with you?" Lesley asked.

The edge in Lesley's voice made Jayne wonder why she was upset.

Mo lifted her hand and drew back. "I didn't think—"

"That I can handle it?" Lesley glared at her. "That's the other thing I wanted to talk to you about. Our arrangement. I know it won't last, so it's off."

Stunned silence greeted her announcement. "Les, there's no rush," Mo finally said.

"Pretending our arrangement will last is only delaying the inevitable. I'll be okay. I'm dealing with it. Why do you think I'm seeing Berry?"

Mo gave her a long look. "We should talk—"

Lesley sliced her hand through the air. "No! As far as I'm concerned, it's off."

Mo raised placating hands. "Okay, it's off. But I'm still not taking Jayne to 72. I'm only going for one night, and the only reason I'm staying overnight is that one shift is late, the other early, and then I'm in a meeting with Ross all afternoon about the practicums starting next week. So there's no point. I'll be flying or busy the whole time."

Not when you're in bed. Jayne couldn't believe the thought had popped into her mind, and wondered if it had entered Lesley's. While the prospect titillated, she wasn't ready for that, and Mo probably felt the same way. They hadn't even kissed.

"Fine." Lesley sat stiffly. "I just wanted you to know that it's off. You don't have to worry about me."

But Jayne *was* worried, and she could see the concern in Mo's eyes.

"Where do you want me to drop you?" Lesley asked.

"Home," Mo said flatly. Less than a minute later, the craft landed in the Middleton Estate holding area. "Come over here after your meeting and we'll have supper together," Mo said as she unbuckled her seatbelt.

"I don't know, the meeting could run late," Lesley said. "I don't want to make you wait for me."

"Even if it runs two hours, you'll be here before 19:00. But it won't. You said an hour."

Lesley shook her head. "I have studying to do for my class tomorrow."

"Come on, you can do that afterward."

"I have things I need to do tonight, okay?" Lesley snapped. She glanced over her shoulder. "Don't forget your sketchbook."

Jayne had already picked it up. "I have it, thanks." She hesitated. "It would be nice if you joined us for supper."

"Yeah, come on, Les."

"I really should get going, or I'll be late for my meeting."

Mo frowned at Lesley. "Take us with you. We'll walk around the grounds while you're in your meeting. All we'll do here is hang out and talk, so we might as well do it there."

"I wouldn't mind seeing the grounds," Jayne added, though under other circumstances, military headquarters wouldn't be high on her list of places to stroll.

"We'll meet at your aviacraft afterward and go for supper," Mo said.

Lesley threw up her hands. "Okay. If that's what you want, okay." The craft lifted off again. Mo glanced over her shoulder and caught Jayne's eye.

After landing, they walked with Lesley to the bottom of the steps rising to the military headquarters entrance. "I shouldn't be more than an hour," Lesley said. With a nod, she climbed the stairs and disappeared inside.

Mo motioned for Jayne to walk, and didn't start talking until they were on a tree-lined path away from the entrance. "I don't know what she thinks she's doing."

Jayne suspected that Lesley was trying to prove something to herself. But what if she failed? What then? "What do you think we should do?"

Mo met her eyes. "I don't know. I'd say stick to our arrangement, but she seems determined to push us together, to the point that she'll be angry if we don't go there, but probably horrified if we do. What are we supposed to do with *that*?"

"Maybe we should speak to Berry."

Mo shook her head. "That would do more harm than good. Les would be upset that we were discussing her with Berry behind her back. I know she's seeing Berry, but that's different." She stopped walking, dug a rock from the path with her boot, and kicked it away. "And now that she's declared the arrangement is off, there's no way she'll admit it was premature and go back on it. But I don't know what she's expecting us to do. Well, maybe I do, but I think it would be a bad idea." She liberated and punted another stone. "On the other hand, if we stubbornly stick to our arrangement, that'll upset her, too." Her hands went to her hips. "No matter what we do, she'll be upset. And I don't blame her. I'd feel the same way." Mo snorted. "If it was me, I'd still be giving both of you the silent treatment."

Jayne smiled. "We can just say okay, the arrangement is off, but stick to it."

"If we say the arrangement is off, and you come to 72 with me, or I spend time at your apartment, she'll assume the worst, and it'll kill her. I know it will."

"She wants to show that she can handle it."

"But she can't!"

"I know."

"So what do we do? If we don't act like the arrangement is off, she'll think we're trying to protect her, which to Les means we think she's weak. If we act like it's off, I don't know what she'll do." Mo released an exasperated sigh, then looked at Jayne. "We can trust ourselves, right?"

Jayne nodded. She'd worried about being alone with Mo, but now her concern for Lesley would prevent her from doing anything stupid.

"Then let's stop walking on eggshells and see what happens."

"What do you mean?"

"Let's treat the arrangement as off." Mo swallowed. "I don't know about you, but even with it off, I want to take things slow—really slow. Things are going to feel weird for a while. If we take it slow, that will give Les time to . . . I don't know, accept it? Adjust? We can see how she deals with it. If she can't deal with 72 or us hanging out in your apartment drinking tziva, we need to know—and then maybe involve Berry."

What exactly was Mo proposing? "So . . . we don't worry about being alone and how it will affect her? I don't think I can do that."

"Of course we'll worry, and she'll hate every minute we're alone together in private. But apparently she'd rather that than have us coddle her. So unless we want to antagonize her, let's give her what she wants. If she falls to pieces the first time I tell her we spent time together at your apartment, even though I've told her nothing happened, we'll beep Berry."

"She obviously wanted us to spend the evening alone together." And maybe more? Didn't Lesley think they cared about her?

"No, she wanted to show us that she wouldn't fall to pieces. But I won't let her hurt herself."

"*We* won't."

Mo grinned. "There really is no point in you coming to 72 with me this week, though. I wasn't lying about that. Anyway, come on. Let's walk."

She strolled away; Jayne reached her side in two strides. Would holding Mo's hand be going slow? Wishing she hadn't left her sketchbook in the aviacraft, she shoved her hands into her cloak pockets.

MO NODDED AT two fellow pilots as they passed on their way out of the canteen. She checked her comm unit, and silently cursed when her lips tightened.

"Am I boring you?" Ann asked. "You've checked your comm unit three times since we sat down."

She shook her head. Les and Jayne would meet in fifteen minutes, and she was already wondering what they'd talk about and how long they'd spend together. Two Chosens, double the jealousy. If she didn't learn to control it—to trust them—she'd make herself ill.

"Go, already!" Ann urged. "I have to fly in an hour."

Mo glared at Ann and took a bite of her sandwich, then slid a card from her hand and dropped it onto the table.

Ann studied her cards. "So I finally heard about Peggy. Is it supposed to be a secret? You didn't mention anything last time you were up, and it took Andrew long enough to tell me."

"What did he say?" Mo asked, eyes on her own cards.

"That your papa surprised you all at the supper I wasn't invited to." Ann threw a card onto the pile.

"It was for family only. You didn't miss anything exciting."

"I missed seeing your eyes bug out of your head."

Mo resisted the urge to kick her under the table and took the top card from the deck.

Ann shrugged. "Doesn't matter. I'll meet her at the Festival of the Way."

Mo looked at her. "What do you mean?"

"I'm spending it with Andrew."

Oh, great. "Don't harass her, okay?"

Ann drew back. "I won't. Oh, were you accepted to the military orchestra? I heard Steve was."

"I was too, but I turned it down."

"Why?"

Because she already had enough to worry about without practices and concerts. "I don't really have the time. When I read over the info Ross sent me for the meeting this afternoon, I realized the practicums will be more work than I thought."

Ann picked up a card. She smiled and laid her hand on the table, face up. "Chalk another one up for me!"

Mo sighed and threw her cards down.

"You're not paying attention. What's bugging you? I thought it was Peggy, but you don't seem too bothered about her."

Only because Peggy had to get in line behind Les and Jayne.

Ann's eyes narrowed. "Why isn't Jayne with you?"

"She's busy." Mo ignored Ann's dubious look. "She's meeting Les for lunch today."

"Ah. You'd better check the time again, see if they're together yet." Ann continued on before Mo could retort. "So how *are* things between you and Lesley? You never told me if I was right about . . . everything."

"You were right," Mo admitted, knowing she wouldn't get away with lying to Ann for long. One lie would lead to another, and then another, until she tripped herself up. She felt herself smile; she'd love to tell Ann that Jayne felt the same way, but that would be asking for trouble and betray Jayne's trust. "Things are a little tense right now, but we'll work it out." *Ha!* She was lying to herself again. She *hoped* they'd work things out, and was starting to appreciate that doing so would take time—maybe months. Les would have to see that Mo's feelings for her hadn't changed. Telling her wasn't going to make a difference.

"So what happens now? With Jayne?"

Mo didn't have to consider lying to answer that question. "Nothing." Not at the speed she and Jayne had agreed to move. They had plenty of time to get involved—the rest of their lives.

Ann's brow furrowed. "You're not going to tell her?"

Argamon! Tread carefully . . . "With the way things are with Les—"

Ann's eyes lit up. "She's not up here because you don't trust yourself. I knew it!" She grinned. "Another game?"

"Sure," Mo said, pleased that her evasive answer had satisfied Ann. While Ann shuffled the cards, Mo popped the last bit of sandwich into her mouth and fought the urge to check her comm unit.

Would they talk about her? Would Les lash out at Jayne? Would either of them beep to let her know how it went, or mind if she beeped them to ask?

"Should I deal?" Ann raised a brow. "Or do you want to check the time first?"

Mo tapped the table with one hand, sat on the other, and vowed to spend more time with Les, even if she had to read announcements while Les studied for her tests. Les and Jayne hadn't declared feelings for each other, but thinking of them together tied Mo up in knots. Imagine how Les must feel!

LESLEY THANKED THE server and pulled out the chair across from Jayne in an eatery in D2. The awkwardness at their last lunch together still made her cringe, and the change of venue wouldn't make any difference. Lesley already felt as if they were talking about everything except what was on both of their minds. Sipping her water, she decided to dispense with the small talk. "Mama has suggested that you stay at the estate on the night of the festival supper. Otherwise we'll have to fly you home, only to turn around and pick you up again in the morning."

Jayne lifted her napkin and unfolded it. "Would you mind, if I stayed?"

It would be better than Jayne staying at the Middletons', and Lesley wasn't angry with her. Any time resentment toward Jayne stirred, Lesley's intellect quickly set her back on the rational path. Jayne hadn't decided to develop feelings for Mo, and vice versa. Lesley could resent how things had turned out, ache over what she'd lost, and feel frustrated that there was nothing she could do except learn to live with it. She couldn't be angry with or resent *them*, and she was grateful that she was thinking straight enough to recognize that. Otherwise she'd throw her water in Jayne's face, not sip it while she pondered what to say. She set her already half-empty glass on the table. "No, I wouldn't mind. It makes sense. Mo will stay over, too."

When Lesley had mentioned Mama's suggestion to her, Mo had made it clear that if Jayne stayed, *she* stayed. While ruminating over Mo and Jayne's fledgling relationship, Lesley had also recognized that if she'd developed feelings for Jayne first, she would have kept them to herself and made sure that her manner toward Jayne never gave Mo a reason to suspect. She dearly loved Mo, but that didn't mean she was blind to Mo's weaknesses. With Mo's jealousy, there was no telling what would have happened. This way . . . as much as Lesley hated it, if it had to happen, the burden was better placed on her shoulders.

"I'm not looking forward to the morning program." Jayne's face reddened. "I—I'm not saying I don't want to celebrate the Way," she quickly clarified. "But . . . I usually go on my own."

Even Lesley's reflexive politeness couldn't prevent her from barking a laugh. "You're not looking forward to spending it with us?"

Jayne's eyes widened; she thrust her hand out, almost knocking over her water. "No! I just don't relish the thought of sitting through the Adams skit, wondering who's looking at me. Usually I sit at the back, not caring what anyone thinks. This time . . ." She swallowed. "It will matter to me," she finished quietly.

"We've already decided that we'll sit in the back. And we've seen the skit before." But not while sitting with an Adams. Would people turn to gawk? Would everyone shun the Thompsons and Middletons during the intermissions, when Rymellans milled around the snack tables and chatted? Did it matter? Between the two families and their friends, they'd have plenty of Rymellans to socialize with, no matter what happened. And . . . "Laura and her family will be attending the festival in C3. She thought it might be prudent to be there, since it will be your first one with us."

Jayne didn't appear surprised, and Lesley wouldn't have been so blunt if she'd thought Jayne would be offended. "She said she might sit next to you, for support."

"Some Rymellans will assume she's there to keep me in line," Jayne said.

Lesley realized with a start that the thought had never crossed her mind. It certainly would have before she'd met Jayne.

The server interrupted them and took their orders. When they were alone again, Lesley raised a subject that had been in the back of her mind since her conversation with Laura. "Since I'm the Principal, people have fallen into the habit of seating me between you and Mo. But that doesn't mean I have to be in the middle when we're sitting at an event like the festival. If you'd like to sit next to Mo . . ."

Jayne shook her head. "I think you should be in the middle."

"Are you sure? Since you're already worried that you'll feel uncomfortable, I'd understand if you'd rather sit next to Mo."

"But . . ." Jayne moved her hands below the table. "You're my Chosen, too. Sitting next to you will . . . help just as much as sitting next to Mo."

"I feel I'm in the way right now," Lesley admitted, surprising herself. It was as if she had so much on her mind, she couldn't hold it all in. "I'm an obligation." She lifted her hands and dropped them to the table. "Our lunches are an obligation."

Jayne blinked at her. "No, they're not. I look forward to them." Her voice softened. "I wish we could see each other more often."

The tenderness in Jayne's voice . . . Lesley met Jayne's eyes—and saw what she'd seen outside Government Hall on the night of the awards ceremony. Jayne was saying something, but Lesley wasn't listening. Could she be mistaken? After the ceremony, she'd figured her agitation over admitting that Jayne was her Chosen had led her to see something in Jayne's eyes that wasn't there. But with recent developments, the last thing she'd do was imagine that Jayne was developing feelings for her. She hadn't imagined things when she'd first suspected Mo's feelings for Jayne. "I'm sorry, what did you say?"

"I said, I know the situation is difficult for everyone, but you're bearing the brunt of it."

"I'd rather it be me than Mo." Not only because of Mo's jealousy. Mo had already gone through enough with her mama's death, and Lesley wanted Mo to be happy. Mo wore her emotions on her sleeve. Watching her try to deal with a relationship between her two Chosens would have been too painful to bear, and could still happen. Lesley hoped that Mo falling for Jayne first would help when—if—Lesley ever fell for Jayne. Argamon, she'd have to be a lot more careful about what she said to Jayne from now on. Her feelings for Jayne were still purely platonic, but that didn't mean she didn't care about hurting her. "And when I said our lunches are an obligation, I meant it feels that way because we only see each other for Berry. We don't spontaneously get together, I guess."

"What would we do, if we did?" Jayne asked. "Read cases?"

Lesley chuckled. It was a good question. Her thoughts turned to what she and Mo did when they saw each other. Their lives were so intertwined that it felt as if they were already Joined. Spending time together could mean Lesley reading while Mo typed dispatches to her friends on the *Falcon*. Before their separation, they'd gone to the Dance Hall and the odd concert or play, but those activities were triad activities now. They still hadn't gone to the lake, and spent too much of their time together discussing the triad. Their quiet companionship had fallen to the wayside. Lesley missed it. Perhaps next time they saw each other, she'd suggest a walk and declare certain topics of conversation off-limits. Was that the key to retaining the uniqueness and specialness of their relationship—ensuring that their time alone together was truly theirs? Of course, Jayne would always be with them to some degree, but right now she hung over them to the extent that Lesley could almost see her when she wasn't there.

The same would hold true for Mo and Jayne—they needed their time together . . . And so did she and Jayne? The notion felt alien to Lesley, perhaps because these lunches were their only experience of time alone together. They'd soon Join. It would be prudent for Lesley to know her second Chosen more than she did now. She had a sense of her, but she didn't consider them friends. She was closer to Laura, which didn't seem right.

Her mind returned to their conversation. "You do seem to enjoy discussing cases more than Mo does, which isn't difficult to achieve."

It was Jayne's turn to chuckle.

"I don't expect you to discuss cases with me, though," Lesley added. What could they do? "You haven't seen much of the estate. Perhaps we can go for a bike ride next time I'm off, so I can show you around, or at least show you the highlights. It's too big to do in an afternoon."

"What about Mo?"

"I'll definitely have to talk to Mo about it first." She'd make it clear that the lake wouldn't be one of the stops on their bike tour. "I'll suggest that we meet her for supper afterward."

Jayne hesitated. "I'd like to, but I don't have a bike."

Lesley shrugged. "You can use Mama or Papa's."

"If they don't mind, okay. I'd like that."

The server arrived with their lunches. They ate their salads in a more companionable silence than Lesley had expected possible. She looked forward to spending time with Mo and trying to simply enjoy her company, and she wouldn't mind showing off the estate to Jayne. Her mood had improved ever so slightly, perhaps because she felt something she'd thought would permanently elude her: hope. For the first time since

Mo had confirmed her suspicion about Jayne, Lesley could see a dim light through the storm.

JAYNE GLANCED DOWN at the festival program she clutched in her hand. Her stomach knotted. Everyone else had rested their programs on their laps or slotted them into the back of the chair in front of them, but she needed something to hang onto. The more she tried to slow her breathing, the faster her chest rose and fell. Her muscles were already aching when everyone applauded the group who'd re-enacted the evolution of Article CT77. She wouldn't have thought that her jaw could tighten any further, but somehow it did when the announcer introduced the next skit.

The "Adamses" stumbled onto the stage. Jayne felt as if an elephant was sitting on her throat. The program she squeezed cut into her hand. Her cheeks burned. She wondered what was running through Lesley and Mo's minds, but she didn't dare turn to them.

Laughter rang out at the antics of the two actors onstage—but not around her. The Thompsons, Middletons, and Finneys occupied the two back rows, and those rows remained silent. Tears stung Jayne's eyes. What were they all thinking? Were they uncomfortable, embarrassed, ashamed? Her presence had dampened the day for them, families who didn't deserve to share in the Adams taint. Would they object if she headed for the train station as soon as the morning program was over? The Thompsons were usually all-day attendees, but maybe they'd want to run away and hide, too.

The audience roared again. Jayne resisted the urge to lower her head. Stupid—nobody could think less of her, so what would it matter if they caught her hanging her head? Oh, who was she trying to fool? She cared about what they thought: Lesley, Mo, Adelaide, Laura, choose a random Rymellan from the audience. Everyone must have snickered when she'd entered the tent and sat between a commodore and a lieutenant commander, upstanding Rymellans with flawless bloodlines who'd never imagined themselves sitting next to an Adams at the Festival of the Way. Worse, next year Lesley would *be* an Adams.

She turned when she felt a hand on her right arm. Lesley met her eyes. "You all right?" she murmured.

Jayne swallowed and nodded.

Lesley lifted her hand and turned back to the stage.

Jayne straightened as well, and when the audience booed at the usual point in the skit, her head remained high. She thought back to the awards ceremony, remembered watching Lesley receive her medal and listening to her speak. Despite the situation with Mo, Lesley had still thought to . . . As far as Jayne was concerned, Lesley deserved the Medal of the Protector and every other medal in existence.

For the rest of the morning, she sat straight and stared down the handful of Rymellans who turned around to sneer at her, not for herself, but for her Chosens. When everyone rose at the conclusion of the morning program to say the *Words Every Rymellan Knows*, Jayne tried not to hold Lesley's hand too tightly and proudly said them along with her: Disobedience means death. Death to those who commit a Chosen Violation. Death to those who disobey. Death to those who violate the Way.

MO SWALLOWED A mouthful of cookie and gaped at Ann. "The Dance Hall?" Argamon, Ann should know better than to bring that up.

Andrew nodded. "Come on, Ann has to go back to 72 tomorrow."

What a shame! Mo gave Les a sidelong glance. "By the time the afternoon program is over and we've had supper, it'll be . . ." 19:00? Okay, forget that excuse.

"Let's go." Les turned to Mo. "We've been talking about going."

Only because Les kept bringing it up.

"It probably won't be as packed tonight," Ann pointed out.

Now Mo glanced at Jayne, who'd probably appreciate a half-filled hall—though after this morning's program, maybe she'd prefer to hide from Rymellans for a while. Not that she had anything to be ashamed about.

Jayne caught Mo's eye. "I'm okay with going, if that's what you two want to do."

"Come on, Mo, don't be the party pooper," Ann pleaded. "Let's go. We'll have been sitting down all day."

She sighed. "Okay."

"Let's eat supper out," Andrew suggested, then his eyes narrowed as he looked past Mo. "Oh, I want you to meet someone." He grasped Ann's arm and pulled her away.

Mo tutted. "I guess we'll be eating supper out. He could have—"

Papa and Peggy joined them. Now Mo understood why Andrew had beaten a hasty retreat.

"The food is better this year," Papa said.

"The lemon cake was delicious." Peggy's smile was strained. "I wonder if they served the same cake back home."

"What sector do you come from?" Les asked.

"D7."

"Not far from Government Hall."

Peggy nodded. "Most of the support staff is from D6 and the surrounding sectors."

Mo scrambled for something to say, so she wouldn't appear rude. "What do you do?"

"I'm a researcher."

Papa's face lit up. "That's how we met." Mo's jaw tightened when he slipped his arm around Peggy's shoulders, then she felt bad when he quickly dropped it, though she appreciated the gesture.

"I was assigned to a committee your papa was on." Peggy's gaze shifted to Jayne. "What sector do you live in?"

"E6," Jayne said.

Mo gave Peggy a point.

"Can I speak to you for a moment?" someone behind Mo asked, though the question wasn't directed at her.

Les looked over her shoulder. "Excuse me," she said, then walked away with Laura.

"We should move on, too," Papa said. "I want to introduce Peggy to a few more people before the afternoon program starts. Will we see you at supper?"

"No, we're going out with Andrew and Ann, then to the Dance Hall."

Peggy raised her brows. "Sounds like fun."

"It does," Papa said. For a moment Mo thought he'd suggest that he and Peggy go dancing, but he said, "We'll see you inside the tent," and steered Peggy away before Mo had a chance to say good-bye.

She turned to Jayne. "That wasn't so bad."

"She's trying."

Yep, and Mo gave Peggy another point for not bringing up the morning program. Had Papa become involved with her before the triad? Either way, Peggy had stuck by him, not abandoned him because his family was linked to Jayne's. Suddenly Peggy's decision to spend the Festival of the Way in C3 took on a new significance. "She cares about him." And that was all that mattered. "I'll grow used to her, I guess." Mo looked up at Jayne. "You sure you don't mind going to the Dance Hall?"

"I don't mind. It'll be a new experience, going out for the evening on the festival day."

Right; Jayne usually spent the day by herself, and went home straight after the morning program. Mo could understand why. The Adams skit had mortified her, especially since she'd laughed along with everyone else in previous years. She couldn't imagine how Jayne must have felt. Mo had noticed the few Rymellans who'd turned to stare, and that nobody except the Thompsons, Middletons, and close friends spoke to her when she was with Jayne. "If it was up to me, we wouldn't stick around for the afternoon program."

Jayne shrugged. "I haven't seen it in years." Her face froze. "Please tell me there isn't another Adams skit."

"Not unless they've added one since the last time I came to the festival with family." She'd always skipped the afternoon program on the *Falcon*, sometimes because of her shift schedule. "If there is one, I'm sure Les would have mentioned it." When her words didn't ease the dread on Jayne's face, Mo couldn't resist taking one of her hands and squeezing it. "Maybe someday they'll drop the morning one."

"I doubt it."

Mo would have said, "You never know," if she wasn't fighting the desire to pull Jayne into a hug so she could hold her in front of all the idiots and tell her that the skit didn't matter. As it was, she hadn't let go of Jayne's hand, and caressed its back with her thumb.

LESLEY PEERED AT the schedule on her comm unit. "No, there's no way I can do it. I'll be at the Military Academy that week. I won't have time to write opinions, and I don't have time to write one in advance. She's already given me enough work to do." She slid the unit into its holder. "Why is she worrying about this today?"

"You know Blair, when she's not sleeping, she's working. And I guess she's not attending the afternoon program." Laura pursed her lips. "She seems keen for you to write the opinion. I'll suggest that she request a delay, but the overseers might not grant it."

"Thank you."

"Sorry for pulling you away, but she knows we're both here, and she wanted an answer this afternoon."

"Aren't *you* the commodore?" Lesley said dryly.

Laura chuckled. "She's so good at scheduling your time with me, rather than going behind my back, that I try to accommodate her. She knows where the line is. Anyway, I should get back to Brian before he feels abandoned."

Lesley said good-bye, then turned and— She squinted. Were Mo and Jayne holding hands right in front of everybody, or were her eyes playing tricks on her? Blood pounded in her ears. Her first impulse was to walk in the opposite direction, grab the first person she even vaguely knew, and engage them in conversation. But what would everyone think? Would they wonder why she was the odd one out? Feel sorry for her? See through her attempt to hide? This had to happen sometime, she knew. But why today, at the festival?

She took a deep breath and walked toward them, feeling as if everything was moving in slow motion. By the time she reached them, they'd let go of each other's hands. Since nothing had registered through her shocked haze, she didn't know if that was because they'd noticed her approach, or if they'd spontaneously moved apart.

"Was it something serious?" Mo asked.

She shook her head, worried that, if she opened her mouth, nothing but a croak would emerge.

"We were just discussing the afternoon program. I haven't seen it for a while. There isn't another skit about the Adamses, is there?"

Lesley glanced at Jayne, remembered Jayne's face as she'd watched the morning skit. Jayne had tried to mask her dismay and shame, but hadn't entirely succeeded. If she'd felt even a tenth of what she'd shown . . . and yet she'd managed to smile as they'd eaten sandwiches, had agreed to go to the Dance Hall, and would sit through the afternoon program when she probably wanted to leave. Lesley had come to appreciate Jayne's strength, and recalled Jayne's words at their last Berry lunch: *I know the situation is difficult for everyone, but you're bearing the brunt of it.* Lesley could say the same to her today, and was torn between throttling her and supporting her. That went for Mo, too.

Mo blinked up at her. "Les?"

"No, there isn't a skit this afternoon," Lesley said, relieved that her voice sounded normal. "Probably because the afternoon focuses on the Law."

A voice announced through the large exterior speakers that the afternoon program would begin in ten minutes. "We might as well go back to our seats." Eager to stick her nose in a program, Lesley sauntered away, and quickened her pace when Mo and Jayne followed.

She'd agreed to the Dance Hall outing because she'd already seen Mo and Jayne dance together. But if her reaction to them holding hands was any indication, she could be in for a rough night. It wouldn't be suicidal for Lesley to march onto the dance floor and demand that Mo dance with her, nor would she behave so rudely. But seeing them in each other's arms would grate, dishearten, and make her want to cry. She'd have to constantly remind herself that not being Mo's Chosen would have been worse, though in her weaker moments, she wondered if that were true.

WITH MIXED FEELINGS, Jayne accepted Mo's hand and walked with her onto the dance floor. Lesley had given them the go ahead, but her mood had darkened since the lunch break at the festival. Had Laura upset her, or had Lesley spotted them holding hands? Jayne hadn't expected Mo's tender caress. The gesture hadn't upset her, and she appreciated the support, but she wished they'd been somewhere more private. Everything she and Mo did, or contemplated doing, felt wrong—and right. The three of them were falling over each other to consider feelings and be accommodating, but all they gained was more awkwardness, and the tension that grew when nobody was saying or doing what they really wanted to say or do.

She was starting to agree with Lesley that they were delaying the inevitable and perhaps harming the triad in the process. On the other

hand, if they threw caution to the wind and Lesley couldn't handle it . . .
Jayne wasn't worried that the triad would spiral out of control, but only
because Lesley would take it all onto her shoulders and let it crush her.
She wouldn't violate the Way, but would she die inside and go through
the motions for the rest of her life?

"Ready?" Mo asked.

Fortunately Jayne remembered how to assume position. They fell
into step with the music. A minute later, she grimaced. Apparently
she hadn't forgotten how to step on feet, either. "Sorry," she said, at
the same time Mo did. They both smiled. "Why are you sorry?" Jayne
asked. "It was my fault."

"I usually know to move my foot out of the way," Mo said with a grin.

"Oh." She'd thought she was doing well, a sentiment that must have
shown on her face.

"Don't worry, you're doing great," Mo said. "This is only your second
time here. Trust me, Les used to step on my feet, and vice versa. I'm
sure we looked like idiots when we were first learning how to dance."

She would have loved to have seen them, and wasn't jealous at all of
the lives they'd shared until that day at the Chosen House. If anything,
it grieved her that they'd never share the life they'd both wanted.

"Not that I'm implying you look like an idiot," Mo quickly added, her
cheeks reddening. "Argamon, I get the feeling I'll be pulling my foot
out of my mouth a lot around you, and not because of your last name."

Jayne's heart skipped a beat at Mo's sheepish grin. If they weren't
on the dance floor and she wasn't worried about Lesley . . . "Do people
kiss on the dance floor?" she blurted. Mo's scarlet face deepened a shade.
Mo wasn't the only one with a mouth that worked faster than her brain.

"Not usually," Mo croaked.

"I was just wondering, because I've never seen anyone kiss on
the . . ." Why continue, when she wasn't fooling anyone, especially since
Mo knew this was only her second time in a Dance Hall. "Never mind."

Mo lifted her eyebrows, then frowned. "What's wrong?"

"It's Lesley." Jayne had glimpsed her over Mo's head.

Mo waited until she'd taken a look to reply. "She's reading her comm
unit."

Yes, but the way her shoulders were hunched . . . "Maybe we should get off the dance floor."

"No, she'd hate that. Let's wait until the dance is over."

"Will you be okay when she dances with me? I mean, because *she's* dancing with me, not because I'm dancing with her." She wasn't surprised to see confusion in Mo's eyes. *Spell it out!* "Will you be jealous because she's dancing with someone else?"

Mo took her time answering. "I hate to admit it, but yeah, I will be. This will sound horrible, but I think of her as mine, and I think of you as ours. Not that anybody owns anyone else."

"I understand what you're saying." For Jayne, they were her Chosens and she was theirs. They were a unit, and their relationship was the primary relationship in the triad. Her relationships with them—romantic or platonic—would always be secondary, and she had no quibble with that. She'd never have to struggle to transition from thinking in terms of "mine" to "ours." They were hers, she was theirs, and they were each other's. Maybe their relationship would eventually stop overshadowing her relationships with them, but she wouldn't be upset if that never happened. "Lesley probably thinks in the same terms you do. You're hers. It will take time for her to see you . . . differently."

"Tell me about it. I don't know how I'll handle it when the time comes."

Maybe she wouldn't have to. Jayne would understand if Lesley never developed feelings for her; in fact, she'd never expected a romantic relationship with either of her Chosens. She was still flabbergasted that Mo liked her in that way, to the point that she sometimes didn't believe it.

"To be honest, when Les talked to me about your bike ride, I had to restrain myself from insisting that I go with you. I—" Mo broke off while they completed a dance step, then continued. "I know it's a double standard, and I don't have any right to be upset about it. But I don't know how much I'll get done that afternoon. I'll be looking forward to supper."

"We're just going to ride around the estate."

"I know." Mo shook her head. "Tell that to the irrational part of me."

They stopped talking and focused on dancing. When the band segued into the next piece and dancers who'd had enough walked off the dance floor, Jayne felt both relieved and disappointed. Lesley's comm unit was in its holder when Jayne and Mo approached her.

"I have to go to the bathroom," Mo said. Jayne wasn't sure if she was telling the truth, or offering an excuse for leaving the dance floor after one song. Either way, Jayne was left alone with Lesley, who looked up at her with a strained smile.

Jayne sat next to her and searched for a conversation-opener. "I'm looking forward to our bike ride."

"I'll have to work out the most efficient route for what I want to show you," Lesley said.

Jayne envisioned them racing from spot to spot. "I hope I'll be able to keep up."

"We can take our time. I want to avoid too much backtracking and zigzagging, that's all."

Taking their time appealed to Jayne very much. Their first lunch had been more leisurely than she'd expected, but the subsequent ones had felt rushed because of Lesley's schedule. No server interruptions and worries about those at the next table overhearing their conversation would also be a welcome change. What would they talk about? Jayne made a mental note to come up with a list of topics beforehand, in case awkward silences started to outweigh conversation—like now, for example! "Where are Ann and Andrew?"

"They went to get a drink." Lesley paused. "Would you like a drink?"

Not really, but it would give them something to do. "Sure." She started to rise.

"No, no, I'll go. You should stay here, so Mo doesn't wonder what happened to us." Without waiting for a reply, Lesley hurried off.

Jayne sank back down. Maybe she shouldn't worry about discussion topics for their bike ride. She'd probably spend the better part of it staring at Lesley's back as she rode behind her.

LESLEY THREW A stone into the lake and dug around in the sand for another one.

"I'm shocked," a voice rang out behind her. She turned around. A smiling Mo strode across the sand. "Don't you have a test tomorrow?"

"I always have a test."

Mo swung up her comm unit and feigned a gasp. "But it's only just gone 19:00," she said, pressing her hand against her chest. "Surely you couldn't have finished studying for it." She let the hand holding the comm unit drop. "So can you blame me for almost fainting when you beeped me and told me to meet you here? Not that I'm complaining. I don't think I've ridden that fast in a while."

Lesley chuckled, glad that she'd overcome her hesitation to beep Mo. "Let's walk."

Mo fell into step with her. Her forehead creased. "So what do you want to talk about?"

"Nothing." Lesley took Mo's hand. "In particular." Mo's hand tightened around hers. "I just thought it would be nice for us to spend some time together," Lesley said, hoping to reassure Mo that she hadn't summoned her because they needed to have a serious talk. "We don't do that anymore. Well, not without the triad hanging over us. I'm not saying we can forget about it. I can't. But if we make time for each other—just us—it might help."

"Is that why you're going on that bike ride with Jayne? To make time for just you and her?" Mo's face was relaxed, but tension strained her voice.

"We've only ever seen each other over those lunches for Berry. I have to build a friendship with her that's separate from you."

Mo blew out a sigh and stopped to kick a stone into the lake. "I know. And I know I have no right to hate the idea." She let go of Lesley's hand and sat in the sand. Following Mo's lead, Lesley also sat, but several feet away from her. Mo hugged her legs to her chest and turned her head to Lesley. "I like this, though. And I'll have to be respectful of your time with Jayne. You're trying to do the same for me, and you have more reason to be upset about it."

If Lesley did what all Chosens do and developed feelings for her second Chosen, Mo would eventually have reason to be upset. Hopefully Mo would have grown used to Lesley spending time alone with Jayne by then. "I saw you holding Jayne's hand at the Festival of the Way." She hadn't intended to bring it up, but it kept nagging at her. "It was a shock, but I'll get used to it."

"We didn't mean to—I think it shocked Jayne, too." Mo paused. "I felt bad for her. It must have been horrible sitting through that skit and knowing we were all thinking about her. I just wanted to let her know it didn't matter. I'm sorry."

Lesley shook her head. "You shouldn't have to apologize. I meant it when I said our arrangement is off. But there will be shocks and wobbles as we figure it all out."

"You're too flaming reasonable sometimes, you know that? If the situation was reversed, I'd be kicking sand in your face."

"You haven't done that in years."

Mo grinned. "Yeah, because we figured out that kissing on the beach is more fun than fighting on the beach."

Lesley's throat tightened. "See, we eventually figure things out."

Mo let go of her legs and slid over to Lesley. They both stared out at the water. "So is being together like this helping?" Mo asked.

Lesley closed her eyes when Mo pressed against her. She lifted her arm and slipped it around Mo, so Mo could lay her head on her shoulder. "Yes, it is."

LESLEY STEERED HER bike onto the path that would avoid the lake and glanced over her shoulder to make sure she hadn't lost Jayne. No, she was keeping up, but probably tiring. Lesley's own muscles ached, and she regularly rode a bike. She kept her eye out for a good place to stop. Five minutes later, she signalled and braked. "Do you want to rest for a bit here?" she asked when Jayne skidded to a stop next to her. "We can sit under those trees."

"Sure," Jayne said breathlessly.

They dismounted, walked their bikes over to one of the trees, and leaned them against it. Thirsty, Lesley grabbed her water flask from her bike.

"How much longer do you want to ride?" Jayne asked as she reached for hers. "I'm just wondering if I should pace the water."

Lesley studied Jayne's heaving chest and red face. "I figure we can head back now. I've shown you most of what I wanted you to see. Not very exciting, I know."

"It depends on what you mean by exciting." Jayne sank onto the grass and sat against another tree. "I might want to sketch a couple of the sights. That tree formation didn't look natural, even though it was."

"Lightning created it." Lesley sat next to her and sipped more water.

Jayne nodded. "Nature as artist. My papa—" She broke off.

"Your papa what?" Lesley prompted. Getting to know Jayne included her life before the Incident, uncomfortable as the topic may be.

Jayne hesitated. "Well, he loved seeing art in the clouds and rock formations and sand—everywhere. On cloudy days, he'd point up and ask me what I saw." She set her water flask down and drew her legs to her chest, reminding Lesley of her evening with Mo at the lake. "Anyway, that old stone wall is fascinating. How many years do they think it's been there?"

"Several thousand. This *is* one of the oldest sectors. You should get Mo to show you around the Middleton estate. You can pick up the wall there. I guess the part of it in between crumbled."

"If she decides to give me a tour, all three of us could go."

"She's not with us today, so . . ."

"Only because we thought we'd try a spontaneous outing that wasn't for Berry." Jayne's mouth turned up at the corners, but Lesley detected a hint of sadness in her voice.

"Do you wish Mo was here?"

"No. I wouldn't mind if she was here, but I don't need her to be here." Jayne shook her head, then picked up a twig and traced a line in the dirt. "I'm not explaining myself very well. I agree with Berry that all the couples need time alone together. I don't see you alone very often, so I don't mind that Mo isn't with us. I wouldn't mind you being with us when—if Mo shows me around the Middleton estate, because I already spend a lot of time alone with Mo."

It sounded as if Jayne saw herself and Lesley as a couple, strengthening Lesley's suspicion that Jayne had feelings for her. Then again, if they weren't in a triad—if she and Jayne had been Chosens to each other and nobody else—they would have been a couple from the moment they left the Chosen House after their notification meetings, feelings or no. "I'm sure Mo wishes she was here."

Jayne smiled. "Yes. I'm glad we're meeting her for supper." She paused. "It's different for me than it is for you and Mo." The line in the dirt became an *X*. "I'm not facing the issues you two are. I'm the interloper."

Lesley frowned. "Not intentionally, and I think interloper is too strong." Or at least it was now. At their notifications, Jayne certainly *had* been an unwelcome intruder into their lives.

"I feel that way." Jayne added another *X* to her growing collection. "Not because of anything you and Mo have done. You're both being great. I don't know how I'd react in your position, and that's just it—I'm not in your position. I have it easier than both of you. At the Dance Hall, I was thinking about how I met both of you at the same time, so you'll always be *the* couple to me. I'll never resent the time you spend together. I can't be jealous because I never had either one of you to myself. For me, it would be strange for you and Mo *not* to be together. And Mo sort of sees it that way, too. She said she thinks of you as hers and of me as both of yours. To be honest, that's the way I see it, too, in terms of what I am to the two of you, and I'm fine with it."

It wasn't fair, though. There shouldn't be a primary relationship, with the third triad member tacked on. But given that Lesley and Mo had been a couple long before Jayne, perhaps that was the only way the triad could work for them.

"I told Mo that you probably think in the same terms she does." Jayne dropped the twig and gazed at Lesley.

"I do, but I'd like to think that our view of you will change over time. It might take a while, but it will change."

Jayne's brows shot up. "You really believe that?"

"Yes." In twenty years, would she and Mo still see Jayne as secondary, after Joining, and sharing a home, and raising children together? Somehow Lesley doubted it, even though getting to that point seemed almost impossible right now. "Your view might change, too. Of course, Mo and I will always be together, but perhaps you'll stop seeing our relationship as the foundation of the triad."

Jayne was silent for a moment. She picked up the twig. "I don't think I will. I can't, because it *is* the foundation. And you know what? I'm glad we have your relationship as the foundation, because it's strong. You and Mo can make it through anything. And you will."

Every time Lesley had told Mo that she'd love her no matter what, she'd meant it. Mo's feelings for Jayne had never threatened Lesley's feelings for Mo. Lesley had worried about Mo's love for *her*, and was starting to believe that Mo hadn't fallen out of love with her, that she was being sincere when she insisted that nothing had changed. Jayne was an addition, not a replacement. Lesley's relationship with Mo was still special, still uniquely theirs. Now it was a matter of her heart catching up with her head. Seeing Mo with Jayne would still sting, especially as they grew more affectionate and shared private moments that would always be theirs alone. But the peace, the acceptance that Lesley had glimpsed on the beach with Mo, was gaining a foothold. It had a long way to go to reach the summit, but at least Lesley believed the mountain could be climbed.

She also appreciated Jayne's support, and the more she came to know her, the more she suspected that Jayne would be a strong ally and someone she could trust. She'd assumed that she'd never develop feelings for Jayne, had even denied her as a Chosen. But now . . . whatever happened, would happen.

Lesley took a long drink of water and watched Jayne draw in the dirt, content to sit in companionable silence until they both felt rested enough to press on.

JAYNE GAVE CAROL a sidelong glance as they sauntered along the path near the White home. Carol hadn't explicitly said that she wanted to talk to Jayne alone, but why else would she insist that they go for a walk while Lesley, Mo, and Ronald discussed the first-year Military Academy curriculum? Carol had practically dragged her outside. Jayne folded her arms. "So Ronald's nephew is thinking about the military?" she said to get Carol talking.

Carol nodded. "You must get tired of all the military talk."

"No. They don't really talk about their roles much. I am starting to think in military time, though." She chuckled, remembering how she'd waited outside her apartment at 16:45, as Mo had instructed.

"I thought supper went well."

"It did. You pulled off the pudding you were worried about."

Carol grunted. They continued to stroll, but not in the comfortable silence Jayne usually enjoyed with Carol. Still, she held her tongue. Carol had asked for this walk. When she was ready, she'd share whatever was on her mind.

Several minutes later, they turned around and headed back to the

White home. Jayne started to doubt whether Carol would ever speak, but after they'd rounded a curve in the path and could see the house, Carol stopped walking and whirled toward her. "I have something to tell you. It's good news," she said, but her forced smile and the tightness around her eyes suggested otherwise.

"What is it? It doesn't involve Robert, does it?"

"No, just Ronald and me." Carol hesitated. "I'm pregnant."

"Oh! Congratulations." She reached for Carol and hugged her. "That *is* good news." But Carol's shoulders were stiff. Jayne stepped back and searched her face.

"We're having a girl."

"You'll be a mama."

Carol nodded. "It'll take some getting used to, but we're looking forward to it."

"When is she due?"

"Six months. We declined the details about hair and eye colour and other particulars. We'd rather be surprised."

"You both must be thrilled." But Carol didn't look overjoyed. "What's wrong?" And why hadn't Carol announced it at the supper table?

Carol blew out a sigh. "When the baby arrives, Ronald's family will constantly be over, and so will mine. Everyone goes crazy when children are involved."

Jayne's heart sank.

"Mama and Papa . . . they know we're close." Carol's finger travelled quickly between herself and Jayne. "Ronald's family knows we see each other often. But with a baby involved . . ."

"What do they think will happen if I hold the baby?" Tears prickled at her eyelashes. She dug her fingernails into her palms. She wouldn't cry over this, not in front of Carol, who'd stuck by her and supported her, and probably saved her life, or at least her dignity and the tiny shred of self-worth she'd managed to cling to. "Will I get to see the baby at some point?" Her pain crept into her voice despite her best efforts.

"Argamon, yes!" Carol's eyes moistened and she bit her lip. "I'm not telling you to stay away. I'm warning you that you might receive a hostile reception if you do come over."

Rymellans usually pulled their children out of her way when she approached, clutching them to their sides and giving her a wide berth, as if breathing the same air she did would contaminate them. Who knew how Ronald's family would react? As for Carol's . . . considering they'd hustled Jayne into her own apartment as soon as they could get away with it, all to spare their younger children the horror of being closely associated with an Adams, she wouldn't expect them to greet her with open arms when she came to see their grandchild. "I'll stay away for a while."

"If it was just Ronald and me, it wouldn't matter. And if you do come over, you know I'll—we'll—stand behind you."

But Carol would be torn, and so would Ronald, and their families had to come before Jayne. "I'll want to see images of what I missed."

Carol smiled through her tears. "I'll do better than that. I'll bring her to you."

"Don't do anything that will cause a problem between you and Ronald and his family."

Carol waved a dismissive hand. "Ronald doesn't care, and his family won't be over twenty-four hours a day. I feel awful warning you away, because our door is always open to you."

"It's okay," Jayne said, even though she felt as if a carpet had been pulled out from under her. Carol was more to her than a cousin; she was a wise older sister who'd taken care of her when she'd most needed someone. Jayne had always thought she'd be there. But things change. They already weren't as close as they were before Ronald, and a baby would only widen the distance between them. "I don't want us to grow apart," she couldn't help saying.

"Neither do I. And we won't," Carol said firmly. "There'll be a flurry of activity when she's born, but it'll die down." Her voice softened. "After Ronald, you're the person I'm closest to. I'm closer to you than I am to my family."

Because she'd made a brave choice, and Jayne sometimes wondered if she regretted it. Now it was Jayne's turn to give back by not making things awkward when the baby arrived. "I'd love to see her, but I don't want to cause trouble."

Carol snorted. "It won't be anything for me to whip out and see you for an hour or two. Ronald will come too, when he can." She frowned.

"Oh, but you'll be living on the estate by then, not in your apartment. Maybe Mo will pick us up and fly us. Can babies go on aviacrafts?"

"I don't know. I'll ask Mo and Lesley." She forced a smile. "Speaking of Mo . . ."

Carol peered at her. "What?"

She scratched her head, suddenly embarrassed and self-conscious. "We're sort of getting involved."

"Sort of?" Carol grinned. "What does that mean?"

She wasn't sure; they were trying to figure that out. But for Carol . . ."I like her. And she likes me." Jayne's smile grew wider and became genuine.

Carol gleefully laughed. "Argamon, that's wonderful! Both our lives are changing!"

Jayne nodded, pleased to see Carol happy. She hadn't intended to tell her about Mo, but had wanted to assuage Carol's guilt by reminding her that she wouldn't sit alone in her apartment while everyone else cooed at the baby. She had two Chosens now.

"What about Lesley?" Carol asked.

Jayne hesitated, then decided to be honest. "I like her in that way. But I don't think she feels the same."

"It'll happen," Carol said. "Give it time." Her eyes widened. "Oh, look who's coming. Time for me to leave."

Jayne spun around. Mo was strolling toward them. "Carol, you don't have to—" It was too late. Carol was already walking away, and waved at Mo, then over her shoulder at Jayne.

"I didn't break up a private conversation, did I?" Mo stopped next to Jayne and watched Carol's receding back.

"No. We were finished."

Mo looked up at her. "Is everything okay?"

Her first thought was to say, "Yes," and wait until she could tell Mo and Lesley about the pregnancy at the same time. But it would be impossible to ensure that both of them learned about developments in her life together. They'd have to accept that sometimes one would be told before the other, and only because of circumstance, not because one was more important. This was more Carol's news than hers, anyway. "Carol's pregnant."

Mo gasped. "That's great!" Her face slackened. "Right?"

When Jayne had first met Mo and Lesley, she would have done her best to hide, or at least downplay, her dismay over her conversation with Carol. She would have fixed a smile on her face and said, "Yes, it's great!" But enough trust had developed between her and Mo—and, for Jayne, with Lesley—to lower her guard around them and be honest. "I'm pleased for her. But it means I'll have to stay away from here for a while after she's—it's a girl—born. I don't want to upset the families."

"Carol doesn't want you around?"

"No, it's not Carol. I don't want to drive a rift between her and everyone else. She'll come visit me with the baby. Can babies go on aviacrafts?"

Mo nodded. "I guess I'll be shuttling a baby around." Her smile at the thought quickly faded. "You shouldn't have to stay away."

"It'll just be until the fuss dies down." Her breath caught in her throat. What about Lesley and Mo's children? The fuss would never die down for them. Would they be teased, ostracized, forced to endure the same treatment she'd experienced at the Indoctrination and Learning Academies? Argamon, it would never end. At least their children would have loving parents to support them, but would that be enough?

Suddenly Mo's arms were around Jayne's neck. "What are you doing?" Jayne asked.

"Hugging you. You look like you need one."

She should deny it and draw away, but she slipped her arms around Mo and pulled her close. She couldn't relax, though, not when she was keeping an eye on the Whites' front door. If Lesley stepped outside, Jayne would try not to push Mo to the ground in her haste to back away.

"I'd kiss you, but I don't want our first kiss to feel like a pity kiss," Mo murmured.

Jayne dared to tighten her arms around Mo. "This is nice," she blurted. She was too shy to add that she looked forward to that first kiss.

JAYNE LEANED BACK against the sofa and smiled as she read Mo's dispatch from 72. Busy with a new wave of practicums, Mo hadn't asked Jayne to go with her. Jayne hadn't minded, and Lesley hadn't pushed, especially when Mo had shared her practicum schedule with them—she'd barely have time to eat. But she *had* found the time to write a dispatch, much to Jayne's delight.

This is the second practicum in the curriculum, so at least the students aren't completely green. I realized earlier today that I actually enjoy doing this. I wouldn't want to teach in a classroom, but it's rewarding to see the students improve, even over the course of one session.

What type of teacher was Mo? Jayne imagined her gently guiding her students and chuckling when someone made a mistake, but Mo took her flying very seriously. Maybe she was all business, barking orders, and berating students who couldn't get it right. No, Mo would never beat someone up for not being perfect. Bark orders? Maybe.

Jayne's comm unit beeped twice just as she reached the end of Mo's dispatch. When she checked the dispatch list, shock jolted through her and she straightened. The dispatch was from the art college where she'd submitted her application. Jayne steeled herself and opened it.

Jayne Adams,

We regret to inform you that your application to study in our art program is declined.
Comments for candidate: None

Yours in the Way,
The Applications Committee

She read it again, then stared at the single word that leaped out at her like a knife driven into her gut: *None.* None? Not even *We hated your painting*? Nothing? Had they even looked at it, or had they tossed it down the nearest recycling chute as soon as they'd read her name?

It didn't matter. She'd known her chances of being accepted were slim. But her shaking hands and blurred vision belied the reassuring words she whispered to herself. Of course it mattered! Nothing? Not one word? Was she that terrible? Had she deluded herself all these years? Had they passed around her painting, laughed at it, hung it in the teaching studio as a lesson of how not to paint?

The comm unit slid from her fingers. She wanted to scratch away the shameful tears that rolled down her cheeks. Why was she crying when she hadn't lost anything? She had no right! Nobody credible had ever praised her work or encouraged her, so what had she expected? She was useless. And now she'd have to tell Lesley and Mo that she wasn't an artist, that her reports from the Learning Academy were true, that she was a talentless Rymellan who wasn't worth the air she breathed. While they continued to excel in their military careers—despite *her*—she'd waste her life away creating artwork that nobody wanted to see.

She should have trusted her instinct and not applied, so she could continue to lie to herself that she could draw and paint, that her teachers were the liars. Now she'd have to face the truth. Her parents were gone, Robert had quickly abandoned her, Carol and Ronald were starting a family, and Lesley and Mo were stuck with her because the alternative was death. Mo claimed to care for her, but Mo had expected Jayne to get into art school. Mo would soon figure out that her second Chosen was beneath her, with nothing to offer.

Jayne's tears flowed faster; she hugged herself as sobs wracked her body. She was tired of giving herself pep talks. How long was she supposed to believe in herself, to fuel the creative energy she needed to pick up a pencil or paintbrush, without a single word of encouragement? Nobody had bottomless drive; without any support, everyone would reach the point where they'd throw up their hands and admit defeat. Well, she'd reached hers.

She was done—done with labouring over drawings that nobody wanted to see; done with telling herself that, if not for her name, she'd have attended art school; done with assuring herself that her life meant as much as everyone else's, that her parents didn't define her. And now she'd burden the lives of two women she cared about, who would have lived the life they'd always dreamed of, if not for her. It wasn't enough that her own life was pathetic; she had to poison their lives, too.

If she wasn't around, Lesley and Mo—and their children—would be free of the Adams taint, Carol would focus on her family without worrying about her inconvenient cousin, and Rymellans would all breathe a sigh of relief that her parents' line was truly dead. Even the planet itself would rejoice; she'd no longer use its resources to produce drawings she'd always told herself Rymellans would love, if only they'd look.

She'd never draw or paint again. Her life no longer meant anything. Everyone would be better off without her.

LESLEY TURNED ON her comm unit as soon as she left the classroom, expecting a dispatch from an overseer in response to an inquiry about a case. She frowned at a dispatch in the list—Mo rarely used the "urgent" marker. Lesley read it, then beeped her.

"Finally! I was starting to wonder if I should come down," Mo said.

"I just finished class."

"Have you heard from her?"

"No."

Silence, then, "Something's wrong. She *always* replies to my dispatches. I was a little worried last night, but I figured that maybe she was spending the day with Carol. But it's been over twenty-four hours now. She usually replies within a couple."

"When did you last hear from her?"

"The day before yesterday."

"Same here." Jayne had written to say that she had an appointment with Catherine Moss regarding the interior design of their future home.

"I even tried beeping her earlier. No answer." Mo cleared her throat. "Look, I shouldn't ask, but can you go check on her?"

Lesley's jaw tightened. "Why shouldn't you ask? She's my Chosen, too."

"I know, but—"

"Mo, I don't hate her because she's fallen for you, any more than I could hate you. I understand that neither one of you is doing it on purpose." She blew out some air, to calm herself. "I'll beep her. If she doesn't answer, I'll go over."

"You'll beep her now?"

"Yes, and I'll head right over, if I have to. I'm walking to my aviacraft."

"I mean, she's probably okay, right? You know how she always takes so long to answer. Maybe I disconnected too soon. Or maybe her comm unit is off." Mo chuckled nervously.

Yes, but what about the comm station in her apartment? Those were always on, so Rymellans wouldn't miss mandatory announcements. "I'll beep you right after I've spoken to her," Lesley said, an anxious knot forming in her stomach.

As soon as they disconnected, she beeped Jayne. The knot tightened when Jayne's message played. When it finished, Lesley said, "Jayne, it's Lesley. I'm heading over to your apartment. If you get this message before I get there, can you beep me right away? Thanks." She pressed the disconnect button and quickened her pace.

By the time she landed in the holding area near Jayne's apartment, she knew that Jayne wasn't with Carol. "No, no, nothing's wrong. I figured she might have turned off her comm unit because she's with you," Lesley had said, easing Carol's worry as her own increased. It wasn't like Jayne to be unreachable. Even if she was angry with them, she wouldn't shut them out. Jayne had bravely demonstrated that she could overcome her shyness and fear when she wanted to raise an issue or was worried about the triad. She valued communication; she knew it was one of the keys to maintaining the triad's harmony.

Nothing appeared amiss as Lesley approached the entrance to Jayne's apartment building—but what had she expected? All sorts of scenarios ran through her mind as she strode up the corridor, including imagining that Jayne might have fallen and hit her head.

When Jayne didn't answer Lesley's knock on her apartment door, Lesley rapped again, calling, "Jayne? It's Lesley. If you're there, come to the door." She leaned closer and listened, then stepped back. Nothing. Well, Jayne could be out drawing, she could be at the Trading Centre . . . but Lesley's instinct said that she was in the apartment. After a moment's hesitation, she grasped the door handle. "I'm coming in," she said, then almost fell into the apartment when the door suddenly opened.

Jayne stared at her with bleary eyes. Her dishevelled hair suggested that she'd just rolled out of bed, even though it was almost 17:30.

Lesley let out a relieved breath. At least she was okay—physically. "We've been trying to beep you. Why didn't you answer?"

Jayne shrugged. "I'm not in the mood to talk," she said, so softly that Lesley strained to hear her. "Do you want tziva?"

Her lifeless voice deepened Lesley's concern. "Yes, please," she said, sure that the last thing Jayne wanted to do was make her tziva. But she wasn't leaving until she found out what was wrong.

Jayne turned and walked away, leaving Lesley to close the door and hang her cloak. Then she followed Jayne deeper into the apartment—and stopped halfway up the hallway. Something was different . . .

The walls. They were bare. Jayne's artwork was gone. A glance into the living room told the same story. Bewildered, Lesley walked into the kitchen and stared in horror at the pile of ripped up papers on the kitchen table. "You haven't ripped up your drawings!"

"No." Jayne sank into a chair, rested her elbows on the table, and held her head in her hands.

Lesley's heart stopped pounding. "I noticed that you've taken down all your artwork," she said, pulling out the chair next to Jayne and lowering herself into it. "Why?" Argamon, hunched over and clutching her head, Jayne looked like a ball of pain.

Jayne chose to respond to an earlier question. "I wasn't answering beeps because I was waiting until I could face all of you." She heaved her shoulders. "But I have to tell you sometime. Might as well be now."

Lesley remained silent while Jayne gathered her courage. Whatever it was must be related to her artwork, but Lesley resisted the urge to guess, not wanting to derail the conversation.

Jayne's hands left her head; she picked up one of the larger shreds of paper and crushed it in her right hand. "My application to art school was rejected."

Too focused on her own training program and Mo and Jayne's growing relationship, Lesley hadn't given much thought to Jayne's application. "I'm sorry."

"The committee didn't have any comments for me. I guess they figured I wasn't worth their time."

Surprise raised Lesley's voice. "They didn't say anything?"

Jayne shook her head.

Then Lesley suspected that they hadn't seriously considered Jayne's application. She couldn't think of a single instance among friends and family where an application to college had been accepted or rejected with no accompanying remarks. But she couldn't be certain, and Jayne deserved more than false hope. "It doesn't mean you can't paint or draw," Lesley said, eyeing the litter pile on the table.

"I don't see the point."

"You enjoy it."

Jayne shrugged. "It's a waste of time."

"It's not a waste of—"

Jayne tossed the ball of paper onto the table and pushed back her chair. She filled the boiler with water and turned it on, then pressed her hands on top of the kitchen counter, her back to Lesley. Her shoulders shook. She lowered her head and wept.

Lesley gaped at her, not sure what to do. Would she sit and watch while Mo sobbed? No. She pushed herself up from the table and, when Jayne didn't move, went to her and put her arm around Jayne's shoulders. She hadn't meant it as an invitation for Jayne to turn and cling to her, but didn't back away when Jayne did. She hesitated a beat, then held Jayne and rubbed her back. "It'll be okay. It's disappointing, but you'll be okay."

"I never should have applied. I didn't want to," Jayne said between sniffles.

"Then why did you?"

"For you and Mo. To do something with my life."

Lesley closed her eyes.

"I have to do more than sit around and draw."

"Many Rymellans are Joined to artists."

"Artists who sell their work, who contribute. I can't do that. I'm not even an artist," Jayne wailed into Lesley's ear.

"Yes, you are. Don't let this rejection take that away. Because of who you are, you might have been refused out of hand." She'd said *might*, despite her certainty that Jayne had never stood a chance. If only Jayne had spoken to her and Mo beforehand . . . they'd thought she *wanted* to apply. If they'd known that obligation and a sense of inadequacy was driving her, they would have talked her out of it, or at least assured her that a rejection wouldn't matter. "We understand why you can't sell your work. All that matters to us is that you derive satisfaction from creating it."

"If I were anyone else, you wouldn't say that."

"If you were anyone else, you'd be fairly evaluated. You're not."

"I don't know if I'm being fairly evaluated. Maybe I am. Maybe I'm deluding myself."

"You've never needed external validation before. Why is it suddenly important?" While Lesley waited for an answer, she realized that Jayne was no longer sniffling. She should let Jayne go and step back, but . . . being in each other's arms, speaking into each other's ears, made honesty easier.

"I'm not sure I need it for me," Jayne murmured after a long silence.

"We don't need it. We see you as an artist. We see it every time we look at your drawings."

"You're just saying that."

"No, I'm not." When she and Mo had first found out about Jayne's sketching—before they'd seen her work—they'd agreed to encourage her, no matter what they thought of her drawings. But that would have been wrong. When you cared about someone, you told them the truth, even though it might hurt. Fibbing about a new pair of shoes was one thing. Encouraging someone to waste her time, to pour effort and energy into a lost cause, wouldn't be supporting her, and it certainly wouldn't be caring about her. Back then, they hadn't cared about Jayne beyond obligation. Things had changed. "You can draw, Jayne. You can paint. If I thought you were wasting your time, I'd tell you. And anyway, for us, your worth isn't determined by what you do. It's determined by who you are."

Jayne chuckled, and Lesley couldn't help but snicker along with her. "Okay, not the best way to put it, but I hope you know what I mean."

In response, Jayne's arms tightened around Lesley's neck; her tears moistened Lesley's cheek. Lesley swallowed; she drew back, let go of her, and pointed at the table. "Those really aren't your drawings, right?"

Jayne wiped her eyes. "No, I tore up an empty sketchbook, to stop myself from tearing up a full one." She sighed. "The drawings from the walls are stacked in my bedroom closet. I don't want to see them right now. I'll put them back up when I feel better."

The boiler snapped off. "Are you desperate for a tziva?" Lesley asked.

Jayne rubbed at her cheeks and blinked at her. "You don't want any?"

"I was thinking that you could go home with me and we'll have tziva there. Bring a change of clothes. I'll fly you home in the morning."

"I'll be okay."

"But why spend the evening alone in your apartment, if you don't have to? Some company will do you good. I'll need an hour to study for my test, but you can read . . . or draw."

Jayne's forehead puckered. "I just tore up my only empty sketchbook."

Lesley bit her lip. "I guess we'll stop at the Trading Centre, then." She paused. "Assuming you'll come. I hope you do."

"Okay," Jayne said with a nod. "Let me pack a change of clothes."

"While you're doing that, I'll feed the recycling chute. Oh, and I'll beep Mo. She's worried about you."

"Tell her I'm sorry. Tell her I'll beep her while you're studying." Jayne stopped in the kitchen archway and met Lesley's eyes. "Thank you." She left without giving Lesley a chance to reply.

It only took a minute and three trips to clear the table of the shredded sketchbook. Lesley pulled out her comm unit, beeped Mo, and filled her in.

"So she applied for us?" Mo tutted. "And they couldn't bring themselves to throw her a single word about her painting? How much trouble would I be in if I accidentally dropped a missile on the college next time I happen to be flying over it in a military aviacraft?"

Lesley chuckled. "How much time do I have to recite the article numbers and remind you of which ones are capital articles?"

"Yeah, that's what I figured," Mo drawled.

Lesley braced herself. "I've invited her to go home with me and stay in the guest room tonight. Otherwise she'll sit around in her apartment and brood."

Mo remained silent.

"Would you rather I let her sit here by herself?"

"No. I mean, of course not. But don't you have to study?"

"She said she'll beep you while I'm studying."

"I might be flying sims with Ann later. Tell her if I don't answer, to write me a dispatch. Tell her I want to hear from her, and that I'll write back before I go to bed." Mo sighed. "I have no right to wish I was there and to worry about the two of you. I shouldn't feel this way."

"You can't help how you feel. Wanting to feel a certain way, to handle a situation with a certain level of maturity—it's easier said than done."

"The voice of experience?"

"Unfortunately, yes." Argamon, Mo knew her well. Lately, how she

felt versus how her intellect said she should feel was a familiar struggle—and a letdown.

"I wish you were as quick to excuse yourself as you always are to excuse
me," Mo said quietly. "Especially since I'm being so flaming unreasonable. I mean, I *asked* you to go check on her, and now I'm worried because
you're supporting her, for both of us. So I'm going to stop. I'll have fun
with Ann tonight, and I'll look forward to hearing from Jayne."

"Good," Lesley said, feeling like a liar. When Jayne had squeezed her
and pressed her cheek against hers, Lesley hadn't drawn back because she
wanted to get away. She'd drawn back because she wanted to get closer.

CHOSENS

.....

Jayne gazed out at the Thompsons' back garden as she sipped her tziva, grateful for the quiet time on her own. She didn't know what Lesley had told Adelaide and Alan about her sudden overnight visit, but Lesley must have beeped and told them *something*, probably while she'd waited for Jayne outside the Trading Centre. The rejection of Jayne's art school application hadn't come up at the supper table, and neither parent had appeared surprised when she'd walked through the front door with Lesley. If Adelaide hadn't already had an inkling of what had happened, she would have bluntly asked.

Jayne had brought her new sketchbook outside with her, in case Lesley had told them the truth. She'd wanted to show them that she wasn't crushed, but it lay closed next to her on the bench swing. She glanced at it but wasn't compelled to open it, fearing how she'd feel when she lifted its cover. Would inspiration come? Would she stare miserably at a blank page?

In front of her, barely visible in the gloom of dusk, two trees towered over the others as parents would over their young children. A majestic family stood before her, its members standing together night and day, remaining loyal not only on sunny days, but on stormy ones, when they would move in unison—*Argamon!* Why couldn't she look at trees and see only flaming trees, like everyone else did? Then she wouldn't have toiled away for nothing all these years, wouldn't have applied—

Her comm unit beeped. *Mo.* Jayne pressed the connect button. "I'm sorry I haven't sent you a dispatch yet. I was going to start it when I finished my tziva."

Mo snorted. "I'm not beeping because you haven't sent me a dispatch. I wanted to see how you are."

"I'm okay." She was also embarrassed by her behaviour and felt even more inferior to her Chosens. "I thought you were flying sims with Ann tonight."

"I'm supposed to be, but I'm starting to wonder if she's going to show up. She's ten minutes late. I've tried beeping her, but all I get is her message."

"She's probably talking to someone."

"Yeah, that's what I figure. Something's up with her. She's been moody since I got up here." Mo paused. "You sure you're okay?"

Jayne blinked away the tears that prickled at her eyelashes. "I'll be okay," she murmured.

"It doesn't matter, you know. I mean, it does because it's important to you, and I know you're disappointed. But it doesn't change how I see your drawings . . . or you." Mo was silent for a moment. "Les said you applied for us."

Jayne blew out a sigh. "I wanted you to see that I was doing something with my life. But maybe I used you as an excuse, too."

"In what way?"

"Maybe I always wanted to apply, but never had the courage. Maybe telling myself that I was doing it for you and Lesley was a way of protecting myself from the inevitable."

"Or maybe you're over-analyzing. Would you ever have applied?"

"I don't know." *Come on*! "Probably not. I always resisted when Carol nagged me about it."

"Then you didn't want to."

But the option to apply to art school had always been at the back of her mind. Now it was gone. She could no longer tell herself that she *could* apply to art school but couldn't be bothered. The situation had changed from her rejecting art school to art school rejecting her, leaving her with one less delusion to draw upon when she needed a boost. No, they didn't want her, and she had no idea if her name had mattered, or if she simply couldn't paint. She'd been afraid to apply, or perhaps smart enough not to burst her own bubble, knowing there'd be nothing left if she did—until Mo and Lesley. She still had them.

Since talking to Lesley, she'd thought about why she'd stupidly applied. She'd known—*known!*—that she was likely to be bitterly disappointed. The possibility that she'd used them as an excuse had turned her stomach, but maybe it wasn't as bad as she'd thought. She *had* wanted to show them that she wasn't worthless, and had perhaps drawn courage from them in a positive, not negative, way. No matter what happened, they'd still be there . . . and they'd still care. They *cared. Please, please, don't let that be another delusion!*

"Jayne? Argamon, I beeped to see how you are, and all I'm doing is depressing you," Mo said. "I should have waited for your dispatch instead of forcing you to talk about it."

"No, I'm glad you beeped. I was thinking about what you said, that's all." Though she wouldn't mind a change of subject. "Lesley's studying. I'm outside on the bench swing. It's a pleasant—"

"Oh, I think I see Ann. Do you want me to put her off?"

"No! I'm okay. Go fly your sims. I'll feel worse if you don't."

"Well, we don't want that." Mo sighed. "I wish I was down there. I'll beep you later, okay?"

"Okay." Silence. Had Mo disconnected?

"Bye," Mo finally said.

"Bye." Jayne cursed herself for not saying that she wished Mo was down here, too. She felt like an idiot, refusing to answer their beeps and then throwing a temper tantrum and ripping up a sketchbook. Stupid, especially since she'd applied because she cared about what they thought of her. Now what did they see? A child who couldn't handle rejection? *Enough! Snap out of the self-pity.* She was entitled to a fit of frustration every once in a while.

Maybe this rejection hurt so badly because she could feel again. She'd cast off the shroud of indifference and isolation in which she'd wrapped herself since the Incident. She'd dared to be optimistic, to dream, to expect more than a lonely life on the fringes of society. Without hope, there could never be disappointment. She'd given up on both when she was twelve years old. It was time to grow up.

MO TORE OFF her helmet, unbuckled her seatbelt, and stomped out of the simulator. Her jaw tightened when she spotted Ann in the corridor. "What is your flaming problem?"

Ann frowned. "You took way too long to disable that escort."

"Too long? I disabled it in 4.3 seconds. Do you understand how good that is?"

Ann shrugged. Mo wanted to throttle her. She'd flown her guts out, mercilessly blasted everything coming her way . . . and enjoyed the carnage too much. Pretending that her opponents belonged to the committee that had rejected Jayne's application had helped—a lot. "Maybe I would have done it in 4.1 seconds, if the other pilot had covered me like she was supposed to." Ann's inattentiveness to the mission objectives had almost cost them an easy mission they normally flew with their eyes closed.

"You were doing fine on your own." Ann strode away.

"I thought you just said I was slow!" Mo shouted.

Ann shrugged again.

Mo hurried after her. "What's wrong?"

"Nothing."

"Don't give me that. Some of my students would have flown that mission better than you did."

Ann whirled and stabbed a finger at Mo. "You know what? Maybe I'm just tired of the whole flaming Middleton family!" She marched off.

Mo stared after her. Great. When she got home, she'd corner Andrew and find out what was going on. This was exactly why she hadn't been thrilled when she'd found out that Ann and Andrew were dating. Their relationship problems were now her flaming problems!

Back in her quarters, she checked her dispatches and smiled as she read a short one from Jayne. If Jayne had been here on 72, she wouldn't have been alone when she'd received the rejection from the art college—at least, not for long, anyway. Mo wanted her here. Argamon, she wanted Les *and* Jayne here, but until Les completed her commander training, she'd only have a day off now and then. Mo usually turned down supply shifts that coincided with Les's free time, but the practicums were a different matter. Les might not want to spend her precious downtime on 72, but Mo would ask. As for Jayne . . . could she and Mo share quarters on 72 and not cross the line?

Honestly—Mo wasn't sure. Restraining themselves for an hour was becoming more difficult; imagine spending hours alone in each other's company, with a bedroom to tempt them. Then there was Les. How would she react to Jayne on 72? Maybe it was time to find out. Insisting that Jayne remain on the planet was starting to feel silly. How long could they keep it up without resenting Les, especially since the same restriction didn't apply to her? She'd said their arrangement was off. Okay, she'd made that grand proclamation because she hadn't wanted her Chosens to worry about her, but she also understood that they couldn't hold each other at arm's length forever. Still, that didn't mean Les wouldn't have a problem with Jayne on 72. A visit to an eatery was one thing; an overnight stay on 72 was something else entirely.

Mo chewed her left thumbnail, then winced and switched to her right. There was only one way to find out how Les might handle Jayne on 72: ask her. If Mo wanted Jayne here, she'd have to do that anyway. Jayne wouldn't agree to come to 72 without Les's "permission," and Mo needed Les's reassurance, too. Argamon, what a weird situation, wanting reassurance from Les that if she ended up in bed with Jayne, Les would still love her! The nerve of even asking . . . but they were in a triad. Someday, Les would ask her for the same reassurance.

Mo sank onto the sofa. If she was going to take this step, she better be sure that she could handle it when that day came. Could she give Les permission to be with someone else? A few months ago, never! But now . . . her feelings for Jayne hadn't changed her feelings for Les, who was as important and special to her as she'd ever been—perhaps more so. Les's struggle to accept Mo's feelings for Jayne, even though it must be killing her, had swept away any doubts Mo had harboured about the depth of Les's love. Who would have thought that falling for Jayne would make Les more special to her? When Les finally developed feelings for Jayne—because she would, she flaming would!—Mo would have to cling to these thoughts and remind herself that Les wouldn't be asking to be with just anyone. She'd want to be with Jayne. So maybe Mo *could* say, "Yes, Les, go ahead. I'll still love you." Because she loved both of them.

JAYNE EXAMINED THE colour charts that Catherine Moss had arranged on the round table. She would prefer lighter colours over darker ones, but would Lesley and Mo? They both lived with their parents; she didn't know how they'd decorate a room or what furniture would appeal to them. They'd said that she could run her choices by them; Jayne hoped they'd meant it.

Catherine swung her chair around and lifted a blueprint from her desk. "Before we work on the second floor, we need to label the bedrooms," she said, slapping the blueprint over the colour charts.

"What do you mean?" Jayne could see at least five rooms labelled *Bedroom*.

"Well, for our purposes, we need to know more than that a room will be a bedroom. We need to know whose bedroom. I'm sure your daughters' rooms will be decorated differently from . . ." Catherine cleared her throat. "Will all three of you be in the same room?" she asked faintly.

Jayne's cheeks felt warm. "I don't know," she mumbled. "We haven't talked about it."

"We'll need to know if any are intended to be guest rooms, too," Catherine said, her eyes on Jayne's face.

Jayne lowered her head and pretended to study the blueprint. They hadn't discussed the sleeping arrangements for their own home, probably because the topic was a loaded one. When she and Mo had stayed at the Thompsons' for the Festival of the Way, she'd slept in a guest bedroom and Mo had slept in Lesley's. Right now that made sense, and Jayne wouldn't mind if she slept in her own room permanently. Three in the same bed would be a little crowded. If anyone was going to share, it would be her two Chosens, which would suit Jayne fine. She was used to being alone. She cherished Lesley and Mo's company, but would relish having her own space, a room that was *hers*.

"Can you discuss it with them and let me know?"

"Sure." Though knowing what she'd prefer wouldn't make talking to them about it any easier.

"Do you know how many daughters you're planning to have?"

Jayne wanted to laugh. One step at a time. "No."

Catherine shifted the blueprint so Jayne could see the colour charts again. "You have an advantage over diff-oriented couples. You can plan exactly how many children you'll have."

"Not all visits to the Reproductive Technology Centre are successful," Jayne pointed out, wishing Catherine would change the subject.

"True. I suppose it's more that there are no unexpected pregnancies."

Jayne nodded, then wondered if Catherine was trying to find out whether she intended to have children. If she didn't feel that it was none of Catherine's business, she'd set her mind at ease. "Can I see the cream chart you showed me earlier?"

Catherine sorted through the pile in front of her, pulled out the cream chart, and handed it to Jayne.

She tapped one of the colour panels. "I like this one for the dining room."

"Oh, I have the perfect dining set to show you. Two, actually."

Jayne listened to Catherine prattle on about possible furnishings for the dining room, relieved that the conversation had turned away from sleeping arrangements and daughters.

LESLEY TURNED OFF her comm display when she heard familiar footsteps thumping up the stairs. Mo burst into the room. "Finished studying?" She threw her arm around Lesley and squeezed her, then plunked onto the bed.

"I'm finished." Lesley stood and rolled her chair under the desk, then turned and noticed Mo chewing her thumbnail. "What is it?"

Mo heaved her shoulders. "I want to talk to you about Jayne and 72."

On her way to sit next to Mo, Lesley continued past the bed and looked out the window instead. She could guess what was coming. How many times had she stared out this window as a child, waiting for Mo to arrive on her bike? How many times had they ridden up to the house together, shouting taunts as they'd raced each other up the path? The two girls had become women; friendship had blossomed into love. Mo had been a part of her for as long as she could remember. All that time, neither had known that there was another girl, and then a woman, who would affect their lives—their relationship—in ways they never could have imagined. Some thought that knowing the future would make life easier, but Lesley wasn't one of them. She wouldn't trade the time she'd had Mo to herself for anything. But those days were over.

"I could tell you that nothing will happen, but I won't lie to you." The bed creaked. "All I can say is that it won't change anything between us. It really won't."

That didn't matter. What had Papa said when she'd told him about Mo's feelings for Jayne? *You'll have something that only two other Rymellans have. Two Chosens. Two women who'll love you and cherish you above everyone else.* She would have been happy with one woman who loved her exclusively.

"If you want more time—"

"More time won't help. You could give me twenty years and it won't make a difference." It would still cut to her core.

Silence, then, "I don't know what to do. I don't want to hurt you."

But she would, and Lesley would forgive her. She had no choice, and neither did Mo. What were she and Jayne supposed to do, wait until Lesley assured them it wouldn't hurt? That day would never come, and they all knew it. The best she could hope for was that it would eventually stop hurting.

"Jayne might not even want to go to 72. I haven't talked to her about it. I wanted to talk to you first."

"She won't refuse forever." Lesley continued to stare out the window. "I don't know what my mood will be like when you get back. You might have to give me some space."

"Maybe I should forget the idea," Mo said, her voice strained.

"Mo, we can't avoid this. Delaying it won't help. Pretending it will never happen won't help." She braced herself and turned around.

Mo had stood. Her moist eyes met Lesley's; her lips trembled. "I don't want you to hate me."

Lesley's own eyes filled with tears. "I could never hate you." She held out her arms.

Mo took a tentative step, then rushed to Lesley and clung to her. Lesley held her close and murmured, "We'll be okay," into Mo's ear, desperately hoping she wasn't whispering an empty promise. Every time they took a baby step, they were afraid they'd fall. So far they'd wobbled, but managed to stay upright. For Lesley, this step would be a barefoot stride across a floor littered with broken glass. She'd bleed; the question was, how much?

"I don't want you to hate Jayne, either," Mo said, her face pressed against Lesley's shoulder and her voice muffled.

"I won't." She didn't know how she felt about Jayne. She'd felt *something* in Jayne's apartment, but had Jayne's distress merely moved her, or had deeper feelings stirred? Either way, she didn't, and wouldn't, hate Jayne. She couldn't allow herself to hate someone who'd live with her for the rest of her life. They'd be okay. They'd be okay. "When you talk to Jayne about going to 72, I'd like to be there. If that's all right."

Mo drew back and wiped her eyes, then her nose, with her sleeve. "Are you sure?"

Lesley nodded. "I want her to be absolutely certain that I know, and that . . . I'll be okay." She'd also check to see if she had an appointment with Berry while they were on 72. If not, she'd schedule one. She *would* be okay, in the sense that she wouldn't be defeated. She'd be in a fighter that had lost all its defences and experienced massive structural damage, but had survived the worst of the opponent's attacks and would fly another day. She believed that love and time would heal the hurt. She had no choice but to believe.

Mo leaned into her again. Lesley closed her eyes, then jumped when two comm units beeped twice in unison, piercing the silence. Thinking that it might be an urgent broadcast to all military personnel or Rymellans in general, Lesley reluctantly reached for her unit, held it up over Mo's shoulder, and softly snorted. A dispatch from Jayne. She read it and shook her head.

"What?" Mo stepped back.

"Jayne has impeccable timing."

Mo chuckled. "That's the first time that's happened."

"She just met with Catherine Moss, who wants to know what our sleeping arrangements will be in our new home."

"You're kidding."

Lesley wished she was. Then again, one uncomfortable conversation would be better than two. "Why don't we all have lunch here tomorrow? Afterward we can talk about this and 72."

"We were thinking of getting together with her anyway." Mo shoved her hands into her pockets. "Are you sure?"

"Yes." Sure that she couldn't hold them back. Sure that she was about to walk through a raging fire, and hoping that she'd make it to the other side, that she wouldn't be trapped in a burning room forever.

WANTING A GLASS of water before she rode over to Les's, Mo bounded down the stairs and headed for the kitchen. Les had insisted that they pick up Jayne together. Even though Mo suspected that Les was trying to show that she wasn't upset about their conversation—or wasn't letting her emotions get the better of her, at least—Mo had readily agreed. Whatever Les needed right now, she'd get, regardless of her reason for asking.

When Mo entered the kitchen, Andrew looked up from a bowl of soup. "You're not at the workshop today?" she asked, only because he'd moped around the house yesterday, too. Would he and Ann please resolve whatever problem they were experiencing?

"I'm not feeling well," he said sullenly.

She filled a glass with water and leaned against the counter to study him. He looked healthy to her, though a little tired. His troubles with Ann must be keeping him up at night. "So what's up with you and Ann?"

"Nothing."

"Come on. She kept snapping my head off on 72, and you've been dragging yourself around the house ever since I got back."

He stared into his soup. "Why don't you ask *her*?"

"Because I'm here, asking you. What's going on? Did you have a fight?"

"She didn't tell you anything?"

"No."

Andrew sighed and stirred his soup. She was about to suggest that he go up to 72 and talk it out with Ann when she realized that, as far as she knew, he'd never visited Ann on 72. They weren't Chosens, but 72 wasn't strictly a military installation. It wasn't against the rules to have civilian visitors. "Why don't you go up to 72 and see her?" she said, interested in Andrew's reaction. When he shook his head, she asked, "Have you ever been up to see her on 72?"

"No."

"Why not? There's nothing—"

"She didn't want me there, okay!"

"Okay, okay." She didn't have to be a mind reader to see that he was hurt by that.

"In fact, she doesn't want me, period. We broke up."

Argamon. "When?"

"Last week. Happy?"

"No!" When she'd found out they were dating, Mo wasn't crazy about the idea, but she'd grown used to it. "What happened? You seemed okay together."

He dropped his spoon into the bowl. "I'm a horrible boyfriend for wanting to be with her."

"What? I don't get it."

"Neither do I. I see her for a few days every flaming three weeks, but apparently I'm smothering her because I'd like to see her more often."

Mortified, Mo watched him blink back tears. Flaming Ann! Her initial suspicion that Ann would intentionally hurt him had fallen to the wayside; over time, she'd come to believe that Ann cared for him. If that wasn't true, the breakup wouldn't still be affecting her a week later. She'd be her usual annoying self, not the snappy, distracted pilot who'd flown sims with Mo. Why would she dump him for wanting more time with her?

"I'm going for a walk." Andrew mumbled. He stalked from the kitchen.

Had he nagged Ann about visiting 72? Why hadn't she ever agreed to it? Mo would have thought she'd welcome him to the space station. Ann spent most of her downtime with Andrew and always looked forward to seeing him—it wasn't unusual for Mo to bump into her in this very kitchen. It couldn't be that she didn't want him to see her quarters. Mo had played cards there with other pilots; Ann didn't have anything to hide. Something didn't make sense.

Papa would eventually drag Andrew to the workshop, but that wouldn't stop him from pining for Ann. His tears had driven home how much he cared about her. Mo sipped her water. Should she talk to Ann? They'd broken up, so doing so couldn't make anything worse. When they'd started dating several months ago, Mo had given them two weeks.

She'd never imagined that she'd try to patch things up between them, and maybe she shouldn't. What if Ann dumped him again?

Well, trying to find out why she'd broken up with him wouldn't hurt; Mo was dying of curiosity to know. Okay, she'd try to get it out of Ann, though if Jayne was with her next time she went to 72, she'd have other priorities.

JAYNE UNROLLED THE blueprint of the upper floor of the house across the table in the study. Lesley and Mo, seated across from her, each held one end and examined the floor plan. "I pencilled in the rooms I thought would make sense for us." Jayne tapped one with her pencil, then the other, and held her breath. This was her way of telling them of her preference for putting them into one room and her into another. "I figured you two would want to share a room," she said when neither of them spoke. "Based on, uh, the arrangements for the Festival of the Way," she felt compelled to add when another long silence followed. They remained focused on the blueprint. What was running through their minds?

Lesley finally looked up. "What made sense for the Festival of the Way might not make sense in the future."

No matter what happened, it would make sense for her.

Mo looked at Lesley. "I always assumed we'd share a room."

"So did I, but . . ."

Jayne silently voiced the question she suspected was on their minds: what would they do with her? "You two sharing a room and me in another room feels the most natural to me. It jibes with the way I see things." She briefly met Lesley's eyes, hoping Lesley would recall the conversation they'd had on their bike ride. Whether they'd admit it or not, Jayne was sure it would feel the most natural to them, too. When the three of them were together, her Chosens always gravitated toward each other. Since only the triad had been at the dining room table for lunch, Lesley and Mo had sat across from her. When they'd entered the study, they'd immediately sat next to each other.

She didn't mind; she wasn't lying, to them or herself, when she said that she viewed them as the primary couple and their relationship as the foundation of the triad. She never felt left out, because they didn't shut her out. At the same time, they were a long-standing couple and behaved like one. She'd never expect or demand that they act as if all their years together had never existed. They'd come to her together, they were together, and she couldn't imagine them anything but together. "I'm being honest. I'm not telling you what I think you want to hear."

Lesley and Mo glanced at each other, then Lesley leaned forward and pointed at the wall that separated the two rooms Jayne had tapped. "Let's put a door here."

Mo snickered.

Lesley turned to her. "On a symbolic level, it connects the rooms together. On a practical level, I'm thinking about when those other bedrooms are occupied. They'll eventually ask why we're in one room and Jayne's in another. We'll be able to say the rooms are connected."

"I know, I'm just being immature." Mo's contrite expression didn't look genuine.

"It'll also give us privacy. They don't need to know when . . . anyone's not in her usual room."

Mo nodded. "It's a good idea."

Jayne agreed, but she didn't look forward to explaining it to William. To her relief, Lesley said, "I'll send William a dispatch and tell him what we want."

"You're okay with this being your room and this being mine?" Jayne asked.

They both nodded. "Is there anything else we need to talk about related to the house?" Lesley asked.

"Now that this is settled, I'll work with Catherine on the bedrooms. Before we go ahead and order anything, I'd like us to get together with her, so we can show you what we've selected. Is that okay?"

"Yeah, sure," Mo said as Lesley nodded.

"If you don't like any of my choices, we can change them. Furniture, ornaments, colours—"

"Yeah, if we don't like something, no big deal," Mo said. "We'll just choose something else."

"Right." Jayne knew it wasn't a test, but it would feel like one. They'd trusted her with the interior design; she'd hate to disappoint them. But enough fretting for today. Now that the conversation she'd dreaded was out of the way, she could relax and enjoy the rest of the afternoon. She rolled up the blueprint, looked up, and . . . why were they both staring at her?

Mo straightened and clenched her hands on top of the table. "Okay, well, now that we've talked about the house, I guess it would be a good time to talk about, uh, something else."

Lesley leaned back in her chair and folded her arms. Jayne slipped an elastic band around the blueprint. She held it on her lap, trying not to crush it.

"I'm going to 72 next week, and I want to know if you'd like to come with me," Mo said.

"I wanted to be part of this conversation, so you'll know that Mo's spoken to me about it and I'm okay with you going—and everything it might involve," Lesley added.

Jayne wanted to openly study her, to determine if that was true. Then she wanted to smack herself. How could it be true? Okay with it? Lesley meant that she'd work very hard to not hold it against them. How many tears and sleepless nights would it take? How much would she torture herself? What imaginary scenarios would taunt her? When they were on 72, how many times would Lesley ask herself whether it had happened yet? Would she want to look at them when they returned?

"You—we—can't avoid it," Lesley said quietly.

Yes, they could. Maybe it was because they'd just discussed the sleeping arrangements for the house and Jayne had thought about what would work best for her, but she knew, without a doubt, what she wanted in this matter. Whether they'd agree to it was a different story.

Mo unclenched her hands and slipped one under the table. "I don't want you to think I'm being selfish and not thinking about Les. We've talked about it."

"We've all known that you and Mo will get physical," Lesley said, her arms still tightly folded. "I won't lie and say it won't hurt. But holding you back would be the wrong thing to do. I don't want to do that, and I don't want you two to do it, either. I know Mo loves me. And I trust that you're . . ." She paused. "I know you're not cavalier about my feelings. I know you've been restraining yourselves out of consideration for me. You can't do that forever."

"It'll be a difficult step for all of us." Mo sighed. "Argamon, I know I'll feel guilty about it. At the same time, we can't—will you go to 72 with me?"

Jayne transferred the rolled-up blueprint to the table and took a deep breath. "No."

"No?" Mo squeaked.

Lesley unfolded her arms and pointed to herself. "If you're refusing because of me . . ."

"I am, but not for the reason you think." *Argamon.* The conversation about the bedrooms paled in comparison to this. Jayne looked at Lesley. "I'll go to 72 when you go to 72."

Lesley frowned. "I won't be able to go to 72 for a while. Even if that wasn't true, it wouldn't be a good idea. I don't think you'd want me there."

"No, I *would* want you there. Not necessarily on 72. Wherever it happens."

Mo shifted in her chair. "Okay, wait a minute. What are we talking about? What exactly would you want her there for?"

Everything. Jayne sat on her hands. Her face already felt hot and she hadn't started talking yet. This wasn't going to be easy, but she had to be honest and clearly state what she wanted. It was too important to hide behind euphemisms. "I met you together." *I fell for both of you together.* "I know I can't tell you both everything at the same time. And I know I'll share my first kiss with one of you. But when it comes to my first sexual experience, I want that with both of you." She could barely hear herself over her pounding heart, but saying it out loud strengthened her resolve that it wouldn't only be the best way for her, but for all of them. One of her Chosens wouldn't hold that first experience over the other for the rest of their lives. Lesley and Mo weren't in competition, but to Jayne, it would create an imbalance between them that could never be remedied. She also believed that it would be easier on them if they shared their first experience with her, rather than having one left out.

She focused on Mo. "If you and I were to go to 72 and end up in bed together, can you honestly say that Lesley wouldn't be there, too? Not physically, but on your mind. I can't. I'd rather she actually be there."

Mo lifted her hand to her mouth, then dropped it. "Of course I'll think of her. I know I'll have mixed feelings about it. Like I said, I'll feel guilty. It's a no-win situation. No matter what we do, we'll suffer in some way."

"Sharing it with both of you would make a huge difference to me," Jayne said. "I wouldn't feel guilty. If it was something we all wanted and we did it together, would you still feel guilty?" She quickly focused on Lesley. "Hypothetically speaking. I know that's not the situation now."

Lesley drew breath, but Mo spoke first. "I probably wouldn't feel guilty under those circumstances. But I haven't thought about this—about all three of us—before. I need to think about it. I mean, it's an interesting idea, but I—" She blew out a sigh. "I need to think about it."

"If we decide that's the way it's going to happen, I'll still be holding you back, but in a different way," Lesley said.

Jayne shook her head. "I'd see it more as waiting for you. To me, holding us back means not letting us do something that's possible for us to do now. If we decide it will be the three of us, then that's not possible yet." She gazed at Lesley, but couldn't read her. "Maybe what I want sounds insane and the last thing you and Mo will want, but I honestly believe that sharing the experience with both of you would be the best way for all of us." Her fingers were digging into the undersides of her legs. She pulled her hands onto her lap and clenched them.

Lesley and Mo turned to each other. "We'll have to talk about it," Lesley said, her eyes on Mo's face. "It's an intriguing idea."

Mo snorted. "Intriguing? That's one way to put it. But yeah, we'll talk about it."

Jayne hoped they'd agree to it. Otherwise she'd have to consider Mo's invitation to 72, they'd probably give in to their desires, and the experience would be marred by guilt, for both of them. Lesley would be a palpable presence in that bedroom, whether she was there or not, and sharing such an important step in her life with only one of them wouldn't feel right. But would her Chosens see things the same way?

AFTER PUNCHING IN the coordinates for the Thompson estate, Lesley leaned back in the pilot's seat and gave Mo a sidelong glance. Since their illuminating conversation with Jayne, Mo hadn't been able to sit still. Was there any nail remaining unchewed on her left thumb?

Now that they'd dropped Jayne off, Lesley could raise the subject that was on both their minds, but she'd have to be careful. Jayne's thoughts about what would work best for her and the triad weren't the only things Lesley had learned from their discussion. When she'd understood what Jayne was suggesting, she hadn't instantly recoiled. The more she'd listened and thought about it, the more it made sense. More importantly, the notion of sleeping with Jayne hadn't repelled her. The feelings that had stirred in Jayne's apartment weren't innocent. "Do you want to talk about it now, or wait until we're home?" she asked Mo.

"Do you know what surprised me?" Mo snorted. "In addition to what she said, I mean."

"What?"

"She was so forward about it."

Lesley chuckled. "When something's important to her, or she thinks it's important for all of us, she forces herself to say it and be straightforward about it. She makes sure we understand exactly what she means." A trait Lesley admired.

"What do you think?" Mo examined her left thumbnail, then lifted her right thumb to her mouth.

"Well, given how she sees the triad . . . in fact, given how we see it, it makes sense."

Mo gaped. "Really? I thought you'd be dead set against it."

"I'm not saying I'd want to do it right now."

"Yeah, the conversation was a little premature for you, I guess."

Not as premature as Mo thought, but now wouldn't be a good time to tell her that the Chosen Council had indeed matched three Chosens together. One thing at a time.

"If I say I hate the idea, you'll think I just don't want to wait," Mo said.

"Mo—"

"You can honestly see the three of us in bed together?"

"To be honest, it wouldn't have occurred to me." Not yet, anyway. It probably would have crossed her mind when they were all living together with only a connecting door separating them. "But when she said it, it made sense. It *would* do away with the guilt. I don't want to hold you back, but I heard you both say that if you sleep together on 72, you'll feel guilty. Is that what you want for your first experience together? Is it what you want for her? It'll be her very first experience."

"Maybe if we wait until you have feelings for her, we won't feel as guilty."

                    RYMELLAN 3

"Do you really believe that? Hypothetically speaking, I'd feel guilty, because I'd know it would hurt you. It wouldn't matter that you . . . love her. It would still hurt you. You'd torture yourself about it, just as I will. You'd wonder when we were doing it, how it went, if I'd still feel the same way about you afterward." She looked at Mo, to reassure herself that Mo wasn't chewing her thumb off. "And I'll wonder if you'll still feel the same way about me."

Mo dropped her hand to her lap. "It won't change the way I feel about you. But I'll feel horribly guilty because I know it'll hurt you. And yeah, when it happens for you, it'll hurt me. Really hurt."

"But you don't like Jayne's suggestion."

"I wasn't expecting it, I guess." Mo was silent for a moment. "It sounds like you think it would be easier for you." She sighed. "And I can see how it would make things easier for me. If it's both of us, if we share the experience . . . I mean, she is *our* Chosen, right?"

Lesley nodded. "I'm not saying it won't feel weird, or maybe awkward would be a better word. But I'd prefer awkward over guilty, especially if it means you won't be hurt. Plus, the guilt will probably be permanent. The awkwardness will be temporary."

Mo barked a laugh. "Once we get going, we'll get over it and enjoy ourselves? Argamon, I never thought I'd have a conversation like this."

Lesley smiled. "Me, either. But when she suggested it, it really did make sense."

"We all have to be ready," Mo pointed out. "Otherwise it'll hurt someone."

"True."

"So I guess it'll be a while, and that's okay. If it means less guilt and hurt, it's worth waiting for."

"Are you sure?"

"Yeah, I'm sure. I wouldn't have thought of it, and when she first said it, I was shocked. But the more I think about it—yeah, when you eventually get to that point . . ." Mo's hand went to her mouth again, "I *would* rather be there than imagine it, and if it's all of us . . . yeah. It'll make a difference."

"And it's what Jayne wants." Lesley held up her hand when Mo drew breath. "I'm not saying we should always do what Jayne wants. But since we're open to the idea, why would we refuse to go along with her suggestion, especially regarding this?"

Mo nodded, then jumped and stared at her thumb. "I just flaming hurt myself!"

"Why don't you do what Jayne does and sit on your hands?"

Mo glared at her. "I guess she won't be going to 72 with me."

"You can still ask her to go."

"You wouldn't mind?"

The conversation with Jayne had made Lesley more comfortable with the idea of Mo and Jayne on 72, not less. Jayne would never do anything to upset the triad's harmony. She'd bravely and clearly stated what she wanted and why she believed it would be best not only for her, but for all of them. Once she knew that her Chosens were willing to give her idea a try, she'd wait. Turning around and sleeping with Mo anyway would shatter the trust they were nurturing and hurt everyone. Jayne would never do that. Lesley trusted Mo too, but Jayne had the edge in this case. "I trust you and Jayne. If we've decided we're going to wait until we're all comfortable taking that step together, then I know you two will stick to that."

"I don't want to put us—all of us—under any pressure. I'm never up there for more than a few days, anyway."

"Mo, if you want her to go up with you, ask her. Or were you only going to suggest it because you wanted to get her into bed?"

Mo drew back. "No!"

"Then don't make it all about that." Lesley glanced at the nav panel. "It's up to you, but I won't mind if you invite her."

"She's still not drawing."

"Give it time."

"Maybe it'll be good for her to get out of her apartment for a few days," Mo said.

Lesley nodded, and marvelled at how the thought of Mo and Jayne on 72 together had gone from threatening to upsetting, all in the course of two conversations. She wasn't naïve; Mo and Jayne would be affectionate with each other on 72. But since the line would be drawn outside the bedroom door, Lesley would torment herself with less terrifying scenarios.

JAYNE HEAVED A relieved sigh and said, "Good." She'd had trouble falling asleep last night, second-guessing herself for being so honest with her Chosens and wondering if they'd concluded that she was insane. On the other hand, the more she'd thought about it, the more convinced she'd become that her suggestion would be the least disruptive and hurtful to the triad, no matter how crazy it sounded.

"So do you want to go to 72 with me?" Mo asked.

"*What?*"

Mo chuckled. "That's what I thought when Les said she wouldn't mind if I still asked you."

"She wouldn't mind? But—"

"She trusts us. We wouldn't do anything to violate that trust, right?"

"No. Absolutely not." Now that they'd agreed to her idea, it would feel almost unnatural to sleep with only one of them, at least initially. Why would she do something so stupid? She wanted to take that step without hurting anyone or feeling guilty, and it was an experience she honestly wanted to share with both of them. Knowing that she could, and that neither Lesley nor Mo's heart would be ripped from her chest and pulverized, would be more than enough for her to restrain herself on 72. "Okay, I'll go."

"Great! I still have a fair number of practicums to do, especially since they fly several times each, so I'll be up and down a lot in the next couple of months. I'd hate it if you could never come with me. I wish Les could come."

"It would be nice for all three of us to be up there together. Not because, uh—"

Mo quickly rescued her. "I know what you mean."

"Who's filling in for you when we Join?"

"Nobody. Ross knew what dates we'd requested. Only the first date was a potential problem, so she scheduled around it. It's only two weeks, right? As for supply, that's always a last minute thing, so they'll just know not to beep me." Mo paused. "I feel sorry for Les. Yeah, she has the two weeks off, but she'll have to catch up. They're not stopping the course for her."

"Maybe we should have waited."

"No, we wanted the *Falcon* to be in dock, remember? We were really hoping for that first date."

"Right." They'd mentioned wanting their pilot friends to attend the Joining supper, but Jayne had known that the desire to put CT134 to rest was the primary reason behind the dates they'd submitted. Otherwise they would have submitted dates six months apart that coincided with the *Falcon*'s docking schedule.

"I have quite a few practicums to fly while we're on 72, so you'll want to bring your sketchbook," Mo said.

"I'll bring it." Whether she'd draw in it was another matter.

MO STEPPED OFF the elevator at Deck 7 and strode down the corridor. Before returning to her quarters and Jayne, she wanted to corner Ann, so it wouldn't be on her mind for the rest of the day. She chuckled as she passed the quarters that Archer had originally assigned to her. Had Jayne believed her when she'd insisted that she hadn't booked a one-bedroom on purpose, that Archer always arranged quarters and she'd explicitly told him she wanted a two-bedroom? At least it hadn't taken him long to remedy the mistake. Now they were on Deck 6.

She reached Ann's quarters and pressed the door chime. The door slid open. Ann stood in the doorway. "Oh, it's you. What do you want?"

Dancing around the subject wouldn't work. "Andrew told me you dumped him."

"Yeah, I did. So what? I've moved on, he'll move on, that's just the way it goes." She folded her arms. "We're not Chosens. We weren't *stuck* together."

Andrew hadn't moved on and, from what Mo had heard, neither had Ann. "Do you want to grab a drink in the canteen and talk about it?"

Ann groaned and rolled her eyes. "Why would I want to talk to you about it? It's over, okay? Get over it."

Mo shrugged. "Okay, I guess we don't need to talk. Andrew told me enough. See you." She turned and walked away.

"Wait!"

Suppressing a smile, Mo whirled.

Ann had stepped into the corridor. "What did he tell you?"

"I thought you didn't want to talk about it."

"He shouldn't be telling you anything."

Mo put her hands on her hips. "No, I'm just his sister and I live with him. You might not care that he's hurting, but I do."

Ann stared at her. "His ego's just hurt. He'll be at the Dance Hall tonight with his next girlfriend."

"You really believe that?" Mo tutted. "You know what I don't understand? Why the one who did the dumping has been down in the dumps ever since. I would have thought you'd be partying."

Ann's chin came up. "I'm not upset about it."

"Give me a break! According to Archer and everyone else, all you do is fly and hole up in your quarters. I want to understand why you don't want to be with him, so I can explain it to him, because I don't think he understands. What's so terrible about him wanting to see you more often?"

Ann's eyes bulged. "That's what he told you? That I broke up with him because he wants to see me more often?"

"Well, yeah," Mo drawled. "Why didn't you ever invite him to 72? You usually only saw him during your downtime, and as far as I could tell, you looked forward to it."

"I wish I'd never met him!"

So she could go on having shallow relationships in which nobody got hurt? Mo kept the thought to herself. "Look, I know you, okay? I know him. You're both miserable. If you're seriously glad you dumped him and you're getting over it, fine. If you're having second thoughts, then let's talk. I might be able to help." Ann wanted to talk, otherwise she would have shut the door in Mo's face long before now.

"I thought you didn't want us to be together."

"When I first found out, I wasn't thrilled. But I was wrong. You were happy together." She ignored Ann's eye roll. "He's my brother. You're my friend, right? So let's go to the canteen. Unless you want to talk about it out here in the corridor."

"If I tell you what's going on, you have to promise never to bring it up again."

"I promise." An easy vow to make, considering she'd never intended to talk to Ann about Andrew beyond the one conversation. After that, her duty was done.

Ann hit the *Close* button and fell into step with Mo. "I guess you're here alone," she said as they entered the elevator.

"No, Jayne's with me. I told her I was going to drop in on you after the practicum."

"Oh, so everyone knows my flaming business!"

"You seriously think she wouldn't find out that you and Andrew broke up? Come on." Mo shook her head.

"So what happened?" she asked as soon as they sat down at a table in a quiet corner with their drinks. Since Jayne was here, Mo's patience would quickly run thin if Ann took her time getting to the point. "He said you think he's smothering you."

"Why couldn't he settle for a few days here and there?" Ann said.

"Were you satisfied with a few days here and there?"

Ann remained silent, but the question was rhetorical anyway. Ann had always grown cranky after a couple of weeks of not seeing Andrew. So . . . "Why didn't you ever invite him to 72? He wanted to come up and see you. Didn't you want to show him around, show him a fighter, show him where you spend most of your time?"

"He might have thought it was serious."

"It *was* serious!" *Was? It still is.* "Is that why you wouldn't invite him? You wanted to pretend to him—and yourself—that your relationship doesn't—didn't matter?"

Ann's face tightened. "Look, I . . . like him, okay? I miss him. But I don't want to live with him."

What? "What do you mean?"

"He asked me to live with him."

Andrew wanted to move Ann into the house?

"Oh, don't worry, he didn't mean under the same roof as you, not that you'll be living there for much longer." Ann sighed, then sipped her juice. "He wants to move out, says it's time. He keeps talking about building a house on the estate and asked me if I'd live there with him. "

Argamon! "So you dumped him?"

"I don't want to live with him!"

"So why didn't you just say no?"

"He's always nagging me to come to 72, then he wants me to move in with him. I had to send a message."

Mo rolled her eyes. "Next time use an inverse laser instead of a missile."

Ann grunted.

"You miss him, and you obviously regret breaking it off."

Ann pulled a face but didn't deny it.

"Why don't you want him on 72?" When Ann didn't answer, Mo tried another tack. "Why are you so opposed to the idea of living with him? You spend all your downtime on the estate. What difference would it make if you stayed in another house on the estate?"

"Moving in with him would mean giving up my room at the Military Academy."

"So what? You never go there anyway." Mo remembered the sterile appearance of Ann's room. It wasn't a home. She'd always assumed that Ann saw it as temporary, but temporary had stretched into months, then years. "If you're worried, hedge your bets. Move a couple of things in with him, but don't give up your room at the Military Academy until you're sure. He doesn't have to know."

"I don't want to move in with him!"

"Okay, so just tell him that, but let him a little more into your life. Maybe he suggested moving in because he was hoping you'd maybe compromise and let him come to 72 every once in a while."

Ann huffed an exasperated sigh. "Why can't he be satisfied with the way things are?"

"Are you?"

"I don't know," Ann mumbled.

Mo did: no! "He sees your relationship as more than a casual one. So do you," Mo held up her hand, "and don't bother to deny it. The only way you can see more of each other is if he comes up here every once in a while, unless you want to run yourself ragged going down to the planet. Not a good long-term plan. So why are you being so stubborn about not inviting him up here?"

"If I invite him up here, let him into my space, introduce him to everyone, he'll think he's . . . I don't know, important to me."

Mo's mouth dropped open. "And wouldn't that be awful." Why was she trying to get the two of them back together? Did she really want to see Andrew with someone afraid to let him know that she cared? In this case, a missile had been the merciful choice, though Ann hadn't intended it that way.

She downed the rest of her juice and pushed back her chair. "I'm wasting my time here. If you don't want to be with him, don't be with him. If you want to be with him, stop pushing him away. It's that simple." Mo stood and walked away, then turned and jabbed a finger at Ann. "Oh, and you both better behave yourselves at the Joining supper." Vowing that she'd stay out of it from now on, she marched off.

JAYNE STUDIED HER quick sketch of the leaf she'd plucked from one of the arboretum's plants—from the area where Rymellans were permitted to take cuttings, of course. Normally she took her time when drawing, but she'd merely wanted to show herself that she could still do it. Should she be exhilarated or upset that, the moment her pencil had moved across the page, she'd felt as if she'd come home?

At the Indoctrination Academy, she'd wanted her compulsion to draw, to capture what she saw in her mind's eye on canvas or paper, to go away. The less she was like either of her parents, the better. But she hadn't been able to resist it. She could no more stop drawing than she could stop breathing. She'd fought to see her passion as a positive thing, not a defect, but was it hurting her? Was she wasting her time; should she try to do something else? Should she be disappointed with herself because she knew that, regardless of the answers to those questions, she'd still draw and paint?

She jumped and closed her sketchbook when Mo burst into their quarters and plopped into a chair with a sigh. "Every time I talk to Ann about relationships, I understand why we have Solitaries," Mo said.

Jayne smiled. "It didn't go well?"

"She's hopeless. Andrew's better off without her. He'll realize that—once he stops moping." She eyed Jayne's sketchbook.

"Lesley beeped me," Jayne quickly said. "She wanted to know if I wanted Robert at any of the pre-celebrations. I'm pretty sure she already knew the answer, but wanted to double-check." And maybe check up on them?

Mo nodded. "Now that it's so close, Adelaide's in full planning mode.

Because things didn't go exactly as we expected at our notification meetings—for any of us—I thought she'd tone it down a little."

Jayne recalled her conversation with Adelaide at the awards ceremony. "I think she realized there's a lot of interest in our Joining Ceremony. They'll probably report more details about our Joining than they usually do."

Mo grimaced. "Yeah."

Jayne sympathized. She wasn't thrilled with the prospect of being on the monitors either. The powers-that-be wouldn't record the ceremony, but the triad arriving at and leaving the Chosen House would be fair game.

"I'm more than happy to let Adelaide handle everything," Mo said.

Jayne was, too—sort of. She had an appointment—Adelaide's wording—with Adelaide next week to "procure what you'll wear." She wasn't looking forward to Adelaide grabbing her by the ear and dragging her down to the Trading Centre.

Mo's gaze settled on Jayne's sketchbook again. "Did you, uh, sketch while I was out?"

Jayne hesitated, then nodded.

Mo's face lit up and she leaped to her feet. "Can I see?"

Jayne's heart sank. "It's—it's just a leaf. I just wanted to do a quick sketch."

"If you don't want to show me, that's okay." Mo plunked onto the sofa next to her.

"No, I . . ." Was that Mo's hand on her back? Jayne flipped the sketchbook open and touched the leaf clipped to the first page. "It's from the arboretum. I went up there and, uh . . ." Her breath caught in her throat when Mo's hair brushed her cheek.

Mo leaned into her and pointed at Jayne's hurried replica. "Are you sure you rushed? If it was in colour, I might mistake it for an image."

"Yeah," Jayne murmured, more aware of Mo's body heat than of what she was saying. She closed the sketchbook, then froze when she felt Mo's hand on her leg. Without thinking, she moved to grasp Mo's fingers. The sketchbook slid to the floor. "Sorry," she mumbled, but didn't bend to retrieve it. She sensed Mo's eyes on her, heard—felt—her breathing. *Okay. Don't pass out.* She swallowed, then turned to Mo, and—the words she'd intended died on her lips when they met Mo's. Her need to wrap her arms around Mo and press her body against hers chased away any worries about doing it wrong. The yearnings she'd suppressed, the sensations she'd never experienced, the lust that surprised her, the pleasure of holding Mo so close and the frustration that she couldn't melt into her . . . the shock and disappointment when Mo pushed her away. Jayne wanted to kiss her forever! "Did I do something—"

"We should get out of here," Mo said breathlessly, then moved in for another kiss that led to another until she pulled back. "Seriously, let's get out of here. We can do this somewhere else."

Jayne had tried not to imagine kissing Mo, figuring that reality would never live up to her fantasy, but she'd had it backward. She understood why they had to leave. She'd never betray Lesley's trust and was sure Mo wouldn't either, but why play with fire?

"Let's go to one of the observation decks." Mo stood.

"Really?"

"Really. We'll check 5. If it's not empty, we'll go to 2. Come on." She grasped Jayne's hand and pulled her up from the sofa.

The sketchbook could stay on the carpet; Jayne wouldn't need it. As she followed Mo into the corridor, one thought rose above all the others that raced through her mind: *I'm sorry, Lesley.*

PASSING TIME WHILE she waited for Mo to show up, Lesley read announcements on the comm station in her bedroom. She could wait downstairs, but if Mo wanted to tell her anything about 72—if she and Jayne had decided not to wait, after all—Lesley wanted to hear it in private.

She selected another announcement, then shook her head when she realized that she'd already read it. Nothing was registering. Up until today, she'd managed to focus on her studies, quickly reassuring herself when she questioned her trust in her Chosens. Now she wondered if she'd been in denial. Something must have happened on 72; they couldn't have completely restrained themselves. But would Mo tell her? Did Lesley want her to?

She couldn't have kept Mo and Jayne apart forever, and insisting that they stick to their arrangement until it wouldn't bother her would

 RYMELLAN 3

have been an avoidance mechanism. No such time would ever exist. Her Chosens weren't intentionally trying to hurt her. She'd have to remind herself of that when—

The front door thumped shut. Footsteps pounded up the stairs. Lesley tensed and stared at the station's display.

The bedroom door swung open. "I thought you'd be finished studying by now," Mo said.

"I'm reading announcements." Lesley forced herself to spin her chair around but was too apprehensive to smile. She searched Mo's face for a clue. When she found one in the set of Mo's mouth and another in her rigid posture, she felt as if she'd taken a direct laser blast to the chest. Her fingers dug into her legs. She wanted to turn back to the comm station and hide, somehow push through the pain until she could be alone, but its intensity surprised and overwhelmed her. She never could have prepared herself for this.

Mo shoved her hands into her pockets. "I don't know what to say—if you want to know." Her voice quavered. "I'm sorry."

"There's no need to apologize," Lesley heard someone say. It sounded like her, but that couldn't be possible, because her head was pounding and she was too focused on not crying to speak.

"I need to tell you. I know that's selfish, but I need to do it." Mo swallowed. "We didn't sleep together. But we did get physical." She bit her lip. "I'm sorry."

Mo's honest confirmation of Lesley's suspicion blew away her defences; all hope Lesley had of maintaining her composure abandoned her. She spun back to her desk, rested her head on her arms, and let the tears flow. How much more would she lose that she could never get back? Would she ever stop hurting? One Chosen. She would have been happy with one Chosen.

"Argamon, Les. I'm sorry. Don't—oh, Argamon."

When Lesley sensed Mo next to her and felt Mo's hand on her shoulder, she slid her hand from underneath her head and reached for her. She hung onto Mo and held her close, aware of Mo's sobs but unable to offer comfort. Mo was hurting too, for a different reason. When would water douse the flames and relieve their agony? Would they ever be happy again, or had they pinned their hopes on an empty promise?

"I'm sorry," Mo whispered again.

"Stop apologizing," Lesley managed to say. "I said this would hurt. I just need to let it out."

"My feelings for you haven't changed."

"I know." If Lesley hadn't already believed that, Mo's distress and the misery in her voice would have erased any doubts Lesley had. She knew Mo still loved her, but that didn't stop her from wishing that she could have Mo to herself. It didn't assuage her grief. She was no longer *the* special person in Mo's life. That wasn't news, but knowing and accepting were two different things. She'd unreasonably clung to her unique specialness while Mo and Jayne were still holding each other at arm's length. Their relationship becoming physical was the final tug that ripped that specialness from her fingers.

She reminded herself that her relationship with Mo was still unique, that they'd share special moments without Jayne. But Mo and Jayne would have their special moments, too. Perhaps that shouldn't bother her, and perhaps it wouldn't, in time. Right now, only the losses were real, and the searing pain they left behind. Everything else was based on hope, or perhaps wishful thinking. Struggling to stem another round of tears, Lesley let go of Mo and lifted her head to wipe her eyes, but she couldn't stop sniffling.

"I want to stay, but if you want me to go . . ." Mo's voice was raw from crying.

Lesley didn't want Mo to leave, but she couldn't pretend everything was okay, not tonight. "I don't want you to go. But I can't seem to control myself, so . . ." She pulled a handkerchief from her desk drawer and held it against her nose. "I'll understand if you want to go."

"I'm staying."

Lesley could only nod. Argamon! She'd known it would tear her to pieces, but she'd hoped to at least outwardly handle it better. It could have been worse. If not for that conversation with Jayne . . .

Mo slipped her arm around Lesley's shoulders. Lesley closed her eyes when Mo's lips brushed her cheek. "I love you," Mo murmured.

Love hurts! Yet she'd wither and die without Mo's love, and could never stop loving her. She drew a shaky breath. "I—"

Someone knocked at the door. Mo jumped away. Lesley quickly wiped her eyes and shouted, "Just a minute," but the door opened.

"Since you're both here, I—" Mama broke off.

"Can it wait?" Lesley asked, eyes on her display.

"No. Mo, give me a moment with Lesley."

"Adelaide, if you don't mind—"

"Go downstairs and prepare tziva!"

Lesley could tell from Mama's hard-edged voice that she'd hold her ground until Mo went. "Go ahead, Mo. I'll join you in a minute." Despite her wet eyes and runny nose, Lesley twisted her head to nod at Mo.

Mo slapped her thighs. "Fine. Who am I, anyway? Oh, just the Chosen," she muttered as she stormed from the room.

Mama tutted and pushed the door shut.

Lesley blew her nose and turned back to the display. "I'm not in the mood for a lecture." Anything Mama might say to her, she'd already said to herself—several times.

"So, Mo's just returned from 72, I know Jayne was on 72, and now you and Mo are both beside yourselves. You've known this was inevitable from the beginning."

Lesley pushed away from the desk and shot to her feet. "So, what, Mama? I shouldn't be upset? I should have prepared myself? Don't you think I've tried? You have no idea what this feels like. It's not what you think, anyway. Not exactly."

"I have eyes, Lesley. They've obviously grown closer."

"Yes, they have. Yes, I'll pull myself together. No, I won't disgrace the family. Are we done?"

Mama frowned and stared at her. "If it had been Karen forced into a triad, I would have worried," she said quietly. "Jason, I definitely would have worried. But you . . . I've worried because it's Jayne. I haven't worried about you. You're the strongest one, you're the one I push. But I would never have pushed this hard. It's . . . difficult to watch you go through this. You have a strong family behind you. You have your papa's and my support."

Lesley's eyes welled up again. "You think I'm weak, that I need your help."

"You are not weak!" Mama snapped. "If you were weak, the triad would have ceased to exist months ago." She slowly exhaled. "This situation would try the strongest of us. There's no shame in your tears. You'll cry, but I know you'll pick yourself up and keep going. You'll also keep it in the family, all right?"

Lesley nodded. Despite Mama's words, she wasn't about to start sobbing her way around the house, and she didn't need Mama to tell her that she had to project a strong public façade—not only for herself and the Thompson name, but for the triad. She'd never show any sign of weakness to her fellow commanders-in-training or her colleagues at headquarters, with the exception of Laura. There was no point trying to pretend with her.

"We *are* here to help, and you have two strong Chosens to support you," Mama said.

"You think Jayne is strong? I thought you were worried."

"Any doubts I had about Jayne disappeared at the Festival of the Way. She has survived. She's a formidable woman." Mama raised a finger. "After a few years under our wing, perhaps she'll realize that."

"Don't push her, Mama. She needs love, not . . . guidance." Especially Mama's type of guidance.

"With two Chosens, I'm sure she'll get plenty of love," Mama said. "I'd be remiss if I didn't help her settle into our family."

And Lesley would be remiss not to watch out for her.

"Now, come downstairs. We have a few details to work out about the Joining supper."

"I'll be down in a minute." Lesley wanted thirty seconds alone to breathe, then she'd try to make herself halfway presentable.

"Don't be long." Mama opened the door.

"Thank you for the talk, Mama," Lesley said. "It helps to know that my current difficulties aren't disappointing you." She hadn't meant to sound bitter, but she did. "It really does help." Not having to pretend that everything was wonderful while at home would make it easier to pretend that it was when she wasn't with family.

Mama's face softened. "I am proud of you, proud to have you as my daughter. You'll get through this." She turned on her heel and left.

Lesley dropped into her chair with a heartfelt sigh. How she'd longed to hear those words! Any other time, they would have overcome her distress, hardened her resolve to succeed, and reminded her of her strong lineage. Maybe tomorrow. Today she'd tread water, though Mama was right about one thing: she'd get through this. Mama was right about something else, too. Lesley had two strong Chosens—who loved each other.

JAYNE WAITED FOR Carol to finish speaking to a friend over her comm unit, then pulled out her own comm unit when Carol mouthed, "Could be a while." Ever since Jayne's unit had beeped twice about half an hour ago, she'd itched to read the dispatch that was probably from Mo or Lesley. *Oh, it's from Lesley.* Jayne hesitated. After returning from 72, she'd agonized over whether to write to Lesley, worried that whatever she did would be wrong. In the end, she'd concluded that having Lesley irritated or upset with her for writing would be better than upsetting her because she hadn't written. The last thing she wanted was for Lesley to think that she didn't care, that she'd not given her a second thought on 72. Nothing could be further from the truth. Not only was she worried about Lesley, she wanted to be there for her. Lesley would probably gag, if she knew.

She read the short dispatch and stared at Lesley's closing words. *I'll be okay.* Not, *I'm okay.* For anyone else, a minuscule difference; for Lesley, huge. Jayne's stomach knotted. Should she be reassured or troubled by Lesley's honesty? Should she be disgusted with herself for deliberately hurting Lesley? No, she couldn't think that way. They'd all known that the alternative—their arrangement—would no longer work, that holding back would hurt them all in the long run. But that didn't make Jayne feel any better about Lesley. It was a difficult situation for everyone, but Lesley was suffering the most.

Jayne wanted to see her, and was still debating whether to throw caution to the wind and suggest that they meet for Berry—*coward*—when Carol lowered her comm unit with a groan.

"Argamon, that woman can talk." She pointed at Jayne's mug on the end table. "More?"

"No, thanks."

"So what were we talking about?" Carol frowned. "Oh, your trading expedition with Lesley's mama."

Jayne smiled. "And Mo. She decided to come along, so we went in her aviacraft." Adelaide hadn't protested. Maybe she'd been as relieved as Jayne. "At least I don't have to worry about what I'll wear now, to the Joining Ceremony or the celebrations." No, all she had to worry about was meeting her Chosens' extended families and their pilot friends and their parents' friends . . . and seeing flaming Robert. If she could keep him away from Lesley and Mo, she would. She would have preferred not to have him associate with them in any way. Fortunately Adelaide hadn't invited him to any of the family gatherings; he'd only be at the Chosen House and the Joining supper. Lesley must have persuaded Adelaide to leave him off the guest lists for everything else. How *was* Lesley? Jayne resolved to somehow pluck up the courage to ask to see her.

"You traded for more than your Joining outfit?"

She nodded. "Adelaide insisted." And Jayne hadn't objected. She didn't have the credits for one outfit, let alone four, and three pairs of shoes, and two cloaks. She'd swallowed her pride and told herself that she was making Adelaide happy and wouldn't embarrass the Thompsons and Middletons—any more than she already had.

Carol raised her brows. "I've only met her the once, at the supper the day after your notification meetings. At the time, I thought you might have a problem with her."

"Everyone was still in shock." Yet the two families had done their best to welcome her, and when the shock had worn off, hadn't wavered. Except Jason. That was another worry; Jayne would meet him at one of the family gatherings before the Joining Ceremony. Mo said he'd calmed down and wouldn't dare cause a scene because Adelaide would never forgive him, but Jayne would still be nervous when Lesley introduced her to him. "They've all been great, Carol. Better than I ever would have expected." Her comm unit beeped twice. Great, now all she'd think about was reading it. "It's probably from Mo," she said, trying to sound casual.

Carol's mouth turned up at the corners. "Go ahead and read it. I was blabbing for fifteen minutes."

"If you don't mind," Jayne said, already reaching for her comm unit. She frowned at the sender's name.

"What is it?" Carol asked.

"It's from one of the members of the art college's applications committee." Jayne remembered reading the name in the college's virtual brochure. She looked up. "What would she want?"

Carol leaned forward. "Read it."

She didn't want to read it, afraid of what it said. Had one of the committee members taken it upon herself to offer a scathing "critique" of the painting she'd submitted? Jayne braced herself and opened the dispatch.

Jayne Adams,

I sit on the applications committee for the C1 Art College. I saw great promise in your painting and would like to take you on as a private student. We would meet one evening a week, preferably Monday or Thursday. As per college guidelines, a third party must be present during our lessons. I always ask the student to bring someone along; it works best if it's the same person every time. Chosens usually bring their Chosens. I expect you'll do the same.

I would appreciate a response to my proposal by Friday. If you accept, we'll decide on the day and time, and I'll forward a list of required supplies.

Yours in the Way,
Joanna Reed

Wariness quickly stifled Jayne's initial burst of shocked excitement. If this instructor had liked her painting, why hadn't she been accepted into the college? And something about the name . . . Oh! Reed! Her paintings were in several of Jayne's art books. Reed was a well-respected nature painter!

"What's it about?" Carol asked.

Jayne handed her comm unit to Carol, her elation dying. Why would someone of Reed's calibre want her as a student?

A smile spread across Carol's face as she read Reed's dispatch. "This is great!"

"I don't know," Jayne mumbled.

Carol's jaw dropped. "What do you mean, you don't know?" She set Jayne's comm unit on the coffee table. "This is what you've always wanted."

"Maybe it's a joke."

"A joke?" Carol's brow furrowed. "Why would an instructor send you a prank dispatch? Not only would it violate Article 663, but what would she be hoping to accomplish?"

To get Jayne's hopes up and then stomp all over them. As for violating an article, that had never stopped anyone from harassing her before.

"She sounds sincere to me," Carol said.

"Maybe we'll set up a lesson, and when I get there, the entire admissions committee will be there to laugh at me and tell me it was a joke."

Carol tutted. "You don't really believe that! Come on, Jayne. It's bad enough that everyone else holds you back. Don't do it to yourself."

"I wonder if those college guidelines were in effect before the Incident."

"You're thinking of your papa."

Jayne nodded. As she'd read the dispatch, thoughts of him and Brenda Stewart in his studio had run through her mind.

"Does it matter why those guidelines are in effect?" Carol asked.

"No, but what if Reed knows details about the Incident?"

Carol's brows drew together. "I'm not following."

"She's an artist. She could have known Papa. She might have heard details about the Incident that aren't common knowledge."

"And, what? She decides to play some type of sick joke by luring you to her studio in a re-enactment of . . . whatever went on?" Carol's forehead puckered. "To what end? Assume this is a genuine proposal, because it *is*."

But what about others who did know what had taken place in Papa's studio? What would they think when they heard that an Adams was taking private lessons? Would the presence of a third party be enough to stop the whispers? *Stop it!* She was being paranoid, at least about that last fear. The files on the Incident were shut tight. Hardly anyone knew the details, and how many of them would know that Jayne was taking private art lessons? She'd be insane to turn down Reed's proposal. The thought of taking lessons did frighten her, because she'd never worked on her art with anyone—not since Papa. Someone would study her technique, make suggestions, teach her new methods—and offer criticism. Real, constructive criticism, not the knee-jerk kind. "You're right."

"Of course I am!" Carol declared with a smile. "Find out if Mo will go with you, then tell Reed you accept."

"No."

Carol's eyes bulged. "Jayne!"

"She said I should bring the same person with me to every lesson. Mo doesn't have a regular schedule. There's no way she can be available every Monday or Thursday night." And Mo wasn't her first choice, anyway. "I'll have to ask Lesley." She wanted to ask Lesley.

"Oh, because Lesley's an Interior officer. Her presence will make everyone think twice about reporting bogus violations."

"No. Because Mo and I see enough of each other already." But balancing her time with her Chosens wasn't the only reason she wanted Lesley to go with her to the lessons. When Jayne had allowed herself to wallow in her disappointment at being rejected by the art college, and had thrown what amounted to a temper tantrum, rudely ignoring beeps and childishly removing all her artwork from the walls, Lesley hadn't judged her. She hadn't told her she was foolish, spouted platitudes, told Jayne to get over it, or twisted the application committee's knife further. She'd listened; she'd comforted. Jayne would feel safe making mistakes in front of her, and wouldn't be consumed by shame when Lesley heard Reed's criticism at the same time she did. Jayne trusted both her Chosens, but for this, she wanted Lesley. "I'll ask Lesley, but I don't know if she'll do it."

"She'll know how important this is for you. Why would she say no?"

Because Jayne had hurt her in a way nobody else could. But, once again, Carol was right. Unless it would interfere with her studies, Lesley would say yes, and Jayne's love for her would deepen—along with her guilt.

MO EXAMINED THE seating plan Adelaide had drawn up for the Joining supper. She peeked at Les, then reached over and squeezed her hand. She wanted to smile and cry when she felt Les's answering squeeze. Here they were reviewing and discussing all the details they'd agreed upon last week, while avoiding more painful topics—or maybe that wasn't true. What was there to say? If Les wanted to talk about it, she'd talk. Mo had expected Les to shut her out of her life while she licked her wounds, but their upcoming Joining Ceremony kept bringing them together, and Les seemed to want Mo around; she'd even invited her along to the Military Academy when she'd attended a half-hour meeting about the next phase of her commander training. Afterward, they'd flown sims together—cooperative sims, not ones in which Les could blast her.

Yep, a week after their Joining Ceremony, Les would be off to the Military Academy. Lousy timing, but at least her Chosens could visit and it would only be for two weeks.

"It looks like Mama did exactly what we wanted," Les murmured.

Mo nodded. All their *Falcon* friends were sitting together. Peggy was at a secondary family table, not at the main table, but it was the best they could do, and more than some families would do, under the circumstances. Ann was at the 72 table, which was comfortably away from the main family table, where Andrew would be. They could try to lob food at each other, but since they wouldn't have a clear line of sight, someone else would end up with potato in their hair. Best of all, Mo and Les had managed to persuade Adelaide to put Carol and Ronald at the main table. Robert Adams and his date would sit with Jayne's other relatives at a secondary table. When they were all on display at the Chosen House, they'd treat him like a brother. At the private supper, where appearances weren't as important, they'd knock him down a notch.

"Should we shake Robert's hand when we meet him?" Mo asked.

Les looked up. "He is family, so we can't snub him. It would be an insult to only nod."

"Do you think Jason will shake Jayne's hand?"

"He'd better."

Mo grunted.

"He will, and if he doesn't, at least it'll happen in private, not on the steps." Les shook her head. "But I don't think we need to worry. I'm sure Mama has told him what's expected of him."

"Yeah." Adelaide wouldn't leave such things to chance. When she'd realized that the Joining of a triad was an "event," she'd decided to go all out on the Joining Ceremony and the celebrations that led up to it. No small gathering of the embarrassed families; no slinking in and out of the Chosen House. Nope. On their Joining Day, the Thompsons and Middletons would behave as if a triad with Jayne was the best thing that had ever happened to their families. Adelaide's tendency to go over the top with every celebration normally irritated Mo. Not this time.

She lifted her elbow when Les tugged at the seating plan. "Let's talk about something else," Les said, moving the plan aside. She met Mo's eyes and hesitated.

Mo forced her gaze to remain on Les's face. So much for not talking about it. "What?" she squeaked.

"The crypt. You haven't been. Don't you think you should visit before the Joining Ceremony?"

"There's been so much going on."

Les's brows shot up.

"I know, I know, when I'm not on 72, I should have time." How often had she practised her violin, played cards with Andrew or Nathan, or kept herself busy while the crypt nagged at her? "It's going to be the one blot on our Joining Day." She drew a shuddering breath and gripped Les's hand. "Most of the time, when I think of her, I'm okay. If I tear up, it's because I miss her, not because . . . I'm blaming myself. But when we're in the Joining Chamber, and when I look around the main table at the supper, I'm going to feel it." Mama wouldn't see her Join, would never know that Mo had been right, that Les, the one she'd loved from the moment she was capable of loving, was her Chosen. Mama would never meet Jayne. "I want to go to the crypt. I thought you wanted to go with me." She sounded whiny and knew she wasn't being fair.

"I do, and we've had plenty of opportunity to go with Jayne," Les said evenly. "But you never suggest it, and I haven't wanted to do it for you."

"Maybe I don't want to be reminded that I'm moving on with life—" Falling in love, Joining, teaching, smiling and laughing "—while Mama lies in the crypt."

Les's forehead creased. "You can't feel guilty for living your life."

She felt guilty for a lot more than that. "Maybe I'm just being selfish. I'm afraid of how it's going to feel, and I don't want to depress myself right now."

"If you don't go, it'll hang over you, from the first party to our Joining Day. You'll feel worse when you look around the main table."

Mo nodded. She wanted her melancholy moments to be pure, not tainted with guilt.

"Let's go on my first day off," Les said. "All we have that day is a gathering in the evening, and Jayne will be living on the estate by then."

"Okay. You might have to drag me."

"You can try to dig in your heels, but there will be two of us. We'll each take a hand."

Despite her surprise, Mo couldn't help but chuckle. Then her love for Les took her breath away. She wanted to stand, wrap her arms around her, hold her tighter than she'd ever held her before, but Les wouldn't want that right now. She wanted Mo to play along, not make a big deal out of every time she managed to crack a joke, or say Jayne's name without punching the table. If their positions were reversed . . . Argamon, when Jayne had told Mo about the art college instructor's offer and the reasons she wanted Les to accompany her to the lessons, Mo had seethed with jealousy. She had no right! She must be supportive. Supportive! "Did you figure out when you and Jayne will see, um . . ."

"Reed? We're meeting on Thursday, just so they can chat and see if they're comfortable with each other. The lessons will have to wait until after I've finished at the Military Academy."

"I guess with that and everything around our Joining Ceremony, there's no point starting now," Mo said, fighting the urge to say, "Hey, I'm around on Thursday. I'll go with you!" She wasn't even sure if she was jealous because Jayne had chosen Les, or because Les was going with Jayne. Probably both. Telling herself that she couldn't be included all the time wouldn't stop her from chewing her thumbnails on Thursday night, but it had prevented her from behaving like a selfish idiot—so far.

JAYNE TOOK A deep breath and slowly exhaled when she spotted the entrance to Reed's studio.

Lesley turned to her. "You all right?"

She nodded, not wanting to poison Lesley's mind with the thoughts running through her own. She hadn't stepped foot inside a proper studio for a long time. Would she always think of Papa and Brenda Stewart every time she came for a lesson? Sometimes she wished it was possible to erase memories, but the lessons she'd learned, the person she was today, would disappear with them, leaving behind someone who didn't understand herself.

They'd reached the door. Nervous, Jayne knocked on it, then jumped when it immediately opened.

"Good, I like prompt students. Come in." Reed—in her fifties, Jayne guessed—stepped aside.

Jayne surveyed the cluttered studio in wonder as she followed Reed inside. The magnificent paintings on the walls, the smell of paint, the draped canvases on their easels . . . and Papa. Why couldn't she have been like Robert and taken after neither of them? She forced her eyes back to the paintings, which covered almost every inch of two walls and most of a third. One painting leaped out at her: her own!

Reed wiped her fingers on her smock, something she did often, from the looks of it. "I've had the same studio for almost thirty years and can't bring myself to part with anything, even the ones I hate."

Jayne's heart sank. Was Reed referring to her painting?

"But where are my manners? I'm Joanna Reed." Jayne nodded and opened her mouth to reply, but Reed continued. "And you're Jayne Adams, but I'm going to call you Jayne and you're going to call me Joanna. And you," her gaze shifted to Lesley, "are Lieutenant Commander Thompson, but that's probably a bit too formal here, don't you think?"

Lesley's expression remained neutral. "Call me Lesley."

"I was hoping you'd say that. Come through to the back." Joanna wheeled.

Jayne followed her, carefully navigating around the odd crumpled sheet, discarded brush, and coloured pencil. Her mouth dropped open when she entered an immaculate room containing a tidy desk, plush guest armchairs, and a carpet she could probably eat off of.

"Let me take your cloaks." Joanna hung them on the row of shiny cloak hooks and swept her arm out. "Sit yourselves down." Jayne lowered herself into one of the comfortable armchairs as Lesley did the same. Instead of going to the chair behind the desk, Joanna went to sit in the remaining free armchair, then groaned and frowned down at her smock. "I'm not supposed to wear this in here, but we won't tell her."

"Who?" Lesley asked, voicing the question in Jayne's mind.

"My Chosen." Joanna sat down and pointed toward the messy studio they'd first entered. "Not long after we Joined, she cleaned the studio. First and last time. We have an agreement. She can tidy up in here. Not out there." She crossed her legs. "Now, let's get down to business. First, I have to apologize to you, Jayne."

Jayne tensed. Had Joanna changed her mind about the lessons? "Why?"

"For not contacting you sooner. I should have sent you a dispatch the moment I left the meeting. But instead I agonized. What would they think if I took you on as a student? Would my reputation suffer? Would I lose my other students?" Joanna tutted. "I let that foolishness go on for too long.

"You did a very brave thing, applying for admittance. When Pauline lifted your painting to show it to us, I was instantly excited at the prospect of having the artist enter our program, but then I read your name, and I knew it would never happen. I don't fight battles I know I'll lose—at least, not anymore," she said with a wry smile. "So I sat silently and fumed while they all came up with reasons why you weren't suitable for the program—all nonsense, of course. I left knowing I wanted to work with you, but I wasn't as brave as you, I'm afraid. I needed time to pluck up the courage. I did have the good sense to request your painting, though. And no, it's not one of the ones I hate. I think it's brilliant. I see your papa's influence, but you're definitely your own artist."

Jayne could hardly believe her ears. "You know of my papa's work?" she asked, struggling to accept Joanna's praise as genuine.

Joanna nodded. "Of course. Your papa was widely known, and very well-respected in the art community. His . . . death was a tragedy on all sorts of levels. You don't need me to tell you that, I'm sure. Anyway, I'm pleased you're here. Have you worked with anyone before?" She frowned. "No, of course you haven't. Can you accept constructive criticism, along with praise?"

Constructive criticism? After years of enduring thoughtless, malicious comments about her work, she'd cherish suggestions and admonitions from an artist who wanted to help her. Working with Joanna would be the oasis she'd dreamed of as she'd dragged herself starving through the unforgiving desert, determined not to die. Every well-meaning comment, whether good or bad, would be a drop of water on a parched tongue. "I want to learn, to improve. I'd like to think I'm getting better, but I don't know."

"You've done remarkably well on your own, though that's not surprising. Your papa had more innate talent in his little finger than most of our students will ever develop. If you inherited even a quarter of it . . . I find teaching most rewarding when I learn as much from the student as the student learns from me. I suspect that will be the case here. Now, what about you, Lesley?" Joanna turned to her. "What will you do while we're working? I don't think we need her staring at us, do we, Jayne?"

"I always have work to do," Lesley said. "As long as I have my comm unit, I'll be busy."

Joanna grunted. "Interior never stops working, does it?" She held up four fingers. "Four siblings, three Interior officers," she said by way of explanation, lowering one of her fingers. "I expect you'll find me more relaxed around you than most. No violations, nothing to fear." Her mouth turned up at the corners. "The conversation around our next family supper table will be quite interesting when I tell them about my new student. Not that I see them very often. They're all up in the L sectors. I moved down here when Abby and I Joined."

Since Joanna wore her Chosen ring on her right hand, that wasn't surprising. Joined couples usually lived in the Principal's home sector.

"But enough chatter. We won't start anything new tonight, of course, so why don't we have a look at your painting and have a little discussion about it? Sound good?"

Jayne nodded. "Yes."

Joanna fixed her gaze on Lesley. "Ground rule, Lesley—and I know you're good with rules. No interrupting, no talking. You will hear me praise Jayne's work. You will hear me criticize Jayne's work. Sometimes she'll get upset with me. Sometimes I'll get upset with her. If we want your opinion about something, we'll ask for it. All right?"

"I'm merely here as the third party," Lesley said. "I'll be quiet."

Jayne cringed. Lesley appeared mildly amused, not offended, but was she regretting her decision to attend the lessons? She was too polite to say anything to Joanna. What would she say when they were alone?

"Good." Joanna pushed to her feet. "Well then, let's go back into the studio."

Butterflies took flight in Jayne's stomach as she rose. It was one thing to say that she was ready to accept constructive criticism, and another to listen to it. It would be difficult—and frightening—but she *would* listen. She *would* improve. She wouldn't squander an opportunity she never thought she'd have. It wasn't a joke. For the first time, someone was taking her seriously as an artist.

She turned when Lesley nudged her arm. A lump rose in her throat at Lesley's encouraging smile. No, Joanna wasn't the first person to take her seriously; she was the first artist to do so. Carol, Lesley, Mo . . . if not for their support, Jayne wouldn't be following Joanna back into the studio. When Jayne's lessons began, Lesley would sit quietly for two hours every week so Jayne could grow as an artist. How many would perform such a kind and loving act for someone who was hurting her, intentionally or not?

Jayne had resolved not to tell Lesley about her feelings for her until Lesley showed signs of reciprocating those feelings. But that might never happen, and Jayne no longer wanted to use it as an excuse to remain silent. Lesley deserved to know that both her Chosens loved her—and Jayne would tell her.

JAYNE SMILED AS she left Joanna's studio. She'd survived! Yes, indignation had stirred when Joanna had pointed out areas for improvement and made suggestions, but Jayne had bitten back any retort, determined to listen and learn. Her pride had soon taken a backseat to her passion for her work. When she'd explained a colour choice in response to a query, and Joanna had grunted and nodded, tears had sprung to Jayne's eyes. To discuss her painting with another artist, someone who understood, who took her seriously . . . she'd forgotten how wonderful it felt.

But she hadn't forgotten Lesley. Every time she'd cast a surreptitious peek her way, Lesley had been focused on her comm unit. Had she overheard the criticism? What had she thought? "Did you manage to get any work done, or were we too much of a distraction?" Jayne asked her.

Lesley patted the cloak pocket containing her comm unit. "I got a lot done. I answered a number of outstanding dispatches."

Good, maybe Joanna's more critical comments hadn't registered with Lesley. "I know what it's like to be so absorbed in what you're doing that the world around you disappears."

"Occasionally I took a break and listened to your conversation." Lesley raised a finger. "But I stayed quiet."

Despite her embarrassment over what Lesley may have overheard, Jayne chuckled. "Sorry. She *is* a little blunt."

"I don't mind. I prefer that to feigned respect, and she wasn't disrespectful." Lesley turned to her. "I respect that she had the courage to take you on as a student, in spite of the potential consequences."

Jayne agreed, especially since Papa had probably committed Chosen Violations in his studio. She shuddered. Had Brenda Stewart been a private student and he'd ignored any guidelines? No, it must have been a group class, but hadn't anyone noticed that Stewart always stayed behind? Or did Jayne have it all wrong? She was only guessing at what had happened—or rather, where it had happened. If any Interior officers who knew the details of the Incident found out that she was taking lessons with Joanna, what would they think? "Thank you for agreeing to come with me. With an Interior officer there, nobody can accuse me of anything."

Lesley was silent for a moment before asking, "Is that why you wanted me to go with you, rather than Mo? Because I'm an Interior officer?"

"No!" Jayne's mortification deepened when she saw Lesley's tight jaw. Had she hurt her? Argamon, why did she always say the worst possible thing? "No, that's not why at all." *I love you and feel safe with you!* But the words wouldn't come out. What if Lesley was horrified? Jayne wanted to tell her, but she'd wait until they landed near her apartment, so they wouldn't have to endure an awkward aviacraft ride. "I asked you because I trust you. I trust both of you, but I go with Mo to 72 and see her other times . . . and we don't see each other much." Wondering how Lesley would respond, Jayne held her breath.

"And I guess it helps that I'm not on an irregular schedule, or at least I won't be after the Military Academy."

"That helps, but it's not the reason I asked you." Her frustration that Lesley hadn't replied to her last point shifted into disgust with herself. If she wasn't such a coward, she wouldn't have to hope that Lesley, of all people, would somehow give away her feelings. "I asked you because I wanted it to be you. But taking private art lessons, being in Joanna's studio . . . I can't help but think of the Incident and what I know about my papa's involvement—or what I think I know."

"If anyone were to accuse you, my presence wouldn't lead to an automatic dismissal of the accusation. I am biased, after all."

"According to Joanna, everyone else brings their Chosens. Why—" Jayne groaned. "I was about to ask why we wouldn't be treated the same as them."

"Actually, we would be, in this case. Their Chosens are biased too. The fact that someone's Chosen was present wouldn't stop me from investigating a tip." Lesley paused. "Having the Chosen or someone else there means that people's suspicions are less likely to be raised, so nobody feels compelled to alert Interior in the first place. If someone does report a suspected violation, a third party presence wouldn't be enough to protect the accused, but the burden of proof would be on us."

"I think your reputation would be a great help in our case. I doubt anyone would believe you'd cover up a violation, especially since it's me. I'm sure everyone thinks you're keeping an eye on me."

"I am," Lesley said. "But not because I'm worried that you're weak in the Way," she added quietly.

Jayne's heart leaped. Because she cared? Of course she cared; they were Chosens. But did she only care out of a sense of obligation, or did she *care*? If Jayne wasn't so afraid to ask, and to share her own feelings, she wouldn't have to wonder. As soon as they landed in the holding area, she'd force herself to say the words aloud.

But by the time the aviacraft touched down, her courage had abandoned her. What was she thinking? Lesley had enough to deal with already. The last thing she needed was a lovesick Chosen pouring her heart out to her. No, it would be selfish to tell her, to burden Lesley with yet another problem while she was still struggling to accept the relationship between her two Chosens. Yes, that would be the epitome of selfish. Lesley would probably ask what else Jayne wanted from her; hadn't she already taken enough? If Jayne truly loved her, the best thing she could do right now was not tell her.

After hastily unbuckling her seatbelt, she mumbled, "Good night," slid the aviacraft door open, and hopped out. But she cursed herself as the aviacraft lifted off. She should have asked Lesley if she wanted a tziva, or at least thanked her again for spending her entire evening babysitting. Then Jayne remembered her sketchbook and wanted to scream. It was on one of the backseats; she hadn't been brave enough to take it into the studio with her. She'd wanted to meet Joanna first, be reassured that it wasn't a joke and her work wouldn't be ripped apart.

In case Lesley remembered it and turned around, Jayne pulled out her comm unit, intending to quickly write a dispatch. She beeped her instead.

"Are you okay?" Lesley said as soon as she answered.

"I'm fine. Sorry, I left my sketchbook on the craft. Maybe Mo can bring it with her tomorrow."

"I'll let her know." Lesley paused. "You sure you're all right?"

"Yeah. I just didn't want you to waste your time bringing it back." And now she felt stupid. Why would Lesley turn around? "Sorry to bother you. Good night."

"Wait!"

Jayne stopped herself from hitting the disconnect button just in time.

"Can I look at it?" Lesley asked.

"What?"

"Your sketchbook."

Jayne swallowed. "Yes."

"Great, thanks. Good night."

"Bye." Jayne stared at her comm unit. Her rapport with Joanna had fed the hungry artist within, thrilling and satisfying her. Lesley's desire to look at her drawings gratified her on a completely different level. She wanted to leap into the air, shout at the top of her lungs, and do cartwheels.

LESLEY CLOSED JAYNE'S sketchbook with a sigh and set it on the night table. She should lie down and turn out the light, but she doubted she'd sleep.

The weight against her right arm lifted. Mo straightened and yawned. "Why the big sigh? You didn't like them?"

Jayne's drawings had evoked not dislike, but a surprising emotion: anger. "I'm glad Joanna Reed has come into the picture, but Jayne should have gone to art school long ago. Her work will never hang in galleries. She'll never be in the art books."

"She can thank her parents for that."

"It's not supposed to be that way!" When she felt Mo's hand on her arm, Lesley took a couple of deep breaths. "Sorry. But it's not. Children aren't supposed to pay for the crimes of their parents. The Adamses were executed. That should have been the end of it."

"Come on, Les, both her parents committed Chosen Violations." Clearly expecting to be blasted, Mo held up her hands. "I agree that she shouldn't have to pay for her parents' crimes. I just think it's naïve to expect that it wouldn't touch her at all."

"Of course people would be a little wary of her, but barring her from art school? All the harassment? She was almost killed outside her apartment!"

Mo lifted a skeptical brow. "And before you got to know her, you believed she was an upstanding Rymellan."

Lesley patted her chest with both hands. "I didn't know she existed until a few days before I met her."

Mo rolled her eyes.

"Okay, you're right," Lesley admitted. "Yes, I wouldn't have wanted to be her friend. Yes, I would have wondered what people would think if they saw me talking to her. But I wouldn't have harassed her, or stopped her from doing what she wanted to do with her life." She narrowed her eyes at Mo. "I suppose you would have been her best friend."

"Hey, I'm not the one getting all indignant about it! I don't like it. In fact, I hate the way she's been treated. But I can't change what happened." Mo's mouth tightened. "I guess going to see Reed with her was a bigger deal than I thought."

It was a huge deal. Lesley hadn't appreciated that until she'd sat quietly on a stool and listened to Jayne and Joanna, heard both the praise and the criticism, noticed the way Jayne's voice had shaken—with outrage, shock, and fear—when she'd first responded to Joanna's less positive comments. She'd seen Jayne's confidence grow through the course of the conversation, along with her determination to learn and her willingness to listen and accept Joanna's suggestions as gentle guidance meant to help, not hurt. At times Lesley had felt like an interloper, eavesdropping on the most personal and intimate of conversations, seeing Jayne at her most vulnerable—and at her strongest.

Sharing tonight with Jayne had alleviated some of the hurt over Mo and Jayne's relationship. Lesley didn't feel as left out. She'd have *her* special moments, too. And Mo was here, right next to her. Lesley's world hadn't come to an end. She'd hurt; she'd cry; she'd have her days when she'd rail against what the Chosen Council had done to her and wish that Jayne had never come into their lives. But she would survive this, and so would her relationship with Mo, and so would the triad. She'd told herself that over and over. Tonight she believed it. "I am glad that she trusted me enough to take me with her. I don't mean to imply that she doesn't trust you. She does." Lesley shrugged. "I think she wants me to feel included." It had worked.

"Well, she chose you to go. I have to respect that," Mo said grudgingly.

"I seem to recall someone wise saying that we're not competing against each other, or something like that."

"Whoever said that is an idiot." Mo collapsed back onto her pillow with a snort. "You already know I'm not going to be half as mature as you about everything, so think about that when I'm spouting nuggets of wisdom, okay? I don't want your expectations to be too high."

Lesley's smile hid her concern. Tonight she'd also learned, or perhaps confirmed, that her feelings for Jayne had grown beyond friendship. On the way home, she'd thought about whether to tell her. She wouldn't keep it to herself forever, but did they need to further complicate the situation right now? No. At the same time, shouldn't Jayne know before they Joined? Then again, if Lesley told Jayne, she'd have to tell Mo, right before their Joining Ceremony—not that there would ever be a good time. Lesley quietly sighed. She had to make a decision, and quickly. Her world hadn't come to an end, but it had certainly changed.

FROM THE SINGLE chair remaining in the living room, Jayne gazed at the empty spot where the sofa had sat. She'd spent the afternoon watching with mixed feelings as her personal movers, as Mo called them, transferred the rest of her furniture from her apartment to a cargo craft. Usually Rymellans engaged a pilot and moving crew along with the craft, but the Middleton brothers had volunteered their muscle, so Jayne wouldn't have to endure sneers and dirty looks. Ronald had joined the group, and they'd emptied the rooms in no time, leaving behind the chair so Jayne would have somewhere to sit while she waited for Lesley—Mo was piloting the cargo craft. She'd drop several of Jayne's items at Carol's, a couple at Karen's, and the rest at a recycling depot—except for a few boxes containing Jayne's books and clothes. Mo knew not to drop those off, or she'd be in trouble! The two bags at Jayne's feet contained her work.

Lesley was flying over right after her class and should be here soon. Then Jayne would leave this apartment for the last time. She'd miss the solitude, at least initially. The coming week was packed with social and family engagements, leaving her little time to herself, or many opportunities to talk to Lesley alone. So today was *it*. Jayne wouldn't lose her nerve, as she'd done last week. If she didn't tell Lesley about her feelings today, she might not have the chance before their Joining Ceremony. The last thing she wanted was for Lesley to feel like a third wheel at her own Joining! Revealing her feelings right before they were going to spend a lot of time in each other's company wasn't ideal, but she'd left herself no choice, unless she wanted to feel horrible during their ceremony.

And how long could she hide her feelings? She'd grinned all day over Lesley's dispatch about her sketches—she was smiling now! *Privileged to view your drawings. Humbled to have such a talented Chosen.* Argamon! But, as usual, a whisper of apprehension marred her pleasure. *Mo.* Regardless of whether Lesley reciprocated Jayne's feelings, Mo would feel threatened, and so Jayne had quickly decided against talking to Mo first. She had to tell Lesley, and let her decide when and how to break it to Mo. Even if Lesley felt the same way . . . well, she didn't. Or maybe she did. No, she didn't. But even if she did, they might decide to keep it to themselves until after the Joining Ceremony, so Mo wouldn't have to deal with it during one of the most social weeks of her life—and during the Ceremony.

On the other hand, hiding her feelings for Lesley from Mo would be just as bad as hiding them from Lesley, wouldn't it? How would Mo feel when she found out that her two Chosens had shared a secret while they'd stood in the Joining Chamber? Maybe Jayne should just keep her mouth shut. She didn't want to hurt Mo and see her pain. She'd desperately want to comfort her and feel hypocritical when doing so.

No, she had to tell Lesley. Here she was, elated over what Lesley had written about her sketches. Now it was her turn to praise. How many times had Lesley encouraged her and told her that her name didn't matter? How often had Jayne appreciated Lesley for her thoughtfulness, her steadfast commitment to the spirit of the Way, and her determination to do what was best for the triad, no matter what the personal cost? Jayne had silently admired her many times, but she'd never told her, maybe because she knew that, the moment she opened her mouth, she'd gush and betray her feelings.

Too bad. She'd taken so much; it was time to give back. Confessing her love to Lesley was the right thing to do; she only doubted her timing. *Will Lesley be grateful that I told her before the Joining Ceremony, or will she wish I'd waited?*

A rap at the door interrupted Jayne's musing. Suddenly nervous, she rose. She was about to find out.

JOINED

.....

LESLEY SQUARED HER SHOULDERS AND WAITED patiently outside Jayne's apartment door. When it swung open, she forced a smile. "They all gone?"

Jayne nodded and beckoned her inside. "They left about twenty minutes ago," she said, her voice echoing around the empty apartment.

The living room contained only a single chair with a couple of bags at its feet. Lesley glanced at the spot where the comm station had sat on a desk, and was surprised to see that it wasn't there. Had Communications worried that nobody would want to use a station touched by an Adams? Would they sterilize the apartment, too?

"They came for it this morning," Jayne said calmly.

Certain that the same thoughts running through her mind had also run through Jayne's, Lesley grunted. After their notification meetings, she'd only seen an Adams whenever she looked at Jayne, but Jayne's family history was no longer the first thing that sprang to mind. Now Lesley saw an artist; a reader; a thoughtful, considerate woman; a Rymellan strong in the Way. A woman Mo loved, who loved Mo in return. A Chosen. A promise of better days to come.

Before Lesley had found out that Mo was her Chosen, she'd always expected to have mixed feelings as her Joining Day approached. She'd been right about her emotions, but wrong about why she'd experience them. She wasn't pining for the woman she loved and wondering if she'd ever be capable of loving the woman the Chosen Council had selected for her. She wasn't worried that she'd have to play-act for the rest of her life. She wouldn't flinch at every mention of the Middletons, wouldn't lie awake at night yearning for Mo. Mo was her Chosen; they would spend their lives together.

She wouldn't miss Mo; she'd miss the exclusivity of their relationship. She wouldn't worry about not loving Jayne; she'd worry about how loving Jayne would affect her relationship with Mo. On the other hand, she would Join in honesty, and would truly honour her Chosens.

As for today, she'd forced a smile because she could appreciate that moving Jayne to the estate was the first step toward her becoming a full-fledged member of the Thompson family. If Lesley wasn't hurting over Mo and Jayne's relationship and still trying to decide whether she should tell Jayne about her own feelings, her smile would have been genuine. That applied to the entire upcoming week. She didn't want to look back on this important time in her life with regret, so she'd put on a smile for all the gatherings by borrowing on the happiness she hoped for in the future. Part of her believed—no, knew!—that this was a positive step in her life. Before their notifications, she'd worried about Mo's conviction that they were Chosens, had seen it as a reckless fantasy that would only lead to despair. Now she understood it, and believed that her hope for the future stood on firmer ground than Mo's ever had.

"Are they coming back for the chair today?" she asked.

Jayne nodded. "Mo said something about Neil and Barbara wanting it."

"I'm sure we could have fit a couple of pieces of furniture into our house," Lesley said, aware that Jayne had let go of everything except her books, clothes, and work.

"It's all old. And I guess I want to move forward. Most of the furniture came from my aunt and uncle."

Lesley nodded. If she were in Jayne's shoes, she wouldn't want reminders of an estranged family around her, either. She lifted one of the bags and slung it over her shoulder. She expected Jayne to pick up the other bag, but Jayne stood silently staring at her. Perhaps she wanted to linger a minute; she was leaving her home of many years for the last time. "Do you want some time alone? I can wait for you in the craft," Lesley said.

Jayne's eyes grew distant, then she heaved her shoulders and reached for the other bag. "No, let's go."

"We have to stop at the Trading Centre," Lesley said as she stepped into the corridor. She waited while Jayne shut the door, and noticed that Jayne didn't stop for one last look over her shoulder. "I have to pick up an order for Mama."

"Okay," Jayne mumbled.

Lesley glanced at her. Jayne appeared pensive, but she gave Lesley a small smile when their eyes met. Perhaps she was fretting over the upcoming events—the fussing, the Joining Ceremony! The constant socializing could wear her down. Lesley made a mental note to keep an eye on her.

JAYNE WANTED TO bang her forehead against the panel in front of her. Why couldn't she open her mouth and tell Lesley how she felt? What was the worst that could happen? Oh, just that Lesley would be horrified or angry, wish that Jayne had remained silent until after the Joining Ceremony, and refuse to speak to her. No, Lesley would be too polite to shun her during all the gatherings, but Jayne would know that every word out of Lesley's mouth, every introduction with Lesley at her side, was fuelled by obligation. Jayne didn't want that, but the alternative—keeping her mouth shut to the point that she was starting to feel dishonest—would mar her Joining Day. She had to speak up—and would, if her brain would let her.

She couldn't believe it when the aviacraft touched down outside the Trading Centre. *We're already here?*

"Do you want to come in, or stay here?" Lesley asked as she unbuckled her seatbelt and rose. She removed a knapsack from one of the cargo containers and offered an apologetic shrug as she added, "It's a special order, so Mama wants me to count all the items, to make sure everything's there. I might not be back for fifteen minutes or so."

"I'll wait for you here," Jayne said, then changed her mind. "Actually, I'll wait outside. I feel like some air." She felt like pacing, to work off her nervous energy. But since she didn't want to draw attention to herself, she'd settle for standing up.

She followed Lesley off the craft and waved as Lesley disappeared through the Trading Centre's entrance. She'd hoped that watching people come and go would distract her from thinking about her predicament, but C3's Trading Centre wasn't a busy one. The same old thoughts were soon running through her mind, taunting her about her cowardice and reminding her in graphic detail of how Lesley's face would look when Jayne revealed her feelings.

The nearby public monitor called to her. Normally she avoided them, but viewing announcements had to be better than the unsettling scenarios playing out in her head, and the monitor area was empty. But when she tapped the *On* button, she was instantly transported back to the day of Owen's execution procession, and the bullying she'd suffered at the hands of the lieutenant and her accomplice.

Jayne's hands clenched as the monitor replayed scenes of Lesley walking in the procession with someone nattering on in the background about how, only a few days later, the lieutenant commander had learned that she was in a historic triad. Curiously, the voiceover didn't mention the identities of the other two triad members. The military was still grooming Lesley for a rise to admiral, so maybe they were hoping that Rymellans would eventually forget that one of her Chosens was an Adams.

The memory of the lieutenant's hand pressed against the back of her head, forcing her to watch the procession, and the lieutenant's mockery of her sketches afterward, made Jayne want to turn off the monitor and walk away. But then the recording of Lesley marching in the procession cut to the moments after the body had been carried through the crematorium's gates. Laura thrust her fist into the air, flowers rained down, and everyone sang the Song of Rymel. The camera zoomed in on Lesley.

Jayne remembered this! Lesley had almost cried. At the time, Lesley's reaction had been noteworthy because Jayne wouldn't have expected an Interior officer to show her emotions at such an event; in fact, she wouldn't have been surprised if Interior officers weren't capable of shedding a tear. Now she was absolutely flabbergasted. Lesley, almost breaking down at a public event? What had been running through her mind? Jayne was sure it wasn't anything to do with the procession itself; Lesley wouldn't get emotional over that.

Then it hit her, with a certainty that took her breath away. *Mo.* They were separated during that period, and not by choice. Had Lesley wondered if Mo was watching? Had she worried about whether Mo still cared? From what Mo had said about the forced separation, Jayne had gathered that they'd had no contact with each other and had vowed not to pester their families for news. They'd stumbled around in the dark, trying to put their relationship behind them while desperately hoping that the other never would. Knowing them as she did, Jayne could only imagine how horrible they must have felt.

When their Chosen Papers had arrived, an indescribable joy must have banished the despair—only to be crushed at their notification meetings. Jayne had done her best to hold her head high when she'd walked into C3's Chosen House that day. If she'd known about their situation, the weight added to the existing burden of her family name would have slumped her shoulders, and the first words out of her mouth upon meeting her Chosens would have been, "I'm sorry." They'd told her about their relationship soon afterward, but she'd been so wrapped up in her concerns about CT134 that she hadn't immediately appreciated how much they loved each other.

Sighing, Jayne turned off the monitor and strolled back to the avia-craft. If she'd found herself in a triad with anyone else under the same circumstances, she wouldn't be worrying about the upcoming family gatherings, how Lesley felt about her, whether she should confess her feelings to Lesley, and how Mo would react. She wouldn't be worrying about anything. An executioner's stick would have ended her life months ago.

Waiting near the craft with her arms folded, she wanted to run and hide when she spotted Lesley approaching a few minutes later. Lesley must hate her. Jayne wasn't responsible for the triad, but did she have to fall for Mo and act on her feelings? She should have stamped out any romantic feelings for either of them. They'd made an arrangement! Yes, Mo had fallen for her, so Jayne wasn't the only one who'd slipped, but she'd forced the issue. If she hadn't shown up at the Middletons' and insisted that Mo explain why their behaviour had changed, Lesley and Mo might have worked through it with their arrangement intact. *No. It wouldn't have lasted.* The arrangement had always been a way to delay the inevitable, and unavoidable, guilt and pain—mainly guilt for her and Mo, and pain for Lesley.

Lesley reached behind her and patted the knapsack on her back. "Everything duly counted. I hope Mama doesn't suddenly remember something else we need for tomorrow night."

A lump rose in Jayne's throat. The woman in front of her deserved honesty. "I don't know how you can stand to look at me," she blurted.

Lesley's brow furrowed. "What?"

"I know it's not my fault—the triad—but I'm the one coming between you and Mo. I'm the one who'll be with you in the Joining Chamber. I know this isn't what you wanted. How could you not resent me?"

Lesley stared at her. "What's brought this on?"

Jayne jutted her chin toward the monitor. "They're replaying some of the execution procession, focusing on you. Part of the lead-up to our Joining Ceremony, I guess." She hesitated. *Honesty, remember?* "When you reached the crematorium's gates and you were singing the Song of Rymel, you . . . you were emotional, for a second. I remember wondering why. Now I know."

Lesley's face tightened. "I wish I could forget that moment."

"I'm sure nobody thought any less of you," Jayne said, guessing that Lesley would have considered her fragile composure an embarrassing display of weakness. "I didn't, and I didn't know you then. Now I do, enough to guess that you were probably thinking about Mo. When your Chosen Papers arrived, you must have thought your dream had come true. Then I came along." Expecting to see resentment, even hate, she forced herself to look into Lesley's eyes. They were unreadable, but not hard.

"I don't resent you," Lesley said. "I won't lie and say that I'm pleased for you and Mo. Maybe I should resent *both* of you. But I can't. I can be sad. I can wish someone else had ended up in a triad. But I can't resent you and Mo."

"I understand why you don't resent Mo. You want to preserve your relationship, not destroy it. You love her."

Lesley almost smiled. "That's why it hurts."

Jayne's throat tightened. "And I'm responsible for that."

"No, you've only done what every Chosen does. You've fallen in love with your Chosen."

If she didn't speak up now, she'd never forgive herself. Jayne wished she had something to hang onto as she said softly, "I've fallen in love with both my Chosens." There, it was out. Her heart raced. She was looking at Lesley, but Lesley's face wasn't registering through her panicked haze. Lesley's voice reached her ears, though.

"Are you saying you have feelings for me? Romantic feelings?"

Jayne swallowed. "Yes."

"I wondered a few times, but I didn't want to presume."

She'd wondered? Jayne should have known that Lesley would pick up on her crush. She felt stupid. While she'd agonized, sure that her feelings were a secret, Lesley had suspected; she'd known about her lovesick Chosen. Now Jayne really wanted to run and hide, but with no apartment, there was nowhere for her to go.

"I'm glad you said something, because you've resolved a dilemma for me."

"What dilemma?" Jayne said, her mind busy analyzing the number of ways she could take "glad" and her heart hoping for one of the more positive interpretations. Lesley could be glad because Jayne had handed her an opportunity to temporarily abandon her politeness and put Jayne in her place, something she'd probably been dying to do ever since her two Chosens had grown closer. Jayne forced her mind to slow down and gave Lesley her full attention, determined to listen and prepared to be conciliatory.

Lesley moistened her lips. "My mood is up and down these days. As I said, you and Mo, it does hurt. At the same time, I've known we have to go through this. So I have my good hours, and my bad hours, and sometimes I'm not sure what I'm feeling." She shifted her weight. "But I do know that I'm feeling something more than friendship—for you—and I've been trying to decide whether to tell you before the Joining Ceremony. I'm mainly worried about Mo. Now that you know, she has to know."

Jayne was struck dumb! Okay, she'd allowed a teeny-weeny part of her to hope that Lesley felt the same way. Well, Lesley hadn't used the word love, but Jayne would take "more than friendship"! But realizing she'd forced the issue again, Jayne somehow found her tongue. "I'm sorry. I'm worried about Mo, too. I also wasn't sure whether to keep my feelings to myself until after the Joining Ceremony. I shouldn't have blurted it out like that."

Lesley shook her head. "No, I'm glad you did. I think it's what I've wanted. The idea of keeping my feelings from Mo hasn't been sitting well. There will never be a good time. I know that from experience," she said wryly. "No, I'm glad everything's out in the open. Having said that, there's already so much going on, not only with all the upcoming social events, but with me coming to terms with you and Mo, that I think it would be best for us to not . . . get more involved until things settle a bit."

Forget about leaping into her arms, then. Jayne pushed the silly fantasy aside. With that heavy knapsack on her back, Lesley would probably tumble backward and crack her head open, anyway. "I agree," she said honestly. She'd require all her energy to get through the incessant socializing, and her relationship with Mo already had her off balance at times. But her emotional turmoil probably paled in comparison to Lesley's. She'd rather they take their first steps beyond friendship when Lesley was hurting less than she was now, when their relationship would feel good, not bad, and be less tainted by their concern for Mo. Right now . . . "What about Mo?"

Lesley stiffened and her eyes grew wary. "We're going to the crypt tomorrow. I'd rather not talk to her about it before then." She frowned in thought. "I'll tell her the day after, in the evening. I don't want to tell her right before we're supposed to go out for lunch and make small talk all afternoon." It sounded like Lesley wanted to talk to Mo alone, a desire that Jayne understood and supported. Lesley cleared her throat. "Shall we go?"

Since Lesley slid open the aviacraft door and motioned for Jayne to board, Jayne took the question as a rhetorical one. As she slid into the passenger seat and buckled her seatbelt, she gave Lesley a sidelong glance. When Lesley caught her eye and smiled, a burst of warmth permeated Jayne's chest and she couldn't help but grin. They wouldn't act on their feelings for a time, but at least she could be honest with Lesley from this point forward.

MO'S GRIP ON Lesley's arm tightened as the triad approached the Middleton family crypt. Lesley turned to give her a reassuring smile, but Mo was focused on her feet. Jayne walked on the other side of Mo, perhaps wanting to offer comfort by taking Mo's free hand. If she did, Lesley wouldn't mind. She'd already quashed one childish fit of jealousy today, when Jayne had offered to embellish the article Mo intended to slot near her mama. Mo had agreed, and Lesley's territorial instincts had stirred. When it came to Susan, supporting Mo was her domain! She'd been there, seen Mo at her worst, and stuck by her. What did Jayne think she was doing, carefully unrolling the article and adding a flowered border? Didn't she have the decency to stay out of it instead of sticking her nose in where she wasn't wanted?

Fortunately Lesley had kept her immature rant to herself, and had felt doubly silly when Jayne had beckoned to her and pointed to a spot in the border where Lesley could sign her name. *Time.* She would eventually adjust to this new world, understand that Jayne hadn't and wouldn't diminish her in Mo's eyes, and accept that love wasn't finite, that giving love to one Chosen didn't take love away from the other. Until then, Lesley would try not to berate herself too much over her inevitable jealousy.

When they reached the crypt's entrance, Mo let go of Lesley's arm and pushed the door open. Lesley and Jayne followed her inside; the carpeted corridor swallowed their footsteps as they walked the length of the crypt. Mo stopped outside a door with a silver nameplate that listed three names. Lesley's gaze lingered on the most recently added one: *Susan Anderson Middleton.* She put her hand on Mo's shoulder. "Do you want a few minutes alone, first?"

"No." Mo swung the door open and went inside.

Lesley followed her, murmuring, "Come on," over her shoulder, in case Jayne wasn't sure whether she should follow, too. She stepped to Mo's side. The offering wall faced the door; the walls to her left and right contained four resting spots each. Mo wouldn't occupy one of the vacant ones; she'd rest in the Thompson crypt. Not knowing what Mo wanted to do first, Lesley waited for her lead, aware of Jayne hovering behind them.

Mo finally stepped toward her mama's resting place and pressed a trembling hand against the cold marble. "Hello, Mama," she said, her quiet voice sounding louder than it should in the hushed room.

Lesley closed her eyes as the memories came flooding back: racing home on her bike in response to Mama's beep, her shock at Susan's death, Mo clinging to life, and the terrible aftermath—Mo sad and gaunt and lost in her baggy uniform, the nightmares, her depression, Lesley's helplessness; her guilt over wishing to have the old Mo back, and her joy when the old Mo returned. She opened eyes filled with tears and looked at Mo now, her dear, brave Chosen, whom she loved so utterly and completely. The triad would never change that. Lesley's feelings for Jayne, which she expected to grow into love, would never change that, nor would Mo's relationship with Jayne.

She glanced behind her when Jayne shifted her weight. Jayne's expression conveyed concern and sympathy. With the exception of the Middletons and Thompsons, anyone else's presence would have irritated Lesley. But Jayne wasn't here to gawk, and she'd be a Thompson soon enough.

As Lesley returned her gaze to Mo, it struck her that Jayne couldn't visit her parents' resting place. Would she want to? If Jayne did, Lesley would have been the first in line to question Jayne's desire—a year ago. Now, she wasn't so sure. Jayne definitely saw her parents as criminals, but they were still her parents. She could condemn their violations without forgetting that they'd raised and loved her, and that she'd loved them, before something went terribly wrong. From the little Jayne had said and Lesley had inferred, Jayne struggled to reconcile two opposing views of her parents; perhaps she always would. If she somehow managed to look back on her time with them fondly, Lesley wouldn't be as alarmed as she would have been before meeting her.

Mo twisted and held out her hand. "Les," she murmured.

Lesley stepped to her side and slipped her hand into Mo's.

"Mama, Les and I, we're Chosens. I was right." Mo didn't smile. "We'll be Joined soon. I wish . . . I wish you were here."

Lesley squeezed Mo's hand and said, "Being Mo's Chosen is what I've always wanted." She felt a bit silly, talking aloud to a dead woman, but this was Mo's visit, and Mo preferred to actually speak, rather than hold the conversation in her head. *I'll take care of her, Susan. I promise.*

"There's more," Mo said. "Les isn't my only Chosen. I have two. Yes, two. They call it a triad." With her free hand, she motioned for Jayne to join them. "This is Jayne. Jayne Adams. Yes, *that* Adams. She's my other Chosen, and Les's other Chosen. We're all each other's Chosen. Oh, and we'll all be Thompsons."

"I'm honoured to be your daughter's Chosen, and Lesley's," Jayne said. Mo grabbed her hand. "I don't really have anything to offer them," Jayne continued, "but I'll always be loyal."

Jayne had more to offer them than her loyalty; she had her trust, her art, her strength. But Lesley kept her thoughts to herself. The last thing she wanted was to make Mo suspicious of her feelings for Jayne. Not here.

"She's a wonderful artist, Mama," Mo said. "She sketches. You'd like her drawings. I wish you could see them. And Les is on her way to commander—no, admiral! But you already knew that." With her fingers, she traced her mama's name on the plaque that marked the resting spot. "I'll be back soon," she said softly, then heaved a loud sigh.

"Good-bye," Lesley murmured, and heard Jayne do the same.

Still holding her Chosens' hands, Mo led them to the offering wall. Lesley reached for Jayne's hand, forming an intimate circle. They chanted together. "Disobedience means death. Death to those who commit a Chosen Violation. Death to those who disobey. Death to those who violate the Way. Death to those who violate the Way. Death to those who violate the Way." Rather than clapping, they merely nodded to each other and broke the circle.

"Look at all the offerings," Mo breathed. "I should have come sooner."

"You came when you were ready," Lesley said as she surveyed the slots stuffed with articles. Soon they'd have to be gathered and placed in the ornamental chest that sat in each room for that purpose.

Mo stepped behind Lesley to open the knapsack on her back. She slid out her offering and read it once more. "The border makes it unique," she murmured. Lesley silently agreed, pleased that her teeth weren't set on edge. Mo stepped to one of the few remaining empty slots and dropped the article into it. "I love you, Mama." She stood silently for a minute, then turned to her Chosens with moist eyes. "Thank you for coming with me."

 RYMELLAN 3

"Thank you for inviting me," Jayne said as Lesley nodded.

Mo managed a small smile. "I had to introduce you. Anyway, I'm ready to go." So ready that she strode from the room without a backward glance. Lesley and Jayne looked at each other, then followed her.

Mo didn't slow her pace until they were outside, walking away from the crypt. "I'm glad I went," she said, taking Lesley's hand and, after a moment's hesitation, Jayne's. "I'll feel so much better at the Joining Ceremony now. I feel so relieved. I'd built up the visit to the crypt into some big ordeal, to the point that I was avoiding it." She blew out a sigh and visibly relaxed. "That's the most difficult part of the week over for me. I can enjoy myself now."

Lesley caught Jayne's eye. Her conviction to tell Mo about her feelings for Jayne deepened. If the guilt she felt over sharing a secret with Jayne while visiting Susan was any indication, there was no way she could stand in the Joining Chamber without Mo knowing.

AS SHE DID every time she found herself alone again, Jayne stood off to one side of the living room and tried not to look uncomfortable. At least she had a glass in her hand, giving her juice to sip while she surveyed the guests. Spending the evening trapped in a room filled with Lesley and Mo's relatives was awkward at times, but not as excruciating as she'd expected. There were so many guests that the formal dining room was also packed. Everyone had greeted her civilly, and a few had engaged her in polite conversation. Most had quickly moved on, satisfied that they'd done their duty. Everyone was clearly delighted that Lesley and Mo were Chosens. They were doing their best not to let the existence of a third Chosen from a disgraced family ruin the occasion.

She sipped her drink again, hoping that someone would come and rescue her soon, before anyone pitied her. Her heart leaped when she glimpsed Lesley, then she quietly sighed. Lesley was talking to Jason, who hadn't hesitated to shake Jayne's hand. He'd even managed to mumble a few words of greeting. Since then, he'd avoided her, but at least he was here, spending time with his estranged sister. Jayne didn't believe that Lesley and Jason had ever been close, but they were siblings, and she hoped their relationship would become less strained. Just because she had a worthless brother and would be happy to never see him again didn't mean that all sister-brother relationships were expendable.

Her Chosens hadn't completely abandoned her all evening. They had to circulate, but they'd made a point of snatching time with her whenever they could, and so had others in their families. Alan had topped up her glass twice, Karen and William had chatted with her, and even Michael and Peggy had made small talk for a few minutes. Adelaide seemed to be taking care of the guests in the dining room; she occasionally popped into the living room for a minute or two, probably to check that Alan was doing his part. Jayne didn't know what had happened to Mo, and felt guilty whenever she saw her. This time tomorrow, Lesley would tell Mo the last thing she wanted to hear.

"What are you thinking about?"

It took a moment for Mo's voice to register. "S-sorry," Jayne stammered. "I didn't see you come over. I'm glad you're here," she said, the familiar guilt snaking through her. "I didn't really know what to do with myself."

"I think I've spoken to everyone at least once, so I can hang out with you now. I figure people will start leaving soon, anyway. We'll see some of them again at lunch tomorrow."

"What are Adelaide's parents like?" Jayne asked. She'd meet all her Chosens' grandparents at the lunch, but Adelaide's parents concerned her the most.

Mo barked a laugh. "Well, her mama's okay, but her papa makes Adelaide look laid-back. The good news is that he'll mainly talk to Adelaide, Alan, and Les. The few times I've spent time in his presence, he's ignored me. I don't know, maybe now that I'm going to be a Thompson, it'll be different. I kind of hope not, though. I'm totally okay with him passing me over. Trust me, you'll know what I mean tomorrow."

Jayne tried not to show her dismay. When she felt Mo's hand slip into hers, she knew she'd failed.

"Maybe you should have invited your grandparents," Mo said, squeezing Jayne's hand.

Jayne shook her head. "They never visited when I lived with my aunt and uncle. Well, they did, but not with me." Their rejection had deepened her suspicion that she'd somehow been responsible for the

Incident. Her adult self had eventually stopped believing that, but as a child, she'd taken it all upon herself and wondered if she could have stopped it. "Honestly, I don't even know if I'd recognize them." And she didn't care. If they ever wanted to see her, they could look up her comm code. Having to invite her aunt, uncle, cousins, and Robert already grated. Carol was the exception, but Jayne thought of her more as an older sister, and having her and Ronald at the main table would make the Joining supper extra special.

Mo's hand felt hot in hers. Should they be holding hands in front of the families? What would Lesley think? Jayne glanced in her direction. Blood rushed to her face when Lesley and Jason quickly turned back toward each other. They'd been looking over here! Was Lesley upset? Had Jason pointed out that Lesley's two Chosens were holding hands, or had they not been staring at her and Mo, specifically?

Jayne didn't want to upset Mo by pulling her hand away, and she liked holding Mo's hand. At the same time, she worried about Lesley, but the harm, if any, was already done. She continued to hang onto Mo, not wanting to perturb both Chosens. Her stomach knotted. After tomorrow night, this balancing act would be a hundred times more difficult.

WITH A WEARY sigh, Mo plunked into Les's chair and waited for her to come upstairs. What was on Les's mind? The moment the front door had shut behind Jayne, Les had said that she wanted to talk and would meet Mo in her bedroom. Maybe she just wanted to get away from her parents and anyone who happened to be visiting. They hadn't had five minutes to themselves since they'd awakened that morning, and tomorrow would be no different. Mo didn't dare lie on the bed; Les would find her fast asleep.

As it was, she jumped when Les shut the bedroom door. Rubbing her eyes, she realized that she must have snatched a two-second nap, because she hadn't heard Les climb the stairs.

Les sat on the bed and beckoned for Mo to join her. "You mean, you want me to move," Mo mumbled. She considered rolling the chair over to Les, then pushed herself up and shuffled over to the bed. "I'm surprised Jayne has the energy for a walk. Then again, she's not used to having people in her face twenty-four hours a day. Leaving the house is the only way she can get any time alone." No wonder she'd insisted that she didn't want company. But . . . "We should have gone with her. She might get lost, and if she runs into a patrol . . ." Suddenly wide awake, Mo dropped onto the bed next to Lesley.

"Relax. Laura's briefed everyone about Jayne. They've seen her image, they know she's living on the estate. Laura won't tolerate so much as a dirty look from anyone. And Jayne has her comm unit. If she gets lost, we'll go find her."

"When's Laura giving up C3?" Mo asked, hoping a change of subject would calm her worry. "I would have expected another commander to take over by now—or will we be getting someone fresh out of your course?" C3 was—or used to be—such a dull sector that a green commander could handle it.

Les shrugged. "I'm not sure. Laura hasn't said anything explicit to me, but I think she's decided to hang onto the sector until she's confident that there won't be any trouble because of Jayne. Admiral Hall obviously agrees with her."

What sort of trouble—Jayne corrupting C3, or C3ers trying to kill her? The latter scenario was likely Laura's main concern. Tomorrow evening would be interesting; the Thompsons had invited many from the nearby estates to a buffet supper. Most had already seen Jayne at the Festival of the Way, but they'd given her a wide berth, which would be difficult to do in the formal dining room. A few families had turned down the invitation, but most had accepted, and a smaller group would also be at the Joining supper. Nobody had turned down *that* invitation, but Adelaide had included only those who had more than a polite, neighbourly relationship with the Thompsons or Middletons. And hey, in twenty years, when hopefully a triad—and an Adams—in C3 wouldn't be such a novelty, they'd probably crow about their presence at the triad's historic Joining supper.

"Tomorrow night, we should stick close to Jayne," Mo said. "I doubt anyone will be blatantly rude, but—"

"I need to tell you something," Les blurted.

Mo instantly grew wary. It wasn't like Les to interrupt. "What?"

"It's happening for me. With Jayne."

Mo sucked in her breath. "What do you mean?" she squeaked,

knowing full well what Les meant. She clenched her trembling hands on her lap.

"I feel something for her. More than friendship," Les stated.

"And you're telling me now?" Mo cried, shooting to her feet. She knew she was being unreasonable, but she'd rather focus on Les's timing—easy—than on Les's message—not flaming listening!

"I didn't want to keep it from you. I didn't want to stand in the Joining Chamber with—"

"Yeah, we're being Joined. In five flaming days!" Mo stomped over to lean against Les's desk, and glared at her.

"What would you have preferred? That we stand next to you—"

Blood pounded in Mo's ears. "We? Who's we? You and Jayne? She knows?"

Les's voice remained even. "I told her a couple of—"

"You talked to her first?" Mo wanted to run from the room, cry, scream, punch something, lift the comm display from Les's desk and hurl it out the window. "What else have you been doing behind my back? Apart from plotting about how you'll tell me about the two of you. No wonder she wanted to go for a walk." Argamon, Jayne! "She can't even have the decency to be here."

"Don't put this onto Jayne. *I* wanted to speak to you alone."

"Well, thank you very much for considering that maybe I don't want to cry my eyes out in front of a crowd."

"You're not crying, you're angry," Les said, in that same even tone that was really, really starting to grate.

"That's because I can't be upset, right? Because you've been so flaming reasonable that I can't . . . be . . . upset. I can just be flaming mad that you've both known for—you knew at the crypt!" Her fingernails dug into her palms. "But I can't cry, right? Because you're not doing anything I haven't done."

"We haven't done anything except tell each other."

Oh, so Jayne also had feelings for Les. Why wasn't Mo surprised? Because Les and Jayne were Chosens. Because everyone kept saying that it was only a matter of time. Oh, and because Les was beautiful and on her way to admiral and everyone would have dated her, if not for her irrational attachment to Mo Middleton. Why would Jayne be any different? She didn't have to settle for the short, plain Chosen anymore—and neither did Les. Yeah, Mo was flaming mad! She'd known it would come to this! No wonder Les had been so flaming reasonable. All she had to do was bide her time until Jayne fell for her. Liar! They were both flaming liars, both of them! How could they do this to her? She hated them!

It wasn't supposed to hurt this much. She *knew* it was possible to love one without diminishing the love for the other. She *knew* that each relationship would be special in its own way. She *knew* that Les's feelings for Jayne weren't a rejection of her. How many times had she told Les that nothing had changed between them? How could she have been so stupid? How could Les have been so reasonable when she hadn't yet experienced having feelings for—loving—two women. Mo's feelings for Les had deepened since she'd fallen in love with Jayne, and yet she still wanted to scream, cry out in agony, hurt Les, hug Les. It must have been infinitely worse for Les. She'd had to blindly believe Mo's assurances; she hadn't had any experience to draw upon. "If I'd known how it would feel, I never would have . . . I couldn't have . . . our arrangement would have been permanent."

Les lifted a brow. "It's a good thing you didn't know, then."

"How could you have been so flaming reasonable? I could see you were upset, but you kept pushing us together."

"I had no choice. Emotionally, it's been a struggle. It still is." Les's chuckle conveyed that as an understatement. She touched her right temple. "Intellectually, I had to accept—believe—that holding you back would hurt our relationship in the long run. Because it would have."

"Still. I get that—now. Especially since I love you more than I ever have. Seriously, Les, I do. My relationship with Jayne will never change how I feel about you. But I still—" Mo balled her hands. Hated them? Wanted to scream at them and throw something at Jayne's head next time she saw her? Wanted to flee from the room, crawl into a hole somewhere, and cry until her eyes burned, her throat was raw, and she'd run out of tears?

Les's expression was sympathetic. "I came to understand that our reaction after the notification meetings was our way of coping until we could face that we're in a triad. I include Jayne in that statement, though I think her reasons for not accepting the triad were different from ours." She stood. "The Chosen Council doesn't make mistakes."

"I get that, too. And I'm hardly in a position to object to you and Jayne, right? But . . ." Mo threw up her hands. The tears she'd fought welled in her eyes. "I'm not as flaming reasonable as you." Her lips trembled. When Les closed the distance between them and wrapped Mo in her arms, Mo leaned into her and sobbed into her shoulder. Howling in pain would have to wait until her social calendar calmed down. She quashed her stirring indignation at Les's timing. Les was right about telling her before their Joining Ceremony. It was bad enough that she and Jayne had known at the crypt, but forgivable under the circumstances. "I have no right to cry," she sniffled.

"Of course you have a right to cry," Les murmured. "You're handling it better than I thought you would."

Mo snorted. "You're not hearing what's running through my mind."

"Tell me, if it'll make you feel better."

"It wouldn't make me feel better. Maybe I'm maturing or something, or maybe it's because I fell for Jayne first, but I know that lashing out at you won't help. That doesn't mean I don't feel like curling up into a fetal position and staying that way for the next year, but maybe how you handled it is helping me to accept that it's not me. You're not rejecting me. You're not out to hurt me. I'm probably saying the same things you said to yourself." When she felt Les's nod, she almost added, "And it probably didn't help to make you feel better, either."

"As I said, all Jayne and I have done is talk about it," Les said. "I don't know exactly how she feels. We didn't say much beyond that we have feelings for each other, mainly because I'm too unsettled right now to even consider, uh, getting involved with her. I'm still conflicted about you and her. I need to feel more comfortable about you, her, us, everything, before we complicate the situation further."

Whereas Mo had plunged forward without a second thought. Well, that wasn't quite true, but she'd accepted Les's assurances as genuine and rushed ahead every time Les had granted her "permission," without considering whether "could" meant "should." Jayne had been the one to slow them down.

Les's arms tightened around Mo. "I'm sorry about the crypt. I wish

I could have told you beforehand, but Jayne and I only discussed this a couple of days ago, and I didn't want to scuttle your visit to the crypt. I just—"

"It's okay. You were right. If you'd told me before, I probably would have backed out of the visit, used it as an excuse." She slipped her arms around Les's waist.

They held each other in silence, until Les said, "What do you want to do now? Do you want some time alone? Do you want me to tell Jayne you've gone to bed?"

"No." Partly because she wanted to do what Les had done—reassure Jayne that she didn't hate her—and partly because the thought of them alone together would now drive her crazy for a while. Yeah, Les had said nothing would happen, but that wouldn't stop Mo from sticking to them like glue. Jealousy wouldn't be her only motive. She loved them. Ironically, she'd draw comfort from them, and need them to get through the coming days. Yep, conflicted was one word for the emotional storm that would now consume her.

It was a good thing she'd fallen for Jayne before Les did. If Les had gone first, Mo would have caved to her worst fears—that Les didn't love her, had rejected her, would abandon her for Jayne. She might have destroyed the triad and all of their lives. Oh, she wouldn't have ended up on the Wall of Offenders, but would her love for Les have survived? She wasn't sure, and would live with that disappointment for the rest of her life.

HER STOMACH CHURNING, Jayne entered the Thompson house, hung her cloak, and glanced into the living room. Mo looked up at her from the sofa. Jayne swallowed at the sight of Mo's red eyes and the slump of her shoulders. So, Lesley had told her.

"Did you enjoy your walk?" Mo asked flatly. Then she blew out a sigh. "I'm not angry with you, okay."

Jayne lowered herself onto the sofa next to Mo. "Where's Lesley?" The moment the words were out of her mouth, she wanted to kick herself. "I'm asking because I hope you're still speaking to her."

To her surprise, Mo smiled. "If I wasn't, we'd be in real trouble, considering we're Joining in a few days." The amusement in her eyes quickly died. "When we saw you coming to the front door, she said she'd make tziva. I guess she wanted to give us a few minutes alone."

"In case you want to yell at me?" Jayne hesitated, then took one of Mo's hands. "You're both my Chosens."

"I know."

A lump rose in Jayne's throat when Mo's fingers tightened around hers.

"I'll deal with it. I'm not saying I'm happy about it, but given this," she lifted Jayne's hand and squeezed it, "at least I understand that she still loves me. I'm not saying it doesn't hurt, but if I didn't know that my feelings for you haven't changed my feelings for Les, that she's still as special to me, I . . . well, I don't know how I would have reacted. I doubt we'd be sitting here like this."

Jayne had hoped that Mo's experience with loving two women would temper her reaction to Lesley's revelation. Their relationship was the foundation of the triad. It had to remain strong.

"I also know that your feelings for Les don't affect your feelings for me," Mo said, but her voice lacked conviction.

"Of course they don't," Jayne said, surprised that Mo might believe otherwise. Then again, their relationship was young; it hadn't grown over years, survived a separation, and persevered through the ups and downs of life. "We have a lot of years ahead of us." To her horror, her voice quavered.

Mo's forehead puckered; she let go of Jayne's hand and pulled her into a hug. "I didn't mean to upset you. I'll be moody for a while, but I know you and Les love me. I do."

Jayne was supposed to be comforting Mo, not the other way around! She held Mo close and, even though she was fighting tears, murmured, "You didn't upset me. And I do love you." In case a tear escaped, she didn't lower her head to press her cheek against Mo's.

"I love you, too," Mo said.

Jayne squeezed her eyes shut, determined not to fall apart. *We have a lot of years ahead of us.* Not just her and Mo—the triad. A family. Love. A life she'd never dared hope for, and one she'd never take for granted. No, Mo hadn't upset her. Jayne was fighting the purest of tears, tears born of love, and joy, and awe. She loved. She felt loved. It no longer mattered how Rymellans treated her. She'd finished paying for her parents' crimes. Her punishment was over.

MO BOUNDED UP the stairs to the Middletons' second floor, entered her bedroom—and her jaw dropped. "What are you doing?" she snapped at Nathan.

He quickly sat up and swung his legs off the bed. "What are *you* doing here?"

"I'm in my own flaming bedroom!"

"It's not yours for much longer."

Her hands went to her hips. "Can you at least wait until I officially don't live here anymore before you start planning how you'll redecorate? Why don't you stick with your own room?"

He shrugged. "This one's a little larger than mine."

"It won't be long before your Chosen Papers come." Mo moved to the closet and slid its door open.

"I'm only twenty-one!" He paused. "I thought you'd taken all the clothes you needed over to the Thompsons'."

She had, but her need to get away from everyone had outweighed her fear of leaving Les and Jayne alone together—not that they were by themselves. She'd left them with Adelaide, who'd wanted to review the timetable for their Joining Day one last time. "All I have to worry about is flying everyone to the Chosen House for 13:20," Mo had said, "everyone" meaning Papa, Jayne, Andrew, Nathan, Carol, and Ronald. Then she'd feigned a shocked look and claimed to have forgotten to bring over the pants and shirt she wanted to wear that afternoon. She might have fooled Adelaide, but doubted her excuse had flown with Les and Jayne. Mo wasn't sure whether she was miffed or grateful that neither one had insisted she stay, or offered to go with her to fetch her clothes. "I decided I want to wear something different today, okay?"

"All the socializing getting to you?"

Mo bit back a retort. Arguing with Nathan wouldn't make her feel any better. "A little, so I came over here hoping to get fifteen minutes to myself." Hint, hint.

"I'll get out of your way, then."

Good, Nathan wasn't dense. Mo pulled a shirt off a hanger, then turned around in time to see Nathan moving to the doorway, where he paused. "While you're here, maybe you can talk to Andrew."

"Why? He's seemed okay at all the gatherings."

Nathan snorted.

"Isn't he at the workshop?" Stupid question. "Oh, no, he wouldn't be." Her family would be at the gathering that afternoon, as usual. "What's wrong with him?"

Nathan clasped his hands over his heart and answered in a high-pitched voice, "He's lovesick."

Flaming Argamon! "I've talked to him. I've talked to Ann. I'm out of it." She had *two* flaming relationships of her own to worry about.

"You introduced them."

"So it's my fault? No way. Look, they're adults. Let them sort it out."

Nathan frowned. "I tried to set him up with someone. He wouldn't even listen! She was his own age, too. Not some old woman."

Old woman? Okay, patience depleted! "That fifteen minutes I wanted is almost down to ten. Get out!" When he grinned at her, she wanted to throw the shirt at him. Maybe her desire showed in her eyes, because he ducked out of the room, closing the door behind him. *Brothers!* A sudden wave of melancholy dampened her exasperation. She was moving out—had pretty much moved out. She'd miss Andrew and Nathan's affectionate teasing. Then she chuckled at herself. She wasn't moving to another sector. She'd see her siblings almost as often as she did now, especially since the Middletons and Thompsons were practically one big family.

Mo sat on the bed and dropped the shirt next to her. Now that she was alone, she wasn't sure what she wanted to do. Cry? No. Break things? Nope. Stoke resentment and anger toward Les and Jayne. She couldn't. Every time indignation stirred or jealousy clenched her hands and tightened her jaw, her relationship with Jayne deftly countered the attack, as if pouring a bucket of water over an already sputtering fire. She couldn't rail at Les, couldn't mentally shout, *How could you turn your back on our relationship?* and *How could you do this to me? How could you hurt me like this?* when she knew from experience that Les wasn't rejecting their relationship, hadn't set out to hurt her, and that a relationship between Les and Jayne didn't mean that Les didn't love her, or that their relationship was somehow less important and special. *And you went first.* Yeah, okay, there was that one little detail. Hadn't she asked herself if she could handle this when the day came? She'd been thinking more about Les and Jayne sleeping together, but still. How had she responded? She'd promised to remind herself that it wouldn't be some airhead. It would be Jayne, who respected her, Les, and, most importantly, their relationship.

All this rational thinking didn't mean that Mo wasn't hurt and didn't feel betrayed. Oh, no! She flaming hurt and knew she was in for a rough time. When Les felt comfortable becoming involved with Jayne, Mo would chew her thumbnails off, slam a lot of doors, and "moody" would be the understatement of the year. But she'd still love Les. She'd still love Jayne. She'd throw her temper tantrums so that resentment wouldn't fester. Her Chosens weren't out to get her, or hurt her, or make her feel as if she didn't matter. Argamon, Andrew was pining after Ann—inexplicably—and probably feeling unloved and unappreciated. Mo had two Chosens who loved her, and she'd cling to that unbelievable, yet true, reality when the hurt threatened to overwhelm reason. Her relationship with Jayne would keep her in line, too. If Les had fallen for Jayne first . . . if Mo didn't *know* that a relationship between Les and Jayne wouldn't mean the end of her relationship with Les . . . she didn't want to think about what would have happened. She did *not* want to think about it.

So why had she run here, under the ruse of fetching clothes she didn't need? Maybe she'd wanted to live up to her reputation as the jealous and hot-headed Chosen of Les Thompson, to show Les and Jayne that she was upset in the only way she could when they were constantly around people. Or maybe she'd wanted to sit in her bedroom and say good-bye to her old life and fantasies. How many times had she lain on this bed, dreaming about being Les's Chosen and the wonderful life they'd share together? Well, hey, she'd got it half right. They *were* Chosens, and you know what? They could still strive for that wonderful life—all three of them. Mo had a few doors to slam first, but each one would bring them closer to that idyllic life—or so she'd tell herself!

She glanced at her comm unit. Argamon, she'd left the Thompsons' twenty minutes ago. The conversation with Adelaide must be over by

 RYMELLAN 3

now. She had to get back! She snatched up the shirt and sprang off the bed, grabbed the first pair of pants she saw from the closet, and raced downstairs.

NOT WANTING TO disturb Mama, who was reviewing the Joining Day agenda on her comm unit one last time, Lesley carefully shifted position on the living room sofa. In one of the chairs facing the sofa, Jayne crossed her legs.

Mama finally looked up. "All right, we're set." She frowned. "Beep Mo and remind her that we have to leave here at 12:30."

"She'll be back in time," Lesley said, hoping her words were true. If she had to go to the Middletons' and drag Mo back here, Mama would demand to know what was going on. Mama's mood was already becoming increasingly high-strung as the Joining Day approached. The prospect of Mo causing some type of scene during the remaining celebrations would keep her up at night.

"She'd better be." Mama rose from the sofa and stalked from the living room.

Lesley and Jayne's eyes met. "Maybe we should have gone with her," Jayne said.

"Mama wouldn't have appreciated all of us leaving. You saw her face when Mo walked out." Mo might have smelled the smoke rising from the two holes Mama's eyes had burned into her back as she left.

Jayne was silent for a moment. "You had to tell her before the Joining Ceremony."

"I don't regret telling her. I expect her to be up and down for a while, but she'll be okay. It would have been better if I could have told her when we weren't expected to constantly have smiles on our faces, but it couldn't be helped." If Lesley had kept her feelings for Jayne from Mo until after their Joining Ceremony, she would have cringed every time she looked back on their Joining Day. Everything—the ceremony, the supper, the grinning faces in the images—would have been lies, and certainly not how Lesley wanted them to begin their lives as officially Joined Chosens. Mo would have been justifiably angry that Lesley hadn't told her earlier, unless Lesley had lied about when she'd recognized her feelings for Jayne, something she'd never do.

They lapsed into an awkward silence. Lesley scrambled for something to say. They hadn't had much opportunity to be alone together since they'd confessed their feelings for each other. As Lesley's acceptance of Mo and Jayne's relationship continued to grow and she regained her equilibrium over her emotions, her friendship with Jayne would naturally evolve into more, in its own time. She didn't want to rush. She refused to pressure herself, and knew Jayne wouldn't pressure her, either. This awkwardness would pass, especially if she stopped thinking about that conversation outside her aviacraft every time they were alone, and focused on simply talking to her Chosen—starting now. "How are you holding up? I'm starting to feel fatigued with all the socializing, so I can't imagine how you must be feeling."

Jayne's mouth turned up at the corners. "I'm okay. At this point, I'm more worried about seeing my relatives."

"Especially your brother?"

Jayne nodded.

Lesley wondered if Jayne would ever explain to her and Mo what had caused the rift with Robert. Maybe they'd find out on their Joining Day, hopefully in a way that didn't involve shouting.

"I'm not looking forward to speaking to the others, either, except Carol and Ronald." She sighed. "Having them all there will feel so hypocritical, but at least only Robert will be in the Joining Chamber."

"And he won't be at the main table."

Jayne smiled. "Thank you for persuading your mama—"

The front door thumped shut. Through the archway, Lesley saw Mo shrug a knapsack off her back and hang her cloak. Mo lifted the knapsack from the floor and strode into the living room. "All done?"

"If you'd waited until we'd finished with Mama, we would have gone with you," Lesley said, curious to see what Mo would say in response. The fact that whatever clothes Mo had fetched—if any—were now a wrinkled mess in her knapsack confirmed Lesley's suspicion that Mo hadn't forgotten her clothes for that afternoon.

"We might not have had enough time," Mo said. "I didn't really need to be here, so . . ."

"So you remember what time we all have to leave the supper to have our images taken? And how long we're expected to greet those arriving at the hall? And what time we're expected to have our first dance?" A tradition that had caused Mama much consternation. How would a triad have a first dance together? After consulting with the Joining Day planner, whom Mama treated more like an advisor, she'd decided to choose a longish song and have each couple in the triad dance a third of it.

Mo's brow furrowed. "You two know, right? I won't be there by myself."

Lesley must love her. She'd want to throttle anyone else. "Are the clothes you have no intention of wearing in that knapsack?" she asked lightly.

Mo's face tightened. "You know, I think I've just hit some type of record, because for the second time in an hour, I feel like throwing something at somebody. I just wanted five minutes to myself, okay?"

"You didn't want us to go with you," Jayne said, perhaps still wondering whether they should have accompanied her.

"No, I flaming didn't! What's next? Do you both want to squeeze into the bathroom with me next time I go?" Mo chuckled at the absurdity of her own remark, then slung the knapsack over her shoulder with a groan. "Look, I know you're both concerned, but I'm okay. Yes, I might be a little snappy now and then, but I'll deal with it. I'm still looking forward to Joining with both of you. Try to remember that when I'm ripping your heads off." She slowly exhaled and shifted her attention to Lesley. "Anyway, I better go upstairs and pretend to hang these clothes before I run into your mama. Why don't you both come with me?" When neither Lesley nor Jayne rose, Mo said, "I'm being serious. I've had my alone time. Come with me."

As Lesley stood, she exchanged an amused look with Jayne. Mo's mood would be all over the place in the coming days and weeks, but she'd put on a brave face in public, and Lesley would be there for her in private. Knowing that Mo would need plenty of reassurance about their relationship was another reason Lesley didn't want to move beyond friendship with Jayne right now. They'd both focus on supporting Mo. Rather than resenting Jayne's involvement, Lesley was grateful that she wouldn't have to look out for Mo on her own. Mo would be a priority, but with her commander training and her own emotional turmoil to deal with, having Jayne there to pick up her slack with Mo would be a relief. She'd never wanted to share Mo, but since she had no choice in the matter, she was glad it was Jayne—someone she trusted, and someone who loved and appreciated Mo, foibles and all.

Jayne nodded gratefully to Ronald when he handed her a glass of water. She took a sip. The cold water eased her dry throat. "Thanks."

He nodded, moved a stack of workbooks from the sofa to an end table, and sat down. "I hope I remember the names of those I've met." He shook his head. "I'm terrible with names."

"What's that?" Carol bustled into the room and placed a tray with two tzivas and a plate of biscuits on the coffee table. She picked up one of the mugs and sat next to Ronald.

"I was just saying that I hope I remember everyone's name."

"Don't worry about it. They won't remember ours," Carol said with a dismissive wave of her hand. She frowned at Jayne. "You all right?"

Was her mounting nervousness that apparent? With most of the socializing behind her, she'd hoped to feel relieved, maybe even excited, on the eve of her Joining Day. Sure, she'd expected apprehension and nerves, but not moments of sheer terror that tightened her chest and made her feel like hyperventilating.

"Jayne?" Carol said.

Jayne drank more water and ignored Carol's question. "I don't know why we have to spend the night apart."

"It's tradition. Though I guess you'll be seeing one of your Chosens before you reach the steps."

Yes, poor Mo had to fly all the way out here to pick them up, when they could have just stayed at the Thompsons'. At least Jayne wouldn't have to walk to the steps with Robert alone. The Adamses and Middletons would walk together. Mo would be with her. There was no reason to be nervous. Her stomach knotted.

"I'm glad we finally got to meet Lesley's brother," Carol said. "She looks like him, much more than Karen."

Ronald reached for a biscuit. "I can't believe how much the Middletons resemble each other."

Carol's eyes widened. "Oh, I know. It struck me when we all went to the Dance Hall. They must resemble their mama, because their papa seems to be the odd one out. Have you seen an image of Mo's mama?" she asked Jayne.

She nodded. Mo had shown her one before they went to the crypt. "They do look like their mama. I wish I'd met her."

"Three young Chosens, and only one mama alive," Ronald murmured.

"That one mama has been very helpful," Jayne quickly said, wanting to get off this subject. Her parents would already be on her mind too much the following day, and she didn't want to brood about the circumstances of Mo's mama's death, either. "She pretty much planned the entire week and agreed to most of my requests."

"Grudgingly, I bet," Carol said.

"Still. It'll be a much happier day for me with you two at the main table." If only she could have bumped Robert from the steps and the Joining Chamber, but tradition was tradition!

Carol set her mug back on the tray. "As I've said before, I was initially worried about Adelaide, but I was wrong. You were wrong, too. You were convinced they'd exercise CT134."

In hindsight, her panic after her notification meeting seemed silly, but all she'd known was that Lesley was a highly regarded Interior officer. That alone had been cause for alarm. When she'd found out that Lesley and Mo were in a long-term relationship, she could excuse herself for having expected to die at an execution site. "You're right. I was wrong about them."

Lesley deserved her reputation in every sense of the word. Upholding the spirit of the Way was paramount to her. She would never have thoughtlessly condemned Jayne based solely on her family history. As for Mo, it would be folly to mistake her lack of interest in cases and article debates as a lack of strength in the Way. Mo was a military officer who'd die for the Way without hesitation. Emotional? Yes. Dedicated to the spirit of the Way? Yes. The two weren't mutually exclusive. As Mo had said, she'd rip their heads off, but do what a Rymellan strong in the Way would do. Jayne had one Chosen who thought her way through challenges, and one who stamped her foot and shouted. Life would be interesting.

If the Chosen Council had asked her—ha!—who she wanted to be in a triad with, Lesley and Mo were the last Rymellans she would have chosen. Military officers, especially an Interior officer? No way! Fortunately the Chosen Council hadn't consulted her; it had introduced her to two Rymellans she'd grown to love and trust. If she'd known her Chosens the way she did now, she would have fainted with relief at her notification meeting, not feared for her life.

How did Lesley and Mo feel when they looked back at their notification meetings? It was easy for Jayne to think that it had all worked out. Her life had changed for the better; they'd been blindsided. Despite their feelings for her—Mo's in full bloom and Lesley's breaking through the soil—there must be a part of them that wished they'd never met her, that the Chosen Council had given them to each other, and only each other. Jayne would try not to feel guilty as she stood in the Joining Chamber. Guilt wouldn't honour her Chosens or the Way. By accepting her and the triad, Lesley and Mo would honour both for the rest of their lives. Jayne wouldn't let them down. She'd follow their lead, leave her guilt at the door, hold her head high, and quash all feelings except love and admiration.

Her Joining Day would be nothing like she'd expected. She wouldn't go through the motions and despair over a life with a Chosen who resented her. She'd Join with two Chosens she loved, and who genuinely cared about her. That her parents had turned their backs on their Chosen bond was even more inexplicable to her now. At the same time, her name would no longer fill her with shame. She would *not* follow in her parents' footsteps. She would redeem her name, but not by convincing Rymellans that she wasn't like her parents—a shallow accomplishment that would offer little satisfaction. No, she'd die a proud Adams because she'd stand by her Chosens for the rest of her life—love them, honour them, respect them, be there for them through the joys and the sorrows.

When each triad member was laid to rest in the Thompson crypt, those gathered wouldn't cringe at the *Adams* on the nameplate, because it was *her* name, someone strong in the Way and whose devotion to her Chosens never wavered. Their daughters, their extended families, and their friends would think of *her*, not her parents. *That* was how she'd reclaim her name, starting tomorrow.

MO JUMPED WHEN Nathan barked a laugh from behind her. He pointed over her shoulder at the image on the study's comm station display. "You both look so young."

"We were young. Or rather, younger." She peered at the smiling faces in the pilot program's graduation image. Where were they now? Most were on tour or on space stations. Only three weren't full-time pilots: Lieutenant Waterman, who'd decided that a career in fighter maintenance was more to her liking, Les, who'd switched to Interior, and Mo, who felt a sudden longing to be on tour. It hurt, but not being Les's Chosen would have hurt infinitely more. Okay, she wasn't grounded because of Les, but because of the triad—military code for Jayne. But with Les being in Interior, and the military wanting her to stay there, tours would have been out of the question, anyway. Sure, Les could have gone on tour as part of an Interior delegation, if Hall and Laura didn't have other plans for her.

Deep down, Mo had known that her tour days would be over if she and Les were Chosens. She hadn't thought about it much because she'd been trying to be realistic about the chances of that happening, and she certainly hadn't considered a triad. Honestly, given how things had turned out, they were better off on the planet, not stuck on some ship, and Mo was content to fly supply and teach. That didn't mean she wouldn't jump at the opportunity to go on tour if circumstances somehow allowed it, but if her last tour on the *Falcon* turned out to be her last tour ever, so be it.

Nathan waved a hand in front of her face. "Hello?"

Mo batted it away and decided not to view any more military images. Seeing Les with a Defence insignia on her uniform reminded Mo of their separation. Yeah, their forced time apart for *nothing*. All the tears, all the sleepless nights when she wondered how Les was, whether Les still loved her, if Les was thinking about her . . . then a few glorious days, and wham! The triad. Good-bye, dream life. Hello, maybe a different type of dream life. Time would tell. She consciously unclenched her teeth and quickly selected another set of images to head off the brooding session she could feel coming on.

Oh, the Festival of the Way after their graduation. Her jaw tightened again. Mama looked so happy. Okay, forget this set. Maybe reminiscing over old images was a bad idea.

"Find one with Papa and his thick moustache," Nathan said.

Despite herself, Mo smiled. "What year would that be?" she murmured, scanning the list. "You were only three, I think."

"I don't actually remember it. I just remember the images," Nathan said, chuckling.

"Here." She stared at the ridiculous mass of hair under Papa's nose. "I don't know how Mama put up with it," she said as Nathan snickered. "No wonder it didn't last long. I think this is the only set with him and that monstrosity." She flipped to the next image and snorted. "Argamon, look at Les! She must have been . . . um, you were three, so she would have been nine or ten, depending on when it was taken." Mo glanced at the date. "Ten." At that time, Jayne would have been eight and oblivious to what was going to hit her in four years. What had she looked like?

"What are you doing?"

Mo turned toward the door. Andrew was leaning against the doorframe with his arms folded.

"Looking at old images." Nathan nudged Mo's shoulder. "Go back to the one with Papa's moustache."

Mo did so and waved Andrew closer. He gazed at the image. "Oh, yeah, I remember that," he said, his tone lacklustre. His mouth didn't even twitch. Mo sighed as he wandered out of the study.

"I don't understand why he's still moping around over Ann," Nathan said.

That made two of them. "I just hope they don't cause a scene tomorrow." Then again, seeing Adelaide and Ann go at it might be worth the disruption. Ann wouldn't stand a chance. She smiled again at Papa's moustache, then flipped back to the image of Les and returned to the question she'd asked herself when Andrew had interrupted. What had Jayne looked like? Mo realized with a start that she didn't have any images of Jayne. "Here, you take over," she said to Nathan as she rose. He eagerly sat down and flipped to the next image. Mo hung around for a minute, then went into the hallway and pulled out her comm unit.

"I wasn't expecting to speak to you until tomorrow," Jayne said. "Everything okay?"

"Yeah. I was just looking at old images, and I realized that we don't have any of you in our family collection. Do you have any you can send me? Recent ones, or of you as a child?"

Jayne was silent for a moment. "No. Well, I suppose Carol has a few, and if you search the public academy archives, you might find me. I don't have any." She paused. "If you do find images of my academy classes, I'd prefer not to see them."

Who could blame her? And Mo should have known better. Jayne's parents' image collection would have been destroyed, or at least sealed. "I'm sorry. I didn't think."

"Don't be sorry. I like that you don't instantly think of my family history every time you think of me."

Warmth surged through Mo. Nope, Jayne's surname wasn't the first thing that came to mind anymore. "Plenty of images will be taken of you tomorrow."

"I won't mind looking at those." Jayne's voice softened. "They'll be our first images as a family."

A lump formed in Mo's throat.

"And the two most important women to me will be in them."

Mo forced a chuckle. "That's funny, I can say the same." Okay, time to say good-bye before she said a bunch of mushy stuff she'd cringe over after they disconnected. "Anyway, I won't keep you from Carol and Ronald. I'll see you tomorrow."

"Yes, you will." Mo could hear the smile in Jayne's voice. "Bye, Mo."

"Bye." Mo slid the unit into its holder, and didn't try to resist the sudden urge that felt so right. She stuck her head around the study's doorframe. "I'm going to Les's."

Nathan spun the chair around. "What? You're not supposed to stay there."

"I won't. It's only nine. I just want to see her one last time before we Join."

Nathan rolled his eyes. "Argamon, talk about lovesick."

"Yeah? I hope you're as lovesick about your Chosen when you've been with her for almost fourteen years." Grinning, and feeling as if she could face anything, Mo grabbed her cloak and almost skipped through the front door.

LESLEY PERCHED ON the edge of the sofa and sipped her tziva as she read Laura's dispatch. When she reached its end, she set her mug on the coffee table and read Laura's words again. When the dispatch had arrived minutes ago, she'd assumed it would contain good wishes for the next day, like every other dispatch she'd recently received. She'd been right, but Laura had added the following to the usual optimistic words:

As your Joining Day has approached, I've been thinking more and more about my family's triad. I suppose that's natural. Eleanor kept journals, and I reread one of them tonight. The journals contain her private thoughts, so I usually don't share their contents. But I don't think she'd mind me sharing this small excerpt with you. In fact, I believe she'd be delighted. See you tomorrow.

Then, the excerpt:

It finally hit me as I watched them approach the steps. Charlotte clutched Miriam's arm, which surprised me. Charlotte's usually the bolder one, but I guess everyone finds some circumstances intimidating. I remember thinking about how I'd like to clutch Miriam's arm.

We must be mad! Almost every triad before us has failed. But what else were we to do? Neither of my Chosens deserved execution and, in time, I can see myself loving both of them. Maybe I already do, I'm not sure. It's difficult to sort through my feelings when I'm growing closer to two women who are also growing closer to each other.

Lesley could relate, in the sense that she was coming to terms with Mo and Jayne's relationship at the same time her feelings for Jayne were changing. She didn't want to initiate a romantic relationship with Jayne until her emotional state had settled. Fortunately, Jayne would be patient. They had plenty of time. She read the rest:

Sometimes I feel insanely jealous and wish I could go out dancing once, just once, with only one of them, but when I do get the chance to snatch some time alone with either of them—when I'm out walking with Miriam or gardening with Charlotte—I miss the other one.

When I stood in the Joining Chamber, I wondered what the chances were

Yes, they'd made it. Fourteen daughters and umpteen descendants, including a commodore. And yes, Eleanor's words had inspired. Lesley had the responsibility of guiding her triad, and her two Chosens were as determined as Eleanor's had been. Of course, their situation was different. Eleanor hadn't faced sharing someone she'd loved for years. She hadn't had a Chosen some regarded as a threat to the Way. But she'd refused to exercise CT134 and had vowed to guide her Chosens through the challenges unique to triads—and she hadn't had a successful triad with fourteen daughters to point to when they had their wobbly moments.

Lesley had Eleanor's—and Miriam's and Charlotte's—success to draw upon. She'd reread this excerpt whenever she needed a reminder that she, Mo, and Jayne could, and would, make it. She and Mo didn't shy away from challenges, and Jayne had shown that she could weather just about anything. As Eleanor had said, *if anyone can do it, we can.*

Tomorrow, as she stood in the Joining Chamber, Lesley would remember Eleanor's words. The next triad would have *two* successful triads in a row to encourage it—and perhaps wouldn't have to deal with CT134? The article's existence rankled—no, offended! An innocent Rymellan should never be executed. Yes, triads were difficult and had a spotty history, but those in them should be treated like every other Rymellan. The Chosen Tradition already covered every imaginable transgression. As Lesley had once said to her parents, when it came to executions, what *could* happen had no place. Her commander training had strengthened her conviction in that regard.

CT134 was on the very short list of articles in the Chosen Tradition that was open to amendments, which included deletion. She could think of two advocates who would relish the challenge, but they didn't specialize in the Chosen Tradition. Perhaps Advocate Phillips would agree to lead the team. Lesley could look past his involvement in Jason and Mary's scheme; he'd only been doing his job, and she'd want the best advocate for this undertaking. She'd help, too. If the others wanted to look down their noses at her because she wrote opinions for the military, so be it; challenging the article was too important to allow pride to get in the way.

The more she thought about it, the more convinced she became that her parents would jump at the opportunity. They'd have to wait until the triad had a few successful years behind it, but they *would* challenge the article. As for Phillips, if he believed the article to be sound, he could take some persuading. Historic case, likely to be covered on the monitors, lead advocate on the team . . . Lesley had time to come up with the carrots she'd dangle. The case he'd written against Jayne could bring his credibility into question, but people were allowed to change their minds, especially when the dire predictions laid out in the case weren't coming to pass. Phillips's about face could actually work in their favour; it would show that he didn't cling to theory when reality countered it. After all, wouldn't the fact that a triad with an Adams in it was surviving—and flourishing—mean that *any* triad should survive? Lesley couldn't deny how satisfying it would feel to turn the hate directed at Jayne into ammunition they could use to strike CT134 from the Tradition.

Her musings came to an abrupt end when the front door swung open. A glance at her comm unit told her it was 21:15. They weren't expecting more visitors, especially at this hour. She felt her face tighten when Mo strode into the living room.

Mo held up her hands. "Don't worry, I'm not going to trample all over tradition by insisting on staying over. I just had the sudden urge to see you. It'll be the last time we see each other before we're officially Joined. We didn't get much time alone together today." She shrugged off her cloak, tossed it over the arm of a chair, and plunked down next to Lesley. "What are you doing?"

Lesley hesitated, then held her comm unit where Mo could read Eleanor's excerpt, sure that Laura wouldn't mind her sharing it with Mo and Jayne. "Laura sent this over. Apparently Eleanor, the Principal of the Finney triad, kept journals. This is an excerpt."

Mo leaned closer. When she grunted and sat back a minute later, Lesley assumed she'd finished and slid her comm unit back into its holder.

"Good to know they weren't sure how their lives would turn out, either," Mo said. "She sounded optimistic, though. I guess they had to trust themselves and believe it would work out." She met Lesley's eyes. "Like we will."

Lesley nodded. "It won't be easy. If we could read her journals after that point, I'm sure we'd find despair and doubt, along with the triumphs."

"Tell me about it." Mo sat forward and brought her hand to her mouth. "I've hardly had time to think over the past few days, ever since you told me about . . . It's going to hit me, you know. I mean, it has, but it's still kind of unreal right now. When you two start getting closer, there will be plenty of despair to go around."

A chill ran up Lesley's spine. She rubbed Mo's back. "I don't want to see you the way you were after your mama died." She'd rather never act on her feelings for Jayne.

Mo shook her head. "I blamed myself for Mama's death. The guilt sucked me into a black hole I couldn't escape, not without help. This is different. I'll be mad. I'll hate both of you—and love both of you. I'll worry about whether you still love me. But I won't feel guilty. Well, not about you and Jayne, anyway."

"You shouldn't feel guilty about you and Jayne, either."

Mo turned toward her. "No? So you won't feel guilty at all about you and Jayne?" There was an edge to her voice.

Point taken. "Well, okay, I—"

Mo groaned. "I didn't come over here to have this conversation. I came over because," she suddenly stood and thrust out her arms, "it's the night before our Joining Ceremony." Her enthusiasm didn't ring completely false. "The night before our Joining Ceremony! What were the chances?" She pointed at herself. "I knew, though. I always flaming knew."

Lesley couldn't help but smile. "Yes, you did. I never should have doubted you."

"No, you shouldn't have. But I know you were only trying to temper my expectations, so I wouldn't have been completely crushed if it turned out that we weren't Chosens—not that there was ever any possibility of that happening, of course. I hadn't factored in the possibility of a third Chosen, though, so we won't exactly have the life I imagined together. But not having you as my Chosen would have been worse. I'm going to do my best to be grateful for what I have, rather than wishing things were different."

Lesley looked up at her. "You really mean that?"

"Yeah. And I'll flaming-well tell myself that every time I want to curl into a ball and cry." She bit her lip. "I couldn't have lived without you, Les. I would only have gone through the motions."

"Me, too." Lesley rose and enveloped Mo in her arms. "So we'll do the best we can."

"I'm glad it's Jayne. I suppose I'd say that no matter who it was, since she'd be our Chosen, but when I first heard Jayne's name, I didn't think I'd ever say it at all."

"Me, either." The thought of sharing Mo with Jayne—with any-one—had angered her. It still did. It still hurt; it still woke her up in the night and would for a while. But they'd make it. *If anyone can do it, we can.* Over the coming years, she'd probably say that to herself more than she said the Words. *If anyone can do it, we can.* And Mo was right. A triad was the second to last thing Lesley would have wanted. Not having Mo as her Chosen . . .

She tightened her arms around Mo, kissed the top of her head, closed her eyes, and thought about their times at the Learning, Indoctrina-tion, and Military Academies, their first kiss, their first night together, the joys, the arguments, the emptiness during their separation. Lesley would endure anything, as long as she had Mo. Endure? It felt that way now, but she believed that, in time, Jayne would enrich her life with Mo, not destroy it. Jealousy, despair, and doubt would wage a campaign, but they would not conquer her triad.

Mo drew back. "I should go, before Papa comes looking for me, or I run into your mama." She put on her cloak and gazed at Lesley. "This is it, then. The next time I see you will be on the steps." Her eyes moistened; she averted them from Lesley's face and walked toward the archway. "Okay, I'm going, or I will be here all night."

Lesley followed her. Without a backward glance, Mo opened the front door and stepped outside. Wanting to say good-bye, Lesley opened

   RYMELLAN 3

her mouth to call out to her, but Mo stopped and spun around. A smile spread across her face as she pointed at the threshold. "Next time I walk through this doorway, I'll be a Thompson. Good night, Les."

Her throat tight, Lesley could only croak, "Good night," in return. She stood in the doorway and watched Mo pull her bike from the rack and ride off, and was still there long after she could no longer see Mo's orange cloak in the darkness.

A LOUD KNOCK at the front door set Jayne's heart racing, even though she'd expected it. Mo, right on time.

"She's here!" Carol squealed as she passed Jayne on her way to open the door. She whirled. "Oh, wait, you do it. You probably want a quiet word with her before we leave."

Jayne wasn't sure her mouth would cooperate. Were Mo and Lesley as nervous? She took a deep breath and somehow managed to walk down the hallway and open the door. Mo looked up at her. "Hi." Her uniform's buttons glinted in the early afternoon sun.

Jayne had last seen Mo in her dress uniform at the awards ceremony, but it was the memory of Mo striding into the room at the Chosen House and introducing herself that flashed through Jayne's mind. At the time, she hadn't appreciated how much of an effort that must have been for Mo. Rather than offering a smile and a handshake, Mo had probably wanted to punch her in the face. What was running through her mind now? Picking up a second Chosen so they could both Join with Lesley wouldn't have been on the list of things she wanted to do in life.

"You look nice," Mo said. "Blue suits you. I've always loved it on you. I guess that's why I really liked this outfit when you tried it on at the Trading Centre."

Her cheeks burned. She'd better say something before Mo asked if she'd lost her voice. "Thank you. You look nice, too."

Mo rolled her eyes. "In the same thing I always wear?"

"You do!"

"It's a good thing I'm not the type to get upset because someone's wearing the same outfit as me. There will be a lot of uniforms around today."

Including on their other Chosen. Jayne cleared her throat. "I guess Lesley is on her way—"

Mo's comm unit beeped; she swung it up and peered at the display. Her brow furrowed. "It's Karen," she said as she pulled the unit from its holder.

Karen? Was something wrong with Lesley?

"We just arrived at the Chosen House," Karen said after the usual exchange of greetings. "Lesley asked me to beep you, to warn you that there are quite a few people here."

"How many is quite a few?" Mo asked.

Silence, then, "The crowd stretches all the way from the Chosen House to the holding area."

Argamon! They'd have to walk through all those Rymellans?

Mo's face looked as tight as Jayne's muscles felt. "Thanks for letting us know. See you soon." She disconnected and muttered, "Sounds like we'll have quite the audience."

"I hope Carol and Ronald won't be stuck at the back." She wished they could be on the steps, not jostling for position among Rymellans who were only there to gawk.

"I say let them walk with us. They can veer off when we're almost at the steps."

"But—"

"If there are as many people as Karen says, everyone will understand." Mo smiled. "At least we know Les is there. Anyway, we should get going. I know she has a short meeting with Watkins, but then she'll be waiting on the steps for us."

"Yes." Jayne turned to call Carol.

"Jayne."

She turned back to Mo.

"Anything I say is going to sound obvious and stupid, but I'll try, anyway. Today is a good day. When I'm in the Joining Chamber, I'll mean every word, and I'm looking forward to a life with both my Chosens. I love you."

Jayne stared at her, suddenly wondering if she was dreaming. She'd expected to have a Chosen who tolerated her existence, and would have put the odds of hearing *I love you* on her Joining Day at zero. When she'd learned that she had two Chosens, both in the military, she'd radically revised that expectation to a short life with no Joining Day. She couldn't

     RYMELLAN 3

have been more wrong. Here she was, all dressed up with tears in her eyes and a proud Chosen in front of her, one she loved, cherished, and respected, and would do so for the rest of her life. She could say she understood that Mo had never wanted a triad, that Mo was making the best of an undesirable situation, and that, for her, the worst was yet to come. But why say it? It wouldn't change anything, and it would trivialize Mo's determination to view her Joining Day in a positive light.

She met Mo's eyes. "I love you, too." Then she was in Mo's arms, not caring whether her outfit would be wrinkled or what the neighbours thought. An Adams in the arms of a military officer in dress uniform! What next? Pink elephants flying through the sky? A year ago, Jayne would have considered the latter more likely to happen.

"LOOK AT ALL the people!" Andrew breathed. "Karen wasn't exaggerating."

Mo hopped off the craft and surveyed the crowd that stood between her and the steps that led to the Joining Chamber's entrance. Okay, once her stomach muscles unclenched, she'd be able to walk. She forced a grin. "The whole sector must be here."

"And then some," Nathan said.

He wasn't helping! Someone gripped her arm; she wasn't surprised to see Jayne's pale face, and reached across to pat her hand. "We'll be—"

"Let's get a move on!" Papa pointed to his left. "There's the rest of the family. Come on."

Everyone fell into step behind him, maybe relieved that he'd taken control. They probably would have stood at the craft all day, otherwise. Fortunately, the holding area was roped off, restricting the crowd to a healthy distance away from the area.

A stranger—with a familiar face—stood with Mo's other siblings. It had to be Robert. Mo would keep his striking resemblance to Jayne to herself, sure that Jayne wouldn't appreciate the observation.

"Good, you're all here." Papa gazed at Robert. "You must be Jayne's brother."

Mary laughed. "That's what we all said as soon as we saw him. You look so much like him," she said to Jayne.

Thank you, Mary. That had to be a new record for putting one's foot in one's mouth at a family event, and undoubtedly only the first of the many similar gaffes that would take place today. Had there ever been a Joining Day on which someone hadn't inadvertently said the absolute worst thing at some point? Mo glanced at Jayne. Yep, Mary's remark hadn't gone down well, but the others probably wouldn't notice the slight tension around Jayne's mouth. She could read Jayne almost as well as she could read Les!

Jayne's smile was strained—to Mo. "Yes, this is my brother, Robert. Robert, this is Mary, and this is—"

"We've already introduced ourselves to each other," Robert said curtly. "Don't you think you should introduce me to your Chosen first?"

Jayne's face flushed. "Sorry, I—" She let go of Mo's arm. "This is Mo Middleton."

"Pleased to meet you," Mo said, grudgingly extending her hand. She'd just broken another record: from curiosity to hate in mere seconds. Moron.

"Pleasure." Robert's handshake was firm and his eyes cool.

"This is my youngest brother, Nathan," Mo said, taking over the introductions and deliberately introducing Nathan before Papa. If Robert didn't like it, tough.

"Are you sure you want us to walk with you?" Carol said when Mo had finished introducing everyone. "We can leave now and find somewhere to stand."

"I want to be able to see them when I'm on the steps," Jayne whispered to Mo.

"We want to make sure you're as close to the front as you can get," Mo said. "Walk behind us and peel off when we're almost at the steps."

Carol frowned. "I doubt people will appreciate us going to the front like that."

"Who cares? We don't know half these people. They're just here so they can say they were here. You and Ronald *should* be—" A loud roar from the crowd drowned out her words and made her heart pound. What the—?

"Disobedience means death. Death to those who commit a Chosen Violation. Death to those who disobey. Death to those who violate the Way. Death to those who violate the Way! Death to those who violate the Way!" Applause and cheers filled the air. As soon as the ruckus died down, the crowd chanted the Words again, and then again, with no sign of stopping. Now that her initial shock had dissipated, Mo understood the reason for the crowd's sudden enthusiasm. Anticipation and apprehension fuelled her racing heart and turned her legs to jelly. The Thompsons were on the steps. Les was waiting for them.

"Time to go," Papa shouted.

Apparently deciding that whether to walk with the families was now moot, Carol grabbed Ronald's hand and pulled him behind all the siblings, who were forming up behind Mo and Jayne. Mo winced when Jayne's fingers dug into her arm, though she sympathized.

Papa stood next to Mo. "Ready?"

She inhaled deeply and slowly exhaled. After everything she and Les had been through, all that stood between them now was a boisterous crowd that would *not* intimidate her. She nodded at Jayne, and smiled when Jayne, who looked terrified, nodded back. "Ready!"

They walked. Mo now acknowledged what she'd noticed as soon as they'd landed, but hadn't wanted to think about: the military presence. Orange cloaks were everywhere, and most weren't worn by her and Les's friends. Interior officers were here to ensure that, no matter how anyone in the crowd felt about the triad and Jayne, they'd keep their mouths shut. Suggesting that the triad would fail because Jayne was in it, or that the triad shouldn't exist, had been tolerated while exercising CT134 was still a viable option. Doing it now, while standing outside the Chosen House as two Chosens walked toward their Principal: suicide.

One of the many military standing guard around the holding area removed a section of rope, and the Middletons and Adamses left their haven and strode through the remaining open space that separated them from the crowd. Then they were engulfed. The noise was deafening; many chanted, some sang on either side of a makeshift aisle formed by military personnel. Mo kept her eyes forward, but she could sense Jayne's panic. She pried Jayne's fingers away, took her hand, and shouted, "Keep your eyes on Les."

Jayne's brow furrowed. She bent her head and leaned closer.

"Keep your eyes on Les," Mo shouted directly into Jayne's ear. Any other time, Jayne would have recoiled, but not in this racket. Mo wasn't sure Jayne could even hear her. "Keep your eyes on Les!"

Jayne nodded and straightened. Mo squeezed her hand. *Keep your eyes on Les. We're walking to Les.* The specks on the steps were coming into focus. There she was! Mo's breath caught in her throat. Her vision blurred. The crowd, the clamour, faded away. *We're walking to Les. We're walking to Les.*

HER EYES PEELED for her two Chosens, Lesley absently chanted the Words along with those assembled. She couldn't wait for Mo and Jayne to arrive, not only because she wanted to Join with them, but to get off these steps. Usually extended family and friends gathered outside to share what Lesley felt was a private moment, even though it took place in public. Well, they would greet each other, smile for the obligatory images, then leave the spectators behind until after the ceremony. They'd already agreed that Jayne would introduce Robert to the Thompsons inside the Chosen House.

The crowd suddenly roared; the chanting grew louder. Lesley fixed her eyes on the path the military had cleared and sensed the excitement of her parents and siblings, who were standing behind her. She'd spent her life preparing for this day, and had expected to force a smile as she waited for a Chosen who wasn't Mo—or walked to that Chosen, if she hadn't been the Principal. But here she was, waiting for Mo *and* a Chosen who wasn't Mo. The situation reminded her of a riddle, or one of the logic problems she'd puzzled over as a child.

Her heart leaped. *I can see them!* She resisted the urge to wave, but couldn't stifle the grin that spread across her face. It wilted as her Chosens approached. They appeared wary and harassed; while she'd stood on the steps resenting being on display, they'd experienced the ordeal of making their way down a narrow path with only military separating them from the crowd pressing in on both sides. She wanted to run down the steps and meet them, but that wasn't done, and her Chosens were strong women who didn't need rescuing.

From the moment Lesley had spotted them, Mo and Jayne had gazed at her, but from a distance. When they reached the bottom of the steps, they could finally *see* her. She nodded at them, then tensed when Mo bounded up the steps with a smile splitting her face, dragging Jayne along with her. The handshake they'd agreed upon was going to be more. Perhaps Mo needed a hug after braving the walk to the steps, or perhaps she was caught up in the moment. Either way, Lesley put aside her aversion to publicly displaying affection and held out her arms, an invitation Mo enthusiastically accepted.

Lesley held her tightly. "I love you."

"I love you, too!" Mo shouted back. Fortunately the clamour from the crowd would prevent anything said—or shouted—on the steps from reaching those below.

Aware of Jayne hovering behind Mo, Lesley drew back, beamed at Mo, then let her go. After Mo had moved to stand at Lesley's right. Lesley met Jayne's eyes and reached for her. "You and I are truly Chosens," she said into Jayne's ear. "This is only the beginning for us."

Jayne's cheek flexed against Lesley's. "It's a wonderful beginning." She paused. "Thank you for never wavering." Then they parted, and she took her place at Lesley's left.

The image taker was already in position in front of them, waiting for the families to line up behind the triad. Robert must be among the group; with her attention firmly on Mo and Jayne, Lesley hadn't noticed. As several in the families changed position in response to the image taker's shouted suggestions, Lesley put an arm around each of her Chosens' shoulders and felt their arms pressed against her back. She didn't need eyes in the back of her head to know that Mo and Jayne's arms were touching each other, and inwardly smiled.

Perhaps sensing the timelessness of the moment, the crowd settled down when the image taker raised his hand and encouraged happy faces. These images of the triad would end up in the history books.

By the time the image taker stepped back and thanked them, Lesley's cheeks ached. She relaxed her frozen smile and lifted her arms from her Chosens' shoulders. Mo turned to Lesley, her eyes alight with excitement. "Time to go in!"

Lesley nodded and turned around. Mama and Papa caught her eye and smiled, then they whirled to follow all the siblings through the doors that two Chosen Council members held open. Since images of Joining Ceremonies were prohibited, the image taker would remain outside. Adrenaline coursed through Lesley. *We're about to be Joined, really Joined.* She reached for her Chosens' hands and held them tightly. Michael disappeared through the doorway, and then it was their turn.

She gave each of her Chosens an encouraging nod. The moment they stepped toward the doors, the crowd roared and the chanting resumed.

The sudden silence when the doors closed behind them was almost disorienting; it reminded Lesley of a crypt's hushed atmosphere. Sighs of relief rose around her. Now that they were safe from scrutiny, it was time to properly greet the families. As she hugged Michael, it struck her that she and Mo would finally unite the Thompson and Middleton families. The two families had such a long history together that they were practically one family already, but today would officially bind them together. When their descendants learned about their lineages, they would see that the two families had finally merged because Lesley Thompson and Mo Middleton were Chosens. Despite it being an event outside her control, Lesley couldn't help but feel proud that she was the Thompson, Mo was the Middleton, and that their love, in addition to the Chosen Council, would Join the families together. Sentimental, yes, but it was the sort of day that encouraged emotional interpretation over rational thought. Just for today, Lesley wouldn't fight it.

After she'd embraced Nathan, she turned to the figure hovering in her peripheral vision. No introduction was necessary—not only did he resemble Jayne, but it could only be Robert, under the circumstances. Still, Lesley waited for Jayne to introduce them. "Welcome to the Thompson family," she said as she shook his hand.

He inclined his head. "Thank you."

"We'll have more opportunity to speak at the supper," she said politely, aware that the others were already being led into the Joining Chamber.

"I'll look forward to it." He fell into step behind Nathan.

Lesley turned to her Chosens, in time to see them roll their eyes at each other. He'd sounded perfectly polite to her, but since Mo apparently wasn't impressed with him, something must have happened. She'd ask Mo later; Watkins had moved in front of them, readying himself to lead the triad. Mo and Jayne took their positions at Lesley's side. Lesley hadn't expected to be nervous; she wanted to Join with the two women flanking her, and she'd do so while surrounded by Rymellans who loved her—with the exception of Robert. But as she reached for her Chosens' hands, her heart pounded, and it would be difficult to tell who was clinging to whom.

Watkins glanced behind him, then stepped forward. The triad followed him. When they reached the stone steps that led down to the chamber, Lesley carefully descended them, not wanting to trip at this most solemn of moments. Watkins reached the bottom of the steps, walked through the chamber's wide entrance that normally saw only two Chosens enter hand-in-hand, and moved aside. Lesley could sense the anticipation from those waiting within. With one last encouraging glance to her right, then to her left, she braced herself and strode with her Chosens into the Joining Chamber, her footsteps reverberating on the stone floor.

The smiling families ringed the circular chamber. Lesley felt herself grin as the triad walked to the centre of the circle. She stopped on the worn, decorative *P* engraved into the floor. Over the centuries, thousands of Principals had stood on this spot and formed a smaller circle by facing their Chosens and taking their hands. Lesley let go of her Chosens' hands, then took them again when Mo and Jayne stood beaming in front of her, despite their nerves. In their case, she could hold only one hand of each Chosen. Theirs was a slightly larger circle than usual.

Footsteps rang out. Watkins closed the outer circle. "Let us begin."

Everyone drew breath and chanted, "Disobedience means death. Death to those who commit a Chosen Violation. Death to those who disobey. Death to those who violate the Way. Death to those who violate the Way. Death to those who violate the Way!" Applause echoed around the chamber.

Mo and Jayne took their respective positions next to Lesley and slipped their hands into hers again as Watkins entered the circle. He nodded to Lesley, then to Mo, then to Jayne. "Today we Join together three families, the Joining of a triad. Before we do, there is the matter of Article CT134. Lesley Thompson, do you and your Chosens waive the rights assigned to you under this article?"

Since the triad had met with Watkins two days ago to review how the ceremony would differ for triads, the question didn't surprise Lesley, and she knew it wouldn't have shocked Mo or Jayne. She squeezed her Chosens' hands. "We waive the rights assigned to us," she said clearly and firmly.

"Very good," Watkins said with a smile. "Then let us remember how you came to be Rymellan." Two Chosen Council members strode up, one carrying three scrolls on a silver tray. Watkins murmured, "Thank you," and reached for the scroll that sat between the other two. He broke the seal, unfurled it, and gazed at Lesley. "Lesley Thompson, your family has a long and illustrious history. As is the custom, we shall limit ourselves to twenty generations. You are Lesley Thompson. You are the daughter of Adelaide Thompson, Joined to Alan Winters. Adelaide is the daughter of Julia Thompson, Joined to David Strong. Julia is the daughter of . . ."

Lesley listened to Watkins recite what she'd learned during her Level Two at the Indoctrination Academy and could repeat from memory to this day. When it was Mo's turn, Watkins repeated the same introduction to Ramona Middleton's family. Since Lesley and Mo had studied their family histories together and tested each other when preparing for the recital exam, Lesley knew Mo's lineage as well as her own and silently recited it along with Watkins. "Ramona Middleton, you are the daughter of Susan Middleton, Joined to Michael Anderson. Susan is the daughter of Colin Middleton, Joined to Donna Matthews. Colin is the son of . . ."

Watkins finally rolled up the Middleton scroll and handed it to his colleague. He lifted the final scroll from the tray and turned to Jayne. "Jayne Adams, you are Rymellan, but you have no family history." With one swift motion, Watkins unfurled the scroll and tore it in half. The rip's echo lingered in the stone chamber. "You are Jayne Adams. Your family history begins today."

Jayne hadn't reacted when Watkins had described this part of the ceremony to her during their meeting. She'd waited until afterward, when the triad was alone, and said, "A new beginning is fine with me.' Then she'd added, "I wish leaving the past behind was as easy as ripping up a scroll." Was she thinking that now? Lesley wanted to glance at her, but didn't want to give anyone in the chamber the impression that Jayne's family history diminished her in Lesley's eyes.

The two Chosen Council members who'd assisted Watkins returned to the outer circle. Watkins cleared his throat. "The Chosen Council is not without compassion. Though it considers both service to the Way and quality of life when selecting Chosens, and has successfully Joined Rymellans together for millennia, it recognizes that, despite its best efforts, a Rymellan may not wish to Join with his or her Chosen—or Chosens. If any of you feel this way, and would prefer to be executed than forever bound to your Chosens, this is your final opportunity to say so. Speak now, and your wish shall be carried out."

The ensuing silence stretched out forever, even though Watkins waited only five seconds before speaking again. "Let us proceed." Despite only two Rymellans having ever opted for execution at this point in the ceremony, and everyone present knowing that the triad intended to Join, the tension in the chamber palpably eased along with the release of pent breath.

The same Chosen Council member who'd carried in the scrolls again approached Watkins, this time with the Chosen rings. Watkins lifted the ring sitting between the other two on the tray. Lesley held out her left hand. As Watkins slipped the Chosen ring onto her third finger, Lesley repeated after him: "I, Lesley Thompson, honour the Way by Joining with my two Chosens, Ramona Middleton and Jayne Adams. I will obey the articles of the Chosen Tradition. I will bring up my children to be strong in the Way. As the Principal, I welcome my two Chosens into the Thompson family." *If anyone can do it, we can.*

"So witnessed," everyone intoned.

Watkins picked the smallest ring up from the tray. Mo extended her right hand. "I, Ramona Middleton, honour the Way by Joining with my Principal, Lesley Thompson, and my Chosen, Jayne Adams. I will obey the articles of the Chosen Tradition. I will bring up my children to be strong in the Way."

"So witnessed," thundered around the chamber.

Now Jayne held out her right hand. At the meeting with Watkins, she'd asked if Mo could recite her vow second, even though Adams came before Middleton alphabetically. Watkins had hesitated, then agreed, since the choice to order the surnames alphabetically in their legal names was just that—a choice not dictated by the Chosen Tradition. Lesley and Mo had supported Jayne's desire to go third. "I, Jayne Adams, honour the Way by Joining with my Principal, Lesley Thompson, and my Chosen, Ramona Middleton. I will obey the articles of the Chosen Tradition. I will bring up my children to be strong in the Way."

"So witnessed."

Watkins nodded. "If you would join hands."

Lesley held out her left hand; Mo and Jayne gripped it with their right hands.

"You are now Lesley Adams Middleton Thompson, Ramona Adams Middleton Thompson, and Jayne Adams Middleton Thompson. You are Joined. Let us witness you say the *Words Every Rymellan Knows* as a Joined triad."

Watkins whirled and walked to the outer circle. Lesley couldn't contain a grin when she met Jayne's, and then Mo's, eyes for the first time as her Joined Chosens. She took Jayne's right hand with her left; her grin widened when she felt the Chosen ring on Jayne's finger. "Disobedience means death. Death to those who commit a Chosen Violation. Death to those who disobey. Death to those who violate the Way. Death to those who violate the Way. Death to those who violate the Way!"

Inside the stone chamber, the cheers and applause sounded as loud as the ruckus from the crowd when Lesley had stood on the steps. She wanted to hug her Chosens—the newest members of the Thompson family!—but that would have to wait until they were on her aviacraft. Watkins and the other Chosen Council members had already moved to the entrance. Lesley took Mo and Jayne's hands. They followed Watkins, their families behind them.

When the triad had almost reached the doors that would open onto the steps, Watkins turned and nodded, then moved aside. Two Chosen Council members swung open and held the doors. Lesley glanced behind her to ensure that their families were ready, then the newest Rymellan family stepped into the sunshine, giving a crowd that needed little encouragement to cheer its first look at a Joined triad, a sight not seen in many years. This time, Lesley didn't mind her ringing ears and the chanting from the crowd while the requisite images were taken. As the triad walked the narrow pathway to the holding area, she couldn't resist lifting Mo and Jayne's hands, and shouting for Mo to lift her right hand, and then basking in the roar that rose from the crowd when the triad's Chosen rings reflected the sun.

MO INWARDLY CURSED when she almost cut a finger on her left hand. While cutting her food, paying attention to the knife rather than to the Chosen ring on her finger would probably be a good idea. But her eyes were continuously drawn to the silver band. Hopefully the novelty would wear off soon.

"Lieutenant Commander Thompson," someone—it sounded like Andrew—said.

Mo forked the piece of quiche into her mouth, then looked up when Andrew repeated, "Lieutenant Commander Thompson!" He met Mo's eyes from across the table, three chairs down. "Would Lieutenant Commander Thompson please pass the rolls?"

Argamon! What was with the formality? Mo swallowed her quiche and nudged Les, then felt herself flush when gales of laughter rose to her right, where her family was seated.

"I told you!" Nathan pointed at Neil and Matthew. "Pay up."

Neil whipped out his comm unit. "I'm transferring the credits to your account."

Mo dropped her fork to her plate. "How was I to know you wanted me, and not her?"

Andrew's jaw dropped. "I was looking right at you!"

She wanted to strangle him, especially when she glanced at Les and caught her grinning. "You better become a commander soon, or this is going to be really confusing!" she snapped, then blew out an exasperated sigh. It wasn't Les's fault, it was her flaming brothers. And Papa! Now his comm unit was out, too. "Do you want the flaming rolls, or not?" she said to Andrew.

He nodded. Mo would love to throw one at him, but why give them the satisfaction? She passed the bread basket to Nathan to give to Andrew. To think that only a few minutes ago, she'd been sitting here feeling all sentimental about Middleton no longer being her surname, which had naturally led to thoughts of Mama. If only she could have been in the Joining Chamber. She would have been so thrilled to see the long-standing bond between the Middleton and Thompson families become official. *See, Mama, you didn't have to worry about me and Les.* But Mama *had* worried; she'd expressed her concern during one of their last conversations together. If only she'd lived. If only she were here, telling Nathan and Andrew not to tease their sister. Nah, Mama would have been in on it, too, her laughter drowning out everyone else's.

"They're only teasing," Les said.

Mo turned to her. "I know. Though it does illustrate that it's a good thing we're not serving together right now." She paused. "Do you think we'll ever serve together again?"

Les's brow furrowed. "Only if I'm transferred to Defence, for some reason."

And with Les in the commander training . . . unless she committed a major misstep on her way to becoming an Interior admiral, the chances of her being transferred to Defence were about . . . oh, what Mo would have thought their chances were of ending up in a triad. She lifted her brows and said, "You never know," then stuck more quiche into her mouth.

JAYNE STOOD WITH the Thompsons and Middletons and watched Lesley and Mo dance the first third of the long piece Adelaide had selected. The triad had practised the dance twice; their comm units would vibrate at the two transition points. Soon it would be Jayne's turn to dance with Lesley. She swallowed and clasped her clammy hands behind her. This would be worse than the Dance Hall. Other couples wouldn't obscure her from those watching; everyone's eyes would be on her as she danced with Lesley and then Mo—including Robert's, and her aunt's and uncle's. So far she'd avoided talking to him, but she'd exchanged a few polite words with them, as acquaintances would. It was hard to believe that she'd lived with her aunt and uncle for five years, though she'd spent part of that time at the Indoctrination Academy.

In addition to Carol, Jayne's other cousins were here. Adelaide had wanted her to invite more relatives, so Jayne had grudgingly agreed to Carol's siblings, and only Carol's siblings. No other aunts and uncles, no other cousins, no grandparents, nobody who'd ignored her existence from the moment she'd lost her parents. Had the sight of her upset her relatives? Repulsed them? Made them feel guilty? Had it been a matter of cutting off what they viewed as a rotting piece of flesh from the familial body?

Jayne Adams, you are Rymellan, but you have no family history. Rather than offending, Watkins' words had liberated. Today was a fresh start, an opportunity to build a new family history with two women she loved.

Adams was still part of her name; it was one of those engraved on the ring on her right hand. But today she'd leave everything that name represented behind and reclaim the identity others had wrenched from her—a true Rymellan, a strong Rymellan, and now a Joined Rymellan who would honour her Chosens until her last breath.

Her comm unit vibrated.

And a terrified Rymellan who'd better not step on Lesley's feet too often! She took a deep breath as she watched Lesley and Mo part and smile at each other, then willed herself to walk, not wanting Adelaide to have to push her and set everyone thinking that she didn't want to dance with Lesley. Mo nodded to her as she approached. Jayne knew her answering smile looked frozen. Every step across the dance floor to where Lesley waited made her feel more exposed; she had to fight the urge to run to Lesley and cling to her. This was as excruciating as the walk to the steps. Mo's voice rang in her ears: *We're walking to Les. Keep your eyes on Les.* And Jayne did. She transferred the spotlight that must be dogging her every step to Lesley, who appeared perfectly at ease in her crisp white dress uniform, her back straight, her chin up, and her eyes encouraging.

When Lesley smiled and extended her right hand, Jayne slipped her hand into Lesley's and her other arm around Lesley's shoulders in one fluid motion. They whirled; they danced; despite stepping on Lesley's feet, Jayne felt graceful and alive and self-assured within the arms of a Chosen she loved and trusted, and bolstered by the supportive voice of her other Chosen playing in her mind.

All those years she'd told herself that she wasn't missing out, that she was content to be on her own, that families only let you down in the end, that the only person she could truly trust was herself . . . how much higher would she soar, now that two women would be there to catch her when she fell? How long would it take for the joyful tears to wash away the shameful ones? She'd believed that the Incident hadn't hardened her heart, that the cold fingers of cynicism and indifference hadn't wrapped themselves around her spirit and squeezed away all hope—until her Chosens' persistent dedication to the spirit of the Way had broken through the barriers she'd erected. Love's light had shattered her delusion and illuminated her huddling and afraid, and trust had coaxed her to take its hand and return to the living, leaving the dead behind.

WITH A QUIET sigh of relief, Lesley turned away from those at the *Falcon* table. Her life had changed so much since she'd last seen her fellow pilots that it felt as if decades had passed since they'd spoken.

"I've already forgotten most of the names," Jayne said when they were out of earshot of the table.

"I wouldn't worry about it. Who knows when we'll see them again?" Mo said.

The sadness in Mo's voice didn't escape Lesley's ears. "Yearning to be back on tour?" she asked.

"No. Well, maybe a little, but only because I miss the camaraderie. I mean, sure, I see the same pilots on 72, but I'm up and down. It's not the same as being in each other's pockets for six months. I guess seeing everyone made me realize that we're growing apart." Mo brightened. "But hey, I enjoy the teaching, I don't mind flying supply, and I'll take you two over a tour any day."

Lesley slipped her arm around Mo's shoulders and squeezed her, then wondered if Jayne wanted to do the same. Jayne rarely touched Mo when the three of them were together. Lesley appreciated her deferential manner. She wasn't ready to throw her arm around Mo, only to discover that Jayne had beaten her to it. Perhaps in time she'd chuckle and rest her arm on Jayne's, rather than wanting to push it away. But not today.

"Oh!" Mo waved and pointed. "There's Ross. Come on, I want to introduce you." She grasped Jayne's arm.

"This Ross is the same one they were all talking about, right?" Jayne said.

Mo nodded. "Most of them graduated from the C6 Military Academy."

Lesley lifted her arm from Mo's shoulders when someone else caught her eye. "You two go ahead. I'll catch up."

Mo followed Lesley's gaze and nodded. Lesley watched her two Chosens walk toward Ross, then maneuvered her way to Laura, nodding at those whose eyes met hers, but discouraging conversation by quickly looking away. Laura was talking to Caroline Johnson, who lived several estates away from the Thompsons. Both women turned to Lesley as she approached. Caroline murmured a hello and quickly excused herself. Laura gazed after her. "She's probably relieved that you rescued her. I don't know why she's always so tense when she talks to me. She has nothing to worry about. Anyway, let me see it."

Lesley opened her mouth to ask what Laura wanted to see, then clamped it shut and held out her left hand. Laura peered at Lesley's Chosen ring. "It's not every day you see three names on the ring," she said as Lesley slowly rotated the ring on her finger.

"Do you have your triad's Chosen rings?" Lesley asked.

Laura's head lifted. "No. I don't know who has them. I assume they went to their eldest daughter and then down that line. I descend from daughter ten, so even if they'd split them up, we wouldn't have them."

"What was daughter ten's name?" Lesley asked dryly.

"Ruth."

"Whose biological daughter was she?"

Laura slowly shook her head. "Tsk, tsk. The only reason I won't tell you off at your own Joining supper is because I know the nuances of the Chosen Tradition in regard to triads aren't at your fingertips, especially regarding children. They will be."

Lesley's face tightened. She hated making mistakes, especially in front of someone like Laura.

"Children belong to the entire triad. Your children will be yours, Mo's, and Jayne's. *You'll* know who the biological parents are. Rymellans who know you will know who the biological parents are. But that information will never go into the public record, and everyone must treat all three of you as the parents, because you will be." Laura's mouth turned up at the corners. "When the time comes, I'm sure we'll issue an interpretation of the relevant articles as a mandatory bulletin. Nobody will have an excuse for doing something like rejecting a permission form signed by the non-biological parent."

When the time comes . . . the triad still had issues to work out, but they wouldn't want to wait too long to start a family.

"To answer your question about Ruth, I don't know, and it doesn't matter. They all brought her up. They're all my ancestors."

Lesley understood the pride in Laura's voice. "Thanks for sending the excerpt from Eleanor's journal. It did inspire. She was a formidable woman. They all were."

"So are you and your Chosens. I'm not worried about this triad, Lesley. I know you'll make it work. The triad couldn't have asked for a better Principal."

Blood rushed to Lesley's cheeks. She could almost forgive herself for her earlier mistake. Almost.

"You know, I might try to find out who has their Chosen rings," Laura said. "We're not close to many of the other families. It's been too many generations. But I wouldn't mind seeing the rings. I'll start by asking my mama how we got copies of the journals."

"If you find the rings, can I—we—see them, too?"

Laura nodded. "I can't think of anything more fitting than your triad examining those rings."

JAYNE WATCHED COMMANDER Ross walk away and felt like pinching herself. The notion of conversing with a commander no longer terrified her. Unbelievably, she'd soon be Joined to one. If her imagination had ever dreamed up a ton of military at her Joining supper, they would have been there to keep an eye on her, not as guests—and her Chosens! She couldn't help but chuckle.

"What are you thinking about?" Mo asked.

Jayne eyed Mo's dress uniform and bit her lip. "I was just thinking that Commander Ross seems nice. There was a time when she would have frightened me."

"You haven't seen her chew out a pilot. She doesn't do it very often, though. You really have to screw up to upset Ross." Mo shifted her weight. "I have to go to the bathroom."

"Okay. I'll go talk to Carol," Jayne said, but she scanned the room for someone else as soon as Mo left. Lesley was still talking to Laura. Good. This would be the perfect opportunity to do what she'd been avoiding all evening. According to the agenda Adelaide had drilled into Jayne's head, they would have to leave soon. She couldn't delay the dreaded conversation any longer.

She found Robert, braced herself, and headed over to him. Fortunately he was with Kelly, and not a bunch of other relatives she'd rather not see. Kelly spotted Jayne first; her face lit up and she beckoned Jayne over to join them.

"Let me see the ring," she said, her voice too shrill. Jayne obligingly held out her right hand and stared at Kelly's bent head. "I'd love to meet your Chosens," Kelly said.

"Lesley's talking to her commanding officer, and I'm not sure where Mo is." Jayne was glad Kelly couldn't see her face. She liked Kelly and wouldn't mind introducing her to Lesley and Mo. Why Kelly had stuck by Robert was a mystery; Jayne could appreciate how difficult that must have been after the Incident. Robert and Kelly had been together for longer than Lesley and Mo. Kelly must see something in him that eluded Jayne. Had Kelly asked Robert why he'd abandoned his younger sister? Had she encouraged him to visit Jayne, or had she been too busy defending Robert to her family and everyone else who'd urged her to dump him? It didn't matter; Robert, not Kelly, should have looked out for her.

Argamon! Robert managed to get under her skin merely by standing next to her. Her resentment, disappointment, and bewilderment at his betrayal . . . they'd never be resolved. He didn't care, and she needed to look forward, especially here, at her own Joining supper. *Say what you came to say and move on.* She gently pulled her hand away from Kelly and forced herself to turn to him. "Thank you for agreeing to stand on the steps with me."

"He's your brother. Of course he'd stand on the steps with you," Kelly quickly said.

Robert scowled at her. "I'm apparently not good enough to sit at the main table, though."

Kelly's face fell. "Rob, don't—"

Jayne held up her hand. "It's not a matter of you not being good enough. It's that we're not close. Carol's been a part of my life all these years. You haven't."

"That makes sense, right?" Kelly patted Robert's arm. "We're at the family table with everyone else."

"It's still a slight," Robert snapped.

A slight? Jayne couldn't believe it. He was upset because she hadn't treated him like a brother for one flaming event? What about him not treating her like a sister for thirteen flaming years? Could he not see past his own nose?

"And I was only on the steps because the other two families wanted me there," he added sullenly.

"The Thompsons wanted you there. I don't think the Middletons cared one way or the other," Jayne retorted before she could stop herself.

"I'm surprised they wanted *you* there," Robert spat.

Kelly gasped.

Robert twisted toward her. "What? I didn't say they didn't want her there. I said I'm surprised that they did. Let's face it, when I heard about the triad, I wondered whether she'd make it to the steps. I couldn't have been the only one. Her two Chosens are in the military, after all." His feigned innocence didn't jibe with the venom in his voice just seconds earlier.

Jayne quashed her rising indignation and the urge to shout that her Chosens had wanted to Join with her. Wouldn't he love to see her humiliate herself by insisting that her Chosens truly cared for her? How many ways would he try to twist her words and, in the process, insult Lesley and Mo? Forget it! She wasn't playing this game anymore.

She'd never understand why he'd written her off when she'd most needed him. Maybe he'd been too shell-shocked to worry about anyone but himself. Maybe he'd been a frightened and hurt seventeen-year-old trying to save his own skin. Maybe, in trying to make sense of an incomprehensible situation, he'd blamed the Incident on her. Or maybe he was a self-absorbed, petty man, who only cared about himself. She didn't care anymore. If he ever wanted to have a mature conversation with her, she wouldn't turn him away. But she was done.

She forced a smile. "It's all right, Kelly. I was surprised, too." Surprised, and gratified, that her Chosens had looked past her name, and that she'd looked past their cloaks. Robert was welcome to read her statement any way he wanted to. "Anyway, I just came over to say hello and to thank you for coming. Enjoy the rest of your evening." With a nod, Jayne whirled and strode away from him.

"Hey, Jayne!"

She looked to her right. Nathan pointed at his empty glass and jerked a thumb over his shoulder. "You want a drink?"

"Sure." She fell into step with him, and blinked back the tears that suddenly sprang to her eyes.

MO LEFT THE bathroom and strolled back along the carpeted corridor toward the reception hall. Two boys were peering into a room off the corridor, giggling and nudging each other. "What are you two—"

They jumped and gaped at her, then raced away.

She shook her head, and slowed her pace as she passed the room. The door was only open a crack. She crept closer to it and listened. Silence. Curiosity got the better of her; she peeked through the crack. Her brows shot up. *Argamon!* It was a good thing she hadn't snacked recently. She quietly pulled the door shut and wished the infirmary could erase the last five seconds of her memory. She didn't need that image of Andrew and Ann sucking face bouncing around in her brain.

What did it mean? Had they reached some sort of compromise regarding Andrew going to 72, or had hormones won the day? She sighed. What was it with those two? Were they infatuated with each other, or was it love? Would they be at each other's throats again tomorrow? *Do I care?* Well, she supposed she did. Two lovebirds were better than Andrew moping around the house and Ann spreading her misery around 72. Next time she felt sorry for someone because they didn't have a dance partner, she'd stay out of it.

As she continued toward the reception hall, she wondered how she'd feel when she saw Les and Jayne kissing. She doubted they'd ever be all over each other in front of her, but even small displays of affection would be jarring. They'd decided they'd all sleep together the first time, but that would be different. Mo would be involved, not a spectator on the sidelines. When she saw them kissing or hugging or patting each other's hands, she'd have to try very hard to remember that they both loved her, too, that she could go right up and kiss them, too, if she felt like it. Her head would still feel like exploding and she'd still want to curl up into a ball and howl in pain, but too bad.

As she grasped the handle on the reception hall's door, her Chosen ring drew her eyes. There was no backing out now, so they'd either learn to accept that they all loved each other, or they were in for one flaming mess of a miserable life. Mo knew which outcome she wanted, and that it would take every shred of self-control and maturity she had to get there. But she'd do it. She'd stay on the right side of the razor-thin line that separated love from hate.

As soon as she entered the reception hall, she spotted Laura talking to her daughter. No sign of Les, but there was Jayne, with Nathan. Mo strolled up to them. "Have you seen Les?"

They shook their heads. "Maybe she's gone to our designated meeting spot," Jayne said.

Mo swung up her comm unit and checked the time. "We're not due there for ten minutes."

"Do you know where Andrew is?" Nathan asked.

She shrugged. "No idea."

"He said he was going to the bathroom. That's the last I saw of him. Maybe he—" The band segued into another tune. Nathan's eyes lit up. "Oh, I like this one. I'm going to dance. See you later."

"Have fun," Mo said absently, her eyes on Jayne. "Do you want to dance?"

Jayne hesitated. "After this one, there probably won't be time for another."

"I doubt Les will hold it against us. It's the last dance for tonight, not of our lives. We have many more dances in our future. All three of us."

"All right." Jayne accepted Mo's hand. "But if we see her, I'll leave the dance floor and tell her to finish the dance with you."

Mo was about to protest, then reconsidered. "No. We'll both leave the dance floor. But only because it's our Joining supper." At some point, they'd have to stop keeping score. She tugged on Jayne's hand. "Come on." Not for the first time this evening, Mo would do what she'd thought impossible when she'd lain awake at night worrying about whether she and Les were Chosens. Leading a Chosen who wasn't Les onto the dance floor at their Joining supper? Nah, she'd considered that possibility. Leading a Chosen *she loved*, and who wasn't Les, onto the dance floor? Not in a million years, or so she'd thought. *Two Chosens*. Argamon.

LESLEY TUGGED AT her collar as she stood waiting for Mo and Jayne in the small room off the reception hall. Funny, it hadn't bothered her at all today—until now. Even on the steps, her concern for her Chosens had eclipsed everything else. But the day was finally winding down, at least for the triad. The supper, the image-taking, the dances; greeting one Rymellan after another and working the large hall . . . she couldn't wait to return home with her Chosens and let it all sink in.

The muffled music suddenly grew louder as the door swung open. Mo and Jayne came into the room and shut the door behind them. "So this is where you're hiding." Mo reached for Lesley and embraced her. "We didn't know where you were," she said as she stepped back. "Last I knew, you were talking to Laura."

"We ended up talking longer than I expected. Sorry I didn't come over when you were still with Ross, but I'll drop in on her when I'm at the Military Academy." When she'd finished talking to Laura, Mo had been nowhere in sight, and Jayne had been speaking with Robert and a woman Lesley didn't know. She'd considered joining them, but since Jayne hadn't seemed keen on spending time with him and hadn't made a point of bringing her Chosens over to him earlier in the evening, Lesley had stayed away. "I had a quick word with Karen and William, then came here."

Mo met Lesley's eyes. "We decided to have one last dance."

"If we'd spotted you, we would have come off the dance floor," Jayne said.

"We figured you wouldn't mind," Mo added.

Lesley could see the uncertainty in Mo's eyes and had heard the anxiety in Jayne's voice. "I don't. If I'd felt like dancing, I would have stayed in the hall."

The door swung open again. "Good, you're here," Mama declared. Papa came in behind her and pushed the door shut. "Well." Mama put her hands on her hips and surveyed them. "Two new Thompsons, and I'm sure it won't be long before there are more."

Mo snorted. "Give us a chance, Adelaide. We've only been Joined for five minutes."

Mama gave her a pointed look. "You and Lesley have been together for how long?"

"The triad hasn't been together for very long," Lesley said.

"They'll want to be in their own home first," Papa added.

Four months. According to William, that was how long they'd have to endure Mama bringing up the subject of children at the breakfast table.

Mama grunted. "I suppose that's true. But even if they were to go to the Reproductive Technology Centre tomorrow, they'd still have nine months to wait."

Longer than nine months, actually, and they had decisions to make, such as who would carry their first daughter. But rather than bringing up these little details, Lesley changed the subject. "Everything went according to plan today. We couldn't have asked for better weather, and everyone seems to be enjoying themselves. Thank you for organizing such a wonderful supper." Lesley's gaze took in both her parents, but Mama had done most of the work, and knew it.

"It was nothing," she said, her face flushed with pleasure. When Mo and Jayne also murmured their thanks, Mama added, "Today we welcomed not one, but two new Thompsons. You're both Thompsons now. You both have a strong family behind you."

Mo and Jayne nodded, even though Mo must have understood that Mama's last words were aimed at Jayne.

"We should go, before the band finishes," Papa said.

Mama nodded. "We'll see you in a few days."

"Thanks for giving us the house to ourselves," Mo said.

"Yes, thank you," Lesley said. The triad wouldn't experience its first night together while Mama and Papa were staying with her paternal grandparents, but she looked forward to the quiet time with her Chosens before her training continued at the Military Academy, and to the evening she and Mo would spend at the lake, watching the sun set. Jayne had insisted that they take one night for themselves, and they hadn't put up much of an argument. "Oh, and when you're back, I want to talk to you about a case you might want to take on. You'll need to work with others, and you won't want to start on it right away, but we'll talk when you get back."

Mama and Papa exchanged a glance. "We'll look forward to it," Papa said. "Good night."

"Good night." As soon as the door closed behind them, Lesley turned to Mo and Jayne. "Time to go home."

"Home!" Mo squeaked. "I mean, I've always thought of your place as a second home, but now it's official."

Yes, it was, and though Lesley believed the triad would eventually find happiness, blind optimism would feel naïve, as if she were hoping everything would somehow work itself out. It wouldn't; the day's giddiness would soon give way to reality, with its jealousies and insecurities. They'd travelled far since their notification meetings, but their journey was far from over—perhaps it would never end. Lesley reminded herself of what Mama had said: she had two strong Chosens who cared about the harmony of the triad. They would travel the road together, supporting and encouraging each other, and catching each other when one stumbled. They would make it.

The muffled music stopped. Lesley swallowed. "We have to go."

"Yeah, we better get out there before your mama has a fit." Mo swept her arms toward the door. "Principal first."

Jayne was being quiet, and looked sombre. On her way to open the door, Lesley smiled at her. Jayne's answering smile didn't reach her eyes. Perhaps she shared Lesley's sense of the gravity of the moment, or reality was already eclipsing the day. Or . . . was she thinking about her parents?

Mama could wait another minute or two. Lesley turned back to Mo and Jayne. The reassuring words she'd intended to say fled her mind. She reached for Mo, held her close, then drew back and kissed her. Hoping Mo would understand, Lesley then embraced Jayne; her lips brushed Jayne's cheek as she patted Jayne's back. She let her go and faced her Chosens. "The Chosen Council did well," she said, then pivoted and opened the door.

The reception hall was deadly quiet; everyone had returned to their tables and joined hands. Lesley climbed the steps to the stage, her Chosens right behind her. Mama and Papa beamed at them, and the five Thompsons formed a circle. Voices echoed around the hall as everyone gathered said the *Words Every Rymellan Knows*.

"Disobedience means death. Death to those who commit a Chosen Violation. Death to those who disobey. Death to those who violate the Way. Death to those who violate the Way. Death to those who violate the Way!"

Applause rang in Lesley's ears. She let go of her Chosens' hands to leave the stage, but grabbed them again when the triad reached the bottom of the steps. The floor shook beneath her feet as they walked the length of the hall, reverberating with the clapping around them. The doorway to the lobby loomed. Lesley tightened her grip on Mo's and Jayne's hands, and kept her eyes forward as the triad stepped over the threshold and into the rest of their lives.

Other titles by Sarah Ettritch

The Salbine Sisters
Threaded Through Time, Books One and Two

Visit Sarah online at www.sarahettritch.com and
www.facebook.com/settritch

Thanks for reading!

www.ingramcontent.com/pod-product-compliance
Lightning Source LLC
Chambersburg PA
CBHW051257210726
48287CB00002B/552